THE LONG WAY HOME

Audrey Howard

WINDSOR
PARAGON

First published 2008
by Hodder & Stoughton
This Large Print edition published 2008
by BBC Audiobooks Ltd
by arrangement with
Hodder & Stoughton

Hardcover ISBN: 978 1 405 68728 7
Softcover   ISBN: 978 1 405 68729 4

British Library Cataloguing in Publication Data available

Printed and bound in Great Britain by
CPI Antony Rowe, Chippenham, Wiltshire

Amy Pearson's family is desperately poor—even by the standards of Edwardian Liverpool—but they have each other. Until Amy is torn from her home by her rich aunt, a woman obsessed by religion and snobbery who wants a girl she can mould as she wishes. Clever and pretty, ten-year-old Amy is perfect for her purposes.

It is the beginning of a long journey for Amy, as she desperately searches for the family she lost, and a home where she can be free at last from her aunt's possessive tyranny. But she will have to endure a forced marriage and a tragic war before she can at last find what she seeks.

Monday's child is fair of face,
Tuesday's child is full of grace,
Wednesday's child is full of woe,
Thursday's child has far to go,
Friday's child is loving and giving,
Saturday's child works hard for a living.
But the child that is born on the Sabbath day
Is bonny and blithe, and good and gay.

1

'Will I light fire before I serroff, Mam? It's terrible cold an' I don't want yer out o' bed till it's warmed up a bit.'

The child hovered uncertainly at the foot of the bed in which lay the still figure of a woman. The bitter winter cold that seems worse just before dawn, and which in mid-winter did not break until eight o'clock, struck a chill right into the bones and the child shivered, pulling her thin shawl about her and doing her best to draw her equally thin nightdress down about her bare feet.

'Mam, are yer awake?' She took another step round the iron bedstead, moving carefully across the huddled shapes of her brothers and sisters who were still asleep on threadbare palliasses, her five sisters curled up on two pushed together, her four brothers top to toe in another. The baby, a boy just one year old, was sleeping peacefully next to Mam. Pa had already left for work on the early shift at the Cammell Laird shipyard in Birkenhead where steam vessels were built and where he had managed to get a job as a casual labourer along with many of the men who lived in and around Earle Street. He and Dolly fought their circumstances tooth and nail in an effort to keep themselves and their children from the workhouse in Arthur Street and he was forced to take any work that came his way. They had, so far, managed to avoid applying for 'out-door' relief. Dolly was one of the lucky women in the area who did not have to struggle against her husband's drunkenness, which dragged many families even further into a soul-destroying poverty. Where their husbands drank their wages away at the Old Swan on the corner of Prussia Street, Pa brought his home every Friday night and put it all in Mam's hand. Next week the screw steamer St George was to be launched which would be in service between Fishguard and Rosslare and Mam had told her eldest daughter she must look up those places in the atlas when she got to school. She was like that, was Mam, doing her best to help them all with their school work.

Amy Pearson longed to crawl back under the worn but neatly mended bedclothes that covered the palliasses and snuggle down beside her sisters, warm herself among them but she knew she would have to get them all up, though they would argue with her, as the older ones, like herself, needed to get ready for school or the school inspector would be after them. It was comp ... comp ... something-or-other, she couldn't remember the exact word, to attend school, which meant they had to go or Mam and Pa would get into trouble. But it was hard when you were only ten years old to make the others do as they were told, what with Mam so sick and Pa at work. Like their Claire who, though six years old, must stop at home today since she was deemed responsible enough to mind the little ones. They took turns, her and the older girls, to stay at home and mind Mam and the youngest. Only until Mam was better, of course, then they could *all* attend Lower Milk Street School. Their Sammy said he would gladly mind them, because he bloody hated school and Claire could go in his place today but Sammy wasn't a trustworthy lad and Mam had told him to watch his language. Mam didn't like language.

The bedroom smelled sad and sour, a mingling of dampness and decades of dirt, old clothes and unwashed bodies, and yet it was considered a clean home, for Dolly Pearson was a good wife and mother. She was a good worker an' all, when she was well that is, going each day to the laundry where she stood at her tub for twelve hours at a time, her younger children about her, and her family were decent. But since she had fallen ill with this dreadful wasting disease, barely able to get out of her bed, it had all fallen on Amy. Amy looked forward to spring, praying that the warmer weather would see Mam on her feet again and back at her job at her tub in the Bath House Laundry on Upper Frederick Street where she washed for the ladies who had no laundry of their own or if they had would be too delicate to tackle it! They badly needed the money Mam was paid, and Amy, being a child of her environment and circumstances, was aware that one wage, and that not always forthcoming, was not enough to keep a family of thirteen.

'Mam, can yer 'ear me?' Amy held the rush-light higher and leaned over her mam. It gave off a very dim light but it was out of the question to buy candles, which were much more expensive. She was vastly relieved when the light showed her mother's chest slowly rising and falling as she breathed, since Amy's one terror was that her mam might die and Amy couldn't bear that for she loved her so much. She loved her pa too because he made them all laugh and had a wealth of stories to tell them from his own childhood.

3

The subdued light revealed the ashen face of her mother, the cheeks fallen in, her bonniness melting away, the veins on her translucent eyelids visible like the lines on a map, the paleness of her lips and the lank tangle of her faded fair hair. Dolly Pearson had been plump and rosy once, a strong healthy woman who had given birth eleven times and, even more to marvel at, every one of her children had lived. She was a good cook when she had the money to buy the ingredients, making nutritious meals on which to sustain the family, cheap meals with food bought at the end of the day when the vegetables and fruit from the market were sold for next to nothing to those patient enough to wait for them. She and Pa, between them, being thrifty, careful parents, had done their best to rear their young as many in the poor district of the dock area failed to do, although Amy, glancing at the baby who lay beside Mam, worried that young Eddy was not getting the nourishment that the others before him had been given in the first year of their lives. Mam's milk had dried up and the baby was weakly, inclined to grizzle and refuse the watered-down condensed milk she and Elsie, who was nine, tried to get down him.

Mam opened her eyes and the long, sweeping lashes, a rich brown tipped at the ends with gold, which most of her children including Amy had inherited, lifted slowly. Her eyes were the colour of pale sherry, golden and almost transparent and she had once had clear, smooth skin, the colour of the cream at the top of the milk, Pa used to say. Not that they had ever had milk with the cream on the top but Pa had when he was a boy and he said

4

Mam's skin was the exact creamy shade. Beautiful she had been when Pa had first seen her working on the north end of Bootle seashore gutting fish from the boats that put in there. Bonny and laughing she had been, Pa said, with her thick curling hair tied up in a kerchief and all the lads round her like flies to a honey pot. She had been sixteen and a year later she, Amy, had been born so Mam was only twenty-seven now. She looked years older, Amy agonised, wanting to go down on her knees at the side of the bed and pray to the God Mr Aspinall at school talked about at prayers. Beg Him to spare her mam who was the best person in the world and loved by them all. But she hadn't time, not with the bairns to get up and off to school and Claire to be instructed on how to look after Mam and the little ones until Pa came home some time in the early afternoon unless he managed to get a few extra hours, which would be a godsend at the moment.

'Amy, chuck,' Mam murmured, lifting a limp hand to touch her daughter's cheek. She did her best to smile, to look cheerful for this good little girl of hers who worried so much, too much, as a child of her age should be playing out in the street with the dozens of other children, hopscotch, skipping rope, alley-alley-o, all the games little girls played. Instead, when she was not at school she was looking after herself and her ten brothers and sisters. It would not do and she, Dolly Pearson, must give over lolling in her bed and get up and see to them herself.

She said so. 'I'm gerrin up terday, chuck. I've 'ad me a good rest these last few days an' it's time I give over. 'Elp me up, lass. Eeh, look, our Eddy's

5

woken. See, lift 'im up an' I'll give 'im 'is feed.' She made a valiant attempt to sit up, straining herself from the unkempt bed, and its far from clean sheets. It grieved her, for when she had been herself she would have whipped them from the bed and down to the laundry, and had them washed, ironed and back on the bed before you could say 'Where's me soap?'

'Mam, yer can't.' Amy was aghast. 'Leave our Eddy, Elsie'll feed 'im.' She aimed her bare foot at the recumbent form of her sister, the next in line to herself. 'Come on, our Elsie, gerrout o' bed an' tekk our Eddie, an' you, Becky, get the others downstairs. Sammy, get the fire lit and fetch in plenty o' coal an' then purron that pan o' porridge. An' yer can stop whinin' or I'll clout yer one. No, Mam, stop where yer are. Claire'll fetch yer some porridge an' yer ter eat it all, d'yer 'ear. When fire's goin' yer can come downstairs but not until, so think on.'

Dolly Pearson, despite her awareness of the seriousness of her condition and the hopelessness of her getting out of bed, smiled to herself. Their Amy was like a small edition of herself, always concerned for the children, ready to boss them about or even box their ears if they didn't do as they were told. She was old beyond her years and Dolly was sorry for it, but what could she do trapped in her bed as she was. She longed to leap from it, leave this mean little room that held nothing but the bare necessities of life and run down the narrow stairs and make sure her children ate their porridge, washed themselves and were warmly dressed—or as warm as they could be in the second-hand clothes Dolly purchased at the market—and were sent off to school with the loving embrace she gave them all. She wanted to weep but she knew it would only upset their Amy so she creased her face into the parody of a smile that seemed to reassure the child.

The family lived in a tiny, back-to-back, one-up, one-down house, one of the hundreds and hundreds built a century ago in rows upon rows that marched inland from the docks to accommodate the dock labourers, the factory and mill workers who had been drawn to the city from many parts of Europe and Ireland bound for the new world across the Atlantic. Liverpool was a vast cosmopolitan centre filled with the thousands of immigrants making for the United States of America and a new life but who had not quite managed to get there. The front door opened directly into a scullery-cum-kitchen and it was here that the family, squashed together like peas in a pod, ate, cooked, washed, laughed, cried and worked. It was the warmest place in the house. They were the poorest of the poor but there was happiness in their home. On one wall stood the kitchen range, once a shining blackleaded testament to the industry of Dolly Pearson, gleaming against the whitewashed walls to which, twice a year, Reuben added a fresh coat. Not so now, for the children and Reuben Pearson had not the enthusiasm that kept Dolly on the go from morning till night. In a corner to the left of the range a stone shelf held a tin bucket that contained the water brought laboriously from the standpipe at the end of the street. There was a sagging couch, a rickety table shored up by bits of wood Reuben, or Ben as he was called, brought

7

from the docks, two dilapidated armchairs reserved for Dolly and Ben and two benches on either side of the table where the children sat. A boarded staircase led to the one bedroom where they all slept, Mam and Pa on the creaking iron bedstead, the children on the palliasses which were stacked neatly against the wall during the day. There were silverfish, mice, rats and cockroaches, for even Dolly's obsession with what she called 'muck' was often overcome by circumstances over which she had no control.

Sammy, who at eight years old was tall and thin like his pa, had got the fire going since, despite his loathing of school and his inclination to be led astray by his companions in the streets he roamed, he was a good-hearted lad and loved his mam as they all did. The pan of porridge was warming on the growing flames and the children were huddled round the range, still half asleep, their bare feet curling against the chill of the worn oilcloth spread on the floor, which Dolly had scrubbed, until recently, every day of her life.

The next hour was frantic, as the children were cold and their hunger not quite satisfied by the bowl of thin porridge doled out to them so that they were lethargic, inclined to argue with their Amy who was doing her best to get them dressed. Eddy was fretful, turning his head away from the spoonful of watery milk that was offered him.

'You'll 'ave ter keep tryin', our Claire,' Amy told her worriedly, 'else we'll 'ave 'im poorly, an' all. Now mekk sure yer keep fire well stoked in case Mam comes down though I don't think she can. Eeh, I wish our pa'd come 'ome, 'onest I do, bur I know 'e 'as ter do extra if it's offered.' She was

8

talking to herself rather than the others and nobody answered. 'Now get yer coat on, our Becky, an' Sammy, if I 'ave ter tell yer again ter comb yer 'air yer'll get such a clout it'll mekk yer ears ring. Elsie, give us a 'and, there's a good lass, an' tie our Billy's bootlaces, an' Claire, when yer've finished wi' Eddy, mekk Mam a cup o' tea an' tekk it up to 'er, will yer. Jesus wept . . .'

They all turned to stare at her, even Eddy, for their pa didn't like language either and certainly not words like that. He called it a word that began with a p—prof . . . summat or other—for their pa came from a family that was chapel-going, so he told them, and he'd been brought up to be respectful of such things. Not that he was religious or anything like that. Not now, and he never talked about the family he had come from. He never went to church and neither did they, but they had prayers at school and they knew it was bad to take the name of the Lord, *and* Jesus, in vain.

Furiously pulling a shawl about her, Amy ran back upstairs to say goodbye to Mam.

'Is that you, our Amy?' the feeble voice asked from the bed.

'Aye, Mam, it's me. We're just off ter school. We've all 'ad our porridge and I medd 'em all 'ave a good wash.' Amy knew this would please Mam. 'I warmed water on't fire an' we took turns. I'll ask Pa ter get down tin bath an' ternight we'll do us all over. Now our Claire's got yer porridge an' a nice cup o' tea so you mekk sure yer gerrit down yer.'

Again, even in the extremity of her illness Dolly had to smile. Their Amy was as old as the hills in her ways, like a little mother with a brood of children, but at the same time it saddened her and

9

not for the first time because the child was just that: a child, and yet she was saddled with Dolly's own job of looking after the children. If only they had a few bob to fetch the doctor in but it was all she and Ben could do to keep the children fed on only one wage.

'What time is it, my lass?' she said weakly.

'Just gone eight, Mam.' The child bent over the bed and took one of her mother's thin, cold hands between her own warm ones. 'Now yer not ter worry . . .' but as she spoke her mother began to cough, the spasm racking her violently, and at once Amy put her arms about her and held her close, willing her mam to rest, to settle, to be warm, to be well, to be as once she had been, her loving heart doing its best to beat strongly for them both.

'Eeh, Mam, I'd best stop wi' yer,' she cried, rocking her mother backwards and forwards, relieved when the coughing abated and her mam managed to speak.

'Nay, my lass, our Claire'll see ter me. She's a good girl an' . . .'

'But wharrabout t'others?' For Dick was only four, the twins Annie and Sidney three, and Phyllis just two years old and how was a child of only six, as their Claire was, to manage? The thought was incongruous coming from a child who was herself only ten years old.

'Nay, chuck, we'll manage. Now get yerself off an' I'll see yer when yer come 'ome.' Dolly collapsed back on her pillows, the effort of speaking exhausting her but doing her best to smile for the benefit of this good child of hers. 'See, give us a kiss,' and when Amy did so and ran down the stairs, tears trickled slowly down her thin

10

cheeks, for how were they to manage without her?

*   *   *

She held the hands of the two youngest with her, Billy and Becky, urging Sammy and Elsie to keep up as they ran along Earle Street, turning the corner into Edmund Street towards Exchange Station. It was already crowded as they skidded past the Station Hotel in front of the station. The hotel was busy with porters trundling luggage on trolleys down the slope and into the concourse which led to the platforms from where guests at the hotel would make their way to many parts of the country. Amy, though she was curious about everything, had no time to consider where these might be as she hurried her little group across the splendid forecourt, for what the rest of the world did was no concern of hers at this moment. They were late and if they didn't get a move on they would be in trouble with 'Miss' when she took the register. As they crossed the front of the station it was so busy they had to dodge irritable travellers intent on gaining access to the trains which whistled and shrieked so shrilly you could hardly hear yourself think, let alone speak, and there was so much steam gushing from their funnels it even escaped into the street.

'Keep up, our Sammy,' she shouted over her shoulder, for anything at all diverted her little brother, who was ready to stop and watch the antics of an organ grinder's monkey which raised its little round hat to him. A horse-drawn tram rattled by, adding to the noise and confusion, and glory of glories, causing Sammy to stop in his

11

tracks, there was one of the new machines known to them all as 'a horseless carriage', weaving in and out of the horse-drawn vehicles, its horn honking, the driver shouting at everything that got in his way: wagons drawn by great shire horses, laden down with bales of raw cotton; carriages carrying ladies to their dressmakers, even as early as this; gentlemen on horseback, bicycles and horse-drawn cabs. On Tithebarn Street two sailors danced a lively hornpipe to the tune of a penny whistle and again Sammy stopped to watch, making Elsie do the same so that Amy was forced to go back and drag him by the arm. There was the sound of high, drunken laughter, the cackle of the gulls that had come inland as bad weather was heralded and above it all the familiar sound of ships' sirens, but Amy hauled them along, immune to everything but the need to get them all to school before the bell went.

They raced along Lower Milk Street until they reached the school gates, tearing across the playground to the door marked 'girls', shoving Sammy and Billy towards the one marked 'boys' just as the bell was being rung. Panting with relief, Amy tagged on to the line of girls, pushing Elsie and Becky in front of her, then watched carefully as they both went to their respective classes before she entered hers. 'Miss' smiled at her, for though Amy was not aware of it she was a favourite of Margaret Hardcastle. It was prayers first, a muttered incantation from twenty children, none of whom knew what the dickens they were saying.

When told to sit, Amy lowered herself on to the seat of the double desk she shared with a girl with nits in her hair and a ferocious squint. None of her family had ever had nits, her mam saw to that, and she sat well away from her companion. Most of the children had thin, peaked faces and stunted frames, all looking strangely alike, which was why Amy Pearson stood out so conspicuously. She was, as far as was possible in this poverty-stricken part of Liverpool, well fed and warmly clad, as were her brothers and sisters in another part of Lower Milk Street Council School. She had hideous boots on her feet but inside them she wore what looked like hand-knitted stockings and Miss Hardcastle, though she had never met her, was acutely aware that this child's mother cared about her, sacrificed for her, made every farthing that came into the house do the work of two. She had several brothers and sisters at the school and they were all a cut above the rest of the scholars who were uncaring and apathetic, the drabness of their surroundings and the poverty in which they had been dragged up numbing their brains to any chance of learning.

But Amy Pearson was delicately lovely and probably the fact that she was clean endeared her even more to Margaret Hardcastle. So many of them had not seen water nor soap for days, or even weeks, and she knew that both were in short supply in the district where the Pearson family lived. But Amy and her siblings were relatively clean and tidy. Amy's hair was a colour that was hard to describe, gold and silver and brown, a bright mixture that wanted to curl but hung in a thick plait to her waist. She plaited it, or had it plaited for her, with a bit of green ribbon tied at the end and the plait was as thick as Margaret Hardcastle's wrist. But curling wisps escaped on to

13

her forehead and over her ears and they were so fair they were almost white. Her eyes were a pale golden brown, the colour of amber Miss Hardcastle decided, surrounded by long brown eyelashes tipped with gold; her mouth was like a peach, with a long upper lip that turned up at the corners and a short, full lower lip. Her features were set in a rich and creamy complexion, but today there were deep bruised shadows beneath her eyes and it was obvious she was tired, for she, who usually sat up with bright curiosity, drooped over her desk.

The teacher was well aware that there were two kinds of poverty in the district from which Amy Pearson and her brothers and sisters came. There was 'clean poverty' where children had enough to eat even if it was nutritionally poor because their fathers were probably decent men who, though they might not be in work full-time, gave all their wages to their wives, and they had no money to spare for anything but the bare necessities of life. And then there was 'sordid poverty' that dragged down whole families. Mothers uncaring after years of childbearing and dealing with drunken husbands, children neglected and sent to school only to get them from under their feet. She watched at playtime as the little Pearsons, with more energy than their half-starved contemporaries, played tig, the girls throwing a ball against a wall or doing handstands. She sighed as she stood at her window, wondering what was going to happen to these pathetic bits of flotsam the world had floated in her direction.

When the bell went at the end of lessons she watched again as they flooded out into the

14

playground, noticing Amy herding her brothers and sisters into a compact group ready for the walk home. She pulled their scarves more closely about their thin necks and made sure her sisters had their shawls wrapped across their chests and tied securely at their backs. One of her brothers, the older one called Sammy, reacted sullenly to her instructions and when she turned her back he stuck his tongue out at her but he followed her, obediently holding his sister's hand.

It was getting dark and a bitter wind blew off the river. Snow clouds were settling over the roof of the Custom House and the first desultory flakes began to fall as the little group passed the forecourt of Exchange Station and turned into Baxter Street.

'Come on, our Sammy,' Amy called over her shoulder, for Sammy had let go of Elsie's hand and was doing his best to get a handful to make into a snowball but there was only a thin film on the cracked pavements. There was no such thing as a pair of gloves in the Pearson household, and his hands were red and chapped so he soon gave up, running to catch the others as they turned into Edmund Street and then Earle Street. Amy could see a tiny light flickering in the window of the family home, put there by Claire or perhaps even Pa who might be home by now. She began to run, dragging a protesting Becky and Billy, slipping in the wet slush that was gathering on the flagstones. Elsie followed closely on their heels, leaving Sammy to run his hands along windowsills in the hope of gathering enough snow to make a decent snowball.

The door was open when he arrived a minute or

15

two after the others and his boy's heart sank devastatingly into his frozen feet as he moved over the doorstep, for, young as he was, he knew something terrible had happened. They all stood there in a huddled group, their Amy, Elsie, Becky and Billy, while at the table Claire sat like a small and mindless figurine carved from ivory. Perched on the bench opposite, all in a row, like birds on a washing line, were the little ones, Dick, Annie, Sidney and Phyllis, bewildered and frightened. The baby, strangely, was fast asleep in his mam's chair.

Pa sat in his sagging old chair, sagging himself as though some terrible nightmare were heavy on his shoulders, his face quite blank, his eyes staring across the kitchen but looking at nothing.

'What's up, Pa?' Amy managed to quaver, her own eyes wide and filled with dread of what he was about to tell them. 'Is . . . is it Mam?' For who else could put that dreadful aura of devastation about her pa?

Pa cleared his throat and shook himself like a dog coming from the water. 'She was badly, chuck, when I got home,' he managed to say. 'I ran up the street to the doctor's on the corner of Old Leeds Street. He came . . . he sent for an ambulance and they took Mam to the Royal Infirmary.' He seemed to rally then, to make a huge effort to put her mind at rest, for the others did not understand. 'She'll be right there, chuck. They'll make her better, you'll see.' He tried to smile but it was very evident to the intelligent child that her pa was frightened and so was she because how was this family to survive without Mam to see to them?

16

2

The woman on the bed turned her face away as the doctor examined her. She made a faint sound of distaste as his fingers probed where even her husband's hands seldom went and her face paled even further. She had lost a great deal of blood.

'All done, Mrs Seymour,' he murmured soothingly, indicating to the nurse that she might replace the bedcovers and preserve his patient's dignity. He put his hand on her forehead and then felt her pulse. Satisfied, he seated himself in the chair beside the bed and took his patient's hand where it lay listlessly, while on the other side of the bed the nurse fussed with the bedcovers, straightening the plain eiderdown and generally doing her best to prove how invaluable she was and deserving of the fee she charged.

Doctor Parsons, who had ministered to the family for over thirty years, assumed the sorrowful demeanour that he had perfected during his career and which he presented to those of his patients who could afford his services. He was old-fashioned and held in contempt the 'new-fangled' methods younger men in medicine practised. He was a great success with ladies!

'Mrs Seymour, we have been unsuccessful once again and I'm sorry to have to say this but I'm afraid it must be our last attempt. It is putting too much strain upon your health and . . . well, madam . . . ahem . . . at your age—'

Zillah Seymour interrupted him coolly. 'It is nothing to do with my age, Doctor Parsons, or the

17

many attempts I have made—*I*, not you—to carry a child. This is God's will and it is our duty to bow down to His wishes and I must not sink into the sin of ingratitude, as I have much to be thankful for.'

'Indeed, Mrs Seymour.'

'If God has ordained that I be childless then it must be for my chastisement. All men are alike in the sight of the eternal Jehovah and all men are set at liberty by the blood of Christ. The most high God has pleased to take unto Himself every child I have conceived.'

A strange glitter shone in Zillah's eyes as she remembered what she had been forced to endure to conceive those children, eight of them in twenty years and each one lost in a disgusting flow of blood. Well, from what the doctor said at least she would be spared that ordeal again and, more to the point, the attentions of her husband which she had endured for the past twenty years. She must have no more children and she would impress on Doctor Parsons that he must inform Caleb exactly what that meant. She had done her best to provide her husband with a son, the son he so ardently required to carry on his work in the flourishing business concern that he himself had inherited from his father. She had failed but she had tried.

Cotton! Manchester was the centre of a wide network of the many townships that served the massive cotton industry, Bolton, Burnley, Blackburn, Wigan, Oldham and Rochdale to name but a few. These townships sent their woven and spun produce to the Exchange in Manchester and from there to the world via the Manchester Ship Canal, and received raw materials that were distributed out from the city by its well-established

18

system of canals and railways. Manchester and a great many small towns and villages surrounding it were responsible for the rapid growth of factories and mills manufacturing merchandise for cotton weaving, spinning, dyeing, fulling and all aspects of the textile industry. 'Cottonopolis' the city was nicknamed, where King Cotton ruled, and Caleb Seymour was one of its ruling princes. And he wanted a son to inherit what he had.

Doctor Parsons patted her hand and placed it reverently on the bed beside her rigid figure. She was forty-two years old and he had attended her at every one of her pregnancies but it seemed her womb just could not hold on to what was planted in it. But if she wanted to put it down to the will of the God about whom she was so fanatical, then that was nothing to do with him. He had done everything he could to help her achieve a full-term pregnancy, medically speaking, and he could do no more. Another attempt would be useless, even dangerous, besides which she was fast approaching that time in a woman's life where the hope of children, or the dread of it in some cases, was ending.

He stood up and moved towards the window to a small table upon which were laid a can of hot water and a plain white bowl, a bar of sensible soap and a clean white towel. As he washed his hands he glanced about the room, pondering that though this was one of the wealthiest families in Manchester there was no sign of it in the house. True, the room was warm and comfortable but austere. There were several paintings on the walls, all with a religious association but nothing that could be called frivolous. It was not like any of the other ladies' bedrooms he had called upon in his capacity as family doctor, ladies of wealth—as this one was—who favoured pretty colours, frills, bows, flowers, lacy feminine things, but here there was a no-nonsense feel about the room, about the woman, about the house. Zillah Seymour had her own money, inherited from her father, which was probably the reason Caleb Seymour had married her twenty years ago but she did not waste it on light-minded extravagances. Plain, simple, even severe, heavy furniture, thick net at the window backed by sober curtains of a hue the doctor could only describe as earth-coloured. The same with the carpet which was of good quality but as plain and colourless as the woman on the bed. Her nightgown was white, of thick lawn with a high neckline and sleeves ending at her wrist without a frill or even a bit of embroidery.

As the doctor dried his hands he glanced out of the window at the wide expanse of lawn which stretched down to the high stone wall that surrounded the grounds. The house was set in a select part of Salford on the broad thoroughfare of Eccles Old Road which the tramway ran along and next to it was the Pendleton Nurseries. There were bare flowerbeds in the grounds with several beech trees growing on the lawn itself and a circle of woodland consisting of nothing but beech trees to the sides and back of the house. In summer they were a lovely sight, he knew, since he had attended Mrs Seymour for the past three months, with smooth, soaring trunks like the columns of a cathedral, forced to grow tall in their constant struggle to reach the light. Their autumn colours had no rivals, displaying a brilliant mosaic of flaming orange and gold which fell to form a carpet that Mrs Seymour's gardeners swiftly raked up and burned at the back of the house. Neat, tidy, lacking individuality, which could have described Mrs Seymour herself. The house was handsome though. A square building with many chimneys and windows, some of them bow-shaped and a pillared front porch that opened on to several steps and the front drive, leading to the wrought-iron gates. The drive wound round to the back of the house where stables were situated and a coach house and, surprisingly, a tennis court! He had never seen it used since the old gentleman, Mr Seymour's father, to whom the house had belonged, had died before his son was married and he had inherited the lot.

He turned his professional smile on his patient. 'Now, I want to see you improving when I visit you tomorrow. Stay in bed, which you would naturally do, and have nothing but light, nourishing food. I myself will arrange it with your cook. I will give you a sedative to help you sleep. Rest, my dear lady. That is the answer. Now I will go and have a word with your husband.'

He had a quiet word with the nurse then left the room, making his way along the sombre, panelled, thickly carpeted landing that led to the wide stairway. The hushed splendour of the hall, which was laid with black and white tiles and was as wide as the staircase, was dimly lit, cool, and as still as a chapel, oppressive with the fragrance of beeswax. The staircase branched to left and right with banisters like ribbons of ebony at each side. It was uncluttered, like its mistress's bedroom, as quiet as a tomb and Doctor Parsons, who had attended the

21

eight miscarriages suffered by Zillah Seymour, wondered vaguely how the eight children who might have been born but who had slipped away on a tide of blood would have survived in this sterile atmosphere. He could not imagine a child running down the staircase, sliding down those elegant banisters, shouting in play or laughing out loud to disturb the church-like peace of the house.

A servant mysteriously appeared, a housemaid in an immaculate uniform, very prim with a crisp white apron and a plain white cap that covered her hair completely. She was pleasant-looking and scrupulously polite, but there was a lurking twinkle in her eyes that seemed to say she had been enjoying a joke with someone beyond the green baize door that led into the kitchen quarters and had assumed her housemaid's expression as she came through it.

'Was you lookin' fer the master, Doctor?' she asked him.

'Yes, I am. Could you direct me to wherever he might happen to be?'

'Is madam ... the mistress feeling any better, Doctor? The servants asked me ter ask you. We was all ...'

The doctor put on his expression of solicitude, one he assumed automatically when asked the condition of a patient. Mrs Seymour would do very well but it was his self-important practice never to say so, not even to this maid. If a patient was made to seem somewhat more poorly than she was, then her recovery, thanks to him, of course, was all the more appreciated.

'She will need great care ... er ... ?'

'Alice, Doctor.'

'She will need to be well looked after, Alice, and it will be some time before she is back on her feet. Somewhat delicate, is your mistress but then I'm sure you and the rest of the staff are aware of that.' He smiled benignly.

'Oh, yes, indeed, Doctor. Is . . . did the baby . . .?' They had all known in the kitchen what had happened to their mistress and not for the first time, it seemed, though Alice had not been employed by the Seymours the last time.

'I'm afraid the baby . . .' The doctor suddenly realised that it was not his place to discuss Mrs Seymour's miscarriage with a servant, at least not before he had spoken to Caleb Seymour who awaited him in . . .?

Alice too became aware of her temerity in questioning the doctor, but then they were Mrs Seymour's servants and were naturally anxious for their mistress.

'He's in his study, Doctor, this way,' Alice said, leading Doctor Parsons down a corridor to the right of the front door. She tapped on a door then opened it and announced him to the man who sat quietly in a large armchair fashioned in a handsome green leather. This room, this inner sanctum belonging entirely to the head of the house, was vastly different from the hallway, the staircase and Mrs Seymour's bedroom in that it was bright, cheerful and vaguely cluttered. There were two windows. A large leather-covered desk stood beneath the window that looked out to the front of the house and another beneath the side window, on which were set many items of interest, such as a globe in a brass meridian on a wooden stand, a telescope, a couple of lamps lit by the

23

comparatively new method of electricity, and strange objects made from quartz, slate and marble, as Caleb Seymour took a great interest in geology. A clock ticked, an imposing thing of fine black marble and ormolu with a golden eagle perched on it. The curtains and blind at both windows were of an attractive pattern of green and red, plants flourished on the windowsills, and the floor was covered with a colourful Turkish carpet. It seemed that Caleb Seymour did not share his wife's taste for austerity in his surroundings.

He was reading *The Times*. He lowered it with what seemed to Doctor Parsons reluctance.

'Ah, Doctor Parsons, do come in. You have news?' but his attitude seemed to indicate that he did not expect it to be good and what's more was not unduly interested. Caleb Seymour had long given up hope that his wife would bear him children. He nodded at Alice who had hung about in the hope of hearing something she could carry back to the others in the kitchen, and she closed the door quietly. She stood outside the door, listening to the doctor's sonorous voice, then she fled silently up the hallway and into the kitchen.

If Doctor Parsons had, for some reason, blundered into the kitchen he would have been thunderstruck by the comparison with the rest of the house. It appeared that wherever Mrs Seymour took little interest, such as her husband's study or the domestic side of the house, as in the kitchen and the laundry, its occupants went their own way. Somerfield was a big house with long hallways and the kitchen was well fortified against noise, the green baize door cutting off sounds of mirth or anger. Not that there was much anger, for they all got on well with one another. In charge was Mrs Abigail, housekeeper and cook with a kind heart and a cheerful disposition who was inclined to be indulgent though she insisted on cleanliness and obedience. Her cooking was superb and had she taken it into her head to throw a noisy party every night Caleb Seymour would have turned a blind eye, for cooks of her talent were hard to come by! There was Alice who was housemaid, Martha kitchen-maid, Jess parlour-maid, Phoebe in the laundry and Primrose in the scullery, all hand-picked by Mrs Abigail, all well paid by the standards of the day and for that reason prepared to put up with Mrs Seymour and her fanatical insistence on chapel-going. Not that they went every day as she did, otherwise, as Mrs Abigail often remarked, there'd be nothing done in the house, but on most Sundays, in their Sunday best, they walked the length of Eccles Old Road, turning right into Langworthy Road to St John's Methodist Chapel on Liverpool Street. Mr Seymour didn't go and neither did Ernie Tingle, who was groom, and since he was the best man with horses Mr Seymour had ever employed and he didn't want to lose him, he had been given permission to absent himself. The others wished they could do the same but it was a small price to pay to keep the decent, well-paid job with which they were blessed.

Mrs Abigail had her head in the oven, set in the centre of the blackleaded range, inspecting the splendid leg of pork from a Berkshire pig which, in Mrs Abigail's opinion, was the best known and most esteemed of all English breeds. She had stuffed it with her own sage and onion stuffing

25

made with four large onions, ten sage leaves, a quarter of a pound of breadcrumbs, butter, salt and pepper, all bound together with the yolk of an egg. It had been roasting for over two hours and would soon be ready for the table but with only Mr Seymour, madam still in her bed, she was anxious that it would not spoil. If the doctor would get a move on she could have it ready for carving and in front of the master in half an hour and though it weighed eight pounds it would not be wasted, for they all loved a good bit of pork, especially that lad in the stables who had come from the workhouse and was as thin as a pipe cleaner. When she'd checked the pork and its accompaniments she meant to make a nice baked raisin pudding. She'd already chopped the suet and stoned the raisins, the buttered pie dish was ready and it could go in the oven the minute the pork and roast potatoes came out. They ate well did the servants at Somerfield House!

'Well, she's lost it,' Alice told them, triumphant at being the one to bring them the news. She was not an unkind person, none of them was, but their lives were so humdrum anything that came to break the monotony was received with great enthusiasm.

'Eeh, no, poor lady,' Mrs Abigail uttered, removing her red, perspiring face from the vicinity of the oven while the others, Primrose in the scullery peeling sprouts, Jess giving a last polish to the cutlery, Martha standing beside Mrs Abigail in her role as kitchen-maid, stopped what they were doing

'An' she's not ter 'ave another.'

'Nay, never.' Mrs Abigail shook her head sadly.

26

'Well, she's tried hard enough, you've got ter give 'er that, poor soul, an' she's not as young as she was but it would've bin nice ter 'ave little 'un about the place. She needs something to take her mind off that . . .' Suddenly she realised that she was doing something that she firmly quashed among her staff and that was gossiping. Well, perhaps not exactly gossiping since she was doing nothing more than commiserating with her poor mistress on her inability to bring forth a living child. It was queer really when you thought about it. Here was a good home waiting to give a decent life to some youngster and in town, even yet in this new century, there were women who gave birth with unfailing frequency to a child every year and reared them as best they could in absolute poverty. They lived in dilapidated houses, damp and without running water except what ran down their walls, with their men bringing in a weekly income of four shillings. Immigrants poured in so that it was said that the Irish were taking over the place and Joe had told her that most of the inmates of the workhouse were Irish Catholics. That's where he'd come from so he should know. Mind, he had also told her things were improving. It seemed he followed the reports of the Manchester Unhealthy Dwellings Committee with which the mistress was involved and that sewage disposal was a worry and that even now in 1908 only one-third of the city's privies were water closets. That's quite enough of that, she told him, for the subject was hardly one to be discussed in her spotless kitchen. He was a clever lad despite his poor beginnings and it was woe betide Alice if she threw away the master's copy of *The Times* before Joe had read it!

27

'Well, Alice,' she said now, 'that's sad news but life must go on and though it's hard for the master and mistress they still have to get on and so do we. Now go and set the table in the dining room, just for one, I suppose, unless Mr Seymour has asked the doctor to luncheon but we'll be told when he's ready.'

*   *   *

Caleb Seymour had not asked Doctor Parsons to luncheon. He had taken the news of his wife's miscarriage with his normal stoicism, a stoicism that could often appear to be indifference.

'And I'm afraid, my dear sir, that Mrs Seymour must have no children, which seems unlikely in any case, given her age.'

'Quite.'

'You understand what I'm saying, Mr Seymour,' the doctor added, doing his best to treat the delicate subject with the right amount of sensitivity. There was no way, at least in Doctor Parsons's opinion, to avoid pregnancy except by celibacy. Oh, there were those who advocated various forms of birth control, the most popular being withdrawal before ejaculation but Doctor Parsons abhorred this method as it was a great strain on the man. There was douching after intercourse but again the good doctor did not care for this, and then there was a clumsy device made of a length of animal intestine which the man fitted to his member. All unnatural in Doctor Parsons's estimation and certainly none that he would recommend to a gentleman such as Caleb Seymour.

28

Mr Seymour seemed not to feel a great deal of concern regarding the end of his private married life though the doctor felt it must be a sad day when a man could not get himself a son through no fault of his own. He himself had four and three daughters, all grown up and married and he felt no loss of his wife's attentions. Of course he was a good ten years older than his patient's husband.

'Well,' he said, waiting perhaps to be offered a sherry or at least a word, but Seymour merely nodded, holding his newspaper as though waiting for the doctor to leave. 'I shall visit your wife tomorrow, sir, and hope to find her much improved. She is in no danger though at her age she would be well advised to rest for a few weeks.'

'Thank you, Doctor,' was Seymour's vague reply.

Doctor Parsons stood up. A cold fish indeed, he thought. Having just been told that his chances of ever having a son to follow him into the business were nil, he appeared to be as much concerned as though the doctor had informed him that his housemaid was about to give him notice.

'I'll be off then. If I may I should like to talk to your cook.'

'My cook?' It was the first time Caleb Seymour had reacted in any way to the doctor's words.

'Yes. Your wife will need a special diet to . . . er, to build her up and I must instruct your cook on what that should be.'

'Of course.' Caleb Seymour reached for the bell and rang it and when Alice appeared told her to fetch Mrs Abigail.

'Mrs Abigail, sir?' Alice was clearly surprised.

'If you please, Alice.'

Mrs Abigail was mortified. 'What the dickens
. . . Can't you see I'm in the middle of serving
luncheon,' just as though it were Alice's fault that
she had been disturbed. 'See, Martha, make sure
these potatoes are drained well and keep the pork
on the top of the oven when you've got the juices
out of the roasting pan . . . Eeh, I was just about to
do the gravy an' all. What can master want now?'

'Doctor's still with 'im, Mrs Abigail,' Alice said,
trying to be helpful. ' 'Appen . . .'

When Mrs Abigail returned to the kitchen they
could all see she was in high dudgeon, her face
red, her arms folded across her capacious bosom,
which was a bad sign.

'My dear Lord, as if I didn't know how to make
a good broth or a bit of beef tea. Barley gruel, he
ses, with port wine, and plenty of barley water.
Calf's-foot broth and make sure that all the
kitchen utensils is *scrupulously* clean and jelly, he
ses, an' plenty of milk . . . I shall say summat to the
master when that old fool's gone, I tell you. A
boiled egg, if you please, as if I didn't know by now
what the mistress likes. This is the eighth time
she's miscarried and did she fade away with the
others, no she didn't . . .'

The servants stood silently in their places
waiting for the tirade to pass which they knew it
would very soon. Mrs Abigail was good at her job
and they all agreed that Doctor Parsons had
overstepped the mark in trying to tell her what
nourishment the poor mistress should have to get
her back on her feet. But she liked to blow off
steam now and again, especially when she believed
she was being undeservedly criticised. Mrs Abigail
had the running of this house, since the mistress,

30

strangely, took no interest in the domestic side of life. Chapel and her charity work were all that concerned Mrs Seymour which was why they had all hoped this child, this lost child, would bring something to the house that it lacked. It was as though Somerfield House contained two worlds: the cheerfulness of the kitchen and the hushed atmosphere of the house beyond the green baize door. They worked hard, all of them, for Mrs Abigail demanded the best from them but they didn't mind. They were well paid by the standards of the day and with Mrs Seymour being such a Christian lady, they slept in warm beds and ate decent food. Chapel was a bit of a nuisance, and the prayers that Mrs Seymour took it into her head to insist that now and again they attend, but all in all *their* side was a happy one!

But still, a child would have been nice!

3

Doctor James Ferguson was thirty-one years old, tall and thin, pale-complexioned and untidy. He had spent time in Africa tending to wounded soldiers, amputating gangrenous limbs and doing his best to alleviate the suffering of those who succumbed to the typhoid outbreak, to Boer women and children, who had been dispossessed by the fighting.

He had come home at the end of it, not with any particular determination to concern himself with women and children but he was doing it nonetheless. The mismanagement of the

31

workhouse hospital had caught his attention, with the lack of a proper maternity ward, the sanitary arrangements, patients with fevers and bowel disfunction and what the staff liked to call 'social diseases' all lumped together in one ward. He had seen so many unnecessary deaths in the Transvaal that, again with no predetermined intention to do so, he had taken up the task of helping those who could not help themselves, those women who had not the means to pay for the specialist care that many of them needed.

Dolly Pearson was one of these.

The Poor Law Infirmaries maintained proper and sufficient medical care for those who needed it but it was haphazard and the staff were vastly overworked. There were voluntary hospitals where they were treated by specialist doctors, of whom he was one, who did some Poor Law work, most part-time, one of these establishments being the Royal Infirmary which was staffed by well-trained nurses but it did not have the facilities to isolate those with infectious diseases.

James Ferguson lived in a crumbling house at the end of Old Leeds Street where, at any time of the night or day, one might find a distraught woman knocked about by a drunken husband, an abused child, or a young girl giving birth to a baby got on her by her own father and whom he could then transfer to care in the proper place. He was a taciturn man but the twinkle in his eye showed that he was not humourless. He had answered the frantic father's entreaty to come and look at his wife who, the father said, lay unconscious in her bed, the children crying and himself unable to cope since their Amy was at school. The doctor

32

had got out his gig and driven himself and the anxious man back to Earle Street to see for himself.

The next day as he sat in Dolly's chair he dropped ash from his old pipe on Dolly's once immaculate linoleum and looked round at the frightened faces of her family. The father seemed incapable of functioning without his wife who was obviously the driving force in the home, though he thought he saw strength in the pale face of the eldest girl, aged about nine or ten. The baby grizzled and the next eldest girl jiggled him on her knee but he was evidently missing his mother's breast.

'I want one of you to go down to the clinic at the hospital, the workhouse hospital, and tell them Doctor Ferguson sent you for some powdered milk for the bairn. It will keep him going until his mother is back with you.'

At once they all smiled and relaxed against one another, for the doctor had just told them that Mam *would* be back with them. They sat in a line on the benches on either side of the table while the father, Mr Pearson, was hunched in a sagging chair by the small fire which barely warmed the room. It was bitterly cold outside, the pavements rimed with a thick white frost, while inside the window of the room was hazed with an opaque pattern formed by the damp. They were in poor straits, this family, despite the father being in work but they were relatively clean, Doctor Ferguson thought, compared with many of his patients. After examining the mother yesterday he had arranged for her to be taken in at the Royal Infirmary on Brownlow Hill, since he had not liked the sound of her chest and it had more up-to-date equipment than at the workhouse hospital. He did not think they would keep her long even there and would send her to one of the hospitals for consumption and diseases of the chest, away from the pollution of the city where clean air, rest and a good diet might pull her through. Probably City Hospital East on Mill Lane which specialised in infectious diseases.

'You may visit your wife tomorrow, Mr Pearson, if it would set your mind at rest but I must reiterate that she is not in the best of health and complete rest is what I propose for her. The damp here . . .' He glanced round the room. He turned back to the silent rows of the man's family. 'Will the children manage?' He smiled at the girl who looked the most capable and who returned his smile. 'Perhaps, er . . . ?'

'Amy, Doctor.'

'Well, Amy, you know where I live and if there is anything you need, the poor relief can be of great help.'

'We'll not have charity,' the father said harshly and Amy nodded her head in agreement.

Doctor Ferguson had been surprised at the rather well-bred tone of the father's voice, for this was a poor neighbourhood where the inhabitants all spoke with the nasal twang of Liverpool.

'Do you not wish your wife to improve, Mr Pearson?' he asked coldly.

'Of course I do.'

'Then when the child goes to the clinic for the infant's milk she can bring back a tonic for the children. While your wife is in hospital she will, of course, be given what they prescribe for her. At

34

home, she will need feeding up, milk, eggs, nourishing food and—'

'How the bloody hell am I supposed to get such things for her?' The man's voice was bitter. 'We live on scrag end and half-rotten vegetables bought at the market at the end of the day when everything is cheap. Potatoes and stale bread, Dolly bought, and we managed but I have to go to work first thing in the morning.' He put his head in his hands and groaned and the doctor was made to realise that this was one of those families that lived teetering on the edge of poverty, and the mother probably gave most of the food she bought to her children, which was why she had got herself into such a poor state of health.

'The ladies of charity provide soup for those—'

'Stand in a soup line!' It was clear that Mr Pearson was vastly affronted and James Ferguson sighed.

'Do you not want your children to survive this emergency, Mr Pearson? Because they won't if you don't pull yourself together and deal with it.' With the wife in hospital he hoped to God the husband wouldn't go to pieces and let his children starve, but the girl, the one called Amy, stood up and went to her father and put her thin, childish arm about his shoulders. She looked directly at the doctor as she spoke.

'Don't you worry about us, Doctor. I'll tekk over Mam's purse an' do't shoppin'. I know where Mam used ter go an' I can do't same. I know 'ow ter cook an' all. Mam showed me. Pa gives 'is wage ter Mam on a Friday an' 'e can give it me instead. We just want our mam ter get better an' come 'ome, don't we?' she said brightly, looking round the

35

circle of anxious faces and they all nodded vigorously. 'Me pa'll be in ter see Mam termorrer when 'e comes off shift an' I'll see ter't little 'uns.'

She set her firm little jaw and squeezed the shoulders of the man who sat slumped in the armchair. A bit of colour had come to her thin cheeks and the doctor was aware that if anybody could keep this family together it was this child. The father, after his dash to Old Leeds Street to fetch him, appeared to have given up and God alone knew how they would cope. As he examined the mother, she found the strength from somewhere to come from her half-unconscious state and argue feebly with him when he said he was taking her to hospital. Her chest was so clogged she could scarcely breathe and with each breath she managed it rattled and creaked painfully. Even as he placed the end of his stethoscope on her chest she broke into a mighty sweat. Her breath whistled in her throat and her face, which had been like a white death's head, grew flushed. She looked like a crumple of old bones and as he handled her she began to mutter feverishly and he knew it would be touch and go whether she survived. How long had she been like this? He hardly liked to ask in case it upset the child, for might she not think he was criticising her? Anyway, for the moment the woman was in the best place and he'd keep an eye on this family. Like Miss Hardcastle, he was impressed with the girl. Amy, was it?

He stood up and they all did the same except the father, even the girl holding the fretful baby who James Ferguson was not sure he liked the look of. He was flushed, and far too thin. But then

36

they all were.

'I'll call again tomorrow,' he told them, at which the father looked up sharply.

'What for?' he asked truculently.

'I want to make sure you'—meaning the children—'are managing. With your wife in hospital who will care for the children?'

Amy piped up, 'I'll see to them, Doctor.' After all, hadn't she been doing just that ever since Mam took ill?

'What about your schooling? And these young ones?' He glanced round at the youngest, five of them, who it seemed to him were not old enough for school. It was hard to tell with children in these circumstances, since they were all somewhat undersized.

'Oh, our Claire or Becky'll stop wi' 'em,' the child said confidently and the doctor was made aware that this child, this slip of a thing with her mass of hair that appeared to be too heavy for her small skull and undernourished body, would shoulder the burden and work far beyond her childish strength until her mother was well again. If she ever was. He had seen this type of illness before and knew it to be chronically infectious, and though he could not say it to the father he wanted to keep an eye on the rest of the family.

The father remained slumped in his chair but the child, Amy, saw him politely to the door like some small hostess bidding farewell to a welcome guest.

'Take care, Amy,' he said gently, 'and promise me that you will allow the ladies of charity to help you. The soup kitchen at the workhouse hospital will give your brothers and sisters a nourishing meal.'

'Me pa don't . . .' she began, but he hunkered down until he was on a level with her face, which he had time to notice was quite lovely or would be with a bit of weight on her.

'I know you wish to obey your father but a good meal for your siblings—your brothers and sisters,' he added when she looked at him uncomprehendingly, 'will make all the difference. Promise me that when your father . . . is . . . not here you will take them. And your mother's bed will need . . .' Dear God, how was he to convey to this child that the bed her mother slept in must be stripped and washed and, if she understood, where in this house was she to carry out the task?

He stood up, sighing. He put his hand on the child's bright head. 'I'll see you tomorrow, Amy. After school.'

'Thank you, Doctor,' she answered gravely.

*   *   *

So began the long hard days of her mam's illness and her disappearance into the hospital. They were all disconcerted, those of them old enough to understand, when, the second time their pa came home from the Royal Infirmary on Brownlow Hill, he told them that she was being transferred to some special hospital, an isolation hospital it was called, way out in the country near Broad Green where Pa could not possibly visit her. Not in the bit of spare time available to him. Even to get to the Royal Infirmary had been a difficult task, for Pa was tired when he got home from his shift which began so early in the morning and didn't finish until after the children came home from school. He had even tried to borrow a bicycle belonging to one of the men he worked with but the man needed it himself and though he was willing to lend it now and again he certainly couldn't let Ben Pearson have it every day, he told Ben apologetically. Anyway, when Mam went to the isolation hospital it was too far even for Pa on a bicycle.

The next blow was their Eddy. Doctor Ferguson, who came nearly every day to talk to Amy, didn't like the look of him, he told her on the quiet and he feared, though this he kept to himself, that the child suffered from the same ailment as the mother. His lungs had that ominous sound he had come to recognise, he had developed a cough and appeared to be losing weight. Amy confessed that their Eddy sweated a lot which was a bad sign and James Ferguson, to be on the safe side, decided to sound all their chests except for the father who shrugged him off saying he was fine and he couldn't for the life of him see why Doctor Ferguson had to poke about at his children when it was obvious they were all thriving.

'Eddy isn't, Mr Pearson.'

Ben Pearson turned surly. He was not a bad husband or father by the standards of the day and he was doing his best to hold his family together while Dolly, who was his strength and shield, was poorly but he resented the way this doctor was trying to run his life for him.

'What do you intend doing with Eddy then?' as though the doctor had fearful designs on his son.

'I think he should be admitted to the children's hospital for a complete examination.' Doctor

Ferguson had deliberately visited the family in the evening when he knew the father would be at home. The room was warm and they had evidently had a decent hot meal, for there was an appetising smell of meat and vegetables and what he thought might be pastry. Possibly a meat and potato pie? And could he smell freshly baked bread? Had the child cooked it? The room was clean, even what might be called spotless. There was a glowing fire in the centre of the range which itself was shining with blacklead. A kettle sat on the hot plate next to a flat iron and above the range a rack held several old pans and some worn dishes. The floor had been scrubbed and the bed in which Dolly and Ben Pearson slept had been stripped and someone had washed the bedding, for the sheets and two coarse pillow cases were airing above the range.

Into James Ferguson's mind came a nasty suspicion. Everything looked so spick and span. The children were clean, even their boots stood in a row beside the fire and had evidently been polished recently.

'Mr Pearson, may I ask who is keeping your home and your children so ... immaculate? Not that I am complaining, far from it, but it is evident that someone is cleaning and cooking and even, somehow, laundering your bed-linen—'

Ben Pearson interrupted sulkily. 'Someone's got to do it, Doctor, just as someone's got to bring in the money to feed us. With my wife in hospital, which means only one wage coming in to the house, I have to work all the extra hours I can get so—'

'So Amy is being kept from school, is that it? Have the inspectors not been to see you? They do not like a child—'

'No, they haven't. They know at the school how I am placed and that someone has to see to the little ones and ... all the rest. They'll take them away, Doctor, you know that, and put them in care—the poorhouse.'

'Hardly that, Mr Pearson, but you must see that Amy's schooling is very important.'

'So's my family, and I'll thank you to mind your own business. Ever since you came here you've done nothing but interfere—'

'May I remind you that you called me in, Mr Pearson. Had you not done so your wife might now be dead.' At once he was sorry he said that, for the children all began to cry, except Amy. She was folding a heap of clothing into neat piles, probably ready to iron them with the flat iron that stood above the fire but she almost fell as he spoke and her face, which was strained and very pale, turned grey. She was doing work a grown woman would find hard to cope with, keeping the place clean as her mother used to do, shopping, going from market to market to find the cheapest food, a tribe of young ones with her, as five of them were still not at school, cooking and, since there were no facilities for laundry in this tiny hovel, making her way to the Bath House, again working as her mother had done. She seemed even thinner than when he had first seen her and if something wasn't done for this family she would be the next to collapse as her mother had done. And he knew she took her brothers and sisters to the soup kitchen every day while her father was at work, for he had made it his business to observe her there. It was probably what was keeping them from starving.

41

He stood up abruptly and so did Mr Pearson. 'You must have some help, Mr Pearson. I shall arrange for Eddy to be admitted to the hospital tomorrow and a close watch must be kept on your other children. The illness your wife is suffering from is extremely infectious and it would be advisable to have them all examined.' Particularly the child who is taking on the job of a grown woman, one that is beyond her strength. He did not say this last but the child did have a somewhat sudden hectic flush on her face.

'Yer can't tekk our Eddy, Doctor,' Amy said desperately. ' 'E'd fret summat terrible wi'out us. Can't yer give 'im some medsin or let me look after 'im at 'ome? 'E already misses Mam, we all do, an' ter tekk 'im away . . . well . . .' Tears began to run down her cheeks and dripped on to the bib of the white pinafore which evidently belonged to her mother. James Ferguson felt his own heart stir in his chest for this brave child who had already far too much to contend with, but he knew he could not allow his emotions to get the better of him. Consumption, or tuberculosis as it was more often called, had been a killer for hundreds of years. It destroyed its victims more slowly than many other infectious diseases but it was ranked among the biggest killers in the world. Millions of young children and adults succumbed to the lingering disease and he must not let it happen to this family if he could help it. It was cruel but then—a stupid cliché—he must be cruel to be kind.

'Can I count on you to bring Eddy to the children's hospital—you know where it is—good girl. Then I will leave you.' He turned to Ben Pearson. 'I'm sorry, Mr Pearson, but it is for the best and your son will be well looked after.'

'Can we come an' see our Eddy?' ventured Sammy, who thought it might be good fun to see the inside of a hospital since he had never done so. He liked a bit of fun did Sammy and if it kept him off school all the better.

'No, son,' the doctor said kindly. 'Eddy will be kept ...' He had been about to say away from other children but then that might be too hard on this already sad family. Poor little Eddy, fretful for his mother and now to be taken away from those he knew and thrust into a world where he would be all alone, but he must be firm for the sake of the others. They must all be thoroughly examined to make sure none of them carried the disease and something must be done about Amy because the burden she carried was too heavy for her frail shoulders.

'Eddy might even be able to be with your mother,' he told them encouragingly, knowing he was not speaking the truth, 'but in the meanwhile I want you all to come to my surgery on Saturday and I will examine you. And Amy'—unaware that his voice noticeably softened when he spoke her name—'I'm going to see if I can find someone to help you.'

'We can't pay anyone, Doctor,' Ben told him sourly. 'I'm sorry about our Amy but we've no choice. Until my wife comes home she must do what her mother did.'

'Perhaps you might help her, Mr Pearson,' Doctor Ferguson said curtly. 'With the housework, I mean.' The children, even Sammy, sensed that there was tension in the room, an argument between their pa and the doctor, and those on the bench huddled closer together. They had never had much, and were used to it, having known nothing else, but their mam had always been there, standing between them and whatever other children had to put up with. They had known love, the protection of responsible parents, though they could not have worded it so. They had each other, cheerful laughter, a noisy, quarrelsome, carefree life, for their mother had never allowed them to realise that they were forever balancing on the edge of the precipice between desperate poverty and just, *only just* hanging on. Now they had been made to understand—as far as they could—that they might fall over that precipice and end up in that home for the hopeless and despairing, the workhouse!

'Doctor, I can manage, 'onest,' Amy burst out. 'Don't tekk em ter't work'ouse,' although it had not been voiced. 'Me mam'll be 'ome soon an' then I'll go back ter school. Our Elsie'll 'elp me, won't yer, chuck?' turning a desolate look on her sister. 'She'll mind little 'uns while I go ter't market. When she gets 'ome from school, I mean.'

'But you must go to school, Amy, don't you see?'

'No, No, don't *you* see? I'll not let me family be took ter't work'ouse. I'll fetch our Eddy ter the 'ospital termorrer an' on Sat'day we'll all come ter your place an' yer can do wharrever yer want ter do burr I'll not leave 'em. Tell 'im, Pa.'

She turned a desperate tear-stained face to her father who stood beside the fire, one elbow on the shelf above it, his head in his hand. His other hand, hanging at his side, clenched and unclenched in his frustration, not just for his

44

family but for himself, as how was he to manage all this without Dolly? She'd been taken away from them so suddenly he could not pull himself together and organise his family as this bloody doctor was telling him. Even when Dolly had been poorly in her bed she had told him what to do, how to share the work and school among the older children; now he was in a hopeless mess and it was easier if he left it all to Amy who was as capable as Dolly and so far they had managed. He knew the school inspector would be knocking on the door soon to find out why their Amy wasn't attending school but he'd cross that bridge when he came to it. In the meanwhile he'd go to work, while there *was* work and money to be earned, which was surely what a family man was supposed to do. The kids could go to be examined as this damned doctor was insiting and if any of them needed treatment he'd see to it that they got it. What more could be asked of him?

'I'll think on it,' he muttered as he indicated that the doctor should leave, and when he had done so he turned to the anxious group of his children and grinned.

'Well, that's him gone, nosey old sod,' then clapped his hand to his mouth in mock horror because he had said a rude word.

They all fell about in relieved laughter, even Amy, for she still believed her pa was the best in the world.

4

Sometimes she thought that if she didn't have a day to herself with no frantic demands on her time she would . . . well, she wasn't sure what she would do, but from the moment she slipped from the palliasse she shared with Elsie and Becky she was on the go until she fell into bed where they were already asleep. She liked to see her pa off and since he started at six it was about five o'clock when they rose as Pa had to walk down to the Pier Head and catch the ferry to Birkenhead. The children left for school at half past eight so the two hours while they still lay sleeping and the house was quiet she swept and scrubbed and scoured and blackleaded the already shining range. She took great pride in keeping their home as Mam would have done and even managed to donkey-stone the front step, though she drew the line at scrubbing the bit of pavement in front of their house as Mrs Derwent did at number seventeen.

They had all been examined the weekend after Mam went to hospital and sadly, Sidney, one of the twins, had been found to have what ailed Mam and Eddy so that meant he must stop with Eddy at the Children's Isolation Hospital at Toxteth Park. The workhouse and the different departments of the sprawling hospital were right next to Toxteth Park Cemetery which Amy thought a bit sinister but she kept that to herself. They weren't allowed to visit poor little Eddy or Sidney but they had the consolation of knowing that the two little brothers had beds next to one another which the kind

Doctor Ferguson had arranged and which would comfort them.

The children were dragged, protesting, from their beds at half past seven, for with five of them to be got ready for school, washed, dressed, hair brushed and fed breakfast of porridge and perhaps a bit of toast held on a long fork against the bars that contained the fire and spread with lard, it was all go! A hot cup of weak tea, no milk or sugar of course, and then, wrapped up in their scarves and shawls and boots, Sammy and Billy with caps on their straw-coloured thatch of hair, a kiss each and with Dick, Annie and Phyllis hanging on to her skirt, their thumbs in their mouths, she saw them off, trusting to Elsie to get them to Lower Milk Street.

At dinner-time there was a real scramble. She met them at the school gates and, always at a run, for they only had an hour, she raced them to the soup kitchen at the workhouse on King Edward Street. She had to carry Phyllis who was only two years old, wrapping her in her old shawl but at least Dick and Annie could manage to walk it. Mrs Derwent had offered to mind the little ones while Amy picked up the others but then that would mean that Dick, Annie and Phyllis wouldn't get the heartening bowl of soup which was the most nourishing meal of their day, filled with vegetables and bits of meat with a chunk of bread on the side.

She then had to hurry them back to Lower Milk Street in time for the bell before tramping with her basket to St John's Market with her few pennies in her hand to search out the cheapest food she could find. Potatoes mostly, carrots, onions, perhaps a bit of fish—cod, of course—left over from yesterday and almost off, and even a chunk of cheese. Doctor Ferguson said she was to feed the children on fish, cheese and milk when she could get it, which would build them up.

Doctor Ferguson visited them almost every day in Earle Street, questioning Amy on what they were eating and wearing, their sleeping arrangements, always coming when Pa was at work. It was an unspoken understanding that Pa believed Doctor Ferguson to be an unwelcome busybody but he certainly was an enormous help and support to Amy.

She had a tremendous stroke of luck three or four weeks after what she called the disaster had struck them down when kind Mrs Derwent from across the road knocked on her door, an ancient pram beside her. It was black, battered, deep and had no hood or brake, indeed it seemed to be no more than a box on four small wheels with a handle at one end. Inside it had a seat at both ends and a well in its centre where a child could put its feet. The padding was torn and in some places missing and the piece to cover the central well to allow a baby to lie down was also gone.

Amy, with the usual array of thumb-sucking toddlers clutching at her skirts, stared in astonishment.

Mrs Derwent beamed. 'What d'yer think, chuck? I know it's nowt ter look at but yer could put kids in an' better'n carryin' 'em, innit? Our Em's on't change'—which meant nothing to Amy!—'an'll 'ave no more. She were gonner give it rag'n'-bone man burr I thought o' you an', well, 'ere it is.'

Amy was overjoyed. If she had been offered one

48

of the high, elegant prams she had seen on the promenade pushed by trim nannies, with fittings that kept the hood up or down and a porcelain handle, she could not have been more delighted. It meant she could squash their Dick, Annie and Phyllis into the pram and push them at her own speed without constantly calling back to Dick and Annie who, after all, were only four and three, to keep up. It was difficult to carry their Phyllis *and* the shopping and since she seemed to spend so much time running backwards and forwards it would be a godsend. This way she could do everything in half the time and the children wouldn't get so tired. The difficulty, of course, was where to store the pram, as they had no hallway, the door from the street leading directly into the scullery-cum-living room which was already jammed with furniture and so many of the family. She managed, before Pa came home, to juggle a bit of space for it in the corner near the boarded staircase, pushing Mam's chair into the other corner which, of course, would be brought back to the fire when Mam came home, and shoving the table and benches nearer the range. Sammy was enchanted with it, wanting to play in it, make a boat, a carriage pulled by horses like the grand ladies had, even a horseless carriage which he had seen on Lime Street.

Pa wasn't much concerned with it as long as it didn't take up too much room, he said, and he could still rest in his chair, and how kind of Mrs Derwent, he added vaguely. Mind you, Pa didn't come home as early as he had done when Mam was there and on a Friday, though he put his wage packet into Amy's hands, it had always been opened and she suspected a copper or two had been kept out of it. Some nights she could smell the drink on him but poor Pa was sad without Mam so who was she to blame him? With what he gave her and the nourishing bowl of broth the children had each day, they managed.

It was almost April and Mam and the two boys had been gone since January but Doctor Ferguson still looked in on them and told them that all three patients were doing nicely but they must not expect them home just yet.

'Try to get to the park with the children, Amy,' he begged her, concerned that she should have an outing more than the others. 'They are all at home on a Sunday. Take them along the side of the river as far as you can then turn up Park Street. Princes Park isn't very far and if you take the pram'— which he thought was a wonderful gift for the overworked child about whom he worried the most—'the little ones could manage it and you could have a nice sit-down. The spring flowers are out, forget-me-nots and daffodils and—'

'Mam loves daffodils,' Amy said raptly. 'They're 'er favourite.'

Sammy didn't want to go. It was a girl's thing, he said disparagingly, but Amy clapped his hand to the pram handle on one side with Billy on the other and Elsie, Becky and Claire skipping along behind. Dick, Annie and Phyllis were lumped together in the pram and with great excitement, despite Sammy's grumbles, they set off down Earle Street towards the river and the Marine Parade. Mrs Derwent waved to them as they went.

It took no more than an hour and would have been less if Sammy had not had a confrontation with a policeman!

They took turns pushing the pram, Sammy making its occupants shriek with laughter as he ran at full tilt pretending to be a train, giving voice to all the appropriate noises, which they were familiar with living so close to Exchange Station. They had brought a couple of bottles of water and 'doorsteps', thick sandwiches spread with bacon fat.

It was a cool spring day but with a hint of the summer warmth to come. The sky, since it was Sunday when the factory chimneys were at rest, stretched blue and cloudless, unpolluted by smoke, across the river to the Welsh hills beyond. The river was busy, not only with steam ships like the Royal Mail steamer just entering the locks but also with old sailing ships still working their graceful way about the busy waters, alongside tugs such as the *Alexandra* and the *Trafalgar* shepherding a liner to her mooring. A tender, the *Skirmisher*, was ferrying passengers and their baggage to a moored ocean- going liner. A lovely sailing vessel leaning to port headed towards Liverpool after passing New Brighton Stage, and the ferry boat *Lily* was not far behind en route for Liverpool from New Brighton. New Brighton Tower rose majestically on the far side of the river, 620 feet high and said to be taller than Blackpool Tower.

At the start of Princes Parade Sammy abandoned the pram and began to swing on the chains that separated the parade from the river. He swung himself over the dancing, silvery water, almost tipping himself into it. Billy soon copied his older brother and Amy, capturing the pram and screaming at them to 'give over', attracted one of

51

the dock 'bobbies' who sauntered over and grasped each boy by the collar. He was wearing his summer, lightweight helmet which almost fell off his head into the river.

'Now then, you lads,' he roared, 'what would yer mam say if she saw yer riskin' yer life? I bet yer can't even swim.'

'Me mam's in 'ospital,' Sammy piped up and at once the constable softened his approach.

'I'm right sorry ter 'ear that, lad, but yer can't go swingin'—'

''E needs 'is ears boxing,' Amy interrupted, dragging Sammy and Billy back to the safety of the pram and giving the bobby such a dazzling smile he was quite enchanted.

'Right, queen, but keep 'em away from't water, won't yer?'

'I will, mister,' she promised, and, gathering her flock about her, she walked briskly on until at last they reached Princes Park.

For many reasons she was to remember that day until her last hour, speaking of it often in the intervening years. She was sure later on that they must have appeared to be a bunch of ragamuffins to the many respectable families who were strolling in the park that Sunday in April. Well-dressed ladies and gentlemen arm-in-arm beside their well-dressed, well-behaved children. The ladies wore long, fluted skirts, some with frills falling in a cascade down the back and fitted bodices that emphasised their tiny waists. Their hats were like a cartwheel, some decorated with a positive garden of flowers. The gentlemen were in a morning coat of check tweed with trousers to match, it being the weekend, and what was known

52

as a 'bowler' with the brim curved up at the sides and in a colour to match their suits. Their children were miniature replicas of their parents, the boys in tweed suits and a cap with a button on top, the girls in calf-length dresses pouched at the waists and floppy hats shaped like a beret. They stared in amazement at the Pearson boys in their second-hand garments bought at the market, a mixture of short trousers which were still too long to allow for their growing, shirts several sizes too big, jackets that had seen better days but were clean and well mended, and enormous black boots from which their thin ankles protruded. The girls were no better in skirts of worn cotton and bodices that didn't match, with a shawl about their heads and, like the boys, boots, black and well polished. Though they were unaware of it, they made a comical sight. They were stared at with disapproval as they erupted into the park, Dick, Annie and Phyllis screaming to be lifted from the pram, which itself compared unfavourably with the elegant baby carriages pushed by stern-faced, starched nannies.

There was scandalised interest in their noisy appearance as the nine of them simply went mad with joy. They had never seen such a vast expanse of grass on which to race and jump, to play leap-frog and tig, and the small wooded areas, the shrubberies that ran alongside the carefully swept paths, made an excellent place to play hide-and-seek. There were cafés and a bandstand where men in uniforms played stirring tunes, and glass buildings filled with hundreds of colourful flowers. It was behind one of these that they found the clumps of resplendent, large-trumpeted, wild daffodils. Their golden heads were perfect and the children were rapt and silent as they collected a large bunch for Mam, packing them carefully in the well of the pram.

As they left the shelter behind the glass buildings, they sang the song their mam had taught them:

Daffy-down-dilly came up to town,
In her yellow petticoat and her green gown.

She did love daffodils!

They were relatively quiet for a while as they ate their butties and drank their 'Corporation pop', sprawled on the grass beside the pram. The sun had some warmth in it and they relaxed, even Sammy, who, though he could have eaten more of the butties, had been taught to share whatever food his mam, and now Amy, produced for them. He watched in some wonder the passers-by and their children, making some scathing remarks about their appearance just as they made about his.

'Look at tha' lad, will yer? 'E favvers them dummies yer see in Lewis's winder. Talk abou' a mardy beggar. 'E'll 'ave ter mind 'e don't gerris kecks mucky or 'is mam'll clout 'im.'

'Now then, our Sammy,' Amy reproached him mildly, though they were all goggle-eyed with wonder.

They found the small lake after their picnic and at once they were all entranced—and wet!—particularly Sammy who was all for stripping off to his ragged underclothes and would have done so had not Amy restrained him. They splashed and

54

shrieked to one another as they raced round its perimeter, disturbing the ducks who flew across the lake calling their displeasure and further attracting the attention of the other people in the park. Even Amy, since she was but a child herself, forgot the reserve she had developed in the last three months. Nevertheless she kept a tight hold on a protesting Phyllis.

The noise of their excitement and the ducks' irritation drew the attention of the park-keeper who marched in their direction, urged on by the incensed *respectable* folk who had had their peaceful perambulation upset by the horde of common children shouting with laughter by the lakeside.

''Ere, you lot, what d'yer think yer doin'?' he bellowed, his face scarlet with indignation. 'Gerrout o' that lake at once, yer little 'ooligans, an' don't you cheek me,' he added, seeing the words forming on Sammy's lips. 'Out yer get an' tekk that pram wi' yer. I dunno what worl's comin' to when likes o' you can upset decent folk ... sorry, madam, sir,' turning apologetically to an irate couple whose small dog had slipped its lead and ran barking hysterically to join the fun. 'See, you'—pointing at Sammy who had picked up his boots and was racing towards the pram into which Amy had flung the three youngest—'grab that dog fer't lady an' gentleman ...'

'Gerrit yerself,' Sammy shouted gleefully and, still laughing, they all raced off towards the gates, their wet, bare feet leaving imprints on the path.

They all agreed as they made their tired way homewards that it had been one of the best days of their lives and wouldn't Mam love the daffodils.

Did Amy think Doctor Ferguson would take them into her tomorrow after he had called, which he did most days, and they could put them into a bucket of water until he came? The problem of where they would store the water for their own use—since the bucket was used in this capacity—did not occur to them.

'An' don't you put them feet o' yours on them, our Annie,' Sammy warned his little sister as they trudged along Edmund Street and turned the corner into Earle Street.

They all stopped as one at the strange sight of the cab drawn up to the kerb halfway down the street. There were women in pinnies leaning in doorways, their arms akimbo, for the presence of such a vehicle in their neighbourhood was unusual. In fact not one of them could ever remember seeing one before, only the doctor's gig outside the Pearsons' house which was where the cab now stood. The cabbie was perched on his seat and he and his horse had taken the opportunity to fall into a light doze.

''Oo is it, our Amy?' Elsie whispered and for some reason drew closer to her sister. Both Sammy and Billy willingly clung to the pram handle while Becky and Claire grasped their sister's skirt. These children were too familiar with dramatic events in their recent past and they were not sure they liked the look of this.

'Nay, don't ask me,' she murmured. 'P'raps Mam's come 'ome.' But with some reluctance she moved them on towards number twenty-two.

The front door was not locked. She pushed it open hesitantly and peeped inside as the others crowded behind her. Phyllis and Annie had fallen

56

asleep after their hectic day, sprawling in the pram, which remained on the pavement. As she opened the door Pa, who had been sitting as usual in his armchair, leaped to his feet, an expression on his face Amy could not read. It was a mixture of different emotions, too fleeting for her to decipher, but somehow a great, pounding terror filled her, tearing at her heart and unconsciously she began to shake her head in denial, at what she didn't know. Perhaps Mam had ... oh, please, don't let Mam be dead ...

'Amy, chuck,' he began, 'there you are. We've been waiting for you. See, we have a visitor,' and it was then that Amy noticed the woman who sat in Mam's chair which had been dragged from its corner and placed before the fire in the range. *Cheek!*

The children turned their gaze on the woman in Mam's chair and she turned hers on them. It was a cool gaze, one that told them that here was someone who would stand for no nonsense and again, instinctively, like young chicks who have mislaid the mother hen, they drew together.

'Children,' Pa said, his lips forming an artificial smile, 'this is your Aunty Zillah come to visit—'

'Hardly *visit*, Reuben,' the woman said. Her voice was as chill as her eyes. She sat, her back as straight as a board, her feet in black buttoned boots planted together on the linoleum. She was all in black, plain and unadorned, her ugly hat squarely on her head, her gloved hands clasping her handbag on her lap. She was pale, thin-lipped, her eyes the same grey as their pa's but where his were a smoky, velvety grey, hers were like flint.

'And I would prefer *Aunt* to Aunty, Reuben.'

Reuben! Their pa was called Ben.

'No, sorry, Zillah. Now, let me introduce you. There's Amy, she's the eldest, next is Elsie, Becky and Claire, then there's—'

'Have not your girls been taught to curtsey to their elders, Reuben? No, I suppose not in the circumstances . . .' glancing disapprovingly about the room.

'And the boys are—' Pa continued but she interrupted him.

'Never mind the boys.'

'No, sorry, Zillah. There are two more girls in—'

'How old?'

Perplexed, Pa turned to Amy. 'Amy . . . ?'

'Our Annie's three, Phyllis is two.'

'Too young. You certainly have been prolific, Reuben.' Her tone conveyed disgust.

Too young for what, Amy wondered, and what did prolific mean?

'I believe two of your boys are in hospital with your . . . with their mother. How many is that then?'

'Eleven.' He sounded ashamed. 'But how did you know—' Pa continued, but the woman stood up abruptly, lifting her hand to silence him. He stopped speaking at once. Amy had never seen her pa so nervous. He was missing their mam who looked after them all, including him. Mam made the decisions, took charge of everything from his wages, the clothes he wore, *them*, meaning her brothers and sisters, and he had been lost ever since Mam had been taken poorly. She herself had done her best to replace Mam until she came home and pulled them all together, making Pa laugh again, cheerful again. In fact *himself* again.

58

'Well, bring in the others if you please,' the woman said. She looked coldly at Amy who began to feel some slight resentment at the way this woman—Aunt Zillah indeed—was ordering her and Pa about but something in her expression, in her eyes which, strangely, never seemed to blink, the way she stood as though she owned the bloody place—and that was swearing—put a stiffener in her spine.

'They're asleep,' she said shortly.

'Then wake them,' the woman said just as shortly.

Amy looked at her pa for support but he was staring unhappily at some spot on the linoleum, taking swift glances at the woman—she refused absolutely to call her Aunt Zillah, even to herself—and Amy got the feeling she was on her own in this, whatever it was. The children, all of them, even Sammy, seemed to have turned into small, frozen statues, hypnotised by the woman's power over Pa, for it was obvious he was afraid of her. Was she Pa's sister then, if he called her their aunt and what the devil did she want?

Her pa shrugged. 'Best get them in, Amy,' he told her and after a moment's hesitation which tightened the already grim line of the woman's mouth, Amy moved to obey. Both the toddlers were fractious as she carried Phyllis and led Annie by the hand into the silent kitchen.

'It seems discipline is lacking in this household,' the woman said, 'but then that is not my concern. Now then, let me see . . .'

'Zillah, won't you—' Pa began, his face working in the strangest way.

'Be quiet, Reuben. You know what we have

agreed.'

'Yes, but Dolly is—'

'Be quiet, Reuben,' and Pa did as he was told.

For perhaps five minutes the woman studied them in total silence except for the whimpering of Phyllis who clung round Amy's neck like a little monkey. Eventually the woman seemed to come to a decision.

She pointed at Amy. 'That one, I think. She looks the most promising.'

'Zillah, I beg you, she . . . I cannot manage, not with Dolly gone . . . just a loan until Dolly—'

'That's enough, Reuben. You always were a sniveller. Get her things together. On second thoughts, don't bother,' her eyes travelling up and down the worn outfit Amy had on. 'Just a coat, if such a thing is available. Now, do stop idling about. I . . . we have a train to catch.'

5

Caleb Seymour had known nothing but cotton since he had been able to say the word. His father had been the owner of three successful cotton manufacturing mills on the corner of Pickford Street and Union Street. The Union Cotton Manufacturing Mills they were called, which young Caleb had inherited on his father's death, and as well as the mills he owned a warehouse on Moseley Street. As his father had done before him, he had worked beside their own mill hands in every department and process of the cotton trade. First at the lap-frame which cleaned the raw

60

cotton, then the carding engine which formed it into a soft rope or strip. On to the bobbin and drawing frames and from there to the spinning room where the bobbins were placed on the mule spinning wheels. Young Caleb had not only stood at one of these machines, as a boy he had acted as a piecer and a scavenger beneath the lethally moving machinery. He had taken part in the bleaching process, the warping and winding, the weaving, the dyeing and the printing and there was not one process at the mill that he did not know intimately.

They did not call Manchester the Warehouse Town for nothing, since the warehouse played a vital role in its economic life and in the warehouse district of the city was one that young Caleb coveted. It was owned by a man with one remaining child, a daughter by the name of Zillah.

In 1884, when he was twenty-three, Caleb Seymour married Zillah Pearson and when Alfred Pearson died three years later Caleb changed the name on the façade of the wide, three-storeyed warehouse from Pearson's to Seymour's. He had not loved Zillah Pearson whose family were staunch Methodists and she had loved no one other than her God and John Wesley, but they both desired children, he to inherit his thriving businesses, she to bring souls to her God. For twenty years they had done their duty, he reluctantly, aware of the need, she distastefully, to have a child but to no avail.

He heard the vehicle draw up to the pillared portico at the front of the house and though he had known Zillah had left home in her carriage early that morning, which had surprised him, he had assumed she was off on some chapel business. She normally walked the length of Langworthy Road three times on a Sunday, taking as many of the servants as could be spared from the preparation of Sunday dinner to St John's Methodist Chapel, the running of which she was deeply involved in, sometimes, Caleb thought, to the annoyance of the preacher, but as long as she did not expect him to share her fanaticism, her comings and goings held no particular interest for him. She had not joined him in Sunday dinner and he did not enquire of Alice who served him where her mistress might be.

Nevertheless, for some reason he could not explain, when he heard the vehicle draw up he rose from his comfortable leather armchair in his study and wandered to the window overlooking the drive, his newspaper in his hand. He was astonished to see her alight, not from her carriage but from a cab, reaching inside to give a helping hand to a small girl. Well, you could hardly call it giving a helping hand, for it seemed to him she positively dragged the reluctant child on to the gravelled driveway.

Jess, as usual, had opened the front door, gawping as he supposed he was at Zillah and the child, but at a gesture from her mistress the parlour-maid paid the cabby and followed her into the hallway, shutting the door sharply behind her. At the sound Caleb came out of his surprised state and made for the hallway where Zillah was handing her hat and coat to Jess. The child stood, her eyes blank, in what was obviously a state of complete shock, looking at nothing, remaining where Zillah had put her. Caleb himself was in a state of perturbation though it was not his nature to show it. By the expression on his face one might imagine Zillah brought home a small ragged child every day.

And she was ragged! Her skirt and bodice, both a much washed-out grey, were neatly patched and the shawl that drooped from her thin, childish shoulders was so faded the colours were barely recognisable. She wore heavy, black boots that appeared to be too large for her but no stockings. Her hair, a curious but lovely blend of honey, amber, gold and a tawny brown, writhed down her back in wild curls to her waist and his first amused thought was that Zillah would soon change that. But who was she?

He asked Zillah. 'And who is this?'

Zillah had been instructing Jess on the preparation of the small back bedroom at the top of the house for the child, the room where Alice, the head housemaid, usually slept. Alice could share with Jess for the moment, she was saying, until other arrangements could be made. The child needed a bath, something to eat, Mrs Abigail would know what, and Jess was to find the child something to wear and put her to bed and later she, Zillah, would speak to Mrs Abigail.

Jess, who was speechless with amazement, curiosity, resentment at having to share with Alice, and what looked like pity, took the child's hand and led her away. Zillah turned to him as though she had just noticed he was there.

'Who is she?' she repeated. 'She's my brother's child, Caleb, and I am to adopt her.' The flat statement fell on his dumbfounded ears as she moved towards the drawing room, expecting him

63

to follow her, which he did, his usually impassive face slack-jawed.

'Your brother's child? But your brother is dead.'

'No, he is not. He left home before you and I were married, ran away . . .'

'I know that but he died on the Indian Frontier . . .'

'No, he deserted the army and disappeared but my father, who did not get on with Reuben, let it be believed that he had died a hero's death on the Black Mountain expedition. He disinherited him, secretly but legally so that everything came to me . . . and you. It seems he married some low woman in Liverpool who bore him eleven children; can you imagine?' Her face assumed a look of revulsion as though she had stepped in something nasty. 'The mother is ill, tuberculosis. I had kept myself acquainted as to his whereabouts and when I discovered the circumstances I offered to take one of his girls. You saw her. She is ten years old, quite rebellious but I shall soon have her biddable.'

Poor little bugger, was his next thought, but he knew it was a waste of time to interfere. His wife picked up her Bible in dismissal and as he made his way back to his study he felt a certain compassion for the lass. She didn't know what she was in for. It wouldn't affect him since he was seldom at home, but still . . . !

*   *   *

Amy lay in the narrow bed where the lady in the apron had put her, her mind one moment blank and without thought, the next whirling in the

64

nightmare that had come upon her.

She had not understood at first when Pa had said she was to go with the woman. In fact she had laughed, *laughed*, thinking it was a joke or that Pa had lost his mind, for how could the family manage without her to look after them until Mam came home from hospital? The others, not understanding, had stared at the woman, then at Pa, then back at her, fidgeting from foot to foot, but not daring to move from the spot on which they had come to rest as they pushed their way into the house. Only Phyllis, who still clung round Amy's neck, had wriggled.

'Put the baby down, child,' the woman had told her shortly, 'and look sharp. I want to get home before dark. Oh, and here's something to help out, Reuben,' she went on, turning to Pa and handing him some money. 'And there's more where that came from. Give these children a decent meal and put them in serviceable clothes. Of course, you know the girl will be well looked after. I can promise you she will want for nothing.'

'Zillah . . .' her pa croaked.

'Now then, Reuben. You know it's for the best, for all of them. You remember what I said.'

'I know, but she's . . .'

But the woman was losing patience. She stalked over to Amy and dragged Phyllis from her arms. At once Phyllis began to scream, and so did Amy. From what the woman said it seemed Pa was selling her but the woman took no notice of her or of Phyllis who stood where the woman had placed her and wet herself.

The woman took hold of Amy's sleeve and with her in tow marched towards the front door but

Amy was having none of that. She screamed and screamed and dug her heels into the linoleum, scratching its already scuffed surface with her hobnailed boots.

'Pa ... Pa, don't lerrer tekk me, please,' she shrieked, but the woman had her in a firm grip round her wrist. It was then Amy went limp.

'Goodness me, what an intransigent child,' the woman remarked calmly. She picked Amy up and stood her on her feet but Amy merely crumpled again, moaning piteously. They were all crying, even Pa, but the woman appeared to be unmoved by it all.

'Stand up, girl,' she ordered Amy, hauling her once more into an upright position. She turned to Pa. 'Can you not discipline this girl? She must be made to obey her elders.'

'Amy, sweetheart ...' Pa began hoarsely. 'Be a good girl and go with your Aunt Zillah. She'll—'

'No, Pa. No, Pa. No, Pa, don't say that. I must stay' she shrieked at the top of her voice, terrified and at the same time furious that Pa should be agreeing to this. Her voice rose higher and higher and the children cowered away in terror, uncomprehending.

The slap across her face made her reel and she would have fallen had not the woman held her wrist.

'There's only one way to deal with hysterics,' she declared. 'I will not be bested by a child. Now then, since you're quiet we will leave.'

Amy barely remembered anything after that as she fell into the blackest of black shock. Images flashed through her dazed mind: half the inhabitants of Earle Street standing in their doorways wondering what was going on at number twenty-two, the cab drive to Lime Street Station, the curious look on the cab-driver's face, the woman sitting straight-backed beside her, the bustle and clangour of the station, the train ride which, in her right mind, she would have found exciting, unidentifiable noises, people brushing by her, another ride in a cab, the fleeting impression of trees and daffodils, a horse whinnying, voices, steps, warm water in a tub, a smile from a kind face before she fell into a state which, though she was not actually unconscious, paralysed her.

*   *   *

'Poor little bugger,' Jess said as she entered the kitchen, echoing the words her master had said to himself. She held the tattered garments she had taken from the child over her arm, for she had discovered that though they might be patched and darned, they were clean. In her other hand she held the oversized black boots. 'Look what she 'ad on, poor kid, but her ladyship ses they're ter be burned. God knows what she's ter put on 'er termorrer. Honest, yer should see 'er. Like a bit o' white thread, she is, 'er little bones stickin' out an' eyes on 'er like saucers but seein' nowt an' sayin' nowt. Bonny though, or she will be when she gets a bit o' flesh on 'er. An' 'er hair, long an' curlin' right down her back an' the colour—well, I never seen owt like it.'

Mrs Abigail, who was at the stove with a basting spoon in her hand ready to tend to the chicken in the oven, tutted irritably. 'Never mind that, who is she, Jess, and what's she doing here? Did she say?

67

Where's she come from?'

They all gravitated to the centre of the kitchen, crowding round the enormous, well-scrubbed table on which Mrs Abigail did all her work. They were eager to know what 'her ladyship', as they sometimes called her, was up to. The kitchen, in sharp contrast to the hushed atmosphere at the front of the house, was bright, cheerful, even noisy. Ernie Tingle, who had been employed by the Seymours since time immemorial and cared nowt for nobody—meaning those above him in the social strata—had made sure that the connecting door was well insulated by the addition of extra green baize on both sides, for they all liked a bit of a laugh at times. He was the best man with horses Caleb Seymour's father had ever known and would never lose his job, but he was also good with his hands. He could fix anything from a broken clock to a creaking gate and was well aware that he had work at Somerfield for as long as he needed it. He had a cosy little cottage next to the stables, his for life and a pension promised as well. He was sharp-tempered, outspoken and hardworking. He was also kind-hearted, though he did his best to conceal it!

'Don't ask me,' Jess said in answer to Mrs Abigail's question. 'She 'asn't spoken a word, I told you, didn't I. She just stood there like a doll, lettin' me undress 'er an' put 'er in the tub. I kept talkin' to 'er but she never answered an' the mistress said nowt. Just went an' sat down in drawin' room as though it was same as always. An' though she went in't carriage she come back in a cab so we shall 'ave ter ask Thomas where she's bin. 'Appen kid's from work'ouse like Joe. 'As

68

mistress rung the bell fer anythin', Mrs Abigail?'

'No, not a peep out of 'er, nor the master. Now, will I make little lass up a tray?'

Jess clapped her hand to her forehead. 'Dear God, I'd forget me 'ead if it were loose. Give 'er summat ter eat, mistress said. Mrs Abigail'll know what.'

She looked expectantly at the cook who at once sprang into action, for this was an endeavour with which she was very familiar. Feeding folk!

'See, Martha, set the small tray with a cloth ... no, not with the mistress's best damask, you fool, but a nice one, there, that with embroidered flowers Mrs Seymour done. Now, what shall I give her? A boiled egg, I think, soft with some nice buttered toast cut into fingers then she can dip soldiers in. All bairns like that, and there's some o' me fruit cake, an' a glass o' milk. Happen she could get a bit of egg custard down her if she needs building up like what Jess says. Poor little blighter.' And though not one of them except Jess had seen her, they all shook their heads in sympathy for the mysterious child.

'I don't think she comes from't work'ouse, Mrs Abigail,' Jess said, looking round at the assembly who had all resumed their tasks.

'Why not, lass?'

'Well, we know Joe did but she never had 'im in't bath nor put ter bed with a tray.'

They all exchanged glances then shook their heads sagely.

'Oh, an' by't way, Alice,' Jess added as she made for the kitchen door, the tray balanced on one hip as she opened it. 'She's in your room.'

'What!' Alice turned from the tray she was

69

setting for the mistress—with a damask cloth this time—who had rung for tea. Her face was scarlet with indignation.

'Only fer now. You're to sleep wi' me but God knows where the bairn's ter go.'

'Well, I call that a damn cheek,' Alice snorted. 'I wouldn't mind if we knew who she was.'

'I'll try an' get it out of 'er when I tekk tea in,' Jess told her.

'Now then, you two,' Mrs Abigail remarked placidly, for Jess and Alice often argued, going back to her basting. 'We'll be told when it suits madam.'

*　　　*　　　*

The child was lying in exactly the same position in which Jess had left her. Her eyes were wide open, a flat brown gaze that quite alarmed the maid. She did not turn her head when Jess entered the small bedroom. It was furnished with a wrought-iron bed, a plain wardrobe, a dresser on which stood a white jug and bowl, and a tray covered with a lace doily where Alice kept her bits and pieces, a comb, a brush, a small pot of handcream, for Alice liked to keep her hands nice, and a hand mirror. A clean white towel hung on a wooden towel rail.

'Now then,' Jess said cheerfully, 'Cook's made you up a nice tray so you sit up an' tuck in. Yer'll feel better wi' summat inside yer.'

She waited but the little girl did not so much as turn her head on the pillow, which Jess found most disconcerting. She tried again.

'Come on, lass, try an' eat summat.' Jess's speech altered to suit whoever she was speaking

70

to. She wouldn't dream of saying *summat* to the mistress but this child by the look of the clothes Jess had just flung in the fire came from a very poor class. 'Sit up, there's a good girl. Now, what's yer name? Mine's Jess.' But still the child lay motionless, her eyes brown and muddy and unfocused and no matter what Jess said, or how she pleaded, the little lass lay as one dead.

'She won't eat,' Jess cried dramatically to those busy in the kitchen when she returned. 'Look, all this good food what Mrs Abigail's put out fer 'er an' I couldn't even get 'er ter sit up. I reckon she's lost 'er wits, I really do, Mrs Abigail, an' I don't know what ter do.' She put the tray down on the table almost in tears.

'Nay . . .' Mrs Abigail's good heart was shocked.

'She's thin as a stick an' all. If she don't eat . . . d'yer reckon I should tell mistress?'

Alice, who had gathered with the rest of the servants to listen to Jess, shook her head. 'Mistress said nothin'. I sorta hinted, yer know, about who the kid was but you know what's she's like. She were off ter chapel, she said, an' that was that.'

In the narrow, immaculate bed in the narrow, immaculate bedroom at the top of the house, Amy lay, warm, clean and alone for the first time in her life. The lady in the white apron—Jess, was it?—had gone but Amy felt nothing, absolutely nothing and she was truly grateful for it. It would not last, of course, even she, young as she was, knew that; this emptiness, this numbness, would wear off. The desperate misery would return, but for now the horror of it did not touch her. Though her thoughts scuttled about like the cockroaches that invaded the house in Earle Street, some were

71

sensible like the one that had crossed her mind on the train, which was, wouldn't our Sammy have loved this? Others made no sense, it had all happened so quickly: why had Pa sent her away? Did he no longer love her? Even that question did not hurt. Not yet! She knew it would, of course. Had Elsie remembered to sing to the little ones as they were put to bed? The state of the poor old horse that had pulled the cab; she had never been in a cab before, fancy that; funny smell inside it; there was someone whistling outside; the man with the newspaper, who was he? Lovely trees and she had seen daffodils; Mam loved daffodils; the woman, how rude she had been to Pa; the wallpaper was pretty; she was tired; she was frightened of the woman but the lady in the white apron had been nice; cows, she had seen cows from the train; Mam, Mam, where are you? Please, please come and get me. I'm . . .

She fell asleep with her mam's smile imprinted on the inside of her closed eyelids.

*   *   *

In the dining room Zillah and Caleb sat down to the light meal that was traditional on a Sunday evening. Dinner had been served as usual at midday even though the mistress was absent. During the week the master and mistress ate their main meal in the evening since Caleb was at his place of business and did not get home until six or seven o'clock. But today, it being Sunday and Mrs Seymour to be off again to chapel, they ate the chicken and salad Mrs Abigail had prepared. Alice served them, doing her best to blend into the wallpaper so that she might glean some information about the child who, Jess reported, was now fast asleep—lay like one dead was how Jess had described it—in Alice's bed. She was not to be disappointed. Like all those who were used to servants, and as all their acquaintances were wont to do, Zillah and Caleb treated them as though they were not only deaf but also dumb, so that even if they overheard private matters they were incapable of repeating them! Conversations, some quite private, were carried out at mealtimes and, on the whole, well-treated servants did not tattle about their employers' affairs, except among themselves.

'So, are you going to tell me what you are to do with ... well, I suppose she is your niece,' the master said, wiping his lips on the crisp, damask napkin and placing his dessert spoon and fork in the dish before him, which had contained Mrs Abigail's iced pudding. A pint of cream, twelve egg yolks, candied citron, chestnuts and a glass of maraschino and a further half-pint of whipped cream after it had set. Far too much for two people but, as Mrs Abigail said, there were ten of them in the kitchen to feed, weren't there?

'I am to bring her up as my own, Caleb,' the mistress replied calmly.

Alice nearly dropped the dishes that she was removing from the table.

'And am I to have no say in this, my dear?' Mr Seymour asked impassively.

'Do you object, Caleb?' making it quite clear it made no difference if he did. They lived separate lives, Caleb and Zillah. She had her chapel, her charities, her work with the poor and the Poor Law

Unions, the hospitals and the foundation of Manchester's Unhealthy Dwellings Committee. Caleb had his businesses and, unknown to Zillah, a mistress in a smart little villa overlooking Langworthy Park. It amused his sardonic sense of humour that Zillah, on her way to her chapel, had to pass Dorothy's house.

'You are to adopt her? Give her my name?'

'My name since you married me. She is called ... er, let me see ... Amy, so she will be Amy Seymour.'

It was typical of Zillah, Caleb mused, that she was not even certain of the child's name.

'She will be brought up as a Methodist and will help me in my work. She will by my daughter.'

'And mine, I presume?'

Zillah looked startled. 'Well, if you say so but you will see little of her at first. She must have a governess and someone to teach her how to speak properly. She has an appalling Liverpool accent and one can hardly understand what she is saying. She will be groomed to become a young lady of breeding as befits my daughter.'

'And her father was willing to part with her?'

'He has ten other children, two of whom are in the isolation hospital with tuberculosis, as is their mother. I shall help him out financially so that he might move them all to a better part of Liverpool.'

'So you have, in fact, bought her?'

'Don't be ridiculous, Caleb. This arrangement suits us both.' She folded her napkin and pushed back her chair. Politely her husband did the same.

'We will take coffee in the drawing room, Alice, and at once, please. I don't want to be late for chapel. When I return I will speak to Mrs Abigail.

Tell her, if you please.'

Alice bobbed a curtsey. 'Yes, ma'am,' bursting to get back to the kitchen to pass on the amazing news.

6

She came awake to a lovely feeling of comfort and restfulness which lasted for about ten seconds after she opened her eyes, then the full terror of her situation hit her savagely. She cowered beneath the bedcovers as though fully expecting the woman to come bursting into her room and inflict some further horror on her, but when the door finally opened it was the nice lady in the white apron.

'Ah, there y'are, chuck,' she said, as though Amy had been out somewhere and had just returned. 'See, I've brought yer breakfast. Aren't you the lucky one 'avin' yer breakfast in bed?' She carried the tray from which wafted the smell of bacon, something they, meaning her family, only had as an extra special treat, but Amy hunched herself further down the bed, watching as the lady placed the tray on the dresser.

'Come on, chuck,' the lady said kindly, her pale blue eyes soft, but Amy didn't trust her, not in this place where the woman had brought her. The sleep she had tumbled into seemed to have returned her to her senses, the realisation of where she was, meaning that she had been separated from her family and the pain of it scourged her in the middle of her chest where she supposed her heart was. She continued to lie in the bed, her hands clutching at the sheet beneath her chin.

'Chuck, yer've got ter eat,' the lady said. 'Yer don't want ter be ill, do yer?'

Amy didn't care!

'An' the mistress'll want yer downstairs at nine o'clock. It's half past eight now so yer'd best look lively. See, eat yer bacon an' eggs what Mrs Abigail did fer yer. An' there's fried bacon an' a pot, *a pot* of tea.'

They had fought in the kitchen over who was to take the tray up to Amy. Aye, that's what Alice had told them she was called last night and didn't they all want to get a look at the mistress's niece? But Mrs Abigail had decreed that Jess was to do it since Amy—eeh, that was a pretty name—already knew her.

'She'll be nervous enough without another stranger fussing at her,' she said. Alice, who was already annoyed that she had had to share Jess's bedroom, set her face angrily. After all, she was head parlour-maid.

As Jess spoke to her she distinctly saw the child's eyes glaze over. It was when she mentioned the mistress that it happened. Though they had been wary as Jess carried the tray into the room, there had been a gleam of understanding in them; now they were like mud again. She sighed sadly but it did no good hanging about. She could hardly force the girl to eat, could she, but she was concerned that since entering the house not a bite had passed her lips. And her that thin already. Also Jess had heard somewhere that if a body didn't drink there would be serious consequences. She'd forgotten the word. De . . . something. She looked under the bed where she had discreetly left the 'po', for the lass was hardly likely to go to the grand bathroom along the hallway which still hypnotised the servants in its modernity, even if she had known where it was. The po was empty.

Jess shook her head. 'D'yer not want ter . . . ter pass water?' she asked delicately, but the kid remained mute and frozen and Jess was not sure she even knew what Jess meant. Well, Jess had to obey orders so she gently pulled back the covers and lifted Amy—she must call her that, it might help—from the bed. Standing her on her feet, she wrapped her in the large fringed shawl that she had brought folded over her arm, tucking it warmly about her thin shoulders.

'Come on, lovey, you come with Jess.' She took Amy's limp hand, opened the door, and led her along the wide, thickly carpeted hallway and down the stairs. It was dim, hushed, the walls papered in a subdued pattern with a dark-painted dado halfway down. The carpet on the stairs was muted in colours of brown and earth made even more sombre by the coloured glass in the front door which let in little light. The coat-stand, where several coats and a cap hung, was fashioned from iron with an umbrella stand beneath containing numerous umbrellas and walking sticks. One of them had a realistically carved shape of an owl perched on top with glass eyes and for a moment Amy was roused from her somnambulism but it slid by her fleetingly. On the walls were several framed pictures, all of a religious nature, one beseeching those who entered to remember this was a Godly house and to abide by His laws. A free-standing mahogany card-tray with a beaten brass card salver stood on the black and white tiles beside the hallstand. On it were several calling cards.

The drawing room door was open and voices could be heard coming from the other side of it. The maid and the child, who suddenly clung tightly to her hand, entered the room where a good fire burned in the grate.

Mrs Seymour and Miss Leach, who worked, so Jess had been told, in the children's department at Kendal Milne's in Deansgate, were there and neatly folded piles of clothing brought by Miss Leach that morning in a cab lay on tables and chairs.

'Ah, Atkins, you have brought the child. Thank you, that will be all.'

But Jess was worried about Amy and meant to say so. 'Madam, if yer please, she's 'ad now ... nothing ter eat, not since she came—'

Mrs Seymour tutted irritably. 'But I gave instruction for Mrs Abigail to—'

In her concern Jess had the temerity to interrupt her mistress. 'She did, ma'am. A tray last night an' another this mornin' but poor little mite is so—'

'Thank you, Atkins, that will be all,' her mistress said frigidly, while Miss Leach stared in fascination at the girl who was purported to be Mrs Seymour's niece and whom she had been instructed to dress. A big order, for Mrs Seymour wanted six of everything from the skin out, just as though she were dressing a bride. 'I will call Mrs Abigail when the child is dressed. A tray shall be brought in here and I shall see she eats everything on it.'

Jess's kind heart sank. Sweet Jesus, the poor little beggar was to be forced to eat and she *would*

78

eat or the mistress would know the reason why. She was not a woman to be defeated by anyone, let alone a small child. Look how she was about her own inability to bear a child. She'd bloody gone out and *found* one and, so it was whispered, paid for her with cash! Reluctantly she prised Amy's clinging hand from her own and left her standing like some bloody sacrifice—and Jess was not usually one for swearing 'cos her pa didn't hold with it—between Mrs Seymour and Miss Leach, wishing she could stay, give support, help her on with what Jess knew would be expensive, well-made, but drab clothes just like the mistress wore.

As she closed the door she heard Mrs Seymour say, 'Now, Miss Leach, let us get the child into her . . . her undergarments first if we can do it without removing her nightgown.' Heaven forbid that a bit of naked flesh should be revealed, even on a small child!

Amy stood, her senses turned in again, barely aware of being pushed and pulled, twisted and turned as garments were held against her. Both women discussed her and her appearance as though she were a waxwork figure, comparing this with that and that with this and all the time she felt the growing desire to wee and she knew she would wet herself soon if she didn't get to the po.

She was in a pair of drawers and what 'they' called corsets, the very best quality it seemed, though the other woman was talking about the latest 'liberty bodices', much more up to date than corsets which children of Victoria's era had worn, when disaster struck. Amy felt it rush in a great tide, for she had not 'been' since before they went to Princes Park yesterday. It flooded the drawers, ran down her legs and formed a pool between her bare feet on the carpet.

Both women jumped back in alarm and to Amy's horror and sudden sense of fear, the woman hit her, actually slapped her viciously on her bare arm. The second woman looked shocked.

'You dirty girl,' her tormentor hissed, then reached for the bell and as though she had been standing outside the door, which she had, Jess flung it open.

'Yes, ma'am?' she asked, her eyes on Amy.

'Remove this child and clean her up then bring her back. Tell the girl who does the laundry—'

'It's not her day, ma'am. She comes on a—'

'Then you wash them. And send someone to clean the mess on the carpet.'

'Yes, madam.'

Jess took Amy's hand and led her to the kitchen, the nightdress and shawl round her once more but not before Jess had noticed the vivid red mark on Amy's arm, her lips tightening ominously. It was then that Amy felt some life, something that might have been called hope, creep back into her.

There seemed to be dozens of people in the huge, bright, noisy room and every one of them drew closer to her, not in a threatening way, but welcoming, curious, smiling, exclaiming to one another on her appearance, what lovely hair, they said, and a fat woman asked her if she'd like a bacon butty.

Amy nodded her head, then was urged to sit at the table to eat it and drink a big mug of tea that was hot, milky and sweet. She had never tasted anything so delicious in her life. Jess sat beside her on the bench at the table, preening as though Amy

80

were all her own creation.

'There was an accident,' Jess told them delicately, passing the drawers into Martha's willing hands, 'an' she's ter go right back. No, no, Amy, it's all right, lovey,' as Amy huddled up against her. 'We're all here,' she added, not sure what she meant but it seemed to comfort the child who allowed herself to be drawn from the table.

Amy felt a lot better. The butty had gone down a treat and the tea had refreshed her so that she felt able to face the woman again. She was determined to demand that she be taken home immediately. She could not believe that Pa had *really* received money for her. She must have been mistaken and she was sure that if she went back home they would all be glad to see her. After all, she belonged to Pa and Mam, not this woman who was Pa's sister, unbelievable as it seemed. She could not keep her here against her will and she would say so. She felt rested, stronger, and the people in the kitchen had been friendly, so if she told them that she had a home in Liverpool, and a family, that the woman had taken her away from them against her will, she was certain they would stand up for her.

As Jess led her into the room she was greeted at once by the woman who had instructed her to call her Aunt Zillah but who had never once called her by her name.

'I hope you are sorry for what you did, child. There is no greater joy in heaven than in one sinner that repenteth.'

Amy wondered what she was talking about.

'Do you think she shows signs of repentance, Miss Leach, for her appalling breach of good

81

manners? If so I'm sure she will be forgiven. Are you sorry, young lady? Will you promise never to do such a thing again? This is a decent house and your filthy ways will not be countenanced. Punishment will be severe if it is repeated, do you understand?'

Amy did not understand so she stood mute which seemed further to enrage the woman who tightened her lips into a line so thin her mouth completely disappeared. Her face grew puce with rage at what she saw as her niece's defiance and she took her by the shoulders and shook her so that her mass of tawny hair tumbled about her head and shoulders and Miss Leach put her hand to her mouth, for she thought Mrs Seymour was extreme in her behaviour.

Mrs Seymour sighed as though at her wits' end. 'Well, Miss Leach, when we have her dressed I will take her to chapel. Perhaps Our Lord God can help her feel the conviction of her sin.'

Miss Leach, who was not a Methodist, indeed had no particular faith since Sunday was the one day she might rest from her exhausting week, nodded her head humbly.

Another pair of drawers was decently replaced, the liberty bodice—the task performed under the protection of the nightgown—the plain white petticoat, the plain, unadorned, grey, ankle-length dress and the full white pinafore worn over the dress were dragged on to Amy's unresisting body. She tried on several pairs of black buttoned boots until a good fit was found. She was told to walk across the carpet and back until the woman was satisfied. A warm woollen cape of a darker grey was tried on and seemed to suit.

'Now we must do something with that hair,' the woman said, her mouth pursed as though she were sucking a lemon. Jess, who had her ear to the keyhole outside the door, prepared herself to burst in, to protest, even if it lost her her job, which, of course, it would but the mistress was speaking slowly.

'If we cut it it will riot all over her head. Short of shaving it we cannot avoid that; all these curls . . .' speaking as though Amy's head were a mass of writhing snakes.

'Perhaps a plait, Mrs Seymour?' Miss Leach offered. 'I deal with little girls in the shop and I'm sure I could show you how it's done.'

'Oh, I wouldn't be involved,' Mrs Seymour said with a slight shudder. 'One of the maids will attend to her dressing and that would include her hair. I'll ring for Atkins as she has been in charge of the child since she came.' She rang the bell and within five seconds Jess appeared, smoothing down her apron.

'Yes, ma'am.'

'Miss Leach is to show you how to plait the child's hair, Atkins, so watch her carefully.'

Jess almost laughed in the mistress's face, for who the dickens did she think plaited Jess's neat hair-do hidden beneath her cap? Ever since she had come to work at Somerfield the necessity of a prim and modest appearance had been drilled into her. Long sleeves and skirts. Sensible, snow-white aprons. Boots so well polished you could see your face in them. A mob cap that covered every scrap of hair, the hair plaited and dragged back from the forehead so that if you were unlucky enough to have curls it was difficult to keep them in order.

'Very well, ma'am. Shall I fetch a brush an' comb an' pr'aps a ribbon ter tie on the—' At once she knew she had made a mistake.

'No ribbon, Atkins,' her mistress spat. 'Some dark thread will do. Now go and fetch the brush.'

Amy stood rigidly while Miss Leach brushed back her intractable hair. It was springy, wild, rebellious, wanting to curl itself round Miss Leach's gentle fingers. Mrs Seymour and Jess watched her until Mrs Seymour lost patience.

'For goodness sake, Miss Leach, what are you trying to do? You must be firmer.' And she stood up and spun Amy round until she had her back to her. Taking the brush, she dragged Amy's head back with every stroke. She had Amy's glossy hair smoothed to her small skull but in the process the prongs of the brush scratched her scalp. The other two women winced at each stroke but though tears came into Amy's eyes she did not make a sound. It was then for the first time that Jess recognised the latent cruelty in her mistress.

'Now plait it,' Mrs Seymour panted to Miss Leach as though the exertion had taken her breath. Miss Leach, hands trembling and with madam holding the child's head, plaited her wonderful hair. The plait was as thick as her wrist, hanging to just below her waist. She tied on the scrap of black embroidery thread Mrs Seymour produced from her sewing box. For some reason Miss Leach felt a great need to bend down and kiss the child's pale cheek.

'I wonder if we should wind it round her head?' Mrs Seymour mused, looking at the yanked-back hair.

'Then it would not fit under her bonnet,

madam,' Miss Leach murmured, indicating the black, deep-brimmed bonnet Mrs Seymour had ordered. Even before the bonnet was jammed on Amy's head, its brim shadowing her face, wisping curls appeared on her hairline, causing Mrs Seymour to tut irritably and tug the bonnet further over her face.

'No, I suppose not. Well, we shall have to see. Perhaps we could cut half the length away, leaving enough to plait.' She suddenly became brisk. 'That will do for now, Miss Leach, and, Atkins'—turning to the frozen-faced maid servant—'run and tell Thomas to bring the carriage round. I and the child will attend chapel.'

*   *   *

Jess was in tears when she stumbled into the kitchen and it took several minutes before the others could get a coherent word from her.

'Poor little bugger,' she sobbed, 'sorry, Mrs Abigail . . . cruel she was . . .'

' 'Oo? Amy?'

'Don't talk daft'—this to Primrose, the scullery-maid who was not very bright—'the mistress. I swear that bairn's scalp were bleedin'. Yer know the bristles on them brushes what mistress gives us are right sharp. Dig right inter yer scalp if yer not careful. Well, she brushes 'er 'air back then that Miss Leach plaited it. Eeh, it were so lovely, but with that bloody 'at . . . sorry, Mrs Abigail, but it's enough ter mekk a saint swear. Well, they're off ter chapel an' she wants carriage.'

They were having their elevenses, the maidservants and the outside men, the men lounging against the wall by the kitchen door. The spring sunshine streamed through the doorway, the rays falling on a big jar of daffodils Matt the gardener had just handed in. Outside in the cobbled yard a mare was being groomed by the stable boy who murmured to the animal as he brushed her glossy grey coat. He was a tall, lanky boy, just at that age when boys grow out of everything they wear, all knees and elbows and a long thin neck. His hair was a dusty brown thatch, uncut and uncombed, but he was clean in his striped, collarless, open-necked shirt, breeches and knee-high boots and his wide mouth revealed good white teeth.

' 'Ere, Joe, missis wants carriage round t'front. Tell Thomas, will yer, an' look sharp.'

The boy gave the grey a last loving pat, then led her towards the coach house. He helped Thomas bring the carriage into the yard and hitch up the matching greys.

'Shall I tekk it round, Mr Thomas?' he asked politely.

'You will not, my lad. I'll just get me jacket. See, hose down the yard an' then yer can get thissen a cup o' cocoa.'

*   *   *

The ride in the splendid carriage beside the woman, the walk along the path between the gravestones into St John's Chapel itself passed by Amy in a blur. Her determination to demand to be taken home to her family had ebbed away as soon as the two women had put her in the drawers and liberty bodice under the concealment of her

86

nightdress. She had retreated further and further away from reality as every minute passed and the indignity of it all went un-noticed. Even the pain of her hair being wrenched back from her forehead, the harsh brush strokes, the woman's words, seemed to have happened to another child. She hid in the dark place she had made for herself as she was snatched from the kitchen in Earle Street and in which, apart from a small moment in time when there had been kind faces and voices, she had remained. The woman urged her up into the carriage, where she stared, unseeing, at the broad back of a man in a uniform until the woman plucked at her again, indicating she was to alight. They entered the building and sat down in the Seymour family pew at the front.

'Now then, child, we will pray that our Redeemer will bring you into the light. I want you to search for eternal salvation. That your soul will be turned to Christ. I shall ask for you to be baptised when I think you are ready. You will be taught the history and character of Methodism which John Wesley brought into our lives. We believe the written word of God to be the only and sufficient rule both of Christian faith and practice. I am a Methodist, one who has in my heart all that is given me by the Holy Ghost. One who loves the Lord my God with all my heart, with all my mind and with all my strength. God is the joy of my heart and the desire of my soul.'

Her voice droned on as though she had forgotten Amy and a look of exaltation spread over her face. For half an hour, perhaps more, it went on and on until, with the words 'One Lord, one Faith, one baptism, one God and Father

87

through all and in you all', she came to a halt.

It took a full five minutes before Zillah recovered. She took out a plain white handkerchief and wiped her sweated face, then put her face on her hands. She remained thus for another half an hour while Amy stared blindly at the other worshippers, many of them plainly dressed women like the one beside her.

A gentleman, soberly dressed, climbed up some steps at the front of the building and the woman who had brought her here rose from her knees and listened raptly to him speak, as did they all, except Amy who remained in her small, dark place and thought of nothing.

When the man had finished speaking the woman stood up and led Amy from the pew and from there to the door where, in the fading sunlight, the man stood. He shook the woman's hand and looked down at Amy. He had a stern look though his eyes seemed to smile.

'You must read your scriptures, child,' she heard him say, though again she had no idea what the words meant.

'She will, Mr Isherwood,' the woman gushed. 'I shall read them with her.'

'See she sets apart some time, every morning and evening, for the purpose.'

'She shall come to God, Mr Isherwood,' the woman told him firmly.

'With you to guide her I know she will, Mrs Seymour,' and at last they moved out again into the graveyard.

It was then she saw the daffodils clustered in nodding groups beneath the elm trees and, quite clearly, she felt her heart break but no sign of it showed in her blank, lifeless face.

He was there at the front of the house as the carriage drawn by the beautifully matched greys came sedately up the drive and drew to a standstill at the steps. Mrs Seymour wouldn't allow Thomas to proceed at more than a walk. The boy had trundled the wheelbarrow round from the back of the house to the front, doing a favour for Matt, when the girl stepped down from the carriage. He could see nothing of her face or her hair since she wore an enormous bonnet but he had heard about her when Jess had sat him down at the kitchen table with a mug of cocoa in his hand. Jess talked of nothing else and he was curious about this girl who was the mistress's niece.

As she stepped on to the gravel, her small, gloved hand in that of Thomas, the coachman, she turned her head and lifted her face to the sunshine. The light caught her eyes which were a pure, golden brown, deep and translucent, like sunshine on water, flecked with a darker brown and surrounded by incredibly long lashes. He looked right into them and was lost. He was twelve years old but he loved her then with a man's heart and strength.

7

She wore the bonnet because she thought she would attract less attention than without it. In the woman's world, the woman who had stolen her, it seemed girls wore bonnets. She had the dainty little clock wrapped in one of the handkerchiefs

Jess had given her and it was tucked in the pocket of her cloak.

The clock had been on the narrow mantelpiece above the fireplace in the bedroom she had been put in, ticking away in the hushed silence that pervaded every part of the house except the kitchen. It was a pretty little clock which seemed out of place in the bedroom that had little in it: a single straight-backed chair; a small wardrobe in which hung the clothes the two women had decided she should wear; a washstand with a plain white basin and jug; a small chest of drawers in which Jess had placed what the woman called her undergarments; and a narrow bed. The counterpane and walls were white, the fireplace, where no fire burned despite the chilly evening, a dull brown. The floorboards were varnished and well scoured and a small threadbare rug in shades of mud and dead leaves lay beside the bed. It was not quite a servant's room and not one that would house a guest but somewhere in between. It was at the back of the house overlooking the yard and stables which, later, were to become a great source of comfort to her. There was the sound of cheerful whistling and horses whinnying, the clop of their hooves on the cobbles and, from the stables themselves, nostrils blowing into a feed bag. There were men about, one hissing over a curry comb as he tended to a dapple grey carriage horse, another hosing down the yard and a third energetically polishing the splendour of the carriage. All cheerful and noisy and comforting but in the bedroom there was no sound but the delicate tick of the clock that Jess had placed there, unknown to her mistress, in an effort to cheer up the room a bit. Neither Jess nor Amy knew the clock was Meissen, rare and expensive, and not one of the mass-produced copies that were fashionable. There were so many clocks in the house Jess was sure it would not be missed.

It was Jess who had put Amy to bed on that second night, tucking her beneath the crisp white sheet and blowing out the candle. The main rooms of the house were lit by electricity but the servants still made do with candles. The child had come back from chapel looking like a little ghost and had been immediately handed over to Jess.

'See she eats something, Atkins. Mrs Abigail will know. On a tray in the room you have prepared, then put her to bed. Her governess arrives tomorrow and will take over her care and supervision but tonight you will see to her. She has the nightdresses Miss Leach left for her. Good, then I will bid you goodnight, child,' looking down at the still figure of her niece who did not answer. Indeed Zillah Seymour was beginning to wonder if she had made a mistake and had perhaps picked the wrong girl. Was Amy half-witted, slow, feeble-minded, even sub-normal? Then she remembered the bright face and laughter of the girl she had first seen at that ghastly house in Liverpool. No, she was just being obdurate and Zillah knew she could do something about obdurate!

Jess sat on the chair and talked to her all the time as she made sure Amy ate the food sent up on the tray: a good hearty soup crammed with fresh vegetables, a nice piece of chicken with tiny new potatoes and home-grown peas, and a strawberry jelly with the gardener's fresh strawberries set in it smothered with whipped cream. All prepared to

91

tempt a child's appetite and she ate it all, Jess reported in triumph, not knowing that Amy's brain had finally realised that she would need her strength if she was to carry out her plan. She talked at random, telling her about the rest of the staff, expecting no answer by now and getting none but Amy took it all in. Mrs Abigail who was cook/housekeeper and a great one for order and cleanliness as was only right in her position. Martha, who was Mrs Abigail's right-hand man— or rather woman—in the kitchen. Alice was head housemaid and inclined to get above herself if Amy knew what she meant, but goodhearted really. Primrose was in the scullery and Phoebe in the laundry. Then there were the outside men. Thomas was the coachman. Matt and Barty were gardeners, Ernie Tingle and Tim were in the stables and of course there was young Joe who came, poor lad, from the workhouse. He'd had a bad start but Mrs Abigail was fattening him up as though he were a pig going to market, she laughed, then noticed the child had gone to sleep, bless her. She took the tray from the bed and tiptoed out to pass on the good news to the kitchen.

*   *   *

It was dark, full night when Amy slipped down the stairs and along the passage to the kitchen which was the only way she knew. She peeped cautiously round the kitchen door before she entered to make sure they had all gone to bed, then crept to the back door. For a moment the cat with its tail curled round it on the mat in front of the kitchen fire startled her when it lifted its head and miaowed plaintively, but when it settled again as though seeing no chance of a saucer of milk she continued to the door. There was an enormous key in the lock but, thanks to Ernie Tingle's wizardry it turned easily and noiselessly. There were bolts on the door, one at the bottom and one at the top. The bottom one was easy but she had to carry a stool from the corner of the room to reach the top one. Both slid back without trouble.

The yard was pitch black and she could hear the horses moving in their stalls. One of them, hearing her in the yard, made a chuffing sound but she crept round the corner of the house and along the side to the front.

She had a fright as she turned the corner. There was a light coming from a window, its rays streaming across the path and grass and when she cautiously peeped over the sill she saw a man seated in an armchair reading a newspaper. She didn't know who he was so she quietly stepped on to the grass and, remembering the way the carriage had come up the drive, ran beside it, keeping to the lawn until she reached the gate.

Though she had been so stunned as she sat beside the woman in the carriage, her normally astute brain had subconsciously absorbed the direction they had taken. Left out of the gate into a wide road which a sign at the corner told her was Eccles Old Road, down the middle of which ran tram-lines, going, she assumed, into the city of Manchester—and the railway station. There were no trams at this time of night or she would have chanced getting on one but she had no money anyway, only the pretty clock which she meant to pawn. She knew all about pawnshops. Hadn't she pawned a thing or two for Mam when they had been desperate and the pawnbroker had asked no awkward questions. The money she got would buy her a railway ticket home. She thought no further than that. She daren't! A ticket to Lime Street, she would say and hope she got on the right train.

She took her bonnet off as she hurried along Eccles Old Road so that she could see more clearly. When she wore it she felt as if she were wearing blinkers, like the horses that pulled the carriage. She'd put it back on when she reached the station. There was gas street lighting along the deserted road, for this was a respectable district of Manchester, but nevertheless she kept a strict lookout for anyone, man or woman, who might be lurking in the shadows: vagrants, homeless people, any street arab or ruffian who might do her harm. She was a town-bred child who knew the streets of Liverpool and those who haunted them for whatever they could find. They would steal the very boots from her feet, or worse, if they found her wandering alone at night.

But she was getting tired. She had followed the tram-lines that curved out of Eccles Old Road into Broad Street, passing some sort of memorial set in a tiny garden. In one corner was a urinal, in the doorway of which two bundles of rags were snoring loudly so to be on the safe side she broke into a run, her breath rasping in her throat. Stopping for a second, she bent forward and put her hands on her knees until she got her breath back.

On her left was a high wall with an open gate in it, the sign beside the gate proclaiming that this was 'The Royal Museum and Free Library' set in what appeared to be a garden. Venturing just

94

inside the gate the moon suddenly slid out from behind a cloud to reveal shrubberies and flowerbeds and slatted seats with backs to them, all very neat and presentable—and empty. She sighed with relief. She would just rest here for five minutes then continue on until she reached the shopping area of Manchester and the pawnbroker she hoped to find there. Every town and city had a pawnbroker. In five minutes she was fast asleep.

*   *   *

Jess placed the tray on the chest of drawers and drew back the thin curtains saying, as she did so, 'Mornin', chuck, time ter get up. Mistress wants yer in't mornin' room ter meet yer governess by nine.' She pulled a face as she turned to the bed, then gasped in horror. The bed was empty. Like a fool, she was to say later to the others, she pulled back the bedcovers as though Amy might be hiding there, looked under the bed, in the wardrobe and even opened a drawer or two in the dresser. She stood in the middle of the room, fear striking her, for she might be blamed for this, whatever it was, since as yet she didn't know, then she galloped out of the room holding her skirts high, along the landing, down the stairs and through the passage to the kitchen. The child might have gone down there, but then Jess would have passed her, wouldn't she? She might have slipped out into the grounds before they all got up. Hadn't Mrs Abigail been in a temper because Alice hadn't locked up the night before with Alice swearing heatedly that she had. Dear God, there'd be hell to pay when the mistress found out but short of locking the kid in her room none of them, meaning the servants, could keep their eyes on her all the time.

She burst into the kitchen as though there were a high wind at her back and every one of them turned in astonishment.

'She's gone,' she said dramatically, her hand on her thumping heart.

'Who's gone?' Mrs Abigail asked, but knowing all the same. Hadn't Jess just taken up the delicious breakfast Mrs Abigail had prepared for the bairn?

'The kid . . .'

'Gone where?'

''Ow the 'ell do I know? I'd not be askin' if I knew.'

'Now listen here, my girl, there's no need to—'

'We'd best tell men ter look fer 'er. She can't 'ave gone far,' Jess interrupted. 'She'll be in't garden, by't pond, I bet. Kids love water. Oh, God, mistress'll sack me . . .' She began to cry. Jobs like this were hard to come by; well paid, working beside servants she got on with and under a mistress who never interfered with anything on the domestic side as long as everything ran smoothly. In some households, where the mistress took little notice of what went on, slackness would have prevailed, discipline would suffer and chaos reign. The staff would become lazy, take advantage, but Mrs Abigail was not one to allow idleness, in herself or in those beneath her. But now what was to happen? It didn't bear thinking about.

They searched every inch of ground, the men, and even Jess and Alice, longing to shout her name but unwilling to alert the mistress that something was wrong before they had looked everywhere. The master was long gone.

But as nine o'clock approached and the cab drew up to the portico and deposited the woman they supposed to be the governess, and her luggage, they could put it off no longer. Young Joe had been beside himself and had even waded into the shallow pond, disturbing Matt's carefully nurtured water lilies, but as the mistress rang the bell Jess knew she must answer it.

'Atkins, will you fetch the child down now,' Mrs Seymour said in that distant way she had.

Jess, who had bobbed a curtsey as she came into the morning room, bobbed another and cleared her throat. The woman who sat opposite Mrs Seymour looked on impassively. Poor, poor little beggar, Jess had time to think as she looked into the cold, fish eyes of the governess. Between them they would kill her!

'Well, ma'am, it's like this,' Jess began, conscious of the governess watching her intently.

'For heaven's sake, Atkins, get on with it.' Mrs Seymour's voice dripped acid.

'It's . . . Amy . . .'

'Yes?'

'She's not in 'er room, ma'am, an' though we've searched everywhere we can't find 'er. She's gone, ma'am.'

Zillah Seymour asked no more questions, not then. What was the use? She turned to the governess. 'I do apologise for this, Miss Gibbon. My household is not usually in such confusion. Atkins will show you to your room and the schoolroom is next to it. As soon as I have cleared this up I'll come to you. I'm sure the child will be found shortly. I'll supervise the search myself,' just as though the servants were incapable of anything so simple.

She turned to Jess who was terrified that she might burst into tears. Jess, not the mistress! It was as though Mrs Seymour had mislaid her embroidery, or at worst one of her fine carriage horses, carelessly abandoned by Thomas. 'That will be all, Atkins. I will speak to you later. Oh, and ask Mrs Abigail to send up tea, or perhaps you would prefer coffee, Miss Gibbon . . . no, then tea.'

Mrs Seymour did not do anything so human as walking about the grounds calling the child's name. Instead she went into the hall where the instrument stood and telephoned her husband who had connections in the city. As Jess headed towards the kitchen after showing Miss Gibbon to the room she was to occupy—so much more comfortable than Amy's—she heard the mistress say to someone, she thought the master, 'Yes, I know, Caleb, but the first thing she would do would be to make for the railway station . . . No, as far as I know she has no money, unless one of the servants . . . I shall, of course, question them . . . but if you could ask Inspector Grant to put a search in action . . . Yes, constables and such . . . Thank you, Caleb.'

*   *   *

She had left her bonnet somewhere, she supposed in the garden where she awoke to the sounds of people walking along the gravel path to the building. She had been so cold she could scarcely walk when she finally darted out of the garden and into the already busy street, which was how she had come to mislay her bonnet. She began to run, thinking it might help to get the stiffness out of her cramped limbs, and as she did so her hair, which had been in the neat braid Jess had plaited for her last night, became unravelled. It fell about her shoulders in a golden cascade and streamed down her back to her buttocks. As she ran, colour came to her cheeks and passers-by stared at her, though she was not aware of it, for she was an extremely pretty and well-dressed child and it was not often you saw such out alone.

Trams were already rattling by, packed with folk going to work and she followed the tram-lines, for she was sure they must be going into the city. Regent Street, Chapel Street, Blackfriars, still following the tramway, Market Street and finally Piccadilly where it was so packed with shops she was sure to find a pawnbroker's. She kept an eye out for the three golden balls that were so familiar to her. The pavements were swarming with people, men in caps and boaters and bowlers, with stiff collars; women, also in boaters with ribbons down their backs, long skirts and boots like the ones she wore. Dozens of trams, hemmed in on both sides by horse-drawn carriages, cabs, bicycles, drays piled high with bales of raw cotton, for Manchester was the hub of the cotton trade, wagons overflowing with goods of one sort or another, and even one or two motor cars at which pedestrians stopped to stare. There was an impressive statue erected by public subscription, it said, to the memory of the Duke of Wellington, whoever he was. It was all so familiar it might have been the centre of Liverpool and Amy immediately felt at home.

She was filled with anticipation, because in her own estimation she was halfway to being home. But she was very hungry so her search for the 'pop-shop' became even more urgent; the first thing she'd buy when she'd popped the clock was something to eat. Then she'd make enquiries as to the whereabouts of the right station for Liverpool.

She saw the familiar three balls just across the street next to a shop that sold pianos. Taking advantage of a street jam consisting of wagons piled high with crates, trams forced to stop at a corner, pedestrians and a bobby in the thick of it doing his best to bring order, she darted across the road and entered the shop.

A bell pinged and from somewhere in the midst of the usual muddle to be found in such places, a shifty-looking man poked his head above the counter. He had a fag dangling from his lips and his spectacles were pushed up to rest on his forehead just above his eyebrows.

He looked at her suspiciously. She was not the normal scruffy kid who usually crept furtively into his shop doing their best to pawn some worthless bit of junk, sent by their mams in the hope of getting a better price. She was well dressed and pretty and she smiled most politely.

'Yes?' His voice was curt, since he wasn't sure how to treat this extraordinary girl.

As soon as she spoke his suspicion grew, for her voice did not go with her dress.

'Me mam sent me. 'Ow much fer this?' and she produced from her pocket a bundle wrapped in a lace-edged handkerchief.

When she unwrapped it and he saw what it was his mouth watered, as this was an item several cuts above those he normally received. He took the clock from her outstretched hand and dug from his pocket an eye glass, one that jewellers used to assess the value of a gem. Putting it to his eye, he studied the clock from every angle and underneath he found the mark that told him all he wanted to know. He looked up and gave the girl the same intent attention.

Amy began to wriggle under his scrutiny, then her upbringing came to the fore. 'Well, d'yer wan' it or not?'

He studied her for several long seconds. 'Where d'yer get it?'

'Does it matter? I've not stole it if that's what yer mean.'

'I never said you 'ad. I just wanner know where yer got it.'

'Listen, if yer don't wan' it I'll tekk it up street. There's bound ter be another pop-shop—'

'There isn't. Anyroad, I'll give yer ten bob though it's—'

'It's worth more than tha',' Amy said indignantly, though she hadn't the faintest idea how much it *was* worth.

'Well, tekkit or leave it, chuck. I can't stand 'ere chattin'.'

Amy made a swift decision. Like the pawnbroker, she hadn't time to stand here chatting. She must get over to the station and buy a ticket to Liverpool, for she knew that by now she would have been missed at the woman's house. Jess would have been up to her room and found her gone and the woman would have started a search. She must take this man's money and get out of Manchester as soon as possible.

'Right, I'll tekk it.' She put on a face which she hoped would flatter the man forgetting her hunger in her haste, 'Er, can yer tell me what station'll tekk me ter Liverpool?' She smiled as the man handed her a ten bob note and tucked the clock under the counter. As most men—and women—were, he was fascinated by her sudden impish beauty. He thought there was some mystery here. A well-dressed kid with a working-class way of speaking . . . still, it was nowt to do with him. He was here to make money and he and the kid had just done a bit of business that was in his favour so he directed her to London Road Station, which wasn't far, he told her. Follow the tram-lines until Piccadilly ran into London Road and the station was on her left. She thanked him prettily and left him scratching his head.

She blended with the shoppers who crowded the pavement and when she saw a policeman—she wasn't sure why unless it was the idea that the woman might have alerted them—she stood next to a woman who was looking in a window until he had passed her by.

The station was packed with travellers, some coming into the city, many of them leaving it, and again whenever she spotted a man in uniform she stuck unobtrusively close to a well-dressed woman as though she were with her until she reached the booking office.

The man behind the small window looked at her suspiciously when she asked for a ticket to Lime Street Station in Liverpool, as one did not often see children on their own but there was a long queue for tickets and he was diverted by some altercation at the back of the queue.

'Single or return?' he asked, his eyes on the man who was arguing with a porter.

'Yer what?' Amy asked.

'Single or return? Are yer ter come back?'

'No . . . oh, no,' she answered.

'Single then. 'Alf fare?'

'What?' she quavered.

'It's 'alf fare fer children.' His patience was running out and as the altercation in the queue was sorted out he was beginning to take more notice of the bonny little thing whose nose just peeped over his counter.

'Yes,' she said, and hopefully proffered her ten bob note.

'First, second or third?'

'What?'

'D'yer wanna go first, second or third?'

'Cheapest.'

'Right, third, that'll be one shilling and eightpence. Platform three.' He handed her a ticket and her change—eight shillings and fourpence—which to her was a fortune and, slipping under the arm of the man behind her, she scuttled across the heaving forecourt, thankful that it was so busy.

The third compartment, which she eventually found without asking anyone, since she wanted to draw as little attention to herself as possible, was packed but a fat and kindly woman made a tiny space for her against the window and she gazed out at the scene with great interest, since this time she was going home. Last time on the journey from Liverpool to Manchester with the woman she had been in a state of such terror she had noticed nothing. Now the countryside presented itself in

103

all its spring glory: green, green fields starred with wild flowers, cows who didn't even look up from their grazing as the train thundered by, Chat Moss which was wild and beautiful, stations where passengers alighted and clambered aboard, all knowing exactly where they were going, which impressed her inordinately, stations with names such as Kenyon Junction, Parkside Street, Newton, St Helens which she'd actually heard of, Roby Street and then into the bustle of Lime Street. She was home. *She was home!*

She actually hummed as she hurried along Lime Street, Shaw's Brow, Dale Street and into the cobweb of terraced streets that were so familiar to her and eventually turned the corner into Earle Street. She began to skip and smile, for wouldn't they all be pleased and excited to see her. She pushed the last picture she had of Pa into the back of her mind as she approached home, number twenty-two Earle Street. There it was, just as she had left it, but even as she raised her hand to knock a strange woman flung open the door and looked down at her.

'Yes, wha' d'yer want?' she asked. 'An' be quick about it. I'm late fer work as it is.'

'Pa ... me Pa?' Amy stammered. 'Our Elsie an'—'

'There's no one 'ere called that so push off; 'ang on, what were their name?'

'Pearson.' Amy staggered back a little, for the woman looked threatening. There was a bobby just turning the corner, walking purposefully towards them. The woman banged the door loudly behind her.

'They've gone, so bugger off.' She fled in the

opposite direction to the police constable while Amy sank to her knees on the none too clean doorstep, her last thought being that no one had used the donkey-stone on it since she had last done so ... when was it? She lapsed into a semi-comatose state as the policeman lifted her gently to her feet.

8

Had it not been for the servants she would not have survived the harsh regime of the following months. The servants and, strangely, Caleb Seymour! Miss Gibbon had taken her to Peel Park on several occasions. They had caught the tram on Eccles Old Road, getting off at Regent Road and walking along the River Irwell to the park. An educational walk, of course, with Miss Gibbon constantly reminding her not to slouch; to put her bonnet straight; to take smaller steps since it was not ladylike to stride out; to take heed of the greenfinch stretching his wings on the branch of the horse chestnut tree which was in the glory of its May flowering, and to remember the name of the bird, for she would question her about it when they got home. Notice the plant growing in the tree's roots and she was not to stare at the gentlemen on the bowling green, nor the tennis courts; in fact she was to act as the well-brought-up young girl her adopted mother required her to be.

On that first outing, as they walked along beside the river, she had nearly thrown herself into its sluggish waters so great had been her despair. It was a couple of weeks after her dash for home, the dash that had ended so devastatingly with her being brought back to Somerfield in dire disgrace. Not that she remembered anything about it. Her last memory had involved the mucky state of her mam's doorstep and the next of waking in the narrow bed with the woman standing over her.

'Get up, girl, and get dressed. I shall stay here with you while you do so since it seems you cannot be trusted to remain alone. Miss Gibbon will take charge of you from now on as Atkins cannot be relied upon. Hurry up, girl. Miss Gibbon is waiting for you.'

Amy, still stupefied with sleep and mired in such deep misery she could hardly function, fumbled her way into the clean drawers, the liberty bodice, the stockings fastened by suspenders to the bodice. Next came the shapeless grey dress the woman had laid out for her, then the white pinafore. She struggled with the buttons on her boots and was reaching for the comb on the dresser when the woman snatched it from her and began to drag it through the tangled curls that lay about her head and fell in a thick, streaked mass of gold to her waist. The woman hissed as she worked but Amy did not cry out as the teeth of the comb bit into her scalp though the tears flowed just the same. They flowed not because of the pain, but because of her desolation, her loss, her hopelessness at the thought that she would never see her family again.

'What a cry-baby it is,' the woman snapped, twisting the lively curls, wrenching them back from Amy's forehead into a tight knot at the nape of her neck, furious when vagrant curls kept escaping her

106

cruel fingers.

'There, that will have to do for now,' she said eventually through gritted teeth, 'but I think the scissors are called for. Now wash your hands and face and later you will have a bath in the schoolroom. Marshall will bring up the bath and hot water, since I fear Atkins has forfeited the right to come beyond the kitchen door.'

For a fleeting second Amy wondered who Atkins was, not connecting it to kind Jess who had done her best to help her, then her hand was taken in a tight grip. The woman opened the door and led her along the landing in the opposite direction from the one she had taken to the kitchen. There was another corridor off the landing leading towards the front of the house on which there were several closed doors. The woman opened the first one and pushed Amy in before her.

Miss Gibbon was sitting at a circular table spread with a red plush cloth. She rose to her feet as Amy and the woman entered but she did not smile or bob a curtsey as the female servants did.

'Here is our truant, Miss Gibbon,' the woman cried almost gaily, 'and I trust you will be able to make something of her. No cosseting, mind. As we have discussed, she needs a firm hand particularly after this last silly escapade and unless she is with me on chapel matters she is wholly in your charge. Her accent is appalling and though I believe she can read and write and add up a sum or two, she is sadly lacking in a decent education. I know you will soon rectify that.'

'You can set your mind at rest on that score, Mrs Seymour,' Miss Gibbon answered, her eyes boring menacingly into Amy's.

'Your bedrooms are adjoining, of course,' the woman continued, 'until we can trust the girl not to go wandering off again, and she really needs a bath. She has clean undergarments on; the ones she wore yesterday have been sent to the laundry. Now, I believe she has eaten nothing so if you will ring the bell Marshall will bring you up whatever you think fit. It is a Christian duty to eat the bread of forgiveness but, really, I fear for the girl's soul.' She shook her head then rubbed her hands together as though wiping the whole sorry incident from her memory. 'Now, I must leave at once. I have a meeting at ten with the Dwellings Committee.'

'Thank you, Mrs Seymour. Say "Good morning" to your ... to Mrs Seymour, child,' Miss Gibbon instructed Amy. She was not as yet quite sure what the child was to call her aunt who was, to all intents and purposes, since she was to adopt her, to become her mother. Amy remained silent and both women sighed at the task ahead of them.

The room, the schoolroom, as it was called, was poorly furnished. A good fire burned in the grate with a comfortable easy chair in front of it. That was for Miss Gibbon! Two straight-backed chairs were drawn up to the table and round the drab creamy-grey walls, at waist height, were shelves to store the school books. There were no pictures except those of a high religious or moral tone and several framed texts stating, THOU GOD SEEST ME, THOU SHALL NOT MOCK THE LORD, THE MEEK SHALL INHERIT THE EARTH, all beautifully embroidered by Zillah Pearson, aged nine years old.

And so it began, the subjugation of Amy

Pearson who, as she became Amy Seymour, withered and was almost lost.

The schoolroom looked out on to the side garden of the house, a great sweep of lawn which, as summer began, came alive with the sound of the lawnmower and someone whistling. It was some weeks since she had been put into the care of Miss Gibbon and since she had behaved herself, as Miss Gibbon reported to Mrs Seymour, she had been left alone for five minutes while her governess had several times slipped to the bathroom. Miss Gibbon had eaten rather too well of the gooseberry fool that Mrs Abigail had sent up the previous evening and in consequence, though she would not have said the word, even to herself, her 'bowels' were acting up.

The first time Amy had studiously continued her writing practice, all done in beautiful copperplate. If it was not perfect Miss Gibbon would rap her over the knuckles with her ruler.

My name is Amy Seymour. I live at Somerfield in the district of Salford in Manchester. I am ten years old . . . but the sound that floated in through the open window, open because Miss Gibbon believed in fresh air, even on the most bitter day, for the first time in weeks drew her from the self-imposed hiding place into which she had been driven when she was brought back from Liverpool.

She stood up slowly and moved to the window and there was the boy. He was vigorously pushing a lawnmower and as he moved over the grass he left a foot-wide line of newly mown grass. When he reached a spot at the corner of the house he turned neatly in the lawnmower's width and came back in a line exactly parallel to the one he had just cut. When he reached the corner of the house and the arch that led into the stable yard he turned again and something, though she had not moved, caught his eye and he looked up. He stopped the lawnmower at once.

They studied one another with a strange, fixed and penetrating look, unusual in children of their age. And so it began. The ten-year-old girl and the twelve-year-old boy, motionless, spellbound; then he winked and broke the spell. His face split in a wide grin to reveal his strong white teeth which seemed too big for his deeply tanned boy's face. His dark hair, cut short recently by Ernie Tingle, stood up like a lavatory brush, or so Mrs Abigail said, and his eyes, such a bright and vivid blue, sparkled with fun.

'Mornin',' he shouted up to her and, lifting his hand, he saluted her as though he were a soldier.

In the weeks since she had been returned to the woman she had lost the will to speak and since the woman and Miss Gibbon did nothing but reprimand her, preach at her, throw orders at her, there had been little need. She spoke only when her lessons demanded it of her.

Her day began at seven in the morning when Miss Gibbon, herself fully dressed, entered her room and drew back the curtains. The bedroom was joined to Miss Gibbon's by a connecting door and had once been a dressing room with a small window let into a sloping ceiling. The second door, which presumably led on to the landing, was locked and there was no key. The room contained a narrow iron bedstead covered by a plain white counterpane, a pine dresser bearing a jug and basin in English stoneware painted with sprigs of lavender, and a pine wardrobe. On a stand beside it was a white towel. A candle which Miss Gibbon lit and blew out each night sat on the dresser. On the wall above the dresser hung a framed print of a man with long white hair and a sort of scarf about his neck who, she was told reverently by the woman, was called John Wesley. Next to the print was another which said, 'My Jesus is all in all to me'. Amy was to hear a lot of John Wesley!

Miss Gibbon's bedroom in comparison with hers was positively luxurious with two long windows overlooking the side lawns, a double bed covered by a hand-worked patchwork quilt, a wardrobe and a dressing table with an ornate mirror in painted and gilded papier-mâché. There was a comfortable easy chair, a good carpet on the floor and flowered chintz curtains at the windows. Amy knew all this since she must go through Miss Gibbon's bedroom to reach her own.

She washed and dressed herself in whatever Miss Gibbon decreed, then ate the plain but nourishing breakfast ordered by Miss Gibbon as suitable for a girl her age and brought up on a tray by Alice, called Marshall by the woman. Alice also carried up the coals for the fire.

At eight thirty precisely she and Miss Gibbon started lessons which consisted of reading, writing, arithmetic, geography, history, French, drawing and painting and sewing. An upright piano, heaved up the stairs by Matt and Ernie Tingle, was installed in the schoolroom and she began piano lessons with Miss Gibbon rapping her so smartly across her knuckles at every wrong note that her hands were constantly painful.

They saw little of the woman during those first

weeks.

'I cannot take her about with me, Miss Gibbon, until she has learned to speak without that appalling Liverpool accent and to speak grammatically. She will come to chapel with me on a Sunday, as you will, as the servants do, but there is no necessity for her to speak there. When she is ready she will go to Sunday school and to meetings as well as worship.'

She spoke over Amy's head as though she were not there, which, in many ways, she wasn't!

'I want her taught how to behave at table, for one day she will eat with my husband and myself, and in company, but on no account is she to address, or be addressed by, the servants. Is that understood, Miss Gibbon?'

'Perfectly, Mrs Seymour.'

Zillah's eyes roamed the room where Amy spent her days with a look of approval. Zillah Seymour had suffered a shock and an affront to her person when her niece had given them all the slip and managed to get as far as Liverpool despite the police hunt instigated through Caleb by the Inspector. The clock that the girl had stolen, *stolen*, which was a sin before God, had never been recovered and though Zillah would have liked nothing better than to punish her niece in the most severe manner, instinct told her that the child was in such a state of senselessness it would be a waste of time. At the last her glance fell on the girl who sat quietly at the table, pen in hand, her own eyes staring at nothing in particular.

'She's looking pale, Miss Gibbon,' she remarked. 'Perhaps a walk in the garden might be in order as long as she talks to no one, and then perhaps further afield. Is she eating?'

'Oh, yes, ma'am,' though Miss Gibbon did not add that had she put a dead frog on Amy's plate and ordered her to get it down her, she would have done so in her mindless state. Miss Gibbon was of the same Methodist persuasion as Mrs Seymour and as strict a disciplinarian. Spare the rod and spoil the child, was her maxim; it had been her own father's maxim when she was a child but she had to admit that she had never known a child as compliant, as docile as Amy Seymour. Still, she had given no trouble since she had been brought back from Liverpool and the housemaid who was partly to blame, or so Mrs Seymour would have it, had been demoted to the scullery.

'Me name's Joe,' the boy shouted up to her now. 'I'm stable lad but sometimes I 'elp Matt and Barty out. They're busy in't pottin' shed gettin' ready ter plant up t'beds. It'll be a picture when they're done. Mind you, missis don't like a lot o' colour, Matt ses, but these beds 'ere'—indicating with a sweep of his hand the well-hoed, well-weeded oblongs of soil beneath the windows—' 'll be sorta out o't way so 'e, Matt, I mean, thought she wouldn't notice, like. What d'yer think?'

Despite herself Amy found her glance falling to the beds beneath the downstairs windows while the boy, Joe, waited for her opinion. The lawn he was mowing, which gave off a lovely smell, lay alongside the beds. In a wheelbarrow standing at the corner of the house were tools, a hoe, shears with long handles, a garden fork and a border spade. Next to the wheelbarrow was a garden roller. For the first time in many weeks Amy felt a stirring of interest.

'What d'yer think?' he asked her again. 'Matt ses blue lobelia an' white alyssum. Not too bright, if yer see wharr I mean.' He meant not too bright to incur the wrath of the mistress who thought pinks and reds and yellows were garish and vulgar, even in a garden.

Amy did not answer but she knew exactly what he meant and again she felt that slight lifting of something from her damaged spirit.

Joe waited patiently. Like all the servants he was sorry beyond measure at the fate of the sad little girl who was said to be the adopted daughter of Mrs Seymour. She had run away, they knew that, but nothing else except she had been brought back and they'd never seen her since, all except Alice and Alice was not a chatterbox like Jess. All she did was shake her head sadly every time she came back from the schoolroom.

'It's a cryin' shame,' Jess wept, her hands up to the elbows in soapy water as she scoured Mrs Abigail's pans, upset not only by the loss of her job which she had valued, but by the way the child was being treated. She knew she had not made much difference to the kid's life but at least she had talked to her. 'She's only a bairn an' she's bein' treated like a bloody—sorry, Mrs Abigail—like a criminal. Locked up with that . . . that hard-hearted bitch.'

'Now then, Jess,' Mrs Abigail remonstrated feebly, but they had all suffered from Miss Gibbon's high-handed treatment when she came down to the kitchen to order the child's meals. She strode in when they least expected it as though to catch them out in some wrong-doing which they were not used to. Say what you like about the

114

mistress she never interfered in the kitchen but this one was a tartar.

'That's far too rich for a child of ten, Cook,' she would say of Mrs Abigail's fruit jelly and whipped cream, her custard tartlets, her almond flowers, all made with good ingredients and planned not only to tempt the child's appetite but to cheer up the little mite. Honest to God, the woman would have the child living on bread and jam and she'd half a mind to speak to the mistress, which they all knew she would never do in case it should cause trouble for the bairn.

Amy looked down at the grinning face of the boy who was waiting patiently for an answer.

What a bonny face she had, he was thinking, even with her hair dragged back so tightly it seemed to lift her eyebrows up towards her hairline. He looked nervously over his shoulder and saw her do the same, aware that should she be caught talking to him—she had as yet said not a word—she would be the one in trouble.

They were both startled when the figure of a man, a gentleman by the look of his dress, strolled round the corner from the front of the house. He wore a tweed Norfolk jacket and knickerbockers, which reached his knees, golf stockings, brogues, and a tweed cap on his head. He was smoking a cigar.

Both children froze like young wild animals caught in a glade by a poacher and Caleb Seymour had several moments to get a good look at the girl framed in the window. So this was the child over whom his wife had made such a song and dance? The day he had first seen her came to his mind but he had to admit he had taken little interest except to note that she had been extremely ragged. He had, since then, completely forgotten her existence. He and Zillah shared nothing except the occasional evening meal and then they barely spoke. He had done her a favour in the matter of the child's escape, wondering as he did so why the poor kid who came from an appalling background—Zillah's words—should want to run away from what Zillah called a chance of a good home, a good education and a better life than she had ever known. Of course, Zillah was fanatically religious, obsessive about chapel-going, worship, meetings, this committee and that, where she would brook no argument with her point of view. She was occupied with what she called her missions of mercy in the back streets of Manchester, moving about with Mr Isherwood from the chapel, advising those with eight or nine children that it really was too many and they must restrain their natures at once. She did not tell them how! Mr Isherwood, Caleb had been told, thought she was a marvel. A fine, noble lady without whom his parish would founder. Yes, you might say Zillah was unhinged about her chapel and all she did in its name, so perhaps the child— God, he couldn't even remember her name—was not doing so well out of the situation after all.

'Good morning, lad,' he said affably to the paralysed garden boy who gulped noisily and touched his forelock. Caleb did not look at the girl again but passed on as though he had not noticed her. But he was intrigued.

Making his way to the side door he entered the house, climbed the back stairs and, reaching the door which he thought was where he saw the girl, he knocked and without waiting for an answer entered.

If he had been a black man wearing a breech clout the two occupants could not have been more taken aback! For several seconds they both stared at him then the woman leaped to her feet and began to splutter. She knew who he was, as Mrs Seymour had introduced her to him briefly on the occasion of her second interview.

'Why, good morning, Mr Seymour. We did not expect to ... but what a pleasant surprise. Stand up, Amy, and greet Mr Seymour. Quickly, quickly, remember your manners.'

'Amy, is it? I don't believe we've met properly. I am your Uncle Caleb, I suppose, since your father is my wife's brother.'

Amy rose slowly to her feet and looked into the shrewd eyes of the woman's husband. *Uncle Caleb!* She felt the same quiver of interest that had gone through her when the boy, Joe, spoke to her, for though he must be part of the scheme to steal her from her pa, he had a different look about him from the woman. His eyes did not actually twinkle but they were not cold, like the woman's, nor hard like Miss Gibbon's.

'Say good morning, child,' Miss Gibbon told her sharply, anxious to make a good impression on her employer's husband.

'Good morning,' Amy whispered and bobbed a curtsey as she had been taught. Her voice was so soft it could barely be heard.

Caleb Seymour thought she had a whipped look about her. Cowed like an ill-treated animal and though he was a businessman through and through with no time for sentimentality, he felt a small

117

frisson of shock. Had Zillah and the governess done this to the child? He had not known her in her life before this one so perhaps she had always been withdrawn. He didn't know why but he didn't think so.

'Well, you are comfortable here, Amy?' he asked her.

The enormous brown eyes, the colour of the golden syrup his mother used to spread on his toast, gazed up into his. They were fanned with long, brown lashes, the top row almost touching her eyebrows, the lower her pale cheek. What a beauty she would be, he thought, if only there was life in her face and dead eyes.

Suddenly she spoke and Miss Gibbon could not hide her chagrin at her words.

'Where's me pa? Where's me family?' In her wretchedness she forgot to speak in the careful way Miss Gibbon was teaching her.

'Amy, that's enough—' Miss Gibbon began, but Caleb held up his hand in a way those who worked for him would at once have recognised. It demanded silence.

'Your pa, child? I don't understand.' And he didn't, for his wife had told him nothing about Amy's reckless dash for Liverpool, only that she was lost and the police were needed to find her. He was aware that she had been found but he knew no details about her family apart from the fact that the father was Zillah's brother. He was a man who did not care to be involved in his wife's affairs since they all seemed to be concerned with the chapel, and he began to wonder what Zillah meant to do with this lovely girl. Even with her hair scraped back, Zillah's doing, he was sure, and in the shapeless grey dress and white, frilled pinafore that seemed to be the uniform of the well-brought-up girl of Victoria's era, although Victoria had been dead for seven years, you could not hide her delicate, childish loveliness.

'Me pa an' me brothers an' sisters 'ave gone.'

'Gone?'

'Aye, when I got there they was gone.'

'Amy, will you be quiet at once. Sit down and resume your reading. Mr Seymour does not want to—'

'Thank you, Miss . . . ?'

'Gibbon, sir.' Miss Gibbon felt compelled to bob a curtsey of her own, just as though she were a common housemaid caught by her employer where she should not be.

'Thank you, Miss Gibbon. Now then, child, I shall do my best to ascertain the whereabouts of your family for you, but I think you must resign yourself to . . . to living here with your aunt and myself. Mrs Seymour has . . . she and I intend to adopt you so to all intents and purposes you are now our daughter.'

Abruptly he left the room, wondering why he felt as though he had a rock in the place where his heart was supposed to be. He was not privy to the tongue-lashing Miss Gibbon directed at Amy nor the blankness that slowly clouded Amy's eyes. But this time the blankness hid her thoughts. The man had said he would find out—was that what the word had meant—where Pa and her family were!

9

He waited until they had finished their soup before he dropped his bombshell. He seemed unconcerned that Alice was still in the dining room removing their soup plates, nor that she nearly dropped them as he finished speaking.

'It came to my notice today that your brother and his children have left their home in Liverpool and gone elsewhere. Do you know anything about it, my dear?' he said to his wife. He wiped his lips on his crisp, white napkin and leaned back in his chair, a half smile crinkling the outer edges of his eyes.

Zillah's mouth dropped open so that she looked like the trout she and the master were about to eat, or so Alice, her normal reticence forgotten, was to report to the kitchen. She herself stood motionless with her back to the sideboard, which was loaded with sparkling plate and glass, silver cutlery, and the trout on its serving dish, and the enormous mirror on the wall behind it that reflected the room and its occupants. Alice's own mouth hung open, wondering how she could slink out of the room without being noticed.

'I beg your pardon?' Zillah's tone was icy. She had quickly recovered her composure. She was so accustomed to doing exactly what she liked, here and in the sphere of her chapel, she could scarcely believe that her husband had the temerity to question her actions. As long as he had a clean shirt each day and a good meal whenever he wanted it he left her alone to follow her own inclinations and had never challenged her about matters to do with her religion, her day-to-day activities, indeed the life she led, *nor the child.*

'I cannot believe you are interested in my brother's child, Caleb, since she will not affect you in any way.'

'Perhaps not, but I would like to know if you have any idea where the child's family have got to. Apparently they have vanished and since—'

'Who told you this?'

'The child herself.'

'You have spoken to her? How can—?'

'I saw her this morning in the schoolroom. Idle curiosity, I suppose, to see for myself this girl you have brought into our house. She asked me where her family was.'

'May I ask what you were doing in the schoolroom?'

'I have just told you. I was interested. Is the schoolroom out of bounds, Zillah?' Caleb asked his wife politely.

'I hadn't realised you would be concerned, Caleb.'

'And why shouldn't I be? I was led to believe we were to adopt her. I should also like to be reassured that Reuben is not going to show up asking for a hand-out.'

Zillah looked deeply affronted. 'Of course he won't. Good heavens, he had enough—' She stopped speaking abruptly, suddenly aware that the housemaid was hovering, *dithering*, she would have called it, to the side of her. 'You may go, Marshall. I'll ring if I need you,' she told her imperiously.

When the maid had slipped silently from the

room she turned back to her husband. 'Yes, I have given my brother some financial assistance to further his hope of a better life and to try to alleviate him in his present trouble, I admit it. I thought it was the Christian thing to do. Our Lord says—'

Caleb sighed loudly. 'May we hold a conversation without invoking the name of your Lord?'

'You forget yourself, Caleb. If you would just believe that all men are set at liberty by the blood of Christ He would joyfully forgive you.'

'For what, my dear? How have I sinned?' His tone was ironic.

'If you would just bear witness—'

'Zillah, I want no sermons from you. If we could only have a discussion like ordinary people do and not as followers of Wesley—'

'But I am a follower of Wesley, Caleb. I can be no other way.'

'I know that, but all I asked was what you have done with the child's family?' Distastefully he averted his gaze from his wife's face and the fanatical expression it took on when she spoke of her beliefs.

Zillah lifted her head, her mouth curved in an uplifted smile. 'I have found him a suitable home away from that slum where he lived. His . . . his wife and children are still in hospital but when they are discharged they will live in a decent place and I would like you to find Reuben some suitable employment. With your influence and business connections in Liverpool I'm sure you can be of help to him.'

'You cannot have arranged all this in the few

days—'

'No, I knew what I meant to do and I put into action the plans I had in mind even before I went to see my brother. I consulted a solicitor who found a house big enough to—'

'And in return he has given you a child? A daughter, is that it?' His eyes were cold and disapproving. 'And the child's wishes do not count. She has been dragged from her family and forced into a place beyond her comprehension, separated from all she knows and loves and all to satisfy your desire for a child. Any child.'

'No, not any child. A child with my blood. She will be brought up as a decent, believing Christian with a good education and the prospect, when the time comes, of a decent marriage. A worthwhile life—'

'Where is her family?' he interrupted rudely, while on the sideboard the trout congealed in its own cold juices.

'I cannot tell you.'

'Will not.'

'No! I cannot have her running off every few days to find them, which she will do, at least until she settles down, if you tell her of their whereabouts. Caleb, can you not see that she will have a much better life here with me, and her brothers and sisters will benefit. The mother will regain her health and Reuben will prosper. It is better all round, really it is. You cannot stop me, Caleb, since I have my own money now and can do as I please providing I do nothing to shame us, and you know I would never do that. My good name is precious to me.'

Caleb leaned back in his chair as though

123

suddenly defeated by this strong-willed woman who, determined to have her own child and having failed so many times to produce one, had purchased her own niece to fill the gap. He had no idea what she meant to do with the girl. She could hardly expect her to inherit their vast fortune, nor take on the mills when he was gone, as a son would have done. No, she would have her own way and he could not argue with her, for, he supposed, she spoke the truth. Her brother's family could only benefit from this transaction and the only loser was the poor innocent child, but he might be able to do something to help her endure Zillah's plan for her. Whatever that might be!

'You may be right, Zillah. She will certainly gain in a material way from your interference in her life but in my opinion if she is to be your ... *our* daughter, she must be given not only a decent education which you seem to think that governess'—said with what might have been called a sneer—'can give her but she must be treated as one of the family. Oh, I know you will wish her to ... to follow you in your ... well, I'm sure you will wish her to be *saved*—is that the correct terminology?—and perhaps you might succeed, but I do not wish it to get about among our acquaintances that our daughter has no better quarters than a maidservant. Oh, yes, I made it my business to find out where the child sleeps and it seems to me that if you continue to treat her like a prisoner she will do her best to escape her prison. She must be taught to act as a child of ours would act. A child of both of us, if you see what I mean. No, no, let me finish'—as Zillah would have interrupted—'so if she is given a certain amount of

... I was going to say freedom but I do not mean to wander where she wants out of the garden, but within the boundary of the walls, she may come to accept it. And in the house. Perhaps she might dine with us, or at least take breakfast at the weekend. I know in the old Queen's day it was considered that children should be seen but not heard. Kept to the nursery so to speak, but if this child is to be my daughter I would wish her to be as one of the family.'

There was a long-drawn-out silence as Zillah digested what Caleb had said, one of the wordiest communications he had ever shared with her. She was totally dumbfounded, since it had been her belief that her husband cared nothing for the child or what was done with her.

'I cannot believe you mean me to allow the child to wander at will wherever she fancies,' she said at last.

'As I said, not wherever she fancies but within the grounds where there will be gardeners to keep an eye on her. When it is necessary that she leave the property, Miss What's-'er-name or yourself will accompany her. I know you will wish her to become involved with your chapel and all its activities and I can have no objection to that,' or at least as long as it does not interfere with my own life, he thought, 'but here she must live as a member of our family. I think you might find that if I should instruct my solicitor to say I am willing to adopt her it will go on as you wish but I must warn you that I could, shall we say, throw a spanner in the works and make it difficult for you to proceed. Tell the servants to put her in a more suitable bedroom, one that is fitting for our daughter; allow her to become involved in the family activities and I shall not interfere with your plans.' He could not for the life of him imagine what those family activities might be, for he and Zillah shared none, except their evening meal when he was at home. When he was not at his place of business he spent as much time as he could at his club in town, or at the pleasant little house in which he had set up his mistress. He had given up all hope of a conventional family life, children of his own, family outings and holidays and asked nothing more than to be left in peace with the pleasures life afforded him.

He waited for some reaction from Zillah but she seemed shocked and speechless for once in her life. He turned his head to look hopefully at the sideboard where the trout awaited them.

*　　　*　　　*

'They're 'avin' a right old ding-dong in the dining room,' Alice said breathlessly as she burst into the kitchen.

They all turned to look at her as she spoke. Mrs Abigail was sitting in her own chair before the kitchen fire, her swollen feet up on the tuffet which came out when her chores were done for the day. The trout had gone in with the vegetables for the second course and the apple charlotte that she herself had made only an hour since with eighteen Savoy biscuits, three-quarters of a pint of cream, vanilla and wine, with added sugar and isinglass, taking great pride in her handiwork, stood on a tray ready to be taken into the dining room by Alice. Primrose was scrubbing the kitchen table,

126

her arm moving in great sweeps on the already spotless top and Martha was on her knees giving the inside of the oven 'what for'. They stopped working as one and Jess, her arms soapy since she was, in her demoted capacity as scullery-maid, scouring the pans, came out of the scullery.

'It's about her,' Alice told them dramatically. 'The master wants ter know where 'er family is. "What yer done with 'em?" 'e ses. "Where've yer put them?" That's where she were, see. Gone ter Liverpool ter find 'em. Eeh, poor little lass, all that way on 'er own.' She shook her head disbelievingly and they all began to converge towards the table, eager to hear what she had to say. It was most unusual for Alice to tell them what she heard in the dining room, or indeed any part of the house and it was a sign of her own distress that she should divulge it now. 'Mistress wouldn't tell 'im. You'll only tell 'er, she ses, an' I don't want 'er runnin' off every five minutes ter find 'em.'

'Eeh, never,' Jess said, shocked.

'It's true, I tell yer. She sent me off wi' a flea in me ear and the trout still standin' on't sideboard, cold by now.'

'An' the trouble I took with that fish,' Mrs Abigail retorted indignantly.

'Never mind that, Mrs Abigail. Oh, I know 'ow annoyed you are but what am I ter do? She said she'd ring when she was ready but it's not that but the poor kid, that poor little bugger . . .' And so upset were they all, including Mrs Abigail, no one noticed the swearing which Mrs Abigail could not abide. Since the governess had taken over none of them had seen Amy except in the distance when she walked sedately beside Miss Gibbon in the

127

garden.

The bell on the board above the door rang suddenly and they all looked at it guiltily as though the mistress herself were watching and listening. Alice jumped nervously then with a grimace ran towards the door and up the hallway towards the dining room.

* * *

The next day Alice was summoned to the small parlour where Mrs Seymour spent her time when she was not at chapel or taking her carriage to one of the many committees and meetings that occupied her time. She had wandered about the bedroom floor of the house, unknown to her servants who were all occupied with their tasks in the kitchen. The bedrooms, her own and the second one at the other end of the landing where Caleb slept, had been attended to, the beds made by Alice and Martha who had taken Atkins's place. They had dusted and the carpets had been swept by the very latest carpet sweeper on four wheels with a rotating spiral of bristles and a dust box which could be opened for emptying, a great time-saving device. The spare bedrooms were only cleaned once a week and Zillah had the task of choosing one of these as suitable for the child. The trouble was they were all, in her opinion, too grand for a girl of ten who had slept for the first years of her life not only thirteen to a bedroom but probably at least six to a bed. The rooms had not been furnished with children in mind. They had not even been furnished by her but by Caleb's mother who had inclined towards the pretty, the feminine, the frilly and it was only her own bedroom, once shared with Caleb, that she had furnished and decorated in her own taste which leaned towards the austere. Still, Caleb had been adamant and though she must give way on this small matter it seemed she had been given carte blanche on the adoption and upbringing of the child.

She chose a room on the corner which overlooked the back of the house. It had two windows, one looking over the back and the other with a view to the side and the small stand of trees that had been planted there. It was smaller than the rest but had its own tiny bathroom which meant the child would not wander about in the night should she need the lavatory. From the back window was a view of the stables, the kitchen garden, the paddock where the horses grazed and the stable yard and as a result it was not really suitable for a guest of any importance. The door to the room was directly opposite her own which was an added advantage!

She had taken the hot chocolate that was her customary mid-morning drink and reaching again for the bell she summoned Marshall who, surprised, entered and bobbed her usual curtsey.

'Yes, ma'am?'

'Ah, Marshall, I want you and the other maid, er . . . ?'

'Martha, ma'am,' Alice said, forgetting Mrs Seymour's tendency to call all the servants by their surnames.

'Martha?' Mrs Seymour frowned.

'Murphy, ma'am, sorry.'

'Well, I wish you and Murphy to clean the back

bedroom at the end of the landing, opposite my own. A thorough cleaning, mind, and when it is done I shall inspect it. I might want some of the ...'—she almost said gaudiness—'draperies and such removed. Is that clear?'

It wasn't but Alice said it was.

'Very well, do it at once. Leave your other duties and when it is done report back to me.' Zillah felt as though she were sucking a lemon as she said this, so sour were the words in her mouth. It was a great trial to her to have to give way to Caleb on this matter, for it was her firm belief that children—though she had no personal knowledge of it—should be brought up strictly, as she had been, with none of the softening comforts some parents favoured. The room was as it had been when she came to the house as a bride, furnished by her mother-in-law, and for the life of her Zillah could not imagine why it had been done up in such a fashion. She was not to know that her mother-in-law had lived in hopes of a daughter, a daughter to dress up, to spoil, to take about with her in her carriage, and the bedroom was to have been hers. Zillah had often decided she would change it all to suit her own plain tastes but had forgotten about it since it was never used. The maids cleaned it with the rest every week but now, to her annoyance, the child who was to be *her* daughter was to occupy it. But she would redecorate it as soon as possible and in the meanwhile hang some serious prints, prints with a religious and moral content on the walls, a picture of John Wesley and others of the faith to encourage the child to go in the direction of Zillah's choice.

At her mistress's words Alice bobbed another

130

curtsey and left the room.

'She wants the small back bedroom cleaning,' she announced to the kitchen when she returned. They all gaped at her, for none of them could remember when last they had guests.

'Who's coming then, did she say?' Mrs Abigail wanted to know, her mind filled with menus and recipes and the all-important matter of catering for guests.

'No, she just said get Martha ter 'elp with the cleaning and when we'd finished she'd inspect it.'

'The *small* back bedroom?'

'Aye, the small back bedroom an' why that one is a mystery. It's only big enough fer one.'

Mrs Abigail sighed, perplexed. 'Well, you'd best get on with it then.'

It was the next day when the news reached them that the occupant of the small back bedroom was to be none other than the little girl who had come into their lives so unexpectedly and nobody could have been more surprised and delighted than the child herself.

At Miss Gibbon's prompting she stood up when the woman came into the schoolroom.

'Good morning, Miss Gibbon,' she said with a nod at Amy. 'I'm sorry to interrupt your lesson just as you are beginning but I shall need the child so you may have the rest of the day off. Before you go, though, I must ask you to help me to . . .' It was evident that what she was about to say was not to her liking. 'I shall need your help to move her from the bedroom in which she now sleeps to one that my husband thinks will be more suitable, thought I must say . . .' What she 'must say' was not revealed to the governess, for it suddenly occurred to Zillah

131

Seymour that no matter how she resented her husband's interference in the child's upbringing it was not done to display that resentment to a servant. 'She is to have a room at the back of the house. The end one on the landing.'

Amy had been copying the beautiful copperplate that Florence Gibbon believed was the hallmark of a lady but it was a trying lesson for them both. Amy had only been used to writing with chalk on a slate and the sight of the dazzling white paper and the pen with its pristine nib that had to be dipped in the inkpot was, to say the least, unnerving. The inkpot was small and made of glass with a lid that bent backwards and when the nib was dipped in it had to be lifted out very carefully otherwise a drop of ink might fall on its journey from inkwell to paper. For once she was glad to see the woman!

She could hardly believe her ears and for several long seconds while the woman and Miss Gibbon discussed the difficulties of transferring her belongings from one bedroom to another she merely stood there in a daze. She had no idea where they, or rather *she* was going and could only believe that it could not possibly be an improvement. She followed them from the schoolroom, the woman having told her irritably to come along and stop daydreaming, and when told picked up an armful of the sensible undergarments lying on her bed and waited for instructions as to where she was to go. The two women discussed this and that and told her to hurry up as she stood uncertainly in the doorway.

The landing round the corner from the schoolroom was wide and along its length stood narrow tables bearing bowls of flowers and from the open doors that led into other bedrooms the sun streamed across the rich carpets. She had not been along here since the night when she had escaped and then it had been dark but now, despite the heavy furniture and sombre wallpaper, it seemed bright and almost cheerful.

There was a door open at the very end of the landing and coming out of the room were Alice and another maid who both bobbed a curtsey to the woman.

'Oh, Marshall, you can help Miss Gibbon to move the child's things from her present bedroom to this one. We have made a start but I must get to chapel before ten and she is to come with me. Mr Isherwood is expecting us so ... and will one of you run down and tell Campbell to fetch the carriage to the front steps.'

She turned to Amy. 'Go and fetch your cloak, child, and your bonnet but remember that from now on you are to sleep in here. My room is directly opposite. Now don't forget to wash your hands and face and I think Miss Gibbon had better re-plait your hair.' She pulled a face, for Amy's hair seemed to have an awkward tendency to untangle itself no matter how firmly it was tied up.

Alice and Martha exchanged amazed glances before Martha set off at a run towards the stairs and the kitchen, not only to order the carriage for the mistress, but to tell them that the small back bedroom would now have an occupant and it wasn't a guest.

It was Amy!

10

From that day Amy began to regain the spirit that had been bred in her not only by her mother and her mother's trust in her but by the life she had led in the teeming streets of Liverpool. Though she was not consciously aware of it, she had also inherited much of the character of Dolly Pearson whose cheerful disposition and talent for banter had made her a great favourite with her fellow workers. She had enchanted Ben Pearson with her bonny, laughing face, her golden-brown eyes which had promised something his life had sadly lacked so far and he had been in thrall to her from the moment he had set eyes on her.

In the years since he had decided he had had enough of the Indian Frontier and had fled the army, Ben had junketed about the world, enjoying his freedom, working in casual jobs to feed himself, moving from country to country on cargo boats and tramp steamers until he had landed in Liverpool. He had been thirty years old. Strolling along the docks until he reached Bootle he had stood to watch the fishing boats discharge their cargo and had first seen his Dolly.

Since then he had loved her, leaned on her, depended on her strength and had done his best by her and the many children Dolly bore him. He was amusing, a good laugh, his fellow workers called him, careless, carefree really, for Dolly took care of them all which was why he had gone to pieces when Dolly was taken away from him and committed to hospital. They had lived on the brink of abject poverty but somehow she had fended it off and he had been a contented man.

And now the girl who was Dolly's daughter was beginning to draw on the strength Dolly herself had bequeathed her, fending off the despair and misery she had first known. She learned patience and she learned something else as well: cunning. But that was to come later! She had not abandoned her determination to find her family but she had come to realise that she could not just take off at the first opportunity as she had done previously but must bide her time and wait for the right moment. Wait until she was not watched night and day and of course, now that she was to be put in the bedroom, a bedroom with an unlocked door, as long as she aroused no suspicion, as long as the woman and Miss Gibbon relaxed their vigilance, she would win that precious scrap of freedom.

Despite herself she was entranced with her new room. It was not a big room which, she supposed, was the reason it had been allocated to her, but then where she came from big rooms were scarce. She was amazed that such a *pretty* room existed in this sombre house, unaware, as Zillah had been, that Caleb's mother had furnished it with a daughter in mind. It was light and airy, simply furnished, with a comfortable chair, cheerful sprigged wallpaper and curtains. Old Mrs Seymour, who had been *young* Mrs Seymour then, had herself worked the colourful quilt on the bed in pinks and greens and filled the white-painted shelves with books and even a doll or two. The books, among them *Poor Daddy Long-legs, The Butterfly Ball, The House that Jack Built*, were much thumbed and obviously much loved by young Anne Whitehead, as she had been before her marriage to William Seymour. There was a picture on the wall of Jesus gathering children about Him, colourful and pleasing, and a framed sampler which spoke of many hours of toil with an embroidery needle over alphabet and numbers. Victorian children, young schoolgirls such as Caleb's mother had been at the time, had been skilled in needlework.

The bed was fashioned from brass and had bevelled glass plaques and brass rosettes on the spindles, the brass polished and winking in the sunlight that fell across the room from the side window. There was even a carpet on the floor, patterned in rose pink and apple green. It did not reach the skirting board but was surrounded by richly polished wood. The room was lovely to behold, at least to Amy who had known nothing like it and as she hesitated on the threshold the thought suddenly came to her that the gentleman who had entered the schoolroom so surprisingly was the one responsible for the move. She could not have said why.

'Well, child, do as you're told and get your cloak and bonnet,' the woman was saying, glaring round her at the pretty room as though wondering where to begin to make it over to her own taste. It was obvious she strongly disapproved of her mother-in-law's choice and was amazed at herself that in the twenty years since she had married she herself had not changed it. She was, of course, a busy woman, not inclined to the domestic side of her household and as she never entered the room, or indeed any of the spare rooms since she trusted Mrs Abigail to see that they were cleaned to Zillah's satisfaction, they had remained as they had been in old Mrs Seymour's day.

'It would be as well if you let Miss Gibbon see to your hair,' she repeated sharply, 'since you can hardly attend chapel as you are. Really, I have never known a child who can get herself in such a state as you seem able to do. Stand up straight, for goodness sake and take that petulant look from your face,' by which she meant the expressionless mask that Amy presented to her. Zillah found it intolerable that her husband should have interfered in what she considered to be her upbringing of the child; she had been forced to go against her belief that a plain, unadorned bedroom was more fitting than this fanciful nonsense her mother-in-law favoured and she only wished she had taken more notice of the rooms and changed them earlier. Mind you, in the early days Caleb had invited guests to stay, businessmen who were in Manchester, and had made it clear he did not want them to be put in what he called the style of bleak rooms she favoured.

She and Amy set out for chapel in the carriage since they were already late, Zillah complained, and it was too far to walk and be there on time. As they entered by the chapel door, covered with red baize figured all over with round-headed brass nails, for the first time Amy took an interest in the large building by which the woman set such store. She was not to know it but most of the congregation of St John's Wesleyan Methodist Chapel were well off and liked to worship in comfort. Zillah, despite her wealth, was an exception and would have preferred a more austere atmosphere but nevertheless as she held Amy's hand and led her to what Amy now knew was the Seymour pew Amy began to glance about her. Perhaps it was the influence of the pretty room at Somerfield which she knew would be waiting for her at the end of the day, but whatever it was she was aware that the ice that had enclosed her for the past two months—or was it more? time seemed to have had no meaning since she had been torn from her family—was melting.

The building was cruciform in shape with two long aisles leading down to the transepts that were on either side of the pulpit. In front of the pulpit was a communion table and behind it were the choir seats. The Seymour pew was at the front and Amy was made aware of the importance of the woman who guided her into the pew and indicated that she was to put her hands together, as many of the congregation bowed to her as she passed. The woman sank her head on to her hands and Amy did the same though she did not pray. The woman finally stood straight and handed Amy a hymn book and indicated that she was to take out her own Bible, the one the woman had given her when they first came to worship. The chapel was beginning to fill up with ladies in their furs and feathers, gentlemen holding top hats and kid gloves, and as they settled themselves expectantly the choir filed in followed by Mr Isherwood who mounted the pulpit steps. The organ began to play and there was a rustling as hymn books were opened and the congregation stood to sing the first hymn.

Lord of all being, throned afar,
Thy glory flames . . .

In full voice the hymn rose to the high ceiling. Amy was mute and in her own rapturous rendition of the hymn Zillah did not notice. Her face was uplifted and so, it seemed, was her soul and it was not until the hymn was over that she turned to Amy. She frowned at her and with everyone else they sat and prepared to listen to Mr Isherwood's sermon. It was very long and several times Amy felt herself drifting off almost to sleep. She did her best to keep her thoughts busy, dwelling on the delights of the bedroom in which she was to sleep that very night. The door would be unlocked and although she had no intention of leaving her room, not yet at least, just the fact that she was not locked in as she had been was a joy to her.

She was surprised, as they alighted beneath the portico and entered the hallway of the house, to be met by the gentleman who, it seemed to her, was hanging about looking at the dreary pictures on the wall as though he had never seen them before. It was evident that the woman also was dumbfounded.

'Caleb,' she challenged, 'whatever are you doing? I was led to believe you were to go into the office this morning. Urgent business you said.'

She was clearly annoyed though Amy did not know why. The man was her husband and lived in the house and surely had a perfect right to stand in his own hallway. She listened with interest since it seemed to her that whenever the gentleman appeared something good came of it.

'I finished earlier than I thought and since it is

139

Sunday and Sunday dinner is about to be served I thought it would be . . . pleasant for us to sit down together.' He did not quite smile but Amy was convinced he was pleased with himself.

'Of course, but do we not usually eat Sunday dinner together?' the woman said coolly.

'Indeed we do, but I meant with . . . with Amy.'

Zillah was further thunderstruck, opening and closing her mouth a time or two, then it snapped shut. She had not expected when she took her brother's child into her house that her husband would concern himself with her and now twice he had taken it into his head to interfere with her own plans. She did not agree that the child should be transferred from the plain bedroom, where Miss Gibbon could keep her eye on her, to the rather . . . well, she supposed she would describe the new bedroom as light-minded and not at all the sort of surroundings in which she meant to raise the girl. As a sober, dedicated follower of Wesley and a believer in his teachings, which was surely the only way to proceed, how was she to take her new life seriously if she was to spend time in the frivolous room Caleb believed she should have? Really, Zillah would have to watch this man who had quite taken her by surprise, since up to now he had shown little interest in what she did and had certainly never questioned her movements.

Her eyes narrowed as though she suspected some trick then she lifted her head and swept past her husband, making for the stairs. She held on to Amy's wrist, taking her with her.

'She is not yet ready to sit down with adults, Caleb. Miss Gibbon is training her to mix with—'

'Then this is an opportunity for her to practise

what she has learned. Dining *en famille*, so to speak. If she makes mistakes there will be only you and me to see it and to help her.'

Amy was appalled at the very thought. Miss Gibbon had drummed into her the etiquette of sitting at table, the correct cutlery to use, how to fold her napkin, every detail of dining that she must learn as a young lady of good family, but as yet she had only practised this special way of taking breakfast, luncheon, as she had been told to call it, and the plain meal they ate at teatime, with Miss Gibbon supervising her. The idea of seating herself in the dining room with this man and this woman and actually being watched as she practised her new skills was terrifying. She was sure she would bungle it, spill something, drop her knife or be asked to say something that was totally beyond her. She wasn't quite sure what, but she knew the man, unlike the woman, would talk to her, ask her questions and how was she to deal with that?

But Caleb was not to be put off. Speaking to his wife's ramrod back as she marched up the stairs dragging her niece behind her, he said, 'I do believe that I have some say in this matter, Zillah. You informed me that we are to adopt Amy and if she is to become our daughter she must learn the niceties of good society. And that means sitting at table with us. Miss Gibbon has, so far, been her only companion.'

Zillah turned perilously, almost tipping Amy down the stairs. 'She comes with me to chapel where she is learning the companionship of the Lord Christ and His followers and when she is ready I shall take her to meetings where she will be introduced to many people of our class. She has as yet not mastered the correct way to speak. Miss Gibbon is doing her best to eradicate her accent but she needs practise and until I think she is prepared enough she should remain with Miss Gibbon.'

She turned her back on her husband, the matter, in her mind, quite decided, but Caleb Seymour was used to having his own way in everything he did and though he had found nothing to complain of in the way his home was run and had never meddled in his wife's way of life, for some reason, perhaps not even known to himself, he was resolute in this.

'I shall expect her to be at the dinner table, Zillah, and have you no other garments for her to wear other than that God-forsaken sack? She is a child of . . . what, ten years old—'

'Eleven,' a small voice piped and Zillah and Caleb looked in amazement at the child. And so did Jess who, unseen by Mr and Mrs Seymour, had come through the green baize kitchen door as Mrs Seymour stepped over the threshold of the hall, Amy dragging behind her. She had stopped at once, wondering if she could sneak off back to the kitchen before they noticed her but something made her freeze, hearing in amazement the words spoken between husband and wife. Slowly, over the months since Amy had been brought back from Liverpool, Jess had been reinstated as parlour-maid, for, as Mrs Abigail said, Primrose was hopeless in her attempt to do Jess's work. It was not that she was unwilling. Put her to scour a heap of pots and pans and she tackled them with cheerful vigour but in the front of the house she had to be constantly told by an irritated Alice what she must do. Counting on her mistress's lack of interest in the working of the household, Mrs Abigail had given Jess her old job back and at this moment she was on her way to the dining room to set the table. She carried a tray of cutlery, glassware, all that was needed for the Sunday dinner which was just coming out of the oven ready to be carried to the table where Mr Seymour himself liked to carve the roast. She stood rooted to the spot, hidden just beneath the turn in the stairs where it branched to left and right.

'Eleven! When did you become eleven, miss, and why was I not told?' Zillah made it sound as though Amy had committed some cardinal sin. 'Do you mean to say you have had a birthday and kept it to yourself? Mr Seymour and I would like to know when this happened,' though what she would have done about it Jess could not imagine. A party! Dear Lord, wait until she told the others.

'First o' June. Mam used ter—'

'Thank you, that's enough,' for Zillah had no wish to know what the child's mother had done. She faced Caleb. 'And she has no other garments to wear, only what I consider appropriate for a girl of her age, Caleb, so, if you are determined on what I consider to be a foolish course of action in allowing her to eat with us then you must put up with her appearance, which, I might add, will remain as you see her.'

'She's ter 'ave 'er dinner wi' 'em.' Jess put down the tray which she had been about to carry into the dining room, crashing it instead on to the kitchen table making everyone in the kitchen jump. They all turned to look at her, even the kitchen cat.

143

'Who?' Mrs Abigail began, turning from the roasting tin where she had been basting the nice leg of lamb for the umpteenth time and which she was to serve in the traditional way with mint sauce, roast potatoes, her own delicious gravy, peas and cauliflower, the vegetables all home-grown, of course, and only an hour from the garden.

'The kid, o' course. They're arguin' about it in the 'all but it looks as though t'master's won. She'll never learn, 'e ses, if she only stops wi' Miss Gibbon, an' 'as she nothin' else ter wear but that God-forsaken sack—'

'Jess!'

''Onest ter God, Mrs Abigail, it's what 'e said. Any road, she's ter 'ave 'er dinner wi' 'em. Eeh, I wish I were servin',' she added wistfully. She twirled round to Alice who, like the rest of them, was standing slack-jawed, interrupted in whatever task she had been about when Jess burst into the kitchen. 'Now, Alice, yer'll tell us every word, won't yer?'

Alice nodded her head, her mouth still wobbling open and Mrs Abigail put her hand to her bosom as though in trepidation for the poor child who was to suffer such an unnerving experience.

'An' guess what?' Jess was triumphant in her task of being the bearer of such news.

'What?'

'She's 'ad a birthday while she's bin 'ere.'

''Oo? Not . . . ?'

Jess nodded enthusiastically. 'Aye, Amy, o' course. I'm eleven, she ses, bold as brass, so what d'yer think ter that? First o' June, she ses, an' not a soul knowin'.'

Mrs Abigail's mind instantly turned in the

direction of iced birthday cakes, wondering how she could get such a thing to the poor little kid in the schoolroom.

*   *   *

He did his best to make it easy for her, though it was obvious his wife disapproved most strongly and kept protesting that Caleb should not pester the girl at the table.

'It is not called pestering, Zillah. It is called conversation. That is the point of the exercise. Now then,' he continued, ready to start, turning to Amy who sat like a small frozen statue on the chair at the side of the table. It was an extending table with huge bulbous legs which, when guests were present, could have one or even two pieces added. To match it were balloon-backed chairs with velvet upholstery in a rich wine red. They stood on a Turkish carpet in sombre shades of red and green laid on the polished boards. The table was set first with a baize undercloth to protect the wood and then a damask tablecloth which had been starched and ironed to perfection, with an immaculate glossy surface embroidered by the late Mrs Seymour in what was known as whitework. The napkins, which matched the cloth, were folded in the mitre style by Alice who had been taught the art by Mrs Abigail. At each place, three of them, was a dinner plate, two forks, one smaller than the other, three knives, one bigger than the other two and a soup spoon all of silver, the outer cutlery being the first used as Amy was quick to observe. Above the plate were a small knife and fork and three exquisite crystal glasses arranged in a

145

triangle. There was a cruet set of silver and cut glass with five bottles containing oil, vinegar, salt, pepper and salad dressing and in the centre of the table Alice had placed a cut-glass bowl of roses. Both Zillah's and Amy's glass was filled with water but Caleb, to Zillah's intense and on-going annoyance, had a glass of red wine.

'Caleb,' Zillah said sharply, 'have you not forgotten something?'

'My dear?' Caleb's voice was mild.

'I believe we should start with grace.'

'Of course, I do apologise,' and at once both he and his wife bent their heads over their clasped hands. Amy did the same, for she was familiar with Miss Gibbon's exhortations of thanks to the Lord.

'Dear Lord,' Zillah began earnestly, 'we beseech you to bless us at this table and look kindly on thy servants and help us to do thy bidding in our daily lives. Some of us are negligent in our devotions and for this we ask thy forgiveness and help us to—'

'Zillah! Grace, if you please.'

His wife glared at him, as she was just about to favour her Lord with what often sounded to Caleb like a chat between neighbours over a fence with one neighbour doing all the talking. So often, as with this child she had taken under her wing, she could not understand why the Lord tried her so when she was doing what she saw as her Christian duty. She was conscious of her own virtues and she expected to be rewarded for them and yet here was her husband rebuking her.

'For what we are about to receive may the Lord make us duly thankful,' Caleb gabbled which to him said all that was necessary. He could see Amy peeping through her fingers at him, her eyes wide and wondering and when he reached for his napkin and shook it out he watched her as she did the same. He realised that whatever he did she meant to copy him. Alice entered carrying an enormous soup tureen which she placed on the sideboard, then, after ladling the soup into dishes that matched the plates on the table, she put one on the plate in front of Mrs Seymour, repeating the action for Amy and Mr Seymour, then bobbed a curtsey and quietly left the room, hurrying back to bring the servants, who waited with bated breath, up to date! She had only given Amy half what she had served the master and mistress.

After several sips Caleb turned to the child who was carefully spooning the soup into her mouth. He noticed that she ate very daintily.

'What are you learning in that schoolroom of yours, Amy? French, I believe, and history?'

'*Oui, monsieur,*' she answered and for a moment he was amazed, then delighted, for not only had the child replied but she had done so in an amusing way. Well, it had amused him and he wanted to say well done but his good sense warned him that Zillah would not be pleased.

She confirmed it. 'There is no need to put on airs, child. The Lord says—'

'Zillah, please. Amy was only demonstrating what she is learning with Miss Gibbon and I for one would like to congratulate her.' He turned away from his wife's outraged face and smiled at Amy.

'Can you say any more? Perhaps "good morning" or . . .'

'*Bonjour, monsieur.*' Amy wriggled in her chair

and at once Zillah pounced on her, ready to castigate her but Caleb put up a hand to stop her.

'Well done, Amy. Now then, how about history? What has Miss Gibbon taught you about the past?'

'Some dates, sir. Queen Victoria came to't throne on 20th o' June 1837 an' died in Janry 1901.' She kept her eyes on her plate, wishing the gentleman would let her get on with the delicate task of eating her soup under the disapproving eye of the woman, but it was not until they were spooning the delicious chocolate cream that Mrs Abigail had concocted that the interrogation, which is how it seemed to Amy, came to an end. And it was the woman who ended it.

'Very well, Caleb,' she said, standing up abruptly. 'I hope you are satisfied. The child has things to do and so do I,' and taking Amy's wrist she pulled her from her seat and marched her to the door.

Both Amy and Caleb were made aware that Amy would be made to pay for this!

11

Miss Gibbon put a hand to her stomach, doubled over and groaned in a most dramatic way. Her face had turned a sort of greyish green and when she straightened up she leaned against the stone wall that surrounded the garden of Somerfield.

Amy watched her dispassionately. Miss Gibbon seemed prone to these attacks and when they struck her she was forced to leave her charge and scuttle off to the bathroom. Amy often wondered at her own uncaring attitude but knew that had it been anyone but Miss Gibbon—or *her*, of course,—she would have instantly sprung to help, to do her best to alleviate their suffering, but the two women who had her in their cold and unfeeling tentacles aroused not the slightest sympathy in her. Should a sparrow have fallen in its flight she would have rushed to its aid but Miss Gibbon and Mrs Seymour, as she now called her since she realised she must cease thinking of her as 'the woman', left her not only unmoved but implacable in her dislike. They themselves had changed her from the good-natured, cheerful and optimistic child she had once been into this automaton that for the most part she now was.

Oh, yes, she understood the word automaton. Miss Gibbon had explained its meaning, not in relation to herself, of course, and she had to admit that Miss Gibbon was an excellent teacher. Amy could read and write fluently, was quick and accurate with her sums, though that did not matter so much in the world Mrs Seymour inhabited, and could converse in a stilted, stumbling manner in French. She knew the dates of all the important events in history, English and foreign, and could recite the capitals of most countries and what produce those countries exported. And all in six months. But then she and Miss Gibbon spent eight hours a day in one another's company, in or out of the schoolroom, apart from the times she was at chapel with Mrs Seymour. Her own quick and inquisitive brain helped, soaking up the facts and figures Miss Gibbon poured into it.

They were walking round the perimeter of the garden beneath the beech trees. The narrow woodland was shady though the day was fine but with the sun lower in the sky it was cool. Drifts of leaves littered the ground and the trees were beginning to close down for the coming winter. The fruits of the trees so typical of autumn also fell with the leaves but above their heads the colours glowed with a brilliant display of flaming orange, russet and gold. Soon the foliage would darken to copper and Miss Gibbon was pointing this out in her pedantic way when she was struck down almost to her knees.

'Come with me at once,' she managed to gasp, taking short, painful steps in the direction of the house but Amy ignored her and since Miss Gibbon was in somewhat of a hurry she had no time to insist. With the leaves rustling under her sensible shoes, she darted out from beneath the trees and headed for the house.

They had left the house by the side door that led into the garden on the right, striding out towards the stand of trees and then setting off briskly along the front wall, the small lake busy with ducks to their left, turning at the corner and making their way towards the back of the garden, still under the canopy of the beech trees.

Amy stood for several moments, listening to the sounds of the outdoors, savouring the marvel of being completely alone in it. There were birds singing somewhere and when a flash of scarlet caught her eye she realised that the robins were searching for food among the trees. The sound they made was quite lovely, short liquid phrases running together from the high perch of the branches. A grey squirrel overhead started abusing her and another which had been hidden suddenly scrabbled up the trunk of the beech. Rooks swept confidently across the autumn sky then settled down to preen and chatter among themselves. There was a great oak tree on the other side of the wall on the perimeter of the Pendleton Nurseries next door and from it had fallen a dense carpet of acorns which she suspected the squirrels were after.

She started to walk slowly between the trees, continuing towards the back of the house, skirting the stable yard where there was a great deal of cheerful clatter and the stamp of horses' hooves.

'Fetch me that hoof pick, will yer, Tim. Blossom's picked up a stone. Must 'ave bin when the master rode 'er yesterday.' That would be Ernie Tingle. 'I dunno, what we gonner do when . . .'

She did not learn what Ernie was questioning since she had gone beyond the stable and the buildings that surrounded it. To her left were the greenhouses and the vegetable gardens where Matt and Barty, whom she had learned to recognise, were clearing the asparagus beds ready to mix in some good manure. Not that she knew what they were doing, only that they were so busy they did not notice her go past.

She came to a well-clipped privet hedge which divided the lawn from whatever was beyond it and from where there came the sound of the lawnmower and someone singing slightly out of tune. A male voice. It was not a hymn, which seemed to be the only kind of music allowed at Somerfield.

I kissed her once upon her lips,
I wished I'd done it twice,
I whispered it's so naughty,
She said it is so nice,

Then when he had finished the verse he began to sing it again.

She skirted the hedge and to her surprise came up against a tall wire-linked fence and beyond it was what she knew to be a tennis court. There was a gate let into the side which stood open. She had seen such a thing that last day at Princes Park and more recently in Peel Park when she had walked sedately beside Miss Gibbon and had been ordered not to stare. A tall boy, the one she had seen from the schoolroom window, was pushing the lawnmower vigorously up and down the court. He had removed the net which was draped to one side and with his back to her he was unaware that he was being watched. When he reached the far end he turned with the same neat movement he had shown on the lawn and it was then that he spotted her. He stopped immediately, both the mowing and the singing. Just behind him to the left was a small shed, well maintained as was everything at Somerfield. His face for a moment was dumbfounded then he grinned and, leaving the lawnmower where it stood, he hurried eagerly towards her.

'Mornin', miss. Fine mornin' innit. I love this time o't year, but then I love all't times o't year, me. What about you?' His grin broadened encouragingly and she noticed that he had what she could only call a kink in his nose as though at one time it might have been broken. She had seen

152

enough fights and broken noses in the streets of Liverpool to recognise one. Joe watched her expression relax. They had seen nothing of this little girl who had come to live so unexpectedly among them, not for a long time. Alice and Jess who looked after the bedrooms, served the family meals, took the coals up to the schoolroom, that sort of thing, reported occasionally on her but then the poor kid went nowhere but to chapel with the mistress and whenever she was glimpsed in the grounds she had that bloody woman with her, the one who guarded her from the gardeners and stable lads as though they might contaminate her.

'I like daffodils,' she said unexpectedly.

'Spring, yer right, it's grand when the spring flowers're out.' He glanced about him somewhat furtively, for both he and the lass would get into trouble if anyone saw them together but they were hidden behind the high hedge that divided the tennis court from the rest of the garden.

'I like daffodils,' she said again. 'They're me mam's favourite. When I go—' She stopped suddenly, as this was the first person she had spoken to apart from Miss Gibbon, Mrs Seymour and the old gentleman as she called him. She had been about to divulge her determination that one day she would go back to her family and in her hand would be the biggest bunch of daffodils anyone had ever seen.

'Me name's Joe as I told yer,' he said simply, realising with the wisdom that seldom comes to the young that they were touching on a sensitive subject and wanting to divert her. 'I know yours is Amy,' he continued shyly. 'D'yer fancy a game o' tennis?' Then he laughed. 'I've always wanted ter

153

do more than just mow t'lawn but I've no one ter play with, even if they'd let me. There's tennis racquets an' balls in't shed. I've often wondered,' he continued, ''oo plays ere. I've never seen anyone but someone must've.'

Amy looked about her consideringly. The idea of Mr and Mrs Seymour having a game was laughable. Tennis was a young person's activity and as far as she could tell there had never been any young people at Somerfield. She would have been surprised to know that in his youth Caleb Seymour had been a keen player which was why his father had had the court put in.

'Mmm, I suppose so,' she murmured.

There was a pause while Joe wondered what to say next. He felt drawn to this young girl. From the first time he had seen her standing in the window of the schoolroom there had been something forlorn about her and from what he heard in the kitchen she had a rotten life. Dragged from her own family and adopted by the Seymours with, seemingly, no choice but to accept, she was being turned by the old woman into a copy of herself. Chapel-going, hymn-singing, Bible meetings, class meetings, whatever they were. 'The class of the Lord's redeemed,' he had heard Alice say, for Alice was privy to many of the conversations that went on in the front of the house.

'Every full member o't Wesleyan Chapel is what's called a class member. Every chapel 'as classes each with its own leader. They meet once a week, say prayers, sing hymns and give their testimony,' Alice told them importantly.

'What the devil do that mean?' Ernie Tingle had wanted to know.

'Nay, don't ask me,' Alice had answered while they all sat round the kitchen table and drank their cocoa. 'It's what the mistress was telling Amy in the schoolroom when I took the coals up. She wants the lass to become one when she's old enough.'

'What?'

'Like I said. A leader of a class, I suppose. She just sat there, kid, I mean, starin' out o't winder an' yer could tell she weren't listenin'.'

Now Joe pondered on what he could say to this girl whose face was unutterably sad but who he sensed, with the right words, could be made to smile. She was kind of lifeless and yet there was something that flickered, like the tiny flame in a fire that just needed kindling, a soft breath to bring it to life and she would burst into the cheerful, dancing coals that he gazed into when he sat before the kitchen fire. It was almost quenched but not quite and if he had half a chance he would bring it to life.

'Wheer's old gorgon then? We don't often see yer out on yer own.'

'She . . . she had to run back to the house.' She spoke slowly as though being extra careful to enunciate her words carefully, which she did.

'Well, 'appen it's fer't best. At least it gives yer a chance ter . . . ter . . .'

'Have a game of tennis?' There was a ghost of a smile on her face and her brown eyes glowed with a shy sense of fun.

He was delighted. 'Shall us?' He turned as though to run to the shed for the tennis racquets but she shook her head.

'She'll be looking for me in a minute.' She

155

sighed and Joe felt his heart wrench. 'But if I get a chance to elude her I'll come looking for you.'

Joe wasn't sure what 'elude' meant but he got the meaning of her words. His face split again into its customary grin. 'I've got ter go anyroad as soon as I've finished the mowin'. Me and Tim's to empty one o't stables fer't new motor. Ernie's real mangy about it. 'E can't abide the thought, yer know 'ow 'e loves 'orses, but if master's ter 'ave one it's ter go somewhere. A Lanchester, I 'eard because Thomas ses Mr Seymour won't 'ave nothin' that's not British. I bet yer'll be 'avin' a ride in it soon.' It was obvious he was very envious. He politely lifted the cap that hung on the back of his head, revealing his recently cropped and uncombed hair and smiled sweetly. 'I 'ope we can talk again,' he said, then ran back to the lawnmower and with another grin he finished and pushed it at great speed towards the gate and then on towards the stable yard.

Amy stood where he had left her and thought about Mr Seymour and his new motor. She had dinner with him and Mrs Seymour twice a week, since it was his belief that she must learn to mix with people, to chat to them, to act properly at table, and though Mrs Seymour did not approve she could see the sense in it. The girl would be accompanying her when she was older to all the important meetings and she must be presentable, able to converse with the people she met and she could not improve, especially her speech, if the only person she spoke to or who spoke to her was Miss Gibbon. Miss Gibbon was beautifully spoken having been raised in a decent family and only the sudden death of her parents had forced her to

156

support herself in the only job open to a woman of her class and education, that of a governess.

That evening Amy sat down at the dinner table and waited, as did Mr and Mrs Seymour, for the first course to be brought in by either Alice or Jess. As soon as Mrs Seymour nodded and told Atkins she would ring when they were ready for the main course Amy turned to Mr Seymour and before she could think of the consequences she asked him politely if it was true that he was to have a motor car. She had returned to the spot where Miss Gibbon had left her earlier in the day so the governess, when she came out of the house looking wan and droopy, had no idea that she had moved. Even as she spoke Amy realised she had made a great mistake. Mr Seymour merely looked surprised, his spoon halfway to his mouth, but Mrs Seymour dropped hers furiously into her soup bowl, splashing her asparagus soup on to the immaculate table cloth.

'And who have you been talking to, miss? Who has told you that Mr Seymour is thinking of buying a motor car?' She threw Mr Seymour a savage look, evidently not approving of his madness, then turned her gaze back to Amy while Mr Seymour, after a heartfelt sigh, continued to sip his soup.

'Nobody, madame,' she answered, using the French term of address which Miss Gibbon had told her was polite. 'I just happened to . . .'

'Yes?' Mrs Seymour's tone was ominous.

'I was waiting in the garden for Miss Gibbon who happened to be indisposed and had to leave me for a moment when I overheard two of the men discussing it. I'm sorry but I have no idea who it was.'

She bent her head and followed Mr Seymour's example, sipping her soup which as usual was delicious. She thought she had got out of that one very nicely but told herself she must be more careful in future. In the six months since she had been brought here she had done exactly what she had been told to do. She knew Mr and Mrs Seymour had adopted her legally because she had overheard them discussing it and she now belonged to them and not to Mam and Pa, but that did not mean she was going to continue in this way and totally lose the Amy Pearson she had once been. It was high time she made a stand, she told herself, for what could the old harridan—a word she had learned recently and which she thought described exactly the woman who now glared at her—do to her? The worst had happened. She had been stolen from her own family and was being forced into the mould Mrs Seymour thought was appropriate but she'd had enough and though she meant to do it slyly she also meant to win for herself a speck of freedom. She wasn't exactly sure how she would go about it but she'd snatch at it at every opportunity.

'Are you interested in motor cars, Amy?' Mr Seymour asked her as he placed his soup spoon in his bowl.

'Caleb, please, this is not a subject I wish the child to be concerned with. Motor cars will not be part of her life, nor mine, as I told you when you stated your determination to get one. Nasty, smelly, noisy things and I for one refuse absolutely to ride in one. I think that—'

'But perhaps Amy might find it enjoyable, my dear,' her husband interrupted mildly, putting a piece of bread in his mouth.

'I don't care whether she does or does not, she will not ride in the thing. You may do as you please—'

'Thank you, my dear.'

' . . .you always have done but the child—'

'When are you going to call the child by her name, Zillah? She has been with us for six months, I believe, and not once have I heard you speak her name.'

'Caleb, this is hardly the place or time to be discussing this.' Zillah was breathing hard, clearly out of sorts and Amy watched her calmly.

This woman had ruined her life, in fact she had taken away her life but now that Amy was stronger and could think more clearly she meant to do her best to lead some sort of a life that included people other than Mrs Seymour and Miss Gibbon. And by that she didn't mean the congregation at the chapel. She had the strangest feeling that *Mr Seymour* might have something to offer. She was not sure what she meant by that but lately he had disputed some of the arrangements Mrs Seymour had made and his suggestions had been in Amy's favour. Like the bedroom, for instance, which was a big improvement on the cramped little cupboard in which she had first slept. On several occasions she had waited until the house was completely quiet, Mrs Seymour in her bedroom and the light no longer showing beneath her door, then she had crept out on to the landing, along the gallery and down the central stairs to the big square hall. She had explored all the rooms on the ground floor including Mr Seymour's study, which was fascinating with shelves of books that she would love to read, and she had even sat before the kitchen fire with the cat purring on her lap. It had been intoxicating! When she had crept back to her bedroom she had hung out of the window—it was still summer and not cold—and studied the stable yard and the garden to the side of the house. It was in this way that she was beginning to recognise the layout of the house and one day she meant to let herself out of the side door and wander round the garden and conduct a search of the whole area. Only by knowing her surroundings would she be able to move about without anyone realising it. By that she meant Mrs Seymour and Miss Gibbon. Naturally, she hadn't given up the idea of one day finding her family, of seeing her mam again, of taking her some of the daffodils that grew wild under the trees in the spring but until then she would make her own secret life.

'Yes,' Mr Seymour said now, touching his napkin to his lips, evidently waiting for his wife to summon the maidservant to bring in the next course. 'I have ordered an automobile and it is to arrive in the morning. A mechanic is to deliver it to the house and will teach me to drive. Would you like to watch, Amy?'

'Oh, sir, can I—' she began.

But Zillah had had enough of this nonsense and rang the bell furiously, summoning Marshall. 'No, you cannot, child. Mr Seymour might be carried away by this contraption but you and I will certainly have nothing to do with it. God did not mean us to travel in such things and we will pray together tonight to keep him safe, for there is no doubt in my mind that such machines fly in the face of the righteous and will—'

She stopped speaking abruptly as Marshall entered the room bearing the main course, one of Mrs Abigail's nourishing and delicious steak and kidney pies with the potatoes and vegetables Barty had delivered to the back door no more than an hour since. Alice, sensing the tension in the room, dexterously removed the soup plates and served the steak and kidney pie, then whisked out of the room with the loaded tray.

'Summat's up,' she announced as she pushed through the kitchen door with her hip. 'You could cut the atmosphere with a knife, 'onest. Rowin' over somethin' or my name's not Alice Marshall. Mind you, Amy looked right pleased with 'erself an' master were smilin'. Now then, Joe Newbridge, what you grinning about, yer cheeky monkey? Yer look as though yer'd lost a farthin' and found a shillin'.'

Joe wiped his plate round with a great hunk of Mrs Abigail's bread, making sure he had scraped up every drop of her gravy, and stuffed it in his mouth. Where he came from there had never been enough to eat and what there was of it had been tasteless and made only to be filling. He had fallen on his feet when he had been picked to come and work for Mr Seymour and if it was true about the motor car he meant to do even better. What a day this had been. His stomach was full, a feeling that, years ago, he would never have thought possible and he was well pleased with what had happened today. He had spoken to *her* and made her smile and if he had his way it wouldn't be the last time. Lovely little thing she was and though he had said nothing to a soul, he didn't know why except he wanted to keep the joy of it to himself for a bit, he couldn't stop grinning like a Cheshire cat.

Up in her bedroom Amy curled like the kitchen cat beneath the warmth of the soft blankets on the bed. She had blown out the candle, the one candle Mrs Seymour allowed her, the candle that Mrs Seymour measured each morning since she did not believe in reading in bed, and lay in the dark though it was not really dark. There was a huge harvest moon floating in the sky just above the stable roof and with the curtains drawn back she could almost have read by it.

Suddenly she threw back the bedclothes and jumped from the bed, moving across the carpet until she reached the window that looked out over the back of the house. Not everyone was asleep. There was a light shining from one of the rooms above the stable where she believed the outside men lived. She knew their names were Matt and Barty, the gardeners, Ernie Tingle, Tim and Joe who was stable boy and who had spoken to her today. Play tennis, he had said and at once her active brain began to connive at how this might come about. She would love to play tennis and perhaps if she mentioned it when Mr Seymour was there she might ... A tricky one, she smiled to herself, since she was watched all the time but she was beginning to think that if she set her mind to it she could do anything. Why? What had changed her from the hopeless, despairing wretch of the past few months into this optimistic, cunning creature who meant to survive this? Perhaps it was her encounter with Joe or was it the strange feeling that she might have found an ally in Mr Seymour? Well, whatever it was she meant to hang on to it and never let Mrs Seymour get the better of her. Miss Gibbon's unreliable stomach might be a help. Slipping into bed again she lay back on her pillow, her arms above her head and smiled, while in his narrow bed above the stables Joe did the same and strangely they were both dreaming the same dream!

12

Mrs Derwent's jaw dropped several inches when she saw who stood on her doorstep that she had only just donkey-stoned. When she heard the knock on the door she had flung it open ready to give what for to whoever had had the effrontery to put their mucky feet on it when it was obvious it had just been scrubbed, but the words died in her mouth at the sight of the well-dressed vision who had once been ecstatic at the gift of the old perambulator Mrs Derwent had given her. The one that was so dilapidated even the rag-and-bone man wouldn't take it.

'Mrs Derwent,' the vision said in a totally different voice to the one she had used back then. 'Do you remember me? I used to live at number twenty-two. Amy. Amy Pearson. Me mam'—reverting for a moment to how she had been then—'was sent to the hospital and me little brother—'

'Queen . . . oh, queen, 'course I remember. Last time I saw yer some woman were—'

'Yes, my aunt. I live with her now but I felt I must try to track down my family.'

'Eeh, I can't gerr over it. Little Amy! It must be

wha' . . . three or four year an' yer all grown up and as grand as a princess.' Her eyes ran over Amy's plain attire which despite its drabness did not quench the girl's beauty.

It was all good stuff, even Mrs Derwent, who had never had any, could tell that. A dress that reached her ankle bone and was in a shade somewhere between tobacco and chestnut which Zillah had thought suitably neutral but which, with Amy's colouring, looked strangely attractive. She had in the past year developed small breasts—to Zillah's dismay—which filled the bodice of the dress and emphasised her narrow waist about which she—Amy—before she left the house had tied a sash of bronze satin. She had removed her hideous bonnet at the same time and loosened her hair which rippled down her back to her waist in a mixture of amber, gold, silver and silky blonde. She had on well-polished boots to match the dress and carried a small brown suede handbag in which Zillah expected her to carry her Bible and prayer book and a clean handkerchief but which at the moment held the purse the servants had given her, clubbing together, for Christmas last year. In the purse was her return railway ticket and five and sixpence in change. It was for a taxi-cab should she need it, they had told her sternly this morning, inspecting her in that wave of affection she had aroused in them. Jess had even bent to kiss her cheek, cupping her face with her work-roughened hands. She had worn fine kid gloves when she left home but they were also stuffed in her handbag. She carried an enormous bunch of fresh cut daffodils.

She smiled shyly. 'How are you, Mrs Derwent,

and how is Mr Derwent?' for she remembered the speechless husband of this kind-hearted, loquacious woman who made up for his deficiencies a hundredfold.

'Eeh, my lass,' screeched Mrs Derwent. 'Come in, will yer, an' 'ave a cuppa. Where've yer bin all this time? Us've wondered times, me an' Bert, an' all t'street, what'd 'appened ter yer. I were only sayin' ter Mrs Quinn—yer remember 'er what lives next door ter me?—I wonder wharr 'appened ter them Pearsons, an' that little lass what that woman took away. Eeh, come in . . . come in . . .' and she hustled Amy over her spotless doorstep and into her equally spotless kitchen which, though it had little in the way of comfort, was bright with firelight on her shining pans and dishes.

'See, let me warm t'pot. Kettles on't boil an' I've just fetched some fresh milk. See, sit yer down. Eeh, I can't gerr over it, it seems like yestidy an' 'ere y'are all grown up and lovely wi' it. Wait until Bert gets back from't docks . . .' For like most of the men hereabouts Bert Derwent was a casual labourer in the dock area.

Before she knew it Amy had a mug of tea in her hand, a thick, earthenware mug which was so familiar to her even though she had drunk from nothing but fine china for the past four years, since that was how long she had lived at Somerfield. The tea was as black as the inside of a parson's hat, as her mam used to say, with very little milk in it, and again she marvelled at how she herself had changed into the young lady who only drank the pale and fragrant China tea that her aunt favoured.

'Now then, queen, tell us all about it,' Mrs

165

Derwent instructed, sinking into the sagging chair by the fire and sipping the tea which she had made extra strong for the pleasure of her unexpected guest but which she was relishing since she seldom drank it like this. 'Where yer livin', then, an' what 'appened ter yer mam and all them little 'uns? Yer've certainly gone up in't world, that's fer sure. I wouldn't a' recognised yer but fer yer 'air. Yer allus 'ad lovely 'air, all on yer. Such a bonny colour. Eeh, wait till I tell our Em, she'll be made up. They'll all be grown up then, yer brothers an' sisters an' not in't pram any more. Yer loved that there pram, didn't yer? I said to our Em, I said, she loves that pram an' . . . what is it, chuck?' as Amy did her best to interrupt the flow of words that gushed from Mrs Derwent.

'That's what I wanted to talk to you about, Mrs Derwent.'

'Eeh, yer do talk lovely.'

'Thank you,' Amy said breathlessly, 'but I wanted to ask you if you had heard anything of Mam, or the kids. Where they went, I mean. I know they flitted . . .' She could not seem to avoid saying some of the words that had once been part of her everyday life years ago. 'After I left here I was told that they had gone elsewhere but I don't know where and I wondered . . .' Her voice trailed away, for Mrs Derwent looked dumbfounded.

'Yer mean yer've not seen 'em since that day?'

'No, I'm . . . I'm kept close confined by my aunt.'

'What d'yer mean, queen? Close confined?' Mrs Derwent said the words with some confusion.

'She has adopted me and is bringing me up as her daughter. I live the life of Riley, I can tell you, but I get little freedom.' Her voice had grown

166

bitter as she spoke of the woman who had spirited her family away and could not—or *would* not—say where they had gone, where they were living now. 'I'm getting a fine education. I eat well and I sleep in a warm bed but I'd exchange it all to be back with me mam at number twenty-two.' She glared at Mrs Derwent as though the blame were hers.

'Chuck . . . eeh, chuck, I'm that sorry. I wish I could 'elp yer, I really do bu'—'

'Do you know where they went, Mrs Derwent? You were here when they left and I wondered if perhaps you heard their destination spoken of by my pa, or one of the kids or even . . . well, the doctor who was—'

Mrs Derwent brightened. 'Now there's a thought, queen. Why don't yer go ter't doctor's surgery on Old Leeds Street an' ask 'im. 'E must've kept in touch wi' yer mam seein' as 'ow he put 'er an' yer little brothers in 'ospital. She'll be out now, sure as eggs is eggs, but 'e must've kept in touch, knowin' 'im.'

Amy leaped to her feet, startling Mrs Derwent. Her face was suffused with excited colour. 'Of course, why didn't I think of that? He'd know, wouldn't he? He's bound to have kept in touch with Pa on account of Mam and the boys.'

She whirled about and was making for the door which, like the one in her old home, opened on to the street. She wrenched it open, ready to spill out on to the pavement when Mrs Derwent put a hand on her arm.

'There's no need ter go off 'alf-cocked, chuck. It's tekken yer four years ter gerr 'ere. Another few minutes won't mekk any difference. Sit yer down an' tell me why yer didn't come before.'

167

Amy hesitated, turning back to Mrs Derwent but she did not sit down again. She took in the kindliness that shone in Mrs Derwent's face, wondering as she did so why it was that folk of her own class, as the servants at Somerfield were, the *labouring* class, showed such goodness of heart. Mrs Seymour and Miss Gibbon thought they were superior to those of Amy's rank and yet though they supposedly followed the teaching of Jesus Christ, they showed no Christianity to those they believed to be beneath them. Oh, certainly, Mrs Seymour did what were called 'good works', but it was for her own glory, not the betterment of those whom she thought depended upon her.

'I did, Mrs Derwent,' she answered slowly, 'but they caught me and took me back. Since then I've tried several times but up to a few months ago I was closely watched. This is the first time I've managed to steal away. She'll know, of course, where I've gone when she discovers I'm missing but by then I hope to have found Mam and Pa. That's why I'm in such a hurry. Last time she put the police on me and I was taken back. All I want to know is if my mam and the lads have recovered, but my life has been so closely guarded, so well ordered, and if it hadn't been for the servants who have *become* my family, in a way, I think I would have chucked myself in the Irwell.'

'Irwell . . .?' Mrs Derwent questioned faintly, quite stunned by these revelations.

'It's a river in Manchester. That's where I live.'

As she spoke her memory ranged over the past four years. Each spring when the incredible spectacle of the daffodils gradually showed themselves in a golden, rippling carpet beneath the trees surrounding the house, she had struggled to escape the clinging attention of Miss Gibbon and fill her arms with the glorious trumpet-headed blooms. To make a wild dash to Liverpool and place them before her beloved mam, to let her see that though they were apart she still loved her and wanted nothing more than to be with her again. She knew it was not possible now because, though she didn't know how, she was aware that her mam's health depended on her and her life with the Seymours. She had realised that Pa had received money from Mrs Seymour and because of it he was able to make a better living for Mam and the children. That Mrs Seymour had *bought* her, Amy, and she was now considered to be her daughter but that did not mean, and she meant to tell Mam so, that Amy had abandoned them all. As the months and years passed she would somehow manage to come and see them and this was to be the first of those visits.

Over the past four years they had settled into a routine of which Mrs Seymour approved and, with the prospect of a modicum of freedom that her acquiescence had lulled Mrs Seymour into believing to be real, Amy was able to be on her own for an hour or so. Not only from Miss Gibbon who was still prone to bouts of stomach upsets, but from Mrs Seymour's vigilance. Amy learned to be patient and slowly realised that if she agreed without protest to Mrs Seymour's wish that she accompany her regularly to chapel, attend Bible classes, prayer meetings and all the other events that made up Mrs Seymour's days she was able to . . . well, in the old days and in the speech of her former life, she would have said she was able to

169

cod not only the mistress of the house but her governess too.

'I wish to read a passage from the Bible, ma'am,' she would say meekly, her eyes lowered, 'and I need quiet and privacy. Have I your permission to go to my room?'

'I feel the need of some exercise and while I walk in the garden I will digest the text you gave me to read on teetotalism. The Temperance movement will be undermined by the Balfour Licensing Act, don't you think?' she had asked innocently and from the corner of her eye saw Mr Seymour turn away with a half-hidden smile, for he knew her by now. He was well aware that the Temperance movement meant nothing to her but Mrs Seymour was delighted with her and gave her these small freedoms to roam the garden where the Temperance movement and the texts she lied about were discarded in favour of talks with the gardeners—and Joe.

In other words she lied frequently and imaginatively, making up other excuses to break the chains that bound her. And it helped that Mrs Seymour trusted Miss Gibbon and believing that her adopted daughter was safe in her hands left her to go about her own busy affairs which were vast and time-consuming. She became even more engrossed in the Methodist Sunday school movement, spending almost the whole of Sunday at St John's Wesleyan Methodist Chapel where she had started a class that taught poor children—and there were many of those—from the slums of Manchester to read the Bible. The children were given a bowl of broth and a glass of milk along with their prayers, which prompted their mothers to insist they attend. More importantly in her own opinion, she spent considerable time giving advice to Mr Isherwood on how best to organise his congregation, whether he wanted the advice or not. She did, of course, donate large sums of money to the chapel which probably explained why Mr Isherwood patiently allowed her to give her opinions and try to guide him in what she believed was the right way to go about chapel matters. It was she who organised talks on various subjects, from the iniquities of the sanitation—or lack of it—that prevailed in certain parts of Manchester, to the beauties of the Lakeland, with slides, from a Mr Winston, a chapel member who had just travelled there, and the Life and Times of Jane Cooper, a leader in early Methodism in England, which was more to her taste.

She herself was a good speaker, or so she liked to believe, revealing to a shocked audience that although they were the richest nation on the earth, 30 per cent of the population were still living below an adequate subsistence level and that more than half the children of working men were in this condition. Infantile mortality among the middle classes was 94 out of 1,000 deaths but no fewer than 247 per 1,000 among those who lived in poverty.

She was busy and occupied and, as far as her nature allowed, happy. She had a purpose in life and a daughter to follow in her footsteps, to continue her charitable duties and carry on the work of the Methodist connection, beliefs that she was passing on to Amy, or so she thought. All this made her relax her vigilance and allowed Amy slowly to begin her bid for emancipation.

Before Amy passed on the newspapers collected from Mr Seymour's study to Joe, who was an avid searcher for the truth, she read *The Times* from cover to cover, for along with her own bid for freedom she was absorbed with the policies and tactics of the women's suffrage movement. She devoured the reports of the Women's Social and Political Union, known as the WSPU, which had been founded in 1903. It seemed to her that the women's fight for equality and freedom ran parallel with her own. Their purpose was to secure the parliamentary vote for women on the same terms as for men. She was amazed and elated to read that the first WSPU headquarters was in Manchester at the home of a Mrs Emmeline Pankhurst and it became her goal, when she had gained some freedom of movement for herself, to seek them out.

But that was a long way off. She had begun gradually, making no sudden movements, nor drawing attention to herself, by becoming acquainted with the servants. Miss Gibbon had freed her from the schoolroom one morning when her delicate stomach had been more than usually troubled and she had been forced to remain near the bathroom on the first floor. After her third visit that morning, unable to pretend there was nothing wrong, she had set Amy to translate a passage from *A Profile Of Wesleyanism* into French, then vanished with a vague promise to return as soon as possible. Miss Gibbon was aware that Amy could, should she have wanted to, report Miss Gibbon's awkward digestive system to Mrs Seymour but the child had not done so and therefore Miss Gibbon was prone to be somewhat slack in her supervision. Miss Gibbon was content in her job. She was well paid and lived comfortably and now that Amy had settled down to her new position and was accommodating in the lessons Miss Gibbon planned for her, she was willing to give her perhaps more leeway than Mrs Seymour meant her protégée to have. Miss Gibbon could not quite call her pupil the *daughter* of Mrs Seymour, for not once in the years since she had become her governess had she heard Amy call Mrs Seymour 'mother'. It suited her to allow Amy to wander in the grounds of Somerfield since Miss Gibbon did not care to be too far from the upstairs bathroom for long, and provided Amy was away for no more than an hour and took some work, perhaps a book to read, she felt she was fulfilling her role in a way Mrs Seymour would approve of. Nevertheless she kept her condition to herself.

On this particular day she was having a worse bout of the dreadful loosening of her bowels than usual and had not noticed Amy's absence and the servants, who were in on the secret of her whereabouts, kept their mouths shut.

*   *   *

Amy hurried up Earle Street until she reached the corner of Old Leeds Street where the doctor's house was situated, her neat booted feet making a great clatter on the flags in her eagerness to get there. She ran up the four steps to the front door where to the side of it a brass plate proclaimed it to be a doctor's surgery. She hammered on the door which took a long time to open and when it did she was surprised to be confronted by an ancient woman in a sacking apron and a bedraggled, frilled mob-cap. She looked put out and was ready to give Amy the length of her tongue but Amy pushed past her, to her great annoyance, and stood looking about her in the narrow hall.

'Doctor Ferguson,' she demanded in her new voice and the woman, thinking she was in the presence of one of the upper classes, sprang to attention.

'Nay, miss,' she dithered, 'he's norr 'ere.'

'Is he out on a call?' Amy demanded to know. 'If so, tell me where he is and I'll go to him. This is extremely urgent and I'm in a great hurry. If you would be so good . . .' She had heard Mrs Seymour use these words so many times it came almost as second nature to her to voice them.

''Appen yer'd like ter see Doctor Williams, miss. 'E's in t' surgery but I could tell 'im yer 'ere.'

'No, I must see Doctor Ferguson, if you please. I must see him at once so—'

'Burr 'e's norr 'ere, miss. I keep tellin' yer.'

'Then where is he?'

'Gone, miss.' The woman wrapped her hands in her coarse apron and grimaced helplessly.

Amy could feel her stomach slip in the most dreadful way. She thought she was going to be sick as the words the woman spoke began to take on their true meaning. Gone! *Gone!* Gone where? Surely she didn't mean what Amy had a horrible feeling she meant. He had gone to . . . to the hospital where he worked, that was it. He would be back soon and she, Amy, would sit in his waiting room until he returned and he would tell her where her family lived now. Oh, dear God . . . dear

God . . .

'Please . . .' she quavered, swaying slightly.

The woman put out a hand compassionately, for she thought the child—she was no more than that—was going to fall, then she withdrew it and waited.

'Where?' Amy felt as though she had grit in her throat as she did her best to get out the question.

'Scotland.' The woman's voice had become harsh in her pity.

'Scotland.'

'Aye, 'e comes from there.'

'Right.'

Amy turned and the woman opened the door wider, then watched her as she trailed down the steps and began to walk, not back to Mrs Derwent's house which would have been sensible but in the other direction, for she did not know where to go to get away from the despair, the pain, the awful knowledge that she had lost her family for ever. The only person who might know where they were would never tell her, since Zillah Seymour believed that she was Amy's mother now and had a perfect right to keep things from her daughter. She would be furious when she learned that Amy had gone once again to Liverpool to find her family.

Amy wandered to the end of Old Leeds Street, turning blindly into Old Hall Street, Queen Street until she was walking directly beneath the overhead railway. Trains rattled above her but she kept going until she reached the entrance to Canning Dock and the graving docks where several ships were tied up. It was all suddenly so familiar to her as the smell of shipping and their

175

cargoes wafted over her: new timber, coffee beans, Indian tea, citrus fruits, nutmeg and camphor and over it all lay the fresh tang of the sea itself. The sound of Liverpool, the constant shouting and hooting and whistling as cargoes were unloaded from ship to dock to warehouse, but Amy heard and saw nothing because she was preoccupied by the awful realisation that this would be the last time she came to the city where she had been born. What was there here for her now? The reason for her being here was gone, lost, and though she could barely stand it she must. And she must find her way back to the life that was now hers, since she would know no other, at least for now.

Somehow she made her way back to Lime Street, mindlessly drifting in the direction of the station, stared at by passers-by who stopped to wonder what such a lovely young girl was doing wandering about the busy streets by herself.

Though she scarcely remembered the journey from Liverpool to Manchester, she had the sense to take a cab from London Road to Eccles Old Road, dimly feeling glad that Jess and the others had had the foresight to give her the fare which she showed to the rather surprised cabbie before she climbed in.

He dropped her at the gates, taking her fare and then watched her as she began the journey up the gravelled drive towards the house before he turned and set off back to the city. She knew Mrs Seymour would be waiting for her, incensed and ready to lock her in her room but it did not seem to matter at the moment. Nothing did. The daffodils growing under the trees that lined the drive were bobbing in what seemed like derision as she dragged along and she wondered idly what had happened to those she had picked and carried so carefully to her mam. She must have left them on Mrs Derwent's table, she thought, for she could not remember taking them to Old Leeds Street. Well, Mrs Derwent would enjoy them!

And then he was there, running swiftly round the corner of the house and across the lawn towards her, his frame, which four years ago had been tall, lanky, scrawny, angular with the lack of grace of an adolescent, altered now to the lean, slender, athletic harmony of the young man he had become.

'Lovey,' was all he said, wrapping his strong young arms about her, knowing that all had not gone as she had hoped. She drooped against him, glad of him, glad of his support and his concern, his warmth, his love, for that was what he offered her and she was at that moment fully aware of it.

'They weren't there, Joe,' she told him listlessly.

'Come inter't kitchen, lovey. They're all there. Missis is out, an' master an' all,' which was bloody good job, he was thinking. 'Kettle's on. See, lean on me. Lean on Joe . . .' And she did.

13

Joe Newbridge was born in the workhouse in Newbridge Street at the back of Victoria Station which was where he got his surname. His mother, a child herself—no more than twelve or thirteen in the opinion of the matron—had given him life and had lost her own when he was born. Considering the poor state of his mother he was a well-formed and healthy baby who developed an engaging grin which endeared him to those in charge of him. He rarely cried, probably because he became aware at a very young age that he was one of many and the nurses and carers would take little notice of him if he did. As he grew he quickly learned the house rules set out by the workhouse, the first being that he and the other inmates obeyed the governor and matron in all things. That they be peaceable, were decent and clean and diligent in their work. There were fifteen of these rules but as many of them did not apply to the children they did not worry him overmuch. He was not likely to drink to excess, was he?

He was allowed, with others of a responsible nature, to leave the workhouse on a Sunday after divine service providing he did not stay later than the hour appointed and it was on one of these rambles through the streets of Manchester that he came across Caleb Seymour. He was eleven years old and during his short life had worked in the vegetable gardens of the workhouse, proving himself to be not only a hard worker but with what the matron called 'a green thumb', whatever that meant.

He was strolling up Moseley Street one Sunday making for Piccadilly Gardens where he intended sitting for half an hour in the mild sunshine to admire the flowerbeds. Flowers weren't grown in the workhouse gardens since flowers could not be eaten and every inch of ground was put to the production of vegetables. He had spent the morning sowing cabbage seeds, raking the beds carefully and patting the surface with a flat board to press in the seeds without hardening the ground. He had learned all this and many other facts about vegetable growing from a bent and ancient inmate who had once been gardener to a wealthy cotton merchant. The merchant had turned him out when he became too old to work and old Barney and his wife had been forced to turn to the workhouse. He was even more feeble now but with his vast experience, knowledge of plants and Joe's young strength he lived a useful life.

Joe heard the commotion as he was passing the open gate that led into the yard of Seymour's Warehouse. He hesitated, peering inside, then, when he saw the gentleman lying on the cobbles and what seemed to Joe to be a wild horse rearing over him, quick as a flash, though he had no knowledge of horses, he darted in, leaped up and grasped the horse's reins, hanging on for dear life. The horse whinnied and rolled its eyes but Joe clung on, despite being lifted from the ground at times, until the man rolled clear and stood up.

'Blasted animal,' the gentleman roared. 'I'll have Jack Openshaw in gaol for this. Well bred and kind, he told me, and easy to handle. The damn beast saw something he didn't care for and threw me and then threatened to trample on me. By God, it's a good job you were there, young fellow. Here, let me ... ' for the animal was throwing Joe from side to side doing its best to get free. The gentleman took the reins, cursing as the animal backed away, and gradually got the horse under control. It stood then, quiet as a lamb while Joe, impressed, kept his back to the wall out of harm's way. The gentleman, who wore immaculate riding gear which consisted of a dark grey frock coat, a snowy white stock, black breeches and riding boots with high plain tops, fastened the animal to a hook on the wall and retrieved his bowler hat from a pool of water.

He turned to Joe then, smiling, and reached into his pocket for a coin which turned out to be a crown.

'There, lad, that's for your help and for saving me from a—'

'No, thank you, sir,' Joe said politely but firmly. 'I don't want no pay. Anyone would've—'

'Nonsense, boy. The sight of Pilot here would be enough to put a grown man off and I insist you have something for your trouble.'

'Thanks, but I couldn't, sir.' Joe was equally determined but polite and the man looked him over carefully. Joe was wearing the hand-me-downs, all slightly too big, that were standard clothing for the orphans. Serviceable, warm but well worn and shapeless. His cap, also too big, kept falling over his forehead and was only held up by his ears.

'Where d'you live, lad?' Caleb asked him.

'Newbridge Street, sir.'

'Is that the . . . er . . . ?'

'Yes, sir, the orphanage.'

'How long have . . . ?'

'I were born there, sir.'

'And when was that?'

'They tell me I'm eleven, sir.' Joe's eyes were an incredible and brilliant blue in his tanned face. The colour of the bluebells that stretched in a carpet beneath Caleb Seymour's trees, Caleb found himself thinking. When Joe was not at his lessons he worked out of doors and though he was thin he was healthy.

For what seemed an age to the boy the gentleman looked him up and down then he turned towards the wide door that led into the warehouse. 'Right, lad, I can't force you to take the money but I can thank you, which I do.' He looked back over his shoulder and smiled again.

Joe had forgotten the incident when, a few days later, he was summoned to the governor's office. He was still in his working clothes, breeches held up by a leather belt and braces, a collarless shirt and a cap. He had had no time even to wash his soil-encrusted hands. He had been sowing a second crop of cauliflowers under old Barney's direction and the pair of them had looked at one another in some trepidation, for what had Joe done wrong?

The governor and another gentleman were drinking coffee when Joe knocked at the door and diffidently entered the office, doing his best to wipe his hands down his trousers. At least they were both smiling, he thought, before he recognised the governor's guest as the one with the bad-tempered horse. He grinned, he couldn't help it, and the gentleman nodded pleasantly.

'Ah, Joe,' the governor said.

'I'm sorry, sir, I've 'ad no time ter wash me,' Joe blurted.

'Never mind, boy. You can have a good wash before you leave. In fact a bath might be in order, Mr Seymour.' He turned to the gentleman and beamed.

'Leave, sir?' Joe gasped, looking from the governor to the gentleman in his bewilderment.

'Yes, Joe, you are to go and work for Mr Seymour and you will live in his household. Your time with us is ended. Mr Seymour has told me of your bravery last Sunday and as he has a vacancy for a handy boy he thought of you. You will help his gardeners or indeed any of the outside men who can call on your services. You will learn about horses, is that right, Mr Seymour?' turning deferentially to this influential gentleman.

'Indeed.' Mr Seymour nodded again. With a smile Joe was dismissed, presumably to go and have the bath the governor had advocated.

And that was how young Joe Newbridge fell on his feet, as he was to say gratefully many times in the years he lived and worked for Mr Seymour. And that too, was how he came to know the young girl who had moved not only into the household soon after he had but had slipped stealthily into his steadfast heart.

On this day five years later he had been polishing the already gleaming bonnet of the motor car the master had acquired three years ago, keeping to the back and slightly to the side of the house, out of sight of any of the windows just in case the mistress who, it was rumoured, had gone off in the carriage on one of her charitable visits, came back unexpectedly. The way in which the stable yard, the house and the garden were aligned meant that anyone standing or working in that spot could see the drive and those approaching the front door.

Joe thought the day the motor car was delivered was the most exciting he had ever known. For some reason the Lanchester they had discussed had been cancelled and instead a Rolls-Royce

182

Silver Ghost had glided almost silently up the drive. Mr Seymour, having heard of Joe's consuming interest in this new age of the automobile and having no other individual with whom to discuss it, had engaged his employee in many a long discussion on the merits of this or that machine, sitting side by side on the bench that stood beside the tennis court. France had taken the lead in the manufacture of the motor car, they had agreed on that, shaking their heads sadly, taking in the Daimler with its V-twin engine and the Peugeot and the way the two automobiles had succeeded in motor racing. But then came Dr Frederick Lanchester and the start of the British motor industry and so the man and boy had continued their strange association. They had pored over the magazine *Autocar* together, to the amazement of the other servants, for Joe was only a lad, comparing the Lanchester to the Vauxhall and the Napier but Mr Seymour, who was intensely patriotic, had decided on the Rolls-Royce. Not only was it decidedly British it was actually built in their own city of Manchester. Mr Seymour believed most good things came out of Manchester, which had given him his comfortable way of life. If the servants, or indeed anyone who knew Caleb Seymour thought it strange that a middle-aged gentleman and his stable boy should be on such friendly terms, nothing was said about it, at least to Caleb's face.

It was well known in the Somerfield kitchen that Joe was mad about the horseless carriage as well as being a keen gardener. Indeed Mrs Abigail called him a 'Jack of all trades'. He was good with the horses and when there was no one, meaning the master or mistress, about he often climbed on Pilot's back—Pilot being well trained by now and no longer the bad-tempered beast Joe had met five years ago—and galloped him round the paddock and even up across the meadow and into the woodland at the back of the house. Joe was amiable, easy-going, even-tempered, cheerful, uncomplicated and eager to please and would turn his hand to anything asked of him. His thin boy's body had grown into young manhood with none of the awkwardness many lads of his age inherit. He had long legs, broad shoulders and a graceful way of moving that had the other servants wondering where he came from. Not the orphanage, of course, they knew that, but his antecedents, those who had bred him. He had an air of ... well, it sounded daft, Mrs Abigail was to remark, but the word was *breeding*. Happen his mother had been done down by some toff from the upper classes, she mused. He had taken to playing football every Saturday afternoon, with Mr Seymour's permission, in a local team on Buile Hill Park where there were tennis courts, a cricket pitch and a bowling green.

A grand lad was Joe who, as had been said a dozen times, would do anything for anyone, so why were they surprised to see him leading into the kitchen the wilting figure of the girl they had all become fond of. It was also very obvious to them all and had been for a long time what he felt for her. It showed in his face, in his eyes which his feelings had darkened to a deep blue that was totally different to the brilliance they usually displayed. At once they began to crowd about him, longing to help him with the lass who looked as though she had just had the thrashing of her life. They knew where she had been, naturally, for hadn't they helped her to get there, but by the look of her it had not been successful.

'Sit yer down, sweetheart,' Joe was saying, placing her tenderly on one of the wooden chairs by the table. He knelt at her feet and gazed up into her grey-etched face then lifted a hand to brush back her hair which fell in heavy, disordered curls over her forehead.

'What 'appened, lovey? Was the neighbour not able ter 'elp yer? Did she not know where yer mam had gone?' They all knew by now that when she had gone back to Liverpool years ago to find them her family had vanished, but they had all prayed that this neighbour of whom Amy had spoken might have some clue as to where they had gone. She fretted badly for her mam and pa and her little brothers and sisters, even after all this time, but now by the dragged-down look of her it seemed all hope had gone.

'Tell us, lass,' Mrs Abigail asked her pityingly. 'Did you see the lady what you went to—'

'Oh, yes. Mrs Derwent was there.' Amy's voice was no more than a whisper and Primrose leaned forward and murmured, 'What did she say?' but was hurriedly hushed by Jess.

'An' didn't she know where ... ?'

'No. I went down the street to the doctor's surgery. Doctor Ferguson ... you know, the one who looked after Mam and the boys ...' Her voice was vague as though she had wandered off into another world and was unsure of where she had gone. 'He's in Scotland.'

They all exchanged glances, for what she told

185

them made little sense. Scotland! Had the lass gone pots for rags in her distress? But they were not to get any further with this thought, since at that moment the kitchen door opened with a flourish.

'And what, may I ask, is going on here?' an icy voice asked from the doorway.

For a few moments they all froze then they leaped away from the central tableau as though they had been caught in some disgusting act, all except Joe who slowly got to his feet and took a step towards the mistress, very evidently with the intention of protecting Amy, but a withering glance from Mrs Seymour stopped him in his tracks.

Nobody spoke.

'Well?' Zillah Seymour demanded. Then Amy, in whom the habit of patient obedience had become second nature for the last four years, felt the knot of submission built up in the hope that one day she would see her family again melt and slip away. She rose from the chair where Joe had put her and stood defiantly in front of him, ready to defend him or prevent any action he might take. She faced her aunt with a composure and courage none of them had seen in her before.

'Sweetheart . . .' Joe whispered unwisely and his mistress's face lost every vestige of colour but Amy's words rang out and Zillah was distracted.

'I have just returned from Liverpool, ma'am,' Amy told her coolly, not hearing, or choosing to ignore, the gasps that erupted about her. 'You see, I have never given up hope that one day I would find my family and one day I swear I will. But . . . but not today.' She did not drop her gaze from

186

Zillah's infuriated expression.

'You wicked girl,' Zillah hissed, taking a step forward. They all backed away, all except Amy and Joe.

'Why am I wicked, ma'am? You and John Wesley teach that love, which is what I feel for my family, is—'

'Not earthly love, you shameless creature. Pure love come from God, from loving Him.'

'Is it wrong to love your parents? Surely God does not forbid—'

'If it comes between you and your God it is wrong. You speak blasphemy, girl. The eternal God is thy refuge, and underneath are the everlasting arms. That is what it says in the Bible and we are bound by it.'

The servants looked at one another surreptitiously, not at all sure they knew what the mistress was on about. It didn't seem to make sense to them but then half the things she spouted about God were unclear.

The lass was not concerned. 'Mrs Seymour, you must believe as you wish and as your God wishes but my love is for my mother and father, my brothers and sisters and I can see no sin in that. You have stolen that from me and for their sake, for the sake of their well-being, I have bowed to it. I realise . . . I *hope* they have benefited from what you gave my pa and I suppose in some way I have also gained something—decent education, good food to make me strong—but I must warn you that from now on I shall no longer give in meekly to your wishes. Oh, I shall still accompany you to chapel so that your friends and the congregation will think me the good and proper daughter of

Zillah Seymour but unless you lock me permanently in my room I shall go where I please.'

'How dare you, *how dare you*, speak to me like that, you ungrateful child. You have been treated like a member of my family. As my adopted daughter you *are* a member of my family and you will do as you are told in all things. All things, do you hear? You will not run off to Liverpool whenever you feel like it and as for those who were once your family—'

'I will never give up looking for them, and you cannot stop me. I love them still and will always do so. I don't even know whether Mam and the boys are well again, or still alive.'

'Of course they are,' Zillah said impatiently, then, realising what she had said, closed her mouth like a trap.

There was a breathless silence that seemed to go on for ever. Everyone in the kitchen stood stock still, some of them still clutching the implements they had been using when Amy and Joe entered the room. Mrs Abigail dripped gravy on to the floor from the wooden spoon she had been using to stir it. Martha held a saucepan to her chest and Jess clutched the duster and fork she had been polishing.

There was the sound of a sob from somewhere in the kitchen, probably from Primrose who was so soft-hearted she wept over a crushed spider.

Amy took a deep breath as the implication of what her aunt had said washed over her. Her aunt was saying that her mother and her little brothers were in good health, probably because of the allowance Zillah Seymour gave to Pa. Amy was grateful for that but what she could not forgive was the realisation that this woman knew that Mam and the boys had recovered, which meant she must know where they were. She must have an address to send money, of course, and she must be in some sort of communication with Pa to know of the recovery of Mam and Eddy and Sidney. She had known all along but she had not even had the compassion at least to let Amy know that her mother and brothers were still alive. All these years she, Amy, had lived in ignorance, had lived in hope, had longed to hear, perhaps from Pa, that the family was well and living in a better state than they had in Earle Street. And all the time this cruel woman who stood before her had known and had not had one scrap of the Christian mercy she spouted on about every day of her life to put Amy's mind at rest.

She could feel her mind begin to slip sideways and she thought she might faint because although she knew her aunt was a fanatic, obsessed with her religion, her position in the chapel, in the community and her power over all in this house, she had never before realised that she was such a cruel and heartless monster who must have her own way in everything. She possessed Amy and her family, working them like puppets to her own purpose, but the worst of it was that Amy was in no position to put a stop to it. She could not force Zillah to tell her where her family were and the two trips she had made to Liverpool to search for them had come to nothing. She could not wander the streets looking for them and the only man who might have helped her had gone to Scotland.

'I really don't know what I am to do with you and as for that so-called governess who has had you in her charge all this time, well, it is very apparent she has not been performing her duty and I shall get rid of her at once. I should think by now you have enough education to do without her and so I shall take you into my complete charge.'

The servants looked from the mistress to the little lass who seemed to have gone into the mists of her own wandering mind and stood like one turned to stone by the horror of the mistress's words. Joe hovered at her back but in his own heart he knew there was nothing he could do. There was nothing any of them could do.

'You have been treated like a member of my own family ...' but the diatribe that Zillah continued to let loose on this girl for whom she had done so much and from whom she had received so little petered out as the girl in question turned away from her and walked towards the back door, the servants watching in silent, open-mouthed astonishment as she vanished into the back yard.

Zillah swung to face them, her own mouth hanging open in amazement, then, her eyes narrowing in maddened rage, she turned on them and Mrs Abigail began to think that, really, their mistress was heading for the lunatic asylum in her apparent derangement.

'And what d'you think you're doing idling about the kitchen? Have you nothing to do to earn the wages you are paid? Get back to your work at once.'

They all sprang into action, bumping into one another in their eagerness to be about something, *anything*, that would allow them to escape the nasty expression in their mistress's eyes. All except

Joe. He moved with the rest but he took the direction Amy had taken, his feet flying across the scrubbed kitchen floor, then the cobbles of the yard towards the stable gate that was swinging on its hinges as Amy had left it. Ernie, his pipe hanging from between his lips, watched him go, as he had watched the little lass.

She was sitting on the bench beside the tennis court, her face expressionless. Her bonnet had been mislaid somewhere and her hair still tumbled about her head and down her back in a waving mass that Zillah, no matter what she did, could not tame.

Joe sat down next to her and took her flaccid hand between his own warm, strong ones.

'Sweetheart,' he whispered. He knew if Mrs Seymour caught him she would make sure the master got rid of him but at that moment his whole being was concentrated on the girl beside him. 'Don't let 'er get yer down. Be patient. Summat'll 'appen and yer'll find yer folks. I bet Mr Seymour could 'elp if yer asked 'im. 'E's a good bloke.'

'He can't do anything against her, Joe. She rules me and though he's kind enough he can't help me. Anyway, he's not here much these days,' she said vaguely. 'But I've got to stay with her since she's the only one who knows where they are.'

' 'Eeh, I wish there were summat . . .' Joe sighed.

'One day, Joe, one day.'

191

14

It had snowed in the night, not a heavy fall, just an inch or two but as the night moved on it turned much colder and what lay on the ground froze solid. The pavements were perilous underfoot and though Thomas grumbled, not to the mistress, of course, but to Ernie Tingle, worried about his horses' legs, Mrs Seymour declared that she and Miss Amy, as she called her to the servants, would travel to chapel in the carriage. It was Sunday and Zillah, with her Bible and hymn book under her arm, warmly shook the hand of the man with a professional smile who met them in the vestibule of the chapel, surprising Amy, for her aunt was never more than cool with anyone except the minister. The man, whose name was Randall Hodge, also dazzled Amy with his smile and took her hand, holding it a little too long for Amy's liking though her aunt seemed to approve. He opened the door and she and her aunt entered the chapel and walked slowly down the aisle to the front pew, the Seymour pew, to the right of the pulpit. It was carpeted in red and had a strip of red carpet on the seat. Zillah sank her head upon her hands and Amy did the same. She did not pray. What had she to pray for, she had asked herself a hundred times in the last years, ever since her unsuccessful trip to Liverpool, and if she did would her prayers be answered? She did not think so. She believed in herself and what she would eventually achieve in the search for her lost family. She waited until her aunt sat up then she did the same.

Across the aisle she was aware that the man who had met them in the vestibule was looking at her but she did not return his glance. He was sitting with a woman who turned out to be his plain sister, a spinster of whom her aunt approved, for she was often her companion in her good works.

Amy knew men found her attractive, had known for the last year, and was accustomed to their sly admiration, particularly since she had grown breasts which her aunt did her best to conceal. Her hair, plaited tightly about her head, was still hidden beneath her ugly bonnet which her aunt had specially made for her. The fashion was for large hats with wide turned-up brims, high toques, tam o' shanters and berets made of beaver, plush, velvet and straw, none of which her aunt approved. She wore a sort of bodice under her drab dress, a tight bodice which was supposed to flatten the swell of her growing breasts, which it did, but nothing could hide the fact that she was a very beautiful young girl. Amy did not know it but she was the image of how Dolly Pearson had been at her age. They had called her mother 'bonny', those who admired her and there were many of those but she had been more than that. For a woman of her class she had had a delicate beauty with a skin like a pearl touched at the cheekbone with peach. Her eyes had been a clear and golden brown and her mouth had a long upper lip, the bottom one shorter so that it curled up in a perpetual smile, soft and sweet. The years since she had married Ben Pearson had robbed her of most of her beauty, for hard work and a life of poverty will erode a woman's looks but they had not taken her strength, her spirit and her determination to do the best she could in the circumstances for her family. And her daughter had inherited these traits. Amy was a miniature of her mother.

She still did lessons with Miss Gibbon who Zillah had decided to retain as a sort of keeper, since Zillah was sometimes absent on some committee or other, not apparently suitable for her *daughter* to be involved with. On these occasions Amy would slip away from the schoolroom where she had been left by Miss Gibbon while Miss Gibbon rested from the debilitating illness that was slowly dragging her down. She was ordered to get on with her studies but she escaped into the garden to look for Joe, her dearest friend. Joe was eighteen now, a young man, tall and strong, with a good position as Mr Seymour's chauffeur among his other duties and his devotion to Amy was well known in the kitchen. Amy loved him, as a friend and as a substitute for the brothers she had lost, and she was not to know that Joe did not love her as a sister! He was circumspect with her. He made her laugh, lightening her drab life, discussing with her whatever they read in Mr Seymour's discarded newspapers. During the reign of King Edward which began with the death of the old Queen in January 1901, long before Amy came to Somerfield, he had travelled the world enjoying immense popularity wherever he went until his death in May 1910. Joe had all the events of his life and of the royal family at his fingertips through his wide reading and he kept the kitchen fully up to date with King 'Teddy's' flamboyant concerns. He had gone everywhere, he did everything, living his life to the full with his people. He was an enthusiastic follower of sea sports, he played golf, he gave garden parties and picnics, he went to dances and dinners and all his activities were described in *The Times* and read out by Joe to the servants. The King at Cowes, which bewildered Primrose, for how could His Majesty interest himself in farm animals? Royal concerts, Ascot for the racing, shooting with this well-known family and that and those who listened to Joe felt that they knew His Majesty's social life as well as they knew their own. They were not quite so interested in other news that Joe read out to them: the Education Bill which a section of the community did not agree with regarding the striking out of religious teaching from the school curriculum; the taxation of unearned incomes; the retirement of the Prime Minister, Sir Henry Campbell-Bannerman in 1908 along with Mr Asquith's old age pension scheme the same year and descriptions of the Budget's stormy progress through Parliament. They felt that such things were really nothing to do with them but they listened politely, for Joe seemed most concerned.

On His Majesty's death Joe read out the sad proceedings with a respectful voice and did his best to comfort them all when they wept for their beloved monarch.

The new King George V and his family were of great interest to them all but there was no man could follow good old King 'Teddy', they said to one another as though they knew the royal family personally! Joe often described to them the 'goings-on' of the unladylike women known as 'suffragettes'. Mrs Abigail was horrified and begged Joe not to read any more, for the mistress wouldn't like it but it was said that in Manchester, from where the notorious leader Mrs Pankhurst came, there were fund-raising exhibitions and bazaars, processions in which the women carried placards demanding VOTES FOR WOMEN and KEEP THE LIBERALS OUT. Amy was fascinated for by now she was part of Joe's audience!

'The last time Miss Gibbon and I went to the City Art Gallery in Mosley Street we walked past a dear little shop further down selling china with a pretty design of an angel all in green and white. There were sashes with Votes for women printed on them, badges in purple, green and white, which are the women's colours, and posters with a suffragette dressed as Joan of Arc and many other things. I wanted to go in and buy something but Miss Gibbon said Mrs Seymour wouldn't like it. Oh, Joe, I long to be a part of it, I really do. Freedom for women, think of that . . .' Her voice trailed away disconsolately, for though she was not yet quite a woman she, of all people, was more a prisoner than most females.

The chapel, as it did every Sunday, was filling up. There was much gentle rustling of hymn-book leaves and when the organ began to play it soothed Amy with its sonorous purring. The choir entered, the organ stopped and silence spread through the building. Her aunt's face took on that rapt expression that always accompanied anything to do with her fanatical religious beliefs, for the minister was about to appear. When he did there was a short prayer and a hymn and he announced his text. As he began to speak Amy slipped away into the place where she found a certain peace and her mind turned, as usual, to memories of her family and how she was to locate them. She fingered the small locket Mr Seymour had given her on her fifteenth birthday, of which her aunt had thoroughly disapproved but so long as she wore it under her clothes, which she did most of the time, Zillah made no further objection.

The sermon did not affect Amy in the least since she did not really hear it. Her mind wandered to the last day she had spent in Liverpool. To Princes Park: April, it had been, with daffodils bowing and nodding in the lush grass, the small wooded area where they had played tig, hide-and-seek and leap-frog, and the lake where they had paddled and Sammy had been told off by the park-keeper, and then suddenly she was brought back to the present with the pinch of her aunt's fingers on her arm.

'Stand up, girl. Can you not see that the sermon is over?'

With her aunt's hand still pressing painfully on her arm she walked dutifully beside her towards the vestibule and the crowds of church-goers who hovered in the doorway to shake the minister's hand and tell him how much they had enjoyed his sermon. Zillah inclined her head and told him pleasantly that it had really been most uplifting, pinching Amy again to encourage her to say something and not just to stand there like some tailor's dummy. She would, of course, scold her when she got home. She was never satisfied with this lifeless daughter of hers who though she did as she was told and made no show of the defiance that had erupted earlier, evinced none of the fervour for the teaching of John Wesley that Zillah would have liked.

Amy smiled, for Mr Isherwood was a kindly man who, she thought, understood what was in Amy's mind: that Amy showed only a dumb obedience to Zillah Seymour because she had no choice.

'Thank you, sir,' she murmured. 'It was most enlightening,' which seemed to satisfy Zillah, as with a cool smile she moved out into the pale sunshine, not because there was a press of people behind her wanting to take the minister's hand— she cared for none of them even should she have noticed—but because she wished to speak to the man and woman who waited for her and Amy beneath the wide spreading branches of an oak tree.

The man, the same man who had greeted them in the vestibule before the service, was tall, stout, well but simply dressed. He was old, at least to Amy's young eyes, his greying hair receding from his broad forehead. His lips were full and rather moist and his eyes were a pale blue as though the colour had drained from them. He held his top hat in his hands, bowing and smiling his brilliant smile, his teeth big and yellowing. The woman beside him, dressed as she was in a plain gown and mantle and the sort of deep-brimmed bonnet Zillah herself favoured, might have been his mirror image they were so alike.

'Mrs Seymour,' the man said, 'what a pleasure to greet you and to meet your daughter at last. Of course I have seen her many times with you in chapel and once I believe at Bible class but this is the first chance I have had to speak to her personally. Miss Seymour'—bowing low—'what a pleasure to make your acquaintance.' He took her hand and she was thankful she was wearing gloves, for even through the leather she could feel the heat of his flesh.

'Good morning, Mr Hodge,' Zillah answered agreeably. 'And Miss Hodge, good morning to you. Of course you and I are old friends and colleagues in our endeavours to alleviate the suffering of our fellow man. But you have not been introduced to my daughter. Amy, these are friends of mine, Mr Randall Hodge and his sister, Elizabeth. They are stalwarts of the chapel, having come to live among us just recently.'

Amy bobbed a small curtsey as she had been taught by her aunt, and having disentangled her hand from that of the brother, took that of the sister, murmuring polite words of greeting. She was uncomfortably aware of Mr Hodge's eyes on her though she kept hers lowered. Mr Hodge had a loud voice and evidently believed that what he had to say was important but she noticed he was most polite towards her aunt. Miss Hodge had little to say and after several minutes of discussion on the sermon, the weather and the possibility of further snow Amy was astonished to hear her aunt inviting Mr and Miss Hodge to dine with them on an evening convenient to them all. When would that be, they asked one another and decided upon next Saturday when Mrs Seymour believed Mr Seymour would be free to join them.

'And will Miss Seymour be present?' Mr Hodge asked almost playfully, as though Amy were a mere child who might not be included in the evening's entertainment.

'Of course,' her aunt emphasised as if Mr

Hodge had asked a foolish question.

They bade one another a pleasant good morning and with much pressing of hands, in fact Amy thought for one astonishing moment Mr Hodge might kiss her aunt's pale cheek, they parted, Amy and Zillah making for the carriage where Thomas sat huddled up in his greatcoat, for it was exceedingly cold.

He jumped down and helped them into the carriage and was surprised when Mrs Seymour told him she would have the hood down since the sun was very pleasant. She had a strange look about her, as though she were ready to smile but was not quite sure how to go about it but, obediently, Thomas put down the carriage hood, tucked up his mistress and the little lass with the fur rugs that lay on the seat, jumped up on the box again and clicked to the horses to move on.

Amy sat beside her aunt, glad that the hood was down, for it was lovely to see the primroses starring the grass beneath the trees set along Langworthy Road. The delicate flowers lifted their heads above the light dusting of snow and beside them were the brilliant colours of crocus and the spears of what would be daffodils within a week or two.

They proceeded slowly, since Zillah did not care for speed, until they came to the junction of Seedley Road where Thomas was forced to bring the carriage to a halt to allow a motor car to pass across Langworthy Road. The horses were well used to Mr Seymour's Rolls-Royce by now, for young Joe often cleaned the machine in the stable yard but as he had Mrs Seymour as a passenger the coachman did not wish the animals to do anything untoward.

Amy, who was on the left-hand side of the carriage, looked out at the row of small, detached, friendly-looking houses set back from the road. They had long, narrow gardens that gave them a remote and quiet air though they were so close to the city. They were flat-fronted, of good red brick with a window on either side of the porch and three windows above. The windows seemed to smile in the reflection from the low sun and as Amy watched idly the front door of the one on the corner opened and a woman came out and walked the length of the garden to the front gate. She had a child in her arms. Both she and the child were warmly wrapped up and as she moved along the path she seemed to speak to the child and point up into the leafless trees.

She reached the gate and stood for a moment, turning her head to face the road and as she did so she and Amy looked into one another's eyes. She seemed to hesitate as though not quite sure what to do next, then she smiled, a sweet smile, a soft smile like that of a shy child towards an adult.

Amy could not help but return the smile, then the carriage moved on.

*   *   *

Caleb was vastly irritated with his wife and the whole house knew it. He always ate out at his club on a Saturday night, he told his wife in Alice's hearing. These people, whoever they were, were not his friends so why should he remain at home to dine with them? Could Zillah not entertain them alone? He would have nothing in common with them since they were members of Zillah's chapel and he could see no reason why—

'Because I wish to present them with a picture of our family, you and me and the child,' Zillah interrupted icily. 'They are *my* friends and as such they will be treated with the respect due them. How will it look if I have to tell them my husband is to dine at his club, *his club*; that is in itself a sin against God. "Can a man take fire in his bosom, and his clothes not be burned?" the Proverbs say and if—'

'For God's sake—'

'You take the name of the Lord in vain and you will be punished for it.' Her voice was implacable and Caleb sighed.

'I will be there, Zillah,' he said, giving in for the sake of peace. 'I shall be away for a few days next week on business so I suppose, if only for Amy, who I'm sure will find it as tedious as I will, I will be there.'

Zillah was deeply offended. 'The child will do as she is told. She will behave as she has been taught to behave and that is as an obedient daughter and a believer in God. Mr Hodge and his sister are well educated and well connected. Their grandmother was the daughter of a baronet and I'm sure when you meet them you will agree with me that they are worthy to come into our home.'

Caleb shook his head, defeated, exchanging a glance with Amy who sat demurely to the right of him. Alice took away the soup dishes as Mrs Seymour signalled to her and hurried to the kitchen to break the news to the other servants.

'She's having guests to dine on Saturday an' master's to be there or else,' Alice blurted, as the servants tended to pass on news about Amy of whom they had grown so fond.

Mrs Abigail lifted her head from the magazine she was perusing. She had just sat down for five minutes between courses, or so she said, though they all knew Alice, Jess and Martha could manage without her once the actual cooking was done. She was a superb cook but Mrs Abigail was getting a bit past being housekeeper, head cook and bottle-washer, as Alice described it, and put her feet up whenever she got the chance.

'Is Miss Amy ter be there?' Jess wanted to know.

'Oh, aye. She wants to show her off, I reckon. To present a picture of them as a family, she says but . . .'

'But what, Alice?' Jess looked at Alice more sharply because Alice seemed to be implying something here that Jess could not quite understand.

'Amy'll be sixteen next.' Alice's voice was very quiet.

'So what's that got ter do wi' it?' Jess questioned.

'I'm not sure, really, but I got a funny feelin' there's more to this than meets the eye. You know how Miss Amy is, she'll never measure up to the mistress's high standards as far as chapel goes. She's still a kid really, innocent as t'day, but she's as stubborn as a mule, or will be when she gets a bit older. There'll come a day when she won't want ter go ter chapel every day o't week and then the mistress . . . well, she's done her best ter get the kid to her way o' thinking but I reckon she's not succeeding an' I also reckon she's beginning ter realise it. If she was ter get her off her hands . . . respectable like . . .'

'What d'yer mean, Alice?' Primrose who had come out of the scullery wiping her hands on the bit of sacking she tied over her decent apron, even she looked concerned.

'What else is there but ter marry her off ter someone from't chapel? That way she could pretend that she was a big success, mistress that is, converting her daughter, like. Miss Amy'd still be one of them Methodists but she'd be someone else's responsibility.'

'Nay!' Mrs Abigail was deeply shocked. The little lass was still no more than a bairn. It was quite usual in the social circle in which their master and mistress moved for girls to be married at sixteen or seventeen but not their Amy, surely. Why, she was still in the schoolroom and had never mixed with girls of her own age. She knew nothing about *anything*, particularly men, marriage and what went on between married couples, as the mistress had kept her a schoolgirl ever since she had come to Somerfield.

Mrs Abigail rose majestically to her feet and at once the servants scuttled back to their tasks. They all knew that look. It told them she was seriously displeased and Alice wasn't sure whether it was on account of what she had just told them, which was, after all, only her own beliefs, or whether it was because they had all been gossiping!

The dinner party was not a success, mainly due to Caleb's disapproval of the strait-laced and boring guests and because of Amy's total lack of any conversation or even interest. Mr Hodge was asked to say grace which he did, long and meandering, so that even as he spoke Caleb's sigh could be heard above it and Alice, waiting at the sideboard ready to serve the soup was flustered by the thought that it would be cold before she got it on the table.

Zillah, Mr Hodge and his sister talked at length of the conditions of the poor in the worst parts of Manchester and how they were to alleviate them, the contents of Mr Isherwood's sermon last Sunday and the difficulty of persuading chapel-goers to become class members of whom they were short.

'Why is that, my dear?' Caleb cut in, longing to take the smug, self-satisfied expressions from the faces of these three people who believed that their way of life and their beliefs were the only ones worth having.

Zillah flushed angrily. 'There are those who have not seen the light. Who disassociate themselves from serving God and the love of John Wesley—'

Caleb interrupted her smoothly. 'But do not all those who worship at your chapel believe as you do, so why do they shy away from becoming class members? What is it you have told us, "the class of the Lord's redeemed".'

'Really, Caleb, we must not give Mr and Miss Hodge the impression that there are unbelievers in this house.'

'Of course not, Zillah, do forgive me.' But there was an ironic smile about Caleb's mouth that told Mr and Miss Hodge exactly what he meant. Amy kept her eyes cast down and unless a question was directed at her she did not speak, though Caleb noticed that Mr Hodge tried his best to draw her out.

'My daughter is very shy, Mr Hodge,' Zillah told him and far from being displeased it seemed Randall Hodge was delighted.

They moved into the drawing room after the stilted, awkward meal, though it must be admitted Mr Hodge did try to bring a lighter touch to the evening by telling them of a trip he had just made to London on business. It was only when he mentioned a commotion that had taken place in Kensington High Street as he was passing by that Amy showed any interest. Pontings, a fancy draper's shop, had been attacked by four women with hammers, he told them, and really it was quite incredible that ladies, for they were not mere working-class women as one might expect, should do such a thing.

Amy raised her head from her contemplation of the coffee cup she held in her hand. 'But they are fighting for their rights, sir,' she declared stoutly and Caleb felt his heart sink.

Zillah's face turned a bright red. 'Where on earth do you get these ridiculous ideas, girl?'

Her voice was challenging but at the same time there was a certain satisfaction in it that Caleb did not like. Amy had been subdued for a long time now and Zillah had had no reason to chide her—though she did, of course, for slight things—but now the child had given her the chance to really punish her. He happened to catch the expression on Randall Hodge's face and sickeningly realised that *he* would like to be the one to punish the girl!

It was at that moment that he fully understood with a horror that froze his blood what his wife intended for Amy. The three of them were murmuring what a splendid evening it had been and would Mrs Seymour, and Mr Seymour, of course, do them the honour of dining with the Hodges some time soon.

'And we must not exclude Miss Amy, naturally.' Mr Hodge smiled. 'I think she is old enough now to dine out, don't you agree, Mrs Seymour?' His eyes gleamed.

'Of course, Mr Hodge.'

And before Caleb, in the awfulness of the situation, could protest that he was far too busy and Amy far too young, the Hodges were out of the door and in their carriage with Zillah standing on the top step beneath the porch waving a gracious farewell.

15

Miss Gibbon—still in charge of Amy despite her employer's frequent threats—had decided they would visit the latest exhibition at the Art Gallery and Mrs Seymour, after enquiring what the exhibition might be, in other words which artist it was and whether he would be suitable for a young girl, said that they might go. His name was John Constable, the name unfamiliar to Zillah since she knew nothing about art which she considered could be decadent, but on finding that he painted clouds and mills and piers, innocent enough subject matter for her daughter, she had agreed. She even agreed that they should travel by tramcar because she needed the carriage that day. She had become more involved with the Temperance movement centred in Manchester which organised lectures and meetings to try to encourage members of the public to abstain from alcoholic drink. There was to be a lunchtime meeting outside a factory gate at which she was to speak, expounding the evils of drink. A table was to be set up so that anyone wanting to sign the pledge to give up alcoholic drink might do so. She was so ardent in her determination to convert every working man—and woman—to the glories of total sobriety that she scarcely took note of Amy, or indeed of Miss Gibbon who looked somewhat drawn.

The first pleasure of the day was the tram ride from outside the gates of Somerfield into town. Miss Gibbon was not having a good day and so she gave permission for Amy to go upstairs on the double-decker tram while she remained on the lower deck since she knew the stairs would be too much for her. So far she had managed to hide the true state of her health, which she knew really needed the attention of a doctor, from her employer, for this was a decent job and, as her charge grew from childhood into young womanhood she had less and less to do bar escort her here and there. Of course she knew Amy wouldn't tell tales to Mrs Seymour since her own delicate disposition gave the girl more freedom, so there was an unspoken agreement between the two of them that if Amy kept Miss Gibbon's increasing ill-health to herself, Miss Gibbon would allow her to roam about the grounds unattended though she drew the line at letting her go beyond the gates.

Now Amy sat on the upstairs deck of the tramcar which had an open top and though it was cold she barely noticed it as she was well wrapped up in a lined, dark grey cloak, beneath which she wore a warm woollen dress, thick stockings and sturdy boots. Out of sight of Miss Gibbon she removed her bonnet and let the breeze from the tram's movement blow her hair about. It soon loosened the tight plait and strands of bright golden hair, streaked by the weak sun with shafts of amber and platinum, blew in curly confusion about her rosy face. She caught the eye of many of the passengers, especially the men, but she did not notice. Her whole attention was on the passing traffic, including a brand-new Model T Ford which she recognised from the pages of Joe's *Autocar*. She must remember to tell him!

They were passing the entrance to the Royal Museum and Free Library where she had fallen asleep on her journey into Manchester the first time she escaped and at the back of which was Peel Park when she saw them. A pretty young woman, evidently just come from the park, was pushing a smart perambulator, the latest model, extremely high but very elegant in a rich shade of maroon, the jointed stays that kept the hood open made of brass and the grip on the handle of porcelain. She was bending down to smile at the baby inside and following her was an older man who was smiling indulgently. The woman turned a laughing face to the man and for a moment Amy thought he was about to kiss her. She wanted to smile herself but instead an enormous wave of astonishment ran through her. It was Caleb Seymour!

The tram had stopped to pick up several passengers so Amy had a chance to get a long look at the couple and again astonishment swept through her, for the young woman was the one who had smiled at her several weeks ago from the garden of the house at the junction of Seedley Road and Langworthy Road. She twisted on the wooden bench to stare at them, then the conductor rang the bell and the tram started off towards the city. Slowly she turned back to face the front, to the acute disappointment of the young man who sat behind her. Her mind was in a whirl, for what could Mr Seymour be doing with a young woman pushing a perambulator? Was she a relative? But then surely one of the servants would know of her and have mentioned her? She had never heard of any in all the years she had been at Somerfield. She wondered if Miss Gibbon had seen them, hoping, for some reason she could not determine, that she was sitting on the right-hand side of the tram. It seemed she had not, for she said nothing as they alighted from the tram on Market Street, ushering Amy along the length of Mosley Street until they reached the City Art Gallery. It was a magnificent building with wide steps leading to six enormous pillars beneath which was the entrance.

'I'm going to sit here for a little while,' Miss Gibbon declared, indicating a wooden bench just inside the entrance. 'My . . . well, I did not sleep at all well last night so I will rest a while. I shall trust you to behave yourself and not speak to anyone, especially any gentleman who might approach you,' for it had not gone unnoticed by Miss Gibbon that her charge excited a great deal of attention despite her drab clothing. 'And do not remove your bonnet,' because when her magnificent hair was revealed she was even more noticeable. Amy had stuffed her bonnet back on her head before she

210

came down the stairs on the tram but there were still small curly tendrils about her cheeks and Miss Gibbon had her suspicions. She was fast beginning to realise that as Amy approached sixteen she would soon be beyond her control. There were signs of it already and her own health did not help.

Amy stood for a long time before a picture which declared itself to be *Flatford Mill ('Scene on a Navigable River')*, a wonderful oil painting that seemed to draw her into and on to the track that lay along the river depicted by the artist. *Chain Pier, Brighton*, was presented next and then *Cloud Study* into which she floated as her mind wrestled with the other picture in her mind, that of Mr Seymour laughing with a young woman pushing a perambulator. The young woman with a child in her arms who had smiled at Amy. There was something here that was disturbing, something so puzzling she wondered how she was to deal with it and the only one she could talk to, and implicitly trust was, of course, Joe. It appeared, thank God, that Miss Gibbon had not seen what Amy had seen, though even that mystified her because why should she be glad Miss Gibbon had not seen Mr Seymour? Whatever he was doing coming from the park on a working day and whoever the young woman was, it was neither Miss Gibbon's business nor Amy's. But she had to admit she had never seen him as he had been today. He often smiled, his eyes shrewd and kindly in their nest of wrinkles, his smiles directed at her but never at his wife. His mouth was full of humour and she often wondered what on earth had possessed him to marry a woman such as Mrs Seymour. Amy had become quite fond of the old gentleman, for that

211

was how she saw him, though she had to admit he had not seemed old this morning! Though he did not exactly stick up for her with Mrs Seymour she had always felt his silent sympathy. But her instincts told her that there was some mystery concerning him and the pretty young woman and the child in the perambulator.

She and Joe were sitting shoulder to shoulder in the potting shed when she told him about the morning. He was having his lunch, tucking into an enormous beef sandwich Mrs Abigail had passed to him at the kitchen door and drinking from a bottle of beer. He offered some to her but she shook her head, for it would be time for luncheon with Mrs Seymour soon and, besides, he needed the food the cook pressed on him since, as she said, he was a growing lad.

'So what d'you think then?' she asked him. 'Who d'you think she was?'

'Nay, lass, how should I know? Mebbe a relative, or a friend; the wife of a friend, 'appen.' He was clearly not overly concerned.

'But doesn't it strike you as strange that an old man like Mr Seymour should be out in the park, which is where they were coming from, in the morning when he's supposed to be at work, with a young woman pushing a pram?'

She was evidently spellbound by what she had seen that morning and Joe stopped his hungry attack on his sandwich and turned to look at her. She looked slightly dishevelled as she had not stopped to tidy herself when she dumped her bonnet on her bed and flew down the back stairs and into the kitchen looking for him. Her hair was still escaping from the tight plait about her head and the fair curls that clustered at her hairline on her forehead and neck had become even looser. Her eyes, deep velvet brown with a luminous touch of gold in them, were turned excitedly on him and her cheeks were flushed. She looked glorious and Joe carefully placed his sandwich on the shelf beside him. This was their secret place, at least from Mr and Mrs Seymour, for all the servants knew exactly where he and the little lass went to get a bit of privacy from the prying eyes of that there governess, as they called her, and the mistress. They did not believe for a minute that anything untoward took place because Joe was a respectable young man who would do nothing to harm the mistress's adopted daughter. He loved her, they knew that, with a young man's reverent love and there was no doubt she thought the world of him but since nothing could ever come of it they were prepared to turn a blind eye. They trusted Joe.

Joe gazed at her for such a long time she began to fidget but at the same time she noticed the long, slow drooping of his thick lashes over the incredible brilliance of his blue eyes. His smoothly shaved face was a lovely shade of amber, for he was out in all weathers all year long. As she watched him his hand rose of its own volition and reached out to tuck a springing curl behind her ear. The tip of his finger moved to her cheek and she blinked her own long lashes in the hush that followed. Then, breathlessly, she came from the brown study into which his gaze and his touch seemed to have plunged her.

'What is it?' she whispered, she didn't know why.

'You're so lovely,' he told her. 'And yer don't even know it.'

'Joe . . .'

'Nay, my little lass, don't be mithered,' for he could see she was bewildered, confused, and yet at the same time there was a certain shine to her eyes that had never been there before. Not the usual lambency—a word he did not even know the meaning of—but it was there in the depths of her golden-brown eyes, something different and what he had said to her had put it there.

'Joe . . .'

'Aye, sweetheart, what is it? I can't 'elp but call yer that an' . . . an' . . . about how yer look, an' if it upsets yer, I'm sorry.' He reached out and took both her hands in his and she made no protest, in fact she found she liked it. Joe had a manual labourers' hands, for though he drove Mr Seymour's motor car, always wearing the gauntlets that went with his chauffeur's uniform, he also worked with the horses and in the gardens with the gardeners. 'Yer like a rose, a rosebud, so bonny an' . . . sometimes I can't bear ter see the way she treats yer. One day, 'appen, when I've got summat ter—'

'Aye up, Joe Newbridge,' a voice said cheerfully, 'yer wanted so yer'd best look lively.' Tim, a stable boy, stood in the doorway, a broad grin on his face as he had not failed to notice that the master's chauffeur and the master's daughter seemed to be holding hands. They sprang apart at once, the pair of them, and Miss Amy stood up abruptly but Tim watched as the colour ebbed and flowed in her face. Mind, she was a pretty lass and he didn't blame young Joe if he had a fancy for her. If things

214

were different he could easily have had a fancy for her himself.

Amy tried a wobbly smile, one of unconcern, smoothing down the boxcloth of her skirt. She had come in here to talk to Joe about the astounding scene she had witnessed this morning and to ask him what he thought about it and though she had told him, something else had happened as well. She hadn't the faintest notion what it was because Joe was Joe and so familiar to her she rarely noticed the length of his eyelashes, the beautiful colour of his eyes or the strong line of his mouth but today . . . today she had and Tim's appearance had flustered her.

'Really, I must go,' she said in the clear-cut tones Miss Gibbon taught her. Ladylike, well-bred, the tones of the daughter of the house who should not really be sitting in the potting shed with the chauffeur/handyman though she had done it a score of times before with the knowledge of all the servants, including Tim. But today she felt the constraint and was bewildered by it.

'Don't bother yer 'ead about it, sweetheart,' Joe said now, taking no account of Tim who was older than he was.

'No, thank you, Joe, I'll just . . .' and with a swish of her skirt she fled across the vegetable garden and the yard and into the house by the side door.

The two men watched her go then Joe turned to Tim. 'An' what d'yer think you're gawpin' at?' he demanded to know, his expression one of belligerent anger.

'Same as you,' Tim was unwise enough to say and was astounded when Joe hit him on the point

215

of his chin, knocking him to the damp soil outside the shed door.

* * *

Caleb refused point-blank to become *friends* with Zillah's new acquaintances, saying he personally had nothing in common with them and if Zillah wished to dine with them she was perfectly at liberty to do so but she could count him out!

How many times he had been forced to put up with them at his own dining table he really didn't care to contemplate. There seemed to be no way he could avoid them, for Zillah always invited them when she knew he would be home, sometimes without a day's warning, but he had the choice to refuse—'Tell them I'm too busy at the warehouse'—when she demanded he accompany her and Amy to the Hodges' home in Weaste Lane. 'And why you have to drag that poor child with you is a mystery to me. She has no interest in either of them.'

'They happen to be my friends and I find them the most interesting of companions and I'm sure the child does as well.'

'The child, *the child*. Can you not call her by her name?'

'Since you cannot be active in the chapel what we do there does not mean that . . . that Amy is the same. I wish her to concern herself with all its activities and the Hodges support me in this. Besides, it does her good to mix with people of breeding who have the same beliefs as we do.'

'We?'

'The girl and me. She has attended chapel with

216

me for many years and, I believe, has become one of God's creatures. "The fear of the Lord is the beginning of knowledge," according to Proverbs and that is what I want for my daughter.'

'She is but a child, Zillah. Should she not be allowed . . . ?' Caleb wanted to say some *fun*, but he knew that would be totally inappropriate and how on earth would she get it in this house? He was well aware that she slipped away from her governess and mixed with the servants, as he had on one occasion, when Zillah had been absent, heard her laughing in the kitchen but he kept it to himself. He had his own life to lead away from Somerfield and his many business activities kept him occupied and fulfilled, but Amy worried him at times. Not the girl herself, as she was well cared for, but what was to become of her in this prison Zillah kept her in. He was often rather ashamed of his own weakness in allowing it but he had no wish to face up to Zillah, because there was no doubt that as long as he left her alone she would allow him to lead the life he chose away from their home. As long as he was circumspect and caused no ripple of scandal to wash up against her and her fanatical beliefs, she took no notice of him or what he did. Since she had become acquainted with the Hodges she had been a bit more demanding, wanting him to dine with them and be host at any hospitality she devised.

He did his best with Amy and had even invited her to play tennis with him during the summer months, much to Zillah's annoyance as she thought that any sort of game, particularly on a Sunday which was when he was at home, was a sin against her Lord. He had enjoyed the game when

217

he was a young man, long before he had brought Zillah to Somerfield as a bride, and the equipment, tennis racquets, balls and net were still stored in the shed to the side of the court. But these had proved to be rotted after so many years so, without Zillah's knowledge, he had gone to the sports department at Lewis's Store in Market Street and purchased all that was needed. Amy had been delighted and quickly learned the rudiments of the game and by the end of the summer had begun to beat him. He had also realised that she was playing the game with young Joe, for whom he had a soft spot, and so, his conscience being somewhat eased, he had allowed Zillah her way when it came to chapel matters.

He had begun to notice during the winter months that Zillah was more occupied with what he called her 'good works', leaving Amy with Miss Gibbon while she went about her philanthropic activities and it had surprised him because she had seemed intent on teaching, or *forcing* the girl into her own way of life. Surprisingly, as long as Amy attended chapel once or twice on Sunday she was more or less left to her own devices.

Zillah talked endlessly about the new Methodist Mission that had been opened in Jubilee Street. It had a Sunday school, a Temperance club and a band of hope, a soup kitchen and a night shelter for the homeless. She and Miss Hodge were deeply involved with it and proud to be, so that Caleb began to understand that their compassion was combined with more than a hint of religious zeal, their philanthropy offering them both a route to status in the community. The socially concerned, as Zillah considered herself to be since she was a publicly prominent citizen, were expected to be patrons to the poor and helpless, she told him and Amy at the dinner table. Though she did not speak of it in front of Amy since she was not supposed to know about such things, she took a great deal of interest in 'fallen women', 'girls in moral danger' and had joined the Manchester Ladies Association for the Protection and Reformation of Girls and Women which established a home to provide training for domestic service for these girls in moral danger.

Caleb could see why Zillah would not want Amy to be involved in such an activity since Amy was a young and innocent girl who had no knowledge of the ways of the world and the wickedness of members of her own sex, but he was surprised that she involved her in no activities at all. All that winter and into the spring and summer she left Amy in the charge of the woman who was supposed to be her governess and the child was beginning to develop into what he had always believed she should be. With freedom to roam the gardens and the bit of woodland to the side and the back of the house she lost that dreadful buttoned-up look, that rigid self-control that had been her demeanour ever since Zillah had got her hands on her. She would often be found in the small gazebo to the side of the house, a book in her hand, her bonnet discarded, the top buttons of her dress undone, her plait falling down her back, unravelling as it did so, and her curls wisping about her face and neck in dishevelled abandon, an abandon that Zillah would have deplored. Somehow, though, she always appeared at table just as Zillah wanted her to be, neat, clean, her hair scraped back from her lovely face, her eyes quite without expression. Now and again, when Zillah was occupied with her soup or fish or whatever Mrs Abigail had sent to the dining room, he would catch Amy's eye and wink, enchanting her, he knew, making her screw up her face in an attempt not to smile.

Once his wife caught the tail end of her expression and clattered her fish knife and fork on her plate. Alice froze at the sideboard, for she herself had sometimes seen these exchanges between the master and the lass.

'And may I ask what is the matter with you, miss?' Zillah asked icily. 'Are you in pain that you should pull such a face?'

'No, ma'am,' Amy answered calmly. 'I beg your pardon.'

'Then what is the matter, pray?'

'Nothing, ma'am.'

Zillah sighed heavily. She did wish the child would stop this preposterous habit she had of calling her 'ma'am'. She was her mother, adopted by her years ago and directed by her to use that form of address but not once had she given Zillah her correct title. Mind you, she did not call Caleb 'father' or 'papa', in fact she called neither of them by any name at all.

'Well, I would be obliged if you would refrain from pulling such faces. Now get on with your meal and then afterwards I would like an account of what you have done today. I have already questioned Miss Gibbon but would like to hear your account first-hand. And I can only hope it has nothing to do with that frightful game you play or there will be trouble.'

This was aimed at her husband, he knew, and he also knew that unless Amy gave the same account of her day as that given by Miss Gibbon, she and Miss Gibbon would be in for it. Zillah had this cunning way with her that led her to question Miss Gibbon and her charge separately, hoping to catch them out in a lie. He was often astounded that Zillah did not notice Miss Gibbon's increasing inability to be a companion to Amy, to accompany her at all times, which was what Zillah expected of her. If she had known, of course, she would have dismissed her on the spot as she had once threatened to do. There was something in Zillah these days that he found he did not care for. He couldn't put a finger on it but there seemed to be a smugness about her which baffled him. He thought back to the time when he had had a very uneasy feeling over the dinner table regarding Randall Hodge and Zillah's behaviour towards him which seemed to be linked with Amy in some way but he couldn't believe that . . . well, he didn't quite know where his thoughts were leading since they, his thoughts, were so totally ludicrous.

So the year drew on and he was aware that the child, for despite his protestations to Zillah she was still only that, a lovely, innocent child, roamed the gardens and the woods and every Sunday he and she played a game of tennis on the newly restored tennis court. Matt and Barty, the gardeners, had laid out the lines, whitening them every week and repaired the posts to which the net was attached and the grass was mown so perfectly it could have been played on by those champions at Wimbledon who Amy read about every summer. The only thing his wife would not allow was a

221

tennis outfit for the child, saying it was not decent. The straight dress was too revealing, the ankle-length skirt too short and the three-quarter sleeves not to be contemplated, so that Amy was forced to play in the drab grey cotton dress that was her summer garb.

Nevertheless, in between her attendance at chapel with Zillah, once in the morning and at the evening service, he and she managed to get in a game and her improvement, he decided, smiling to himself, was due to the practice she put in with young Joe.

He might not have been so complacent had he known of the growing attachment between the girl his wife had bought from her parents and presented to him as his new daughter and his own chauffeur/handyman!

16

It had begun for her on the day she had seen Mr Seymour with the woman pushing the perambulator. She became aware of Joe, not as her friend, her confidant, her older brother, but as the young man he had grown into and who suddenly looked different though she could not at first understand how. She only knew that whatever it turned out to be it involved her and changed how she perceived him. Sometimes his face wore an expression that she could not decipher, one that Mrs Abigail called *daft* when he talked to Amy, though Amy didn't quite know what she meant by that. Not daft as in stupid but sort of soft, dreamy,

222

not his normal casual friendly expression. It came over him more frequently when they were alone together and he would stop what he was doing or saying and simply gaze at her, then, with what seemed to be a great effort he would tear his eyes away, clear his throat and with his wash leather continue to clean the Rolls with a furious determination. His mouth would firm up into a tight line as though he were fighting to keep words inside. His arm holding the wash leather would sweep over the bonnet and she found she was watching the strong line of his muscled back and his tanned arms and their fine covering of soft golden hairs.

He was tall, half a head taller than she was and his active life, playing football at the weekend, his manual work about gardens and stables, kept him lean, with broad shoulders, narrow hips and legs that were in perfect proportion to his body. He had grown into a beautiful young man, not in the sense a woman might be beautiful but completely male, virile. His vivid blue eyes glowed with health and his strong, uncompromising young mouth had an endearing curl at each corner and his dark hair curled in the nape of his neck. His step was light and buoyant and his movements were as graceful as the cat that stalked the mice in the stable yard with a long, swinging stride. The female staff had become aware of his attractiveness, even Alice, and they vied with one another to make him a cup of tea or a sandwich. But they all knew, without voicing it for it would not be proper, that Joe was . . . well, they didn't quite know how to describe it since they were not particularly literate and did not have a way with words, but Joe was sweet on

223

their little lass, though much good it would do him, knowing the mistress.

Amy, whenever she could get away from Miss Gibbon, found she was hanging about where she knew Joe might happen to be and when she saw him her heart seemed to move in her breast. Well, it might be her heart, she wasn't sure, but something stirred beneath the smooth material of her plain cotton bodice and her breath quickened.

She was reading *Jane Eyre* for the third time and was in that romantic mood the book seemed to arouse in all young females so perhaps that was why she let it happen; or was it because she had been aware for the past year that Joe treated her quite differently to the way he treated the other females in the house. Of course, she was 'the daughter' of the house and not a servant but on this particular day she was deep in Mr Rochester's longing for Jane when a shadow fell across the wide doorway of the gazebo where she lounged and there was Joe with a great bunch of wild flowers in his arms. Not the cultivated roses or dahlias so lovingly tended by himself or Barty or Matt but a mixture of golden buttercups, creamy meadowsweet, crimson poppies and white lady's smock, their names as pretty as the flowers. He had tied a bit of ribbon round them and as she stared in wonder he held them out to her wordlessly.

'Joe, how lovely, but . . .' She sat up and closed her book and as she did so a stray beam of sunlight touched her hair and he caught his breath at the beauty of her. She took the flowers and held them to her face and he sat down beside her.

'Yer know what yer mean ter me, Amy.' His

voice was hoarse with emotion and yet he made an effort to control it. 'Yer've known fer a long time. I've nowt ter offer yer, only meself, an' God knows what I'm doing sayin' this to yer. Even if I were made o' money mistress would have me out of here soon as look at me. But I can't go on wi'out tellin' yer how I feel.' His face spasmed and his hands curled into fists as though he would dearly like to hit someone, preferably the mistress, in his frustration, but very gently Amy put her own hand over one of them.

'I know, Joe. Though nothing has ever been said between us, I know how you feel and ... and I think I feel the same. You and I are ... orphans of the storm, I suppose, though that doesn't say what I mean but ...'

Joe lifted her hand to his lips and with great delicacy kissed each finger. His eyes were shining and yet at the same time soft with his love for her. His lips were warm and slightly rough and as his flesh touched hers she felt something stir in the pit of her stomach and at the same time a long sigh of deep contentment flowed through her. This was so right. There was a sudden peace between them, an awareness of one another, not as Joe the servant and Amy the daughter of his employers but as a young man and woman. They had been friends for a long while, now they were more, much more than that. She turned to him and sat quietly, trusting him completely. They studied one another gravely, knowing how impossible it was going to be but believing it would happen one day. It was a beautiful moment. He put his hand to the back of her head then bending his he placed his lips on hers for their first kiss. He lifted his head to see her reaction and she was smiling. Her lips parted and, still smiling, both of them, they exchanged a second kiss, then a third, their mouths warm and sweet and soft and innocent. He pulled her to her feet and put his arms about her and drew her willing body to his.

'I love you, love you . . .' and his pronunciation of the words had none of the careless northern accent with which he usually spoke. 'My love, my little rosebud . . .'

She did not answer but pressed her young mouth to the bare flesh of his jaw and throat, just above his open collar and at once he stiffened and drew away, for he was a man and his body reacted the way a man's did.

'I must go, sweetheart. God, I love you, you are my heart's sweetness. Do you . . . love me?'

'Yes, oh, yes, Joe . . .'

And so that spring and early summer they met whenever they could in the secret depths of the woodland at the back of the house, talking, not saying much, but in the way of those who loved, speaking of it all the time with their eyes. He was careful with her, for she was only just sixteen and knew nothing of the world or of what happened between a man and a woman though perhaps he would have been surprised at how much she *did* know. Had she not slept in the same bedroom as her mam and pa who had often loved one another in the dark of the night? They talked vaguely about the future, neither of them unduly concerned with it at the moment since they were happy just to be in one another's company whenever she could escape Miss Gibbon, or, worse, the clutches of Zillah Seymour.

226

Amy and Zillah dined frequently with the Hodges who often gave circumspect dinner parties at their house in Weaste Lane for those of like interests as themselves. The house was set in a select area of Salford, a narrow, leafy thoroughfare where solicitors, bankers and moneyed people lived, lying well back from its ornamental iron gate in a pool of tree shadow. The hall was dimly lit, as indeed was the rest of the house, cool and hushed like the chapel they all attended. It had a subdued elegance with an uncluttered dining room and a sombre drawing room. Glass-fronted cabinets displayed many frail and lovely porcelain figurines by Wedgwood and Meissen and others Amy could not identify. The dinner table was set with fine crystal, silver cutlery, damask napkins, all, Amy felt, to show off the wealth and status of Randall Hodge but which meant nothing to her and her indifference often caused harsh words from Mrs Seymour when they were in the carriage.

'She's in trouble again,' Thomas would report to the others but then when was she not, for it would take a bloody saint, as he put it, to please the mistress. When he entered the kitchen hoping for a hot drink, the maidservants were taking their ease round the kitchen table, drinking a cup of cocoa before making their weary way to bed, listening in varying states of indifference to Joe as he read to them from the newspaper. Apparently there were suggestions that there might be a war, though for the life of them they couldn't understand why. Germany was rattling its sabres, whatever that meant, but Joe seemed to think it was important. Some archduke who was the heir to the crowns of Austria and Hungary had been murdered in June and as a result someone had attacked a place called Serbia which the Germans supported who then, for another reason unclear to them all, though Joe seemed to understand, were all for declaring war on Russia. And Belgian neutrality came into it somehow. Oh, it was all too much for them, they yawned, and, besides, as Mrs Abigail remarked, their King and the Kaiser were cousins so was it likely they would go to war against each other. It stood to reason, blood would not fight blood and Joe was to stop frightening them all with his talk of war.

She and Joe were playing tennis when disaster struck, not the international crisis that the newspapers talked about but something much nearer to home. As she reached for the ball which he had hit low over the net into the furthest corner of the court, she flew across the grass, tripped on the skirt of her long dress, careered off the grass and fell heavily on to the gravel path that surrounded it. She went full-length on the rough surface. With a hoarse cry he leaped the net, dropping his racquet as he jumped over.

'Sweetheart . . . lovey, are yer hurt? Let me see . . . Jesus, yer went a real cropper. See, let me help yer . . . no, don't try ter stand up, stay there an' I'll get yer up. Are yer legs . . .'

'Joe, Joe, really, I'm not hurt. I just scraped my hand and the knuckles on the other one on the gravel. Help me to my feet and . . .' But the palm of her left hand on which she had fallen and the knuckles of her right hand which held the racquet were scraped raw and beginning to bleed.

Gently he lifted her to her feet and as the tears began to ooze from her eyes he put his arms about

228

her, holding her close to him crooning his loving concern, bending to kiss her cheek and her eyes and her lips, then as she stumbled away from him, taking her hands and dropping light, tender kisses on her wounds. As he did so there was some frightening transmission between them. Something electric, something purely *physical* that had not been there, or at least only on the very edge of their consciousness but which they had kept at bay. Joe meant to make something of himself. He was an experienced driver by now and had learned, from manuals and with his head under the bonnet of the machine he drove, the mechanics of the motor car and had it not been for Amy he would have been looking for a better job. He wasn't quite sure what but he was no longer just a handyman, a stable hand or a gardener. Chauffeur/mechanics were in demand, for there were so few of them at this, the dawn of the motor car era. But his love for Amy kept him at Somerfield.

'We'd best get yer inter't kitchen, my little love. Them hands need cleanin' and Mrs Abigail'll have summat ter put on 'em. See, lean on me, or shall I carry yer?' for she was trembling with what might have been pain but was not. Joe wasn't really aware of what he was saying, his longing for her, which he had kept tight within him, rushing to the surface and overwhelming him.

'Joe . . .' She didn't know what she was about to say, she only knew that it was very comforting; no, more than that, she was honest enough to admit to herself, something she wanted from Joe, something she could only get with Joe and though she did not put a name to it she knew it was to do with desire. With what her mam and pa had!

She leaned trustingly against him, his strength holding her up as she allowed him to lead her from the tennis court, along the path that led to the stable yard and to the kitchen door. For God's sake, her practical mind was whispering, you've only grazed your hands, but it was so lovely, so sweet, as he led her like a precious treasure newly gained into the kitchen. Yes, he treasured her, she knew that and she had not been treasured since the day her mother had been taken from her. It was all there in his eyes which had changed to the soft blue of a summer sky, in the way he held her and she felt the warmth of her own feelings rush to her heart and fix themselves there for ever. Oh, she knew they were all fond of her, Mrs Abigail, Alice, Jess and the rest, but Joe loved her and she loved him and his arm round her was like a comforting, protective blanket that he would never let go. This realisation was nothing new, of course, and as he looked down into her eyes and hers looked up into his it seemed all barriers had dissolved between them and what was Joe and what was Amy touched and communicated and needed to be consummated. It lasted only a second but it was enough.

'Dear Lord, whatever's up?' Mrs Abigail ejaculated, rising with alacrity from the chair into which she had just thankfully sunk. The sight of Joe with his arm round the daughter of the house, for that was what Amy was, shocked her immeasurably and yet why should it, she was to ponder later for they all knew what Joe felt for the little lass.

'She fell, Mrs Abigail, and hurt her hands on the path round't tennis court. Look, she's tekken skin

230

off 'em and . . .'

'Give her here, Joe. See, sit down, lovey, an' let me have a look,' dragging Amy from Joe's arms and placing her tenderly in a chair by the table. 'Primrose, fetch my box.' Mrs Abigail had a medical kit where she kept everything that might be needed for an emergency in her kitchen, such as minor burns, cut fingers, or other injuries required some of her ointment or a bandage. Not that her girls were clumsy or inexperienced in the ways of the kitchen but accidents could happen and she was prepared for them. The maids clustered round sympathetically, pushing Joe to one side where he stood helplessly. They 'oohed and aahed' but Mrs Abigail was having none of that.

'Alice, fetch a bowl of warm water and Jess, bring me a towel . . . no, not that old one, yer daft happorth, run up to Miss Amy's room and fetch a good one.'

While the maids scurried about longing to help, wincing with her as Amy's hands were plunged into the bowl of warm water to which Mrs Abigail had added a large dose of iodine, Joe hovered at their backs, getting in everyone's way until Mrs Abigail ordered him to get back to work.

'I can't, Mrs Abigail,' he said desolately.

With clean cotton wool the housekeeper was bathing Amy's cuts, gently picking out the bits of gravel that had become embedded in the grazes. 'And why not, pray?' she asked coldly. 'There's nothing for you to do here—'

But she was interrupted by Amy. 'No, don't go, Joe, stay, please.' Her eyes pleaded with him, for he was her comfort, her rock, her one happiness in

231

the drab days of her life with Mrs Seymour. She found that her mind and her body were at peace when he was close by.

They petted her tenderly while the painful business of cleaning the grazes was attended to and watched as Mrs Abigail bandaged her hands with clean white gauze. Mrs Abigail tied the bandages neatly then ordered a nice hot cup of tea be put in Amy's hand, 'with plenty of sugar, mind, for the lass has had a shock'. Joe still dithered at her back to Mrs Abigail's annoyance and only when Jess lifted Amy from her chair and with an arm round her led her from the kitchen did he reluctantly leave for his own room above the stable.

'I feel such a fool,' Amy was murmuring, as Jess, who had been her friend from the very first day, helped her out of her dress and prepared to dress her for dinner with Mr and Mrs Seymour. Not that the 'evening' gown was any finer than the ones she wore daily, plain and of a drab olive colour but at least it was of faille, an unwatered moiré with the usual high neck and long sleeves.

'I reckon yer'd best wear gloves, lovey,' Jess said. 'Them white ones'd do, otherwise missis'll be bound ter want ter know what happened to yer hands.'

But handling first a soup spoon, then a knife and fork with gloves on, for they were not the sort of fine evening gloves young ladies wore, was difficult and her aunt noticed them at once.

'May one ask why you have taken to wearing gloves at the dinner table, miss?' she enquired in a soft, deceptive voice which was the one they were all, including the servants, afraid of. 'You are dining with your family and as we are not people who dress for dinner when we are alone I am at a loss to understand why you should feel it necessary. Do you know, Caleb?' she asked, turning to her husband whose heart sank.

He too had noticed Amy's gloves and for some reason, though he did not know why, he sensed trouble brewing. 'No, my dear, but if Amy is perhaps . . . cold . . .'

'In this heat?' For the summer of 1914 had been one of the warmest on record and even at the end of the day it was still very close. 'Well?' She turned back to Amy, contemptuously discarding her husband's half-hearted explanation. 'What have you to say?'

'Nothing, ma'am.' Amy kept her eyes on her plate and Alice wanted to turn her face to the wall because, like her master, she knew a storm was coming.

'Nothing! You are wearing gloves on a hot summer's evening and have no reason for doing so. Take them off at once and then perhaps you can eat gracefully as is expected of a young lady.'

'I would rather not, ma'am.'

Zillah's face turned a peculiar shade of purple and Caleb watched her with interest. One of these days she would have a stroke, he was sure of it, and it really couldn't come quickly enough for him. He knew that Amy was hiding something beneath her gloves and though he could not imagine what it could be, and dreaded it, he felt pity for the child wash over him.

'Take them off at once,' Zillah thundered, 'or shall I take them off for you?'

'No, I will do it myself.' Slowly, finger by finger,

233

for her hands were stiff and sore, she pulled the gloves from her hands and the neat bandages that Mrs Abigail had so lovingly applied were revealed. Even Caleb leaned across the table to study them with amazement.

Zillah was the first to find her voice, her *ominous* voice, the one that was quiet and yet terrifying. 'What is the matter with your hands? Why are they bandaged like that?'

'I . . . I fell.'

'Doing what, pray?'

'On the gravel.'

Alice moaned a little in the back of her throat though no one noticed it. She wanted to run away and hide in the kitchen, babble to them all that their little lass was in deep trouble because if the mistress found out how the child had hurt her hands there would be a disaster, not just for her but for them all.

'I did not ask where, but how. A well-brought-up young girl does not fall when she is merely walking along a path. A well-brought-up young lady does not run or skip like a child, and I would also like to know where Miss Gibbon was when this . . . this *fall* took place. Why did she not report it to me when I spoke to her less than an hour since? Now then, young lady, I will have the truth.'

'Oh, for God's sake, I was playing tennis.' Amy's voice was shrill with defiance. 'There, does that satisfy you? Tennis! An innocent game which is recognised as a perfectly proper way to exercise.'

'Not by me! *Not by me.*' Zillah turned on her husband. 'And I suppose you encouraged her in this flagrant contempt for my wishes. "A virtuous woman is a crown to her husband: but she that maketh ashamed is as rottenness in his bones."'

'What the devil are you ranting on about, woman? Amy has no husband and I agree that there is no harm in a game of tennis but, believe me, I was not playing with her. Oh, God, oh, sweet Jesus . . .' as he suddenly realised what he was saying in his anger and so did Zillah.

Her face became a mask. 'I see,' she said softly. 'And may I say I am appalled at your taking the name of the Lord in that way. But that aside, let us first find out with whom this wicked child played tennis. Well?' She turned to Amy and waited, her face rigid, her eyes like icy slivers and yet there was a strange expression on her face which seemed to speak of . . . could it be triumph?

Amy remained silent though in her heart was a fear so great it lurched sickening in her breast. She didn't know why—did anyone ever know why they were so afraid of Zillah Seymour—for what could she do to hurt Joe? Dismiss him, but then Mr Seymour would surely not allow that for such a simple thing as a game of innocent tennis? Joe was an expert chauffeur, a mechanic of great talent and Mr Seymour would not want to lose him.

'Well?' the woman said again. 'I am waiting.'

'It was nobody,' Amy said bravely, knowing what a ridiculous answer that was.

'It is not possible to play tennis with nobody, you stupid girl. Tell me who it was at once and you will not be punished,' as what she had in mind for her niece was not punishment in her eyes. 'I suppose it was one of the servants?' she asked casually and was instantly alerted by the averted face of the girl who sat, her head hanging in despair, at the side of her.

'Zillah, really, does this matter?' Caleb was unwise enough to say.

'Keep out of this, Caleb, if you please. We will now go through a list of the servants one by one and be assured I shall find the culprit. It may be that some person has trespassed on our land and he or she is the girl's partner in this crime but I cannot think so. Now then, shall we start with . . . with Marshall.' She turned like a snake to the trembling maid at the sideboard but already Alice was shaking her head in terror, backing away as though the mistress were about to stand and strike her.

'No, I thought not. Perhaps Mrs Abigail or Atkins . . .' She mentioned the names of all those who worked in the house then began on the men servants. Holden, Tilsley, who were both gardeners, Campbell the coachman, all quite ludicrous for they were not young men. Ashby, Ernie Tingle and then . . . Newbridge. Joe Newbridge who had been brought to this house against her wishes by her husband from the orphanage and being the woman she was, with a knowledge of deception bred in her by her own fanatical obsession with wrong-doing, she was instantly aware that this was the one. Amy did her best not to react to Joe's name but the tiniest indrawn breath gave her away and at once Zillah sprang to her feet. She said nothing, merely gripped Amy's arm and dragged her to her feet. Alice began to weep silently and Caleb rose in his chair to protest but Zillah was like a woman possessed.

Amy was wrenched, unprotesting, towards the door, along the hall, up the stairs and thrust into her bedroom. The last thing she heard was the key turning in the lock. She collapsed, dry-eyed, on to the bed.

17

Zillah looked dispassionately at the wary face of the woman who sat opposite her. She noticed what a bad colour she was, and she seemed to have lost weight since she had employed her as governess years ago so perhaps it was time to do what she had to do. And besides which, it gave her another weapon to fight with.

'You don't look well, Miss Gibbon. Is there something wrong?'

'Oh, no, Mrs Seymour,' Miss Gibbon hastened to assure her, her mind instantly dwelling on the awful prospect of being dismissed because of her health, but Mrs Seymour gave her a tight smile, one that said she had nothing to worry about.

'I'm quite well,' Miss Gibbon babbled, her face losing even more colour. 'I am sometimes prone to ... to indigestion but a dose of salts puts me right. And of course, Miss Amy is inclined to be somewhat energetic at times and I endeavour to keep up with her which ... well ...' She began to flounder, while conscious that Mrs Seymour was watching her closely. She began to despair but suddenly her employer smiled again.

'Well, that brings me to what I have to say to you. To *ask* of you. It is, of course, about Miss Amy. As I'm sure you know, or at least will have guessed, my husband and I are hoping for a match between my daughter and Mr Hodge. You are surprised, Miss Gibbon?

'No, oh, no; but I had thought that . . .'

'You thought Miss Amy was not in favour, but I'm sure you will appreciate that parents know what is best for their children and Mr Hodge is an excellent match. Miss Amy needs a strong hand to guide her. She is becoming . . . as she gets older she is becoming headstrong and is proving obstinate. But that is nothing that need concern you. Mr Seymour is to be away for a week or two and I would like to have this problem resolved by the time he returns. Now, there is something you might help me with . . .'

'Of course, Mrs Seymour. Anything, anything at all.' Miss Gibbon would be overjoyed to help her employer, her attitude said. She would kiss Mrs Seymour's feet if necessary. If it meant that she would keep her employer's approval, short of committing a crime she would do her utmost to help Mrs Seymour to obtain what she needed. She had heard rumours about Mr Hodge who was a frequent guest and she had noticed that he was very taken by Miss Amy. She was young to be married, but Mr Hodge was an influential and wealthy gentleman, a chapel-goer like Mrs Seymour and a suitable prospect for marriage. It was well known that older gentlemen required young wives to bring them children, heirs, and who could be more fitting than Mr Hodge for Miss Amy. Miss Amy was beginning to turn intractable and Miss Gibbon had become afraid that Mrs Seymour would soon find out that Miss Gibbon no longer had the influence she had once had over her young charge. In fact she was getting out of hand and it would not have been long anyway, since Amy was sixteen now, before she herself would be out of a job. Of course, if Amy was to marry, if Miss Gibbon was to help Mrs Seymour to bring her daughter to the altar with Mr Hodge beside her, she, Miss Gibbon, would earn Mrs Seymour's approbation and influence in finding another position.

Her attention was drawn to her employer's hand. She watched, fascinated, as Mrs Seymour withdrew something small from her pocket and with careful fingers let whatever it was lie in the palm of her hand. She drew in her breath as she recognised the silver locket that Mr Seymour had given Amy for her fifteenth birthday.

Mrs Seymour let the chain of the locket dangle from her fingers then she smiled. 'This morning I noticed that Miss Amy was not wearing her locket, the one that Mr Seymour had given her for her birthday and when I enquired as to its whereabouts she told me she thought she had dropped it in the garden, that it must have slipped from her neck when she was walking. I thought this was strange, especially as she looked somewhat . . . shall we say *uneasy*. Remembering her escapade on the tennis court with . . . well, with someone of whom I disapprove I went personally to the court and there found the locket in the gravel. Now here's what I want you to do, Miss Gibbon.'

*   *   *

Amy sat down obediently when directed to do so by her aunt. She had been locked in her bedroom since the incident on the tennis court, until, a few minutes ago, Alice had let her out and with a face on her that looked as though she had recently been weeping told her that she was wanted in the drawing room.

'I have good news for you, child,' her aunt said, her face creased with what might have been a smile of triumph, 'which I wanted to impart as soon as it was confirmed. Mr Seymour agrees that at sixteen it is time for us to think about your future and since a young woman in your station of life has only one road open to her which, of course, is marriage we have been looking round for a suitable partner. We have been approached by a gentleman of the highest respectability and have decided that he would be an excellent match. Your position in society would be assured. You would be a prominent member of the chapel, a lady of quality. Mr Hodge, of course you know Mr Hodge, is kind, generous, a respected gentleman, successful and would be a very suitable husband for any woman. You are very lucky to have captured his'—Zillah could not quite bring herself to utter the word *heart*—'his attention and as there is no need to wait the wedding is set for two weeks this Saturday. You will need time to be fitted for a wedding gown, something plain, of course, and a trousseau, since I am told by Mr Hodge he wishes to take you away on what is called a honeymoon.' Her face twisted in distaste, remembering her own. 'Mr Seymour will be home by then and will give you away as is customary.'

She sat on the sofa, impatience beginning to show on her face, waiting for the explosion she had expected, as she had begun to realise that this girl

240

she had kidnapped from her family was becoming more and more awkward to control and that the years under her rule had not quite resulted in what Zillah had planned for her. Best get her off her hands then, and who better to do it than Randall Hodge who had lusted after her for months now. Besides which it would keep the girl in the ways of Methodism which was what Zillah had planned for her from the outset. A very satisfactory outcome and if the arrangements could all be accomplished before Caleb returned home, apart from the actual ceremony, Zillah was sure Caleb would have no reason to object if the girl was primed and Miss Gibbon did as she had been ordered.

Amy sat as though turned to stone, nothing showing in her face. The horror she felt, the terror, the revulsion were well hidden, for deep within her was the certainty that Joe would not let this happen, nor would Mr Seymour. She knew Mr Seymour was fond of her and did not care for the Hodges but since he was a man who liked peace and harmony he had gone along with his wife's obsession with the chapel and her passion for 'good works' which he did not share. As long as she did not interfere with his life he did not interfere with hers. But surely, despite his liking for a quiet life and his reluctance to face up to his wife, he would never allow her, Amy, to be married off to an old man like Mr Hodge?

As if on cue there was a timid knock on the door which opened to reveal Miss Gibbon, her colour high and her eyes bright.

'Miss Gibbon, do come in,' Zillah said pleasantly, so pleasantly Amy began to feel a worm of renewed fear twist in her stomach. When was

Mrs Seymour ever pleasant to her servants? She spoke to them as though they were creatures from another world, one much lower in the order of things than her own, born to do her bidding and woe betide them if they didn't. Whenever she gave an order they sidled about with their eyes down, glad to be out of her presence. Here was Miss Gibbon, smiling as though she and her mistress were the best of friends, which did more to frighten Amy than anything that had gone before.

'Well, Miss Gibbon, did you do as I asked?' her aunt said.

'I did, Mrs Seymour. I searched all the servants' rooms as requested, knowing they were all in the kitchen, even the outside men, as you ordered.'

'And . . . ?'

'I have the locket here.' Triumphantly she dangled Amy's locket from her fingers, delighted, it seemed, by its silvery twinkle. Amy's eyes widened. She had scarcely missed the locket since her incarceration in her bedroom, just vaguely wondered where it could be and meaning to search for it when she was free. She could feel the ice beginning to creep along her veins as though her mind did not know what was happening but her senses, her heart, the very essence of her was well aware and the conclusion was too terrible to contemplate.

'And where did you find it, Miss Gibbon?' Zillah stood up and took the locket from Miss Gibbon's hand, gazing at it as though she had never seen anything so precious. Her eyes gleamed and her face was flushed. She seemed to tower over Miss Gibbon and Amy felt a great need to cringe back into the sofa and curl up like a small child who has

242

been naughty and is waiting for retribution. Amy knew something devastating was going to happen but seemed unable to do more than cower away from this disaster that her instinct told her was about to descend on her.

'It was under the pillow of the man who looks after Mr Seymour's motor. Newbridge, I believe is his name. There were also these rings and a bracelet.'

'Does he know you have found his ill-gotten gains, Miss Gibbon?' Mrs Seymour was salivating as though she could not wait to get her teeth into some succulent dish.

'Oh, no, ma'am. He is still in the kitchen with the rest of the servants.'

'Very well. Telephone the local constabulary and ask them to send round a constable and a wagon at once. There has been a burglary and the culprit is awaiting arrest.'

Miss Gibbon bustled importantly from the room and Amy could hear her on the telephone but somehow she herself could not move or speak. She was paralysed with terror, not just for herself but for Joe. Her aunt stood over her threateningly as though daring her to make one move, to protest in any way and something inside her withered away and died a slow death. She must fight, she knew she must, but her aunt was a figure of such formidable strength, such absolute doom, and she, Amy, had no one, not even Mr Seymour, to protect her. If they took Joe away . . . Oh, God, oh sweet, loving Jesus . . . If only she could throw off this terrible lethargy, this frozen shock, get up and scream her defiance . . .

Her cheek began to twitch and she put up a

hand to stop it and Mrs Seymour smiled.

'You must agree, my dear, that Mr Seymour and I have found you a wonderful husband. Surely all our thoughts for you cannot displease you?' She watched dispassionately as Amy began to choke, then put up her hand to her eyes where, she found, the tears she had not known she was shedding had wet her cheeks. The tears did not stop but dripped on to her gown leaving large dark grey spots on the pale grey bodice.

'Come, come, girl, there is no need to take on. This affair of the stolen jewellery has nothing to do with you. Oh, I know you have become ... acquainted with this man, this servant and I strongly disapprove as you must know, but we need say nothing to Mr Hodge. The thief will be taken away and put in prison until he is charged and that is the last we will hear of him. When the case has been heard you will have your locket returned to you.'

She crossed the room and looked out of the window. 'Ah, here is the police van. How very prompt. I must go and speak to the constables, two of them I see, and have the man arrested. Perhaps it might be as well if you were to go to your room.'

Amy sprang frantically to her feet. 'Please, please, Mrs Seymour, don't blame Joe.'

'*Joe!* You dare to call the man by his Christian name,' Zillah thundered. 'He comes from the orphanage and who knows what tricks he picked up there. Other items have gone missing in the past and now we know who is the culprit.'

'He would not steal from you or from me, madam.' The 'madam' infuriated Zillah even further. 'There has been some terrible mistake. He has worked for Mr Seymour for years and is honest as the day. Ask the others.'

'There is no need to ask the others. The police will take him to the police station and question him there, then decide if he is to be charged but I hardly think he could be found otherwise. The ... the ... er, *goods* were discovered under his pillow by—'

Amy's voice was passionate. 'Rubbish! They were put there by the woman who is your creature and would do anything you asked.' Tears poured unchecked from her eyes, drowning them, drenching her waxen cheeks. Even her nose dripped and Zillah looked at her with disgust.

'For pity's sake, girl, pull yourself together and wipe your nose. You still seem to have guttersnipe tendencies, I see, even after the years of training to be a lady. Now I must go and attend to the matter.'

The doorbell rang but it was not Alice who answered it, for she had been instructed to stay in the kitchen, but Miss Gibbon with Mrs Seymour close behind her and at her back was Amy, crying distractedly, babbling incoherently, her terror so great she gave the appearance of being half demented.

The two constables who stood sternly on the doorstep were obviously astonished by the scene that met their eyes as the door opened. The mistress of the house was struggling with some young girl who seemed to be having hysterics but a cruel and vicious smack across the lass's cheek, which made even the constables wince, not only nearly lifted her from her feet but quietened her. She fell against the wall, one side of her face as pale as fresh fallen snow, the other a vivid scarlet.

245

'Do come in, Constables and go through to the drawing room,' Mrs Seymour—who was well known in Manchester for her charitable work—told them pleasantly, 'while my companion and I get my daughter to bed. She is obviously distraught at this turn of events.'

The constables, still shocked by the blow struck on the young lass, were bewildered as to why the daughter of the house should be so affected. They removed their helmets, placed them carefully under their arms and stood awkwardly where they were put.

'I will be with you in a moment,' Mrs Seymour told them, then she and the other lady half led, half carried the almost insensible young girl up the stairs where they disappeared for five minutes. The policemen shuffled their feet uneasily and looked about them, exchanging glances, waiting dutifully. When Mrs Seymour reappeared, she smiled at them. As one remarked later to the other privately, it reminded him of the smile of a hyena, a picture of which he had seen in his son's picture book.

'Now then, if you will come through to the kitchen I will point out the culprit of this wicked crime. And please understand I want him taken away at once. You saw how my daughter reacted so the sooner the villain is out of our home the better. These items—' pointing to the jewellery laid out on the table—'were found by a trusted friend, this lady here,' nodding at Miss Gibbon who stood becalmed by the door. 'She was instructed by me to search the servants' quarters when my daughter's locket was found to be missing—'

'Madam, if I could say a word . . .' One of the

constables was unwise enough to interrupt her but a venomous look from Mrs Seymour, who was after all the wife of one of the most powerful business gentlemen in the city, brought him to a stuttering halt. He was only here to investigate a man who had been accused of theft and it was not up to him, thank God, to prove him guilty or not guilty. When the man was incarcerated at the police station his job was done.

'Yes, Constable?' she said coldly.

'Well, madam, us only 'as the word . . .'

'Yes, Constable?'

'Well'—totally routed—'p'raps if we was ter 'ave a word wi't servants, like, one at a time an'—'

'Not in my home, if you please. I merely want you to apprehend the man under whose pillow these items were found. I want him taken away and questioned. The others can be . . . questioned later though it is beyond me why the word of two respectable *ladies* could be in doubt. You know who my husband is, of course?'

'Yes, madam. P'raps if we could 'ave a word wi' Mr Seymour an' all.'

'Unfortunately Mr Seymour is away on business but I can see no reason why you cannot deal with me in his absence.'

'Well, madam . . .'

'I will take you into the kitchen then. Perhaps if you could take the police van round to the back of the house it would be easier to facilitate the removal of the culprit.'

The extra green baize that Ernie Tingle had applied to the door between the kitchen and the hallway had done its duty well. The servants had been aware of something going on but had heard

247

nothing of what it might be. They had obeyed Mrs Seymour's instructions to remain in the kitchen, imagining that she might have some announcement to make to them all. They had chafed and muttered and speculated, drunk innumerable cups of tea, grumbled at the waste of time, since Mrs Abigail had a roast to see to and Joe was eager to get his head under the bonnet of the Rolls from where a strange ticking sound could be heard.

When the mistress entered the kitchen accompanied by two policemen, they were all astonished, staring with wide eyes and open mouths. Primrose dropped the roasting pan which, though already meticulously scoured, she had been told to wipe round. The noise made them all jump and brought them to their senses.

'I see you are all here,' said the mistress. 'I will not keep you long from your duties but these policemen also have a duty to perform. There has been a series of thefts . . .'

A collective gasp lifted into the air and again the constable did his best to intervene. 'Please, madam, it is my job to—' he began but Zillah Seymour was having none of him.

'Thank you, Constable. There is the man I wish you to question'—pointing a finger at Joe whose jaw dropped even further—'but not in my home. Take him away. If he is found guilty he will go to prison. If he is innocent, which I doubt, then he will be freed. You'—turning to the second constable who had been mute throughout—'fetch the wagon to the back door and quickly, then come back here for the prisoner. I wish to have this disgusting episode over and done with as soon as

248

possible. Now I must go and comfort my daughter,' who was locked safely in her room with Miss Gibbon but Zillah was concerned with what commotion she might cause.

Joe instinctively backed away when the constable, a burly chap, moved towards him and several of the men, Ernie Tingle among them, made a move as though to defend him.

'Now, now lads,' the constable said, feeling there was something not quite right about all this but powerless to do other than he was ordered. Thankfully the sergeant at the station would take over when they had the lad under lock and key. At that moment the second constable came in through the open back door and as respectfully and firmly as they knew how they each took one of Joe's arms and led him, uncomprehending, unresisting, to the van. He was put inside. The door clanged behind him and the van drove off, disappearing round the corner of the house.

They stood for perhaps a full minute before they came to life.

'Bloody, bloody 'ell,' from Ernie Tingle who crashed his clenched fist on the table. 'She'll do fer 'im, she'll bloody do fer 'im.'

'Not our Joe,' Mrs Abigail whispered. 'Many's the time I left cash on't table ter pay the butcher an' never so much as two brown halpennies went missing.'

'It's our fault,' moaned Jess, 'we let 'em get fond o' one another. She found out an's gettin' rid of 'im.'

'Aye, poor lad; poor lass . . .' Alice threw her apron over her head and wept uncontrollably.

They heard the screaming then, even through

the thickness of the baize-covered door and Primrose fell to the scullery floor which she had just scrubbed.

*   *   *

The old doctor had been and gone. Amy lay on her bed, wide-eyed and unseeing. Her lovely face looked as it might when she had breathed her last. She had seen the 'paddy wagon', as it had been called where she came from, draw away with her life in it and though Miss Gibbon had done her best to hold her she had driven her clenched fist right through a pane of glass, screaming his name. But he was inside the wagon by then with the heavy door closed and did not hear her.

Doctor Parsons had shaken his head after they, himself, Mrs Seymour and the governess had forced the draught down her throat. Her hand was bandaged, needing a couple of stitches and would be scarred but not noticeably, he told Mrs Seymour, who he saw draw a deep breath since it was her left hand, though he was not to know she was thinking of wedding rings and not the child's welfare. He wondered out loud what had caused Miss Seymour to smash the window in such a way.

'She is highly strung, Doctor. She is to be married very shortly and you know how these young girls are.'

No, he didn't, but he was intrigued and going beyond his normal careful respect and, yes, his wariness when dealing with this woman he was emboldened to ask, 'Really, may I ask who the lucky gentleman is?'

'Well, it is not announced officially yet but I can

tell you he is a prominent member of the Church.' Mrs Seymour actually bridled, something the doctor thought was most unattractive. It was as though she had personally brought off a great feat and was rather proud of herself. 'His name is Mr Randall Hodge. We, Mr Seymour and I, are delighted since he is a man of substance, a man to whom we can entrust the future happiness and security of our daughter.'

They were descending the stairs as she spoke and only Miss Gibbon heard their conversation. She had instructions to dart back upstairs to lock the door to Miss Amy's bedroom door as soon as the doctor had left the premises and to make sure that it remained locked at all times. It would not do for Doctor Parsons to know that his patient was to be kept in close confinement until the day she left Somerfield for her new home in Weaste Lane. Zillah had had the foresight to ask the good doctor, who had no reason to deny her, for a further supply of the draught which would keep her daughter calm until her wedding day, that's if it was needed.

'I shall call again, my dear lady, perhaps tomorrow, to see how your daughter is doing and to dress her hand. We do not want it to fester, do we?'

'Is there any likelihood of that, Doctor?'

'No, not if it is kept clean. Perhaps a glove—'

'Then there is no need to bother you, Doctor. I can do all that is necessary and, by the way, my husband and I would be gratified if you and your wife would be guests at our daughter's wedding. The invitations go out tomorrow.'

Doctor Parsons too was gratified, so much so he

251

did not argue but climbed into his carriage and drove off. Mrs Seymour was a sensible woman and would call him if she needed him. He smiled as he imagined Mrs Parsons's delight when he told her that they were to be guests at the Seymour wedding.

18

It was the strangest, one might even call it the saddest wedding they had ever been to, the servants agreed, those who were given time off and told to attend. More like a bloody funeral, Ernie Tingle was heard to mutter in the back pew where they were seated. Little lass dressed in white but very plain, reminded him of the lily-of-the-valley that grew in great swathes beneath the trees, even her head drooping down like the top petals of its bell-shaped flowers. She looked overshadowed by her portly groom who was also plainly dressed in black. Her responses to the minister could not be heard by the congregation though the groom spoke out clearly and loudly. The mistress and master and the groom's sister sat side by side in the front pew, the master looking totally bewildered since he had only returned home the previous day but he had done his duty, leading Miss Amy—why did Ernie keep thinking 'sacrificial lamb'?—to stand beside the groom before sitting down next to the mistress. *She* looked well pleased. In the second pew sat that there governess looking very smug, a new fur tippet round her neck and in her pocket, so it was

252

whispered, a glowing letter to the new employer the mistress had found for her. She had been in hospital for a few days, no one knew why, and appeared to be in the best of health. Ernie often wondered how these two tit-bits of gossip had got about!

The organ played and, her hand in the crook of her new husband's arm, the lass moved down the aisle like a sleep-walker towards the chapel door which stood wide open, allowing the golden sunshine to pour across the threshold in a cheerful stream totally in contrast to the sombre mood within. Jess was sobbing openly and not for joy! The lot of them wished they were anywhere but here as the ghost-like child, for she was no more than that, was led into the porch by her triumphant husband. Mr and Mrs Seymour and Miss Hodge followed them, though to be honest Ernie thought the master was visibly distressed.

The servants all stood when the guests did, following them from the chapel, clustering in a group beside the path. Congratulations were exchanged. Smiles and pleasantries as the guests moved towards their carriages. There was to be a reception at Somerfield before the newly married couple set off on their wedding journey. The sister, Miss Elizabeth Hodge, was to be the overnight guest at the home of Mr and Mrs Seymour, as Mr and Mrs Hodge would spend their wedding night at Mr Hodge's grand home in Weaste Lane before continuing the next day to London and then on to the Continent, though Ernie wondered how far they would get with the way events were shaping up. Not that Ernie was knowledgeable about what seemed to be a looming crisis but he knew enough to know that trouble was coming. What Russia and Germany and France, and now Great Britain, were wrangling over was a mystery to him, but there, he was an old, uneducated man and now that Joe had gone they were all sadly lacking in explanation of the news. Serbia, wherever it was! What had that got to do with anything the British working man could understand?

They had all agonised over what had happened to Joe, missing his cheerful disposition, his willingness to help out with anything, no matter what, his mischievous cheek which was never rude. With him in prison on a daft charge, and the little lass fastened in her bedroom with the missis, the house was misery and doom. The women cried at the drop of a hat and the men grumbled over nothing.

They walked behind the procession of carriages, Jess and Primrose arm-in-arm comforting one another, Ernie and Matt and Barty following silently, for what was there to say? Even Barty's offering of a small posy for the bride had been refused by the mistress.

None of them noticed the tall, rigid figure of a young man who hid behind the broad trunk of a hawthorn tree, nor, when they had passed by saw him sink to his knees and weep broken-heartedly. None of them saw him get to his feet, clinging to the tree as though mortally wounded, then stumble off in the direction of the city.

*   *   *

He kept touching her. From the moment they were alone in the closed carriage, his large, damp hand was laid on her knee, her cheek, the smooth flesh of her throat so that she wanted to scream as she shrank away from him.

In the drawing room at Somerfield he stood close to her with his heavy arm about her waist which many of the ladies present though somewhat vulgar. They drank toasts, as Zillah, so enraptured by the success of her plans, had even provided champagne, then Amy was led away to the bedroom in which she would never sleep again, her white wedding gown removed by Jess and Alice who both wept silently. They put her in the drab green outfit, her 'going-away outfit' as the mistress had artfully called it, a new bonnet and boots. She was led down the stairs where her husband was waiting for her. The guests simpered and nodded, the ladies wondering if this childlike waif would be equal to the ordeal that lay ahead of her, the gentlemen thinking the groom to be a damned lucky fellow and wishing themselves in his place. Not only was she the adopted daughter of Caleb Seymour, powerful and immensely rich, but she was sixteen and exquisitely pretty. No life in her though. She walked stiffly, mindlessly, as though she were drugged and at the last moment only came to life to cling to some weeping maidservant.

Randall's own carriage took them on the short journey from Eccles Old Road to Weaste Lane. It stopped opposite the three steps that led up to the front door where he jumped eagerly from it before the coachman had time to get down and open the carriage door.

'Come, my dear.' Randall almost pulled her from the carriage, urging her to the door which was opened by an elderly housekeeper. 'Put the

255

carriage away, Webb,' he called to the coachman. And to the housekeeper, 'My wife and I shan't need you again tonight so you may retire, Mrs Rogers . . . No, no, we need nothing to eat. We had plenty at the reception.'

His hand was in the small of Amy's back, hurrying her up the staircase. Mrs Rogers watched in astonishment, for it was not yet dark.

He began at once. He had waited months for this. He knew nothing of Joe and the wicked plan carried out by Mrs Seymour to persuade this girl, who was backing away from him in terror, to go through with it.

'Now then, my dear,' he said thickly, 'there is no need to be afraid.'

It was as though after two weeks of existing in the half-dark, stunned and afraid for Joe, the hollow shell of Amy Seymour had crouched beneath a glass dome like the one which lay over the dried flowers in the drawing room; the loud voices and the voice that whispered threateningly, she now finally became fully conscious.

'Once upon a time they used to hang a man for a theft over forty shillings,' the voice had said, which Amy knew was not true now but the thought of Joe in prison was horrific, so she had bowed her head and agreed to marry Mr Hodges if Mrs Seymour dropped the charges. Today was a blur, a blur of faces that smiled, or wept as Jess and Alice had done. Now it was here, the moment she had barely thought about. This man was her husband and could do as he liked with her which he proceeded to do.

He began to take her clothes from her, tearing her dress in his haste to have her naked. Randall

256

Hodge considered himself to be a pious man, a decent chapel-goer, doing his best to curb his ferocious sexual appetite. Only in marriage could a man be free from sin. Now and again he paid for the faceless body of some woman in town but was plagued afterwards with guilt. Besides which he ran the risk of being recognised. Now he could do as he liked, for a wife could not refuse her husband. It was the law.

He stripped her naked, gloating as he did so. At first she resisted and he hit her, knocking the sense out of her for a moment, then he laid her on the bed, arranging her to his satisfaction on her back like a starfish. After removing his own clothing he flung himself on her. His male member was as thick as Amy's wrist, long and hard as iron and when he penetrated her she screamed in agony. In the kitchen, Mrs Rogers, hearing her cries, cowered in her chair, alone, for Mr Hodge had given the rest of the servants the day off. She could do nothing to help the lass since she was old and was afraid for her job, though her heart was sore for the poor girl.

He brutalised her again and again, so carried away was he. It was not until he came to his senses and saw what he had done to her face that he realised she could not be seen in public in this state and would have to stay in their bedroom for a while. At this point, aware of her stillness, he thought he had killed her so he slapped her again until she blinked. They would have to postpone their honeymoon but that didn't matter. He rather liked the idea of locking her in, having her waiting for him whenever he fancied her. He would have to persuade Elizabeth to go and stay with relatives until his wife was fit to be seen.

On this happy thought, satiated and pleasantly tired, he fell asleep, his sweaty face pressed to his wife's bruised breasts.

She waited an hour. He was snoring heavily as she eased her wounded body, gently, slowly, inch by careful inch, from under his. He grunted but did not wake. She stumbled across the bedroom, finding it difficult to walk. There was her gown where he had dropped it. She struggled into it, her trembling hands holding the torn front of the bodice together where he had ripped it. She did not dare stop to find her boots, terrified he would wake. Closing the door silently behind her, she looked about in some confusion, for it was dark by now and she had never been upstairs in this house before and did not know the layout. But there in the dimness ahead of her were the stairs. Her bare feet made no sound on the carpet. Praying that the front door would be easy to open she reached for the knob. The door was bolted top and bottom. Remembering another door in another life, she carried a chair to it, stood on it and slid the top bolt. The bottom bolt was easy. She put the chair back, not wishing to draw attention to anything out of place, closed the door behind her and began to run. She knew exactly where she was going!

*   *   *

Dorothy Collins or Dodie as she was called, was just about to turn out her bedside light when there was a gentle knocking on the front door which she might not have noticed had Rags not barked. Who on earth could it be at this time of night? Not

258

Caleb, for he would be forced to remain at home on the day and possibly the night of his daughter's wedding. Besides, he had a key. Rags was barking furiously. She heard Myrtle go downstairs muttering about waking the child and, having got out of bed, was opening her bedroom door when she heard Myrtle shriek.

'Dear sweet God! Miss Dodie, Miss Dodie, come quick. Oh, ma'am . . .'

When she reached the bottom of the stairs, her heart in her mouth, Myrtle was on the floor holding in her arms the figure of a woman so badly beaten about the face that Dodie did not recognise her. She was barely conscious, moaning pitifully, her limbs contorted every which way as though she were no longer in control of them, her bare feet bleeding. Myrtle was patting her, saying, 'There, there, you're safe now, chuck,' though she did not know from what. Rags had stopped barking, sniffing round the supine figure, then he lay down and whined as though in sympathy.

The woman spoke hoarsely and with difficulty. 'Please . . . close . . . the door,' which still stood open. 'Don't . . . don't let him find me.'

Dorothy, still in thrall to the dreadful apparition on the floor, stepped round her and Myrtle and closed the front door and the woman seemed to relax in the comfort of Myrtle's arms.

'Dear God, Myrtle,' Dorothy faltered.

'Now, Miss Dodie,' Myrtle replied harshly. 'The bugger what's done this wants hanging. But us can't just lie here. We must do summat for't poor lass. Telephone for't doctor and then—'

The woman in Myrtle's arms came alive, clutching desperately at Myrtle as though the devil

259

had come to tear her from the kind arms. '*No*. No doctor. Nobody . . . nobody must . . . know.'

It was then that Dorothy knew who she was. Her hand flew to her mouth and her eyes widened in horror. 'Oh, Lord, oh, dear sweet Lord . . .'

'What is it, my lass?'

Dorothy had seen this woman, girl really, earlier in the day from her bay window, sitting upright in the Seymour carriage on her way to her wedding. Caleb had managed to let her, Dorothy, know he could not see her until Sunday and the reason why. Now that same girl was sprawled on Dorothy's hall floor, battered, bruised, obviously badly hurt and who could have done this to her? Surely . . . *surely not her new husband*!

'Please . . . nobody . . . must know where . . . I am. Please . . . tell no one.'

'But you need medical attention, Miss Seymour. No, it's Mrs Hodges now.'

'*No! No! No!*' the girl began to shriek but Dorothy knelt down beside her and spoke soothingly.

'Amy then; there, don't upset yourself any further. Myrtle and I will look after you.'

Amy's face was swollen and her eyes mere slits in the puffiness so that she could not see the kind face of Caleb Seymour's mistress but she lifted her hand and Dorothy took it.

'Look, Miss Dodie, look at her breasts', for the movement had parted the bodice of Amy's torn dress. 'She's nowt underneath.'

Amy's small breasts were covered with bites and bruises, one of them still bleeding.

Between them they got her upstairs to the bathroom where Myrtle filled the bath with warm water. Both women wept when she was naked, for were they not both female and could feel Amy's pain and shame. They put her in the bath and with careful, gentle hands sponged off the blood and ... and the other *stuff* which they both recognised. Myrtle ran downstairs for hot-water bottles, preparing a bed in the pretty spare bedroom. They patted her dry tenderly, put her in one of Dorothy's dainty nightdresses and Dorothy kissed her cheek. Together they tucked her in the warm bed.

'Leave ... the light ... please,' Amy whispered. 'I'm afraid.'

'Nay, my lass, I'll stay with you. See, there's a comfy chair by't fireplace. Now, go to sleep, chuck. Myrtle's here and you'll come to no harm.'

She and Miss Dodie exchanged a few whispered words at the door and the last thing Amy was conscious of was the kindly presence of the servant, a shawl draped about her shoulders, sitting in the chair which she had dragged beside the bed.

*　　　*　　　*

Caleb was just about to set off on his chestnut mare, Blossom, eager to see Dodie and Willy when the telephone rang. He ignored it, allowing Alice, who had just handed him his bowler hat, to answer it. He was astounded when she held the earpiece from her ear as though the sound of a brass band were erupting from it.

'Excuse me, sir,' she cried at last into the mouthpiece, 'excuse me, I'll get the mistress ... yes, yes, sir, I understand,' though clearly she

261

didn't. She looked helplessly at Caleb as Zillah came from the drawing room and grabbed the earpiece from her.

'Yes,' she said abruptly, then, to Caleb's surprise, gasped and sat down heavily on a nearby chair. 'Yes, Randall ... but she's not ... no, Randall, she's not here ... really, are you doubting my word?'

Caleb moved a step or two closer to his wife.

'Of course not, she is your wife. If she came here I would not let her in. God tells us that a man and his wife ... really, Randall, there is no need to take that tone with me. I cannot believe ... have you searched the house and gardens? Of course I will ensure she is not in our grounds. Please, Randall, calm down, Randall, she will soon be found.' There was a pause. 'What? No police ... but she must be looked for ... Why not? We must have ... well, you are her husband and have the right to ... Very well, if she comes here I will hold her until you arrive.'

Zillah replaced the earpiece then turned to Caleb. 'The girl has gone,' she said simply. 'The boy was discharged yesterday once I had dropped the charge and she promised she would ...'

Caleb felt the rage run through him, knowing the urge to put his hands about his wife's neck and squeeze until she was dead. His hatred was white-hot and his eyes red and deadly. 'So that's how you did it, you bitch. You blackmailed her. Forced her into this ... this marriage. Do you not know that blackmail is against the law and a sin before your God? I hope He strikes you dead and you burn in hell for ever. I cannot bear to look at you. And I will never share a roof with you again. That child,

262

that poor child. If I had been here . . .'

He turned on his heel, ran down the steps and mounted the mare Tim held for him. He had never ridden so hard and so fast in his life in his eagerness to get to the sweetness and sanity of Dodie and Willy. People on the pavement stopped and stared until he reached Langworthy Road.

The home he had bought for Dodie was small, friendly, detached and stood at the end of a long garden. The grass was closely cut and green and the roses were in full bloom. It was of good red brick with a bay window on either side of the porch and three windows above. It was on a corner and as he passed the house and turned into Sandy Lane there was a high double gate let into an equally high wall, the gate wide enough to take a carriage. There was a coach house and stable and beside and beyond that a large, well-kept garden. Opposite the side of the house was a wooded area and he had chosen it because a discreet man, on horseback or in a carriage, could enter and leave with neighbours none the wiser.

He leaped from his horse, opened the gate and led the animal inside. A man, well into his sixties, but spry, ran forward and took the mare, leading it to the stable. Before he had crossed the yard Dodie had run out to meet him, the expression on her face ranging from anger and compassion to downright misery. She fell against his chest and his arms went round her. The man, Angus, turned away hurriedly.

'Dear God, what is it? Not . . . not the child?' Caleb's voice was hoarse.

'No, oh, no, my love. Oh, Lord, I don't know where to begin.'

263

'Come inside, dearest.'

'Yes. Oh, Caleb . . .'

They entered the kitchen where Myrtle was sitting at the table watching William colouring in a book. He looked up, a bright handsome boy of almost three years old, then flew to his father and grasped him round the legs.

'Papa, Papa, come see . . . come see . . .'

'Willy darling,' his mother said. 'Mama and Papa must talk first. You stay with Myrtle because she needs help to make gingerbread men then Papa and I will look at your picture. We might even go for a walk in the wood . . .'

And at once the boy looked enthusiastically at Myrtle, for he did love gingerbread men. Dodie turned and whisked Caleb into the hallway.

'She's here, Caleb.'

Caleb looked bewildered. 'Who's here?'

'Your daughter, Amy.'

'*Amy*, but . . .'

'She came last night, very late. We had gone to bed when she knocked on the door and when Myrtle opened it she fell inside.'

'Dodie, my love, what are you talking about? Amy . . .'

Dodie began to cry broken-heartedly. 'Oh, Caleb, you should see her. She is badly injured.'

'What!'

'Her husband has abused her, bitten her, beaten her, raped her; she is badly torn . . . down there and her body is covered in bruises. Her face, her poor face, she cannot see her eyes are so swollen and can barely speak.'

'Have you telephoned the doctor?'

'She won't allow it.'

'Won't allow it? But she must have medical attention if she is as injured as you describe.'

'She is terrified. She says no one, *no one* must know where she is in case he gets to know. He must be a monster.'

Caleb stared over her shoulder, his eyes hard and unfocused. 'Why did she come to you?'

'I don't know. I saw her once in the carriage with Mrs Seymour on her way from the chapel when I was at the garden gate. We smiled at one another and I remember thinking what a sad smile. Also, somehow, she knew of our relationship and the boy, our son, but she told no one.'

He moved towards the stairs, Dodie still clinging to his arm. 'I must see her, talk to her.'

'I doubt she will speak to you, darling. She is too ill.'

'Then we must employ a nurse. You cannot look after her.'

'I must. She trusts me or she would not have come here.' Her sweet face hardened and he bent to kiss her.

*   *   *

She lay neatly in the bed where Dodie and Myrtle had put her. Nothing could be seen of her injuries except her face on the pillow which Caleb found hard to recognise. It was dark with bruising, so swollen she could not open her eyes. Her mouth was split and torn and Caleb shuddered to think what the covers hid.

It was at that moment he admitted to himself how much he loved this brave child.

265

19

They stood for several moments while Dodie waited for Caleb to recover.

'Let me go first,' she whispered, approaching the bed and placing a hand gently on Amy's forehead. Amy turned towards her and tears seeped from her swollen, closed eyes.

'Who . . . ?'

'It's Dodie.'

'Dodie, you have been so kind.'

'Not at all, sweetheart. I've brought you a visitor.'

At once Amy began to struggle so fiercely and scream so hoarsely one might have imagined her husband had just entered the room. As she did so the covers were dislodged, slipping down her threshing body. She wore one of Dodie's pretty nightdresses, its low-cut revealing neckline exposing her neck and one shoulder and the top half of her small breasts. The bruises and bites were horrific and Caleb gasped in shock. He was speechless and his groan of distress reached the girl on the bed who was fighting with Dodie to escape and reach the window with the evident intention of throwing herself through it.

'No . . . No, Amy, it's all right, really. It is Caleb who had no idea you were here. He is as appalled as Myrtle and me. And I can assure you he will not harm you or reveal your whereabouts.'

'He will. He will tell *him* or *her* and they will fetch me back and if that happens I will throw myself in the Irwell. Oh, please, Mrs . . . Mrs . . .

Dodie, send him away. He gave me to . . . to that man . . . please, let me go. I will . . .'

The gentle voice from the doorway brought her broken-hearted pleas to a halt.

'Amy, my dear, would any man send his daughter back to that . . . that beast who did this to you? Dodie and I and, of course, Myrtle are the only ones who know you are here. I was told you had run away from your husband's house.'

He saw her shudder and collapse against Dodie's shoulder where Dodie held her tenderly for a moment before tucking her back beneath the covers.

'He telephoned this morning to say you were missing and a hue and cry has been set up. But strangely he would not have the police called in.'

'That's because he . . . wants . . . no one to see me like this. To see . . . what he did to me.'

'Yes, my dear. I also want you to know that if I had been home I would not have allowed the marriage. Though I have not been given full rein to show my affection, I am very fond of you and I am ashamed of what I let her . . . do to you. You shall not go back to Mr Hodge, but, my dear, you need a doctor.'

'She does need stitching, Caleb,' Dodie said vehemently.

At once Amy began to thrash about again but Caleb took a great chance and moved from the door to the other side of the bed. He put his hand lightly on hers which lay outside the cover and was appalled when she recoiled as though a cobra threatened her.

'Don't touch me . . . don't, don't . . . oh, please . . .'

267

He withdrew it at once. 'I'm sorry, I can understand why a man's touch would be distasteful'—wondering at his own use of such a stupid word as *distasteful* when faced with the injuries inflicted on this child—'but I just want you to know that Dodie and I promise to tell no one where you are. Dodie and Myrtle will nurse you until you are recovered—'

'I shall never recover.'

He ignored the interruption. 'Then you and only you shall decide what you want to do, where you want to go. We shall call no one, not even a doctor. Myrtle is versed in herbal remedies and will help you to recover. She was a nurse in the Boer War before she worked for Dodie's family and I dare say if it came to it could stitch your wounds. I will go downstairs and ask her to mix you a potion to make you sleep then all you need to do is lie there and get better.' He paused. 'Amy, all men are not as Randall Hodge, my love.'

'Joe . . .'

'Yes, Joe is safe now.'

'I loved him.'

'I know that now and he loved you.'

'Where . . . ?'

'We don't know where he's gone but he's been released from prison. Now rest . . . rest. I will send Myrtle up while Dodie and I talk downstairs.'

Amy turned her head painfully on the pillow and did her best to smile at Dodie. 'I heard . . . is there a child in the house?'

'My son, William. Willy, we call him.'

'I saw you . . . in the park. He was an infant then, in a . . . a baby carriage.'

'And you told no one.' Caleb bowed his head,

268

feeling the tears prick his eyes.

'I was glad . . . glad you had some . . . someone besides *her*.'

'Amy . . . oh, Amy, my dear.'

'I will never have children now,' were the last words she spoke before she turned her face away from them. When Myrtle returned she drank the draught that was held to her lips then fell into the healing of a deep sleep.

*   *   *

'She is a remarkable young woman, Caleb. So brave. You have told me something of her history. Snatched from her family at a young age, her upbringing in the strict Methodist ways but I had no idea . . .' Dodie paced the room in great agitation. 'And I tell you this: I will protect her with my life.'

'And I will protect you both, my darling, with mine.'

Caleb, who sat by the window smoking a cigar, spoke mildly though inside he was raging. The sight of the lovely, abused child who had lived in his home for six years had shocked him unutterably and he would have liked nothing better than to call up a couple of bully boys of his acquaintance, bare-knuckle fighters, to beat the living daylight out of Randall Hodge. Transform him into a eunuch who could no longer damage a woman. But he knew he was bound to respect Amy's wishes. And Dodie's. Dodie was the only woman he had ever loved, the mother of his son. He would die for her, for them both, wondering as the thought entered his head what the gentlemen with whom he did business and knew him for a hard man would make of that statement!

'You give your consent then? For her to stay here?' Dodie asked him, rushing to crouch at his knee.

He placed a loving hand on her shining hair. 'My love, you must do what your kind and gentle heart tells you to do.'

'And you will reveal to no one that she is here?'

'On my son's life, I promise.'

'Then we will make her better.'

*　　　*　　　*

She was a strong and healthy girl and within a week was sitting up in bed, the bruising and swollen flesh fading away from her face and enabling her to see. Myrtle had stitched the wound her husband had inflicted when he penetrated her delicate flesh. A small dose of laudanum obtained by Caleb from a chemist who owed him a favour had put her to sleep and with Dodie's help the wound was carefully pulled together. It healed quickly. Every day they put her in a bath into which a handful of salt had been thrown, old Angus keeping the boy amused and out of their way, and then soothed her bruises and cuts with oil of lavender that Myrtle had made up. Every day she took more nourishment but Myrtle insisted she sleep as much as possible with the help of a draught, also of Myrtle's making. Day by day her body began to heal but it was as though her mind had closed down, shutting itself in some sheltered place where it hid from the nightmare that had engulfed her. She turned her head towards them when Dodie or Myrtle or Caleb entered the room but they got little response from her when they spoke. She ate obediently when told to and even got out of her bed and sat by the window in the rocking-chair, watching the small boy and the little rough-haired terrier roll in play on the lawn at the back of the house. Myrtle or Dodie sat in the sunshine on a white painted wrought-iron garden seat to keep an eye on him, and his childish laughter, the dog's pretended growls drifted through her open window along with the fragrance of roses. The garden was quite lovely, tended by the old man who used a lawnmower pulled by a plump pony to keep the grass smooth. The borders were crammed with flowers of many colours, bright red Livingstone daisies, busy lizzies in shades of pink, red, mauve and white, begonias, sweet william, hollyhocks and lupins, the tallest at the back of the beds glowing against the high, red brick wall. It did not tempt her to leave her room.

Dodie brought her books to read, books she had never read since Zillah would not allow such depravity in her house. *Mansfield Park* by Jane Austen, *Pickwick Papers* by Charles Dickens and *David Copperfield* by the same author. Even *The Times* newspaper, for it seemed war had been declared while she lay in her bed but she showed little or no interest, evincing no more than a polite smile of thanks. She rocked for hours by the window so that they began to believe she would never recover.

Caleb had decided after a long discussion with Dodie and Myrtle, who was more than a servant to them, that despite his last words to Zillah he must return to Somerfield.

'If I don't go back, my love, she will make it her business to find me and that would lead to Amy. I'm inclined to believe that the child would do away with herself, or at least disappear from our lives ending up God knows where if she was found and forced to return to her husband. Yes. Yes! Dodie, she would. Don't you agree, Myrtle?'

He turned to Myrtle who nodded sadly. 'Aye, the lass is not in her right mind now and only t'good God knows what would would become of 'er if—'

'I wouldn't allow it, Caleb,' Dodie cried fiercely.

'He is her husband, my love, and has a husband's rights. Oh, I know the law is changing and that women are becoming more independent and in control of their own lives but I wouldn't trust that … that bugger. I apologise for my language, but until she is more herself she must stay here then get right away from Manchester and start a new life where she is not known—'

'Oh, no, dearest, I could not part with her,' Dodie interrupted tearfully.

'Then what is she to do? She cannot spend the rest of her life within these four walls.'

Dodie was sitting on the floor at his feet, her cheek against his knee and a tear crept down it. Myrtle watched them, well used to the way these two were with one another. She was not sure of Mr Seymour's age, probably in his forties and Miss Dodie was twenty-eight. They had been together for seven years ever since they had met in the home of Dorothy Collins's father. Edward Collins had been a small cotton broker in Liverpool with whom Caleb Seymour had done business. Myrtle had been with the family since Dodie and Bella, her sister, were young girls, when their mother had died.

The scandal, when it became known, had rocked the small social circle in which the Collinses moved, and had Isabel, a year older than Dorothy, not already been married, would have spoiled her chances for ever. Caleb Seymour was a married man. Dorothy Collins was unmarried, unspoiled, sweet and gentle but she was, on this one point, stubborn. She would have Caleb or no one, whatever the outcome. Cast from the family home she and Myrtle had moved to the pretty little house in Langworthy Road and as Myrtle described it had been as happy as two love-birds on a branch. When the boy was born she had been afraid for her young mistress but so far life had run on smoothly. What would happen when Willy was old enough for school was another matter. When this storm broke over Miss Amy, Caleb Seymour had been consulting with a solicitor on the question of a divorce; he would then marry Miss Dodie and his son would become his legitimate heir and perhaps there would be other children. Until Miss Amy was settled safely away from his wife these moves were presumably to be postponed.

The three of them brooded for several long minutes until, clapping the palm of her hand to her forehead, Dodie sat up, her face pink with excitement.

'Why didn't I think of it before?'

'What is it, dearest?'

'She could go to Bella. You know how good-natured she is and so is Johnny. Neither of them give a damn for convention, otherwise she would

273

have cast me out even though we are sisters. And with five young children and another on the way she would be overjoyed to have some help. And Broad Green is well out of the city.' She thought of the lively, cheerful, haphazard state of her sister's home to which, now that her father was dead, she was often invited. When Caleb was in Liverpool on several days' business she often accepted the invitation. She and Willy and Myrtle had enjoyed the happy-go-lucky atmosphere of Bella's home, Willy romping with his cousins and becoming as boisterous as they were. Bella's husband, John Carstairs, was a doctor at the Highfield Infirmary, which was only a five-minute walk from their home. They lived in a large, rambling old house that had been in Johnny Carstairs's family for many years. He had been born there and at the time of their marriage it had seemed only practical to move in with Johnny's widowed mother who was as woefully lackadaisical as her new daughter-in-law. She died in the second year of her son's marriage and since then a series of servants had come and gone, most unable to cope with their young mistress's sad lack of domestic management and the absence of any kind of discipline over Bella and Johnny's growing family. And yet they were the happiest couple Dodie had ever known, completely without prejudice hence their acceptance of Dodie's situation. If anyone could help to ease the pain of Amy's ordeal and at the same time hide her from her tormentors it was Bella and Johnny.

'What d'you think, Caleb? Are not they the very ones to bring Amy back from the terrible pit into which she has fallen and who could possibly find her in Broad Green? Only you and I and Myrtle would know where she was.'

She sat back on her heels and looked up at him expectantly then turned to Myrtle. 'She would be safe, would she not, Myrtle, and best of all I could go and visit her there. And she might even find her own family once she has settled with Bella. Really, I can find nothing wrong with it. I could not bear her to go to a strange place with people she does not know.' She whirled to face Caleb again, waiting.

'Well . . .' Caleb replied hesitantly. He himself would not care to stay in Bella Carstairs's rackety home for long. He liked order and harmony but he had to admit it was very carefree, noisy, of course, but perhaps just what Amy needed since she was but sixteen herself. Their rowdy cheerfulness might heal her, for she would have no time to brood. And Johnny Carstairs was a doctor so again there might be some advantage to it.

'Oh, dearest, do say yes. I know she is your daughter but this way you must see we would know where she is and that she is safe. Oh, please, Caleb.'

'We would have to wait until she is recovered somewhat. She has not even been out of her room yet.'

And it seemed, after four long weeks, she never would. Day after day while the good weather lasted Dodie urged Amy to walk with her in the garden, the back garden which was totally private but Amy resisted all her pleas and had it not been for Willy might have remained there for ever. It was inevitable really, Caleb was to say later, as his son was bright, with a young child's enquiring mind.

She was as usual rocking by the window when the bedroom door opened and when she turned her head listlessly to see who was there, a small, rosy-cheeked face peeped round it. For a moment they surveyed one another then the child, a little boy, the one she had watched in the garden, pushed the door open further and stepped inside. He grinned endearingly.

'My name's William,' he said, 'but my mama and my papa call me Willy. And Myrtle does too. What's your name and what are you doing in my house?'

Amy was taken aback but not afraid. She had spoken to no small child since she had lived with her brothers and sisters and over the last few weeks apart from Dodie, Myrtle and Mr Seymour she had neither seen nor spoken to a living soul. But this was a child, small, cheerful and harmless.

She sat up slowly, pulling the shawl she wore over her nightdress more closely about her though she was not cold and, for the first time in weeks, smiled.

'Amy,' she said.

'Mimi, that's a nice 'ickle name.'

'No, Amy.'

'I yike Mimi. Funnily enough,' he continued in his rather quaint, old-fashioned way, 'I wanted to call Wags Mimi but Mama said Mimi was a girl's name an' Wags looked like a bungle of them, wags I mean, so that's what we called him. Wags is my dog,' he continued importantly. He hopped across the room and rested his elbow on the arm of Amy's chair, his chin in his hand. He looked up earnestly into her face.

'I yike you. You're nearly as pretty as my mama.'

'Thank you, Willy. Your mama is as pretty as she is kind.'

'Yes, I know.'

He now hopped to the window which seemed to be his normal mode of moving from one place to another, leaning on the sill, natural, casual as young children are, expecting nothing from her. 'Oh, look, there's Angus. He's mowing the grass for the last time, at least he damn well hopes so! Did you know it stops growing in the autumn? Angus is my fwiend. You can be my fwiend if you yike, Mimi.'

'Thank you, Willy, I'd like that.'

They both turned as Dodie, flustered and out of breath, flew into the room, looking from one to the other anxiously.

'Oh, Amy, I turned my back for a moment and . . .'

'Dodie, it's all right, really.'

'I found Mimi in here, Mama. She's my fwiend.'

'Mimi?'

'Yes, that's her name.'

As small children often are he was as unconcerned at finding an unknown person in the bedroom as he might a mislaid book or toy. He had opened the door and there she was, accepted as nothing out of the ordinary and yet, as Amy was to find out, he could be as inquisitive, as curious, as questioning as any youngster.

'Why does Mimi sit in the bedroom, Papa?' They had by now become accustomed to Willy's name for her and they all made an effort to call her by it. Should Willy let slip to someone out of the house, a tradesman for instance, that Mimi was

277

staying with them it could not be connected to the missing Amy Hodge who was by now believed to be no longer alive. Willy spoke very well for a child of his age since he mixed only with adults except for Angus who listened to him but rarely answered except with a grunt.

'Because she has been poorly, my son.'

'When will she be better?'

'Soon, I hope.'

'When is that, Papa?'

To a child 'soon' could be in five minutes, an hour, certainly no longer and certainly not 'some time'.

'Not long, Willy. Now go and get your book and I will read to you.'

'But I want Mimi to come and play in the garden with me, Papa.'

'Go and ask her then.'

Which Willy did, time and time again, but though they played some good games in the bedroom, 'lions and tigers', 'camping'—under the tablecloth on the round table—'soldiers', which was very popular now that there was actually a war on, he longed to get her into the garden to run and jump and play with Rags.

'Please, Mimi, please,' he begged until at last she said she would if only she had something to wear.

'I cannot go out in my nightdress, Willy,' she told him, thinking that would be the end of it but in the next few minutes he dragged his mama into the bedroom with a pile of dresses over her arm.

'See, Mimi, Mama has loads of dresses and there is one very pwetty one I think you would yike.'

She and Dodie exchanged resigned looks and before she could speak she was taken behind the screen and, wearing Dodie's undergarments, emerged in the rose-coloured woollen gown, the plainest Dodie possessed. Willy and Dodie were enchanted, clapping their hands and standing her before the mirror where her reflection struck her mute. For years she had worn grey, navy blue or black but with the rosy pink tinting her cheeks she was quite beautiful.

'There,' Willy said triumphantly. 'Now get your shawl and come into the garden, Wags is waiting for us,' towing her through the bedroom door and down the stairs.

*   *   *

Caleb was struck quite dumb when he came home that evening, for she sat in the drawing room with a glass of wine in her hand, clinging somewhat to Dodie but out of the bedroom where she had been hiding all these weeks. She was the same size as Dodie, perhaps a bit taller but the fashion was to show a bit of ankle these days so it did not matter.

Caleb had just come from Somerfield where, as usual, he had listened to Zillah's tirade against life which had treated her so badly. She and Randall were forever at odds because she wanted the police to take over the search for her ungrateful missing daughter, Randall's wife, but he was still adamant that they should not be brought in. Randall was afraid that if she was found before he could get to her she would tell her tale of their wedding night and though there would be no evidence except her own word by now, his reputation might be smeared if it should get about that he had mistreated his young wife.

'What that girl was thinking of I cannot imagine,' Zillah complained, 'after I went to such trouble to find her a suitable husband. "Be sure your sin will find you out" it says in the holy Bible and so it shall. "Upon thy belly shalt thou go and dust shalt thou eat all the days of thy life" and you can be sure that girl, if she is still alive, will live to regret the day she left such a good marriage.'

'If you say so, Zillah,' for Caleb had learned early to switch off the words that fell from Zillah's lips. He had suffered her triumphant crowing when he returned to Somerfield after he had sworn to leave her but at least he knew exactly what was going on in the search for Amy. A private detective had been hired, she had told him and had been furious when nothing had come of it. The girl had disappeared off the face of the earth but she would not give up, and neither would Randall.

It was then he realised that it was time for Amy to leave Langworthy Road and move to Broad Green to the safe haven of Dodie's sister's home.

20

The three women were in the full black of mourning. Veils shrouded their faces and fell almost to their waists and even the small boy who clung to the hand of one of the women was in a diminutive black suit and cap.

The station was alive with soldiers. They made a

280

wide and respectful berth of the three women, for already in this, the fourth month of the war, many families had lost men in the battlefields at the front, as it was called. The BEF, British Expeditionary Force, some 160,000 of them, had opposed the Germans at Mons and the First Battle of Ypres and had been virtually destroyed. Perhaps these women were numbered among them.

But these men, shouting cheerfully, whistling, even singing 'It's a Long Way to Tipperary' which was a great favourite, were not inclined to dwell on that. They were part of 'Kitchener's Army', hundreds of thousands of volunteers who could not wait to get over there. They wore their uniforms proudly, khaki tunics and pantaloons and puttees, a service cap with the badge of the 2nd Lancashire Regiment pinned to the front. A great many belts, straps and pockets hung about them but as yet these raw recruits had no rifles.

The three women, as they drove to the station, had been astounded by the crowds and long queues of men outside the recruiting office intent on volunteering as soldiers. Hundreds of them held up the traffic, excited as boys off on a holiday, cheered by the men and women they had resolved to defend.

London Road Station, the very one from which the young, optimistic Amy had once left for Liverpool in her search for her family, was thirty-one miles from Lime Street, the destination of the three women. They climbed into a first-class compartment which had been reserved for them and even when, with a shrieking whistle and a great chuffing of smoke, the train began to move, the women did not remove their veils.

It had taken many weeks to persuade Amy to leave the safety of Dodie's home and that this was the only way in which she might, if they were careful and cunning, leave Manchester to start a new life in Broad Green.

'Dodie, I cannot expect your sister to feed, clothe and house me. I must make a living.'

'Believe me, dearest, you will certainly earn your keep with Bella. The children are wild and naughty, completely out of hand, five of them and soon to be a sixth. You will be invaluable to her, particularly now, and what's more, you will be safe. Far away from . . . from those who would harm you. Isn't that so, Caleb?'

They had just dined on Myrtle's good vegetable soup, veal chops, home-grown potatoes and newly picked peas, all with the purpose of 'building up' Amy's health; apple pie and thick cream followed by cheese, Stilton which was Caleb's favourite, celery and a glass of port for the master. The ladies drank a decent white wine and Amy certainly looked as though the building-up process was succeeding. She wore one of Dodie's elegant gowns, this time a deep, tawny velvet that matched the colour of her eyes. She had become a lovely young woman since her stay with Dodie, the look of vulnerability, of suffering adding to her beauty. The expression only left her face when she romped with Willy and Rags in the garden. Her long, thick hair, a mass of curls now it was no longer dragged back from her face, was tied with a velvet ribbon to match her gown, small tendrils drifting to her forehead and over her ears.

'It is, darling,' Caleb answered. 'Amy, much as

we are reluctant to part with you, you cannot continue to live here like a hermit, a prisoner.'

'Oh, do not say that, Papa, please,' and at once the four of them, since Myrtle had just brought in the coffee, stared at Amy in amazement.

'I'm sorry,' Amy whispered, realising what she had said, 'but I cannot continue to call you Mr Seymour, nor Caleb. Uncle is . . . and I have a pa . . .'

Caleb stood up, moved across to her, and drawing her to her feet, pulled her gently into his arms. This time she did not flinch.

'My dearest girl, I am honoured . . . honoured to be so named. I think of you as my own and . . .' He could not go on and both Dodie and Myrtle brushed their hands across their eyes. It was a lovely moment. They had moved to the elegant little drawing room where the fire crackled and the flames leaped cheerily, the curtains drawn, for the days were beginning to shorten and the tender scene, so unexpected, was even more poignant.

Amy sniffed then sat down abruptly, as did Caleb, and the discussion continued as it had done many times before and was to do again. Dodie and Bella telephoned one another almost every day and several times Bella spoke to Amy until, at last, knowing she had no other choice, she had agreed and they had it all arranged.

A closed cab was ordered and on the day they were to go, Myrtle, Dodie, Amy and Willy climbed into it, Willy complaining bitterly that Rags was not to go with them.

'Angus will look after him, sweetheart,' Dodie had soothed and at last they were settled. Angus had opened the gates wide at the side of the house

283

to allow the cab to drive into the yard. The cabbie, who had parked at the front, was considerably startled when he was told to go round to the side. The gates were closed behind him, the ladies and the child got in, he climbed on to his seat, the gates were reopened and they were off.

The soldiers were to take another train which would carry them through Birmingham to London and from there to Dover. For the unseasoned soldiers packed into the cross-Channel ferries, the pleasure steamers and the cattle-boats pressed into service as troop ships, this was the exciting gateway to the war, the start of the journey towards the unknown front where the guns rumbled and flashed in the east. Among them was a Private Carter, Joe Carter, who had, as he queued at the recruiting office seen the sign above a business on the other side of the road. *Hire a cart from Carter's*. The name Carter was derived in the old days from a driver of carts and wasn't he a driver? A driver of motor cars not the old-fashioned carts but it seemed appropriate and he was reluctant, for some reason, to use his own name. He just wanted to disappear into the vast anonymity of the army, losing his name and identity and perhaps his life into the bargain. It didn't really matter.

*   *   *

Not until she was safely inside Bella Carstairs's large, rambling, noisy house did Amy relax enough to remove her veil. There was a wooden hobby horse abandoned on the porch, one wheel missing, but even as they climbed down from the cab that had brought them from Lime Street Station there was a sound from inside the house that made her think of a horde of piglets squealing. The door was opened by a red-nosed scrap of a maid with a cold and about her were a tumble of children from a crawling infant to a child, a boy of about five or six, and an enormous dog which at once jumped up at Amy, its paws on her shoulders, knocking her hat sideways. In between the infant and the boy there were three others all jumping with excitement, clutching at Dodie's skirts and behind the group, smiling, her hand to her enormous stomach, was Bella. She appeared to be oblivious to the commotion, and Amy could at once appreciate what Dodie had told her about the Carstairs household. Happiness seemed to emanate from every corner of the huge square hallway and though the children had scuffed boots and grubby pinafores and the place looked as though it needed a good 'seeing to' as Mrs Abigail would have said, it was evident that Bella didn't care a jot. She was not as pretty as Dodie and certainly not half as well dressed but she was surprisingly attractive due, no doubt, to the deep, contented expression on her smooth face.

'Come in, come in, do. Arthur, do not pull at Aunt Dodie like that and do hold Muffin before he has Amy—it is Amy, is it not?—flat on her back. Georgie, mind Georgie, Jack, don't step on him; poor baby, did Jack step on you then?' bending down to pick up the infant and cradling him somehow over her swollen belly.

Amy had been quiet and lifeless during the cab drive from the station along the streets of Liverpool, gazing through her veil at the

285

unfamiliarity and yet *familiarity* of the houses, for the rows and rows of dwellings through which they passed were exactly like the ones where she had grown up. As a child she had never ventured this far away from the river but in this joyful atmosphere she found herself responding to the noise, her spirits lifting at the laughter, the loving warmth between the two sisters. The children never stopped talking, shouting really, every one of them at once, never listening to one another, drawing Willy into their tumultuous welcoming world, begging him to come and see their soldiers, their dolls, their trains, their books and the kittens in the stables. Yes, kittens, real kittens! And the macaroons. They were sure Willy had never tasted macaroons like the ones Mrs Topsy had made for tea and at last Bella, the baby struggling to get down and briskly crawl after the others determined not to be left out, led the three women into an extremely large and untidy drawing room.

'Darling, take off that ghastly hat and cape, and you too, Myrtle, and let me look at Amy. How pretty you are, just as Dodie told me, but you will want tea. Daisy'—to the draggled little maid—'go and ask Mrs Topsy for tea. The children call her that because they can't pronounce her name which is Topladyson, would you believe. She has been here for ever and what I would do without her I cannot imagine. You know how I am at cooking, Dodie. Well, she cooks and cleans with Daisy and a woman who comes in once a week to do the rough stuff but it is the children who need someone, so if Amy thinks she could be happy here I cannot tell you what—'

'For heaven's sake, Bella Carstairs, will you stop

talking for a minute and let someone else have a say. Yes, this is Amy who we all love and you will too, won't she, Myrtle? Amy, my love, do sit down if you can find a chair without something on it. Lord, what *are* those children up to? I never heard such a racket in my life.'

'Oh, they'll be all right,' Bella said vaguely, lowering herself cumbersomely into a deep, wide armchair. 'Oh, Lord, I shouldn't sit in this chair, I keep forgetting. Once I'm in it I can't get up, but only another fortnight, or so Johnny says. Ah, here is Daisy with the tea.'

To Amy's relief nothing was asked of her but to sit in peace and drink her tea. Dodie, Bella and Myrtle talked on and on about anything that came into their heads. The past, the future with this awful war which would, of course, be over by Christmas, everyone said so, the children, the hospital where Johnny worked so hard, for already there were wounded men from the trenches, people they had known as girls though, naturally now, none of them recognised Dodie's existence. It seemed that Dodie was so content with her Caleb it meant nothing to her and she revealed to her sister, thinking that Amy was in that other world to which she sometimes escaped—often happening when they saw from behind their net curtains Mrs Seymour passing in her carriage on the way to chapel—that now the child, with a significant look in her direction, was safe, Caleb meant to move into Langworthy Road and try for a divorce. Quite a scandal but then they had survived the last one so . . .

It was at this point that Myrtle put a hand on Bella's arm to stop the flow between the sisters.

'I think it's time to get the lass settled, Miss Bella, so if you'll tell me which bedroom she's in I'll take her up and start unpacking.'

'Oh, Amy dear, how could we? I'm so sorry, talking about people you don't know but Dodie and I—'

'Please, Mrs Carstairs,' Amy began, wondering what that crash above their heads meant but since Dodie and Bella seemed not to mind, could she interfere?

'*Mrs Carstairs!* Bella, if you please or you and I will have a serious falling out. Now, if someone will get me out of this chair . . .' struggling to rise but Myrtle stood up and took Bella's hand comfortingly in hers.

'Stay where you are, lass. You just tell us and me an' Amy'll find her room then we'll go and see to them children.'

'Oh, really, well, just as you please.' And once more the sisters put their heads together in that careless way that seemed the custom in this happy-go-lucky house.

Amy's room was at the top of the house at the front with dormer windows looking out on the overgrown garden of fading summer flowers. It was large, square and comfortable in a haphazard sort of way, though it was evident Bella had done her best to make it cosy, homely, somewhere Amy could get away on her own if she wanted to with a deep, comfortable armchair to sit in and a shelf for books. It was painted white. Her trunk, which was crammed with Dodie's gowns—soon to be replaced by Amy's own which would be made for her by the fashionable dressmakers in Bold Street—and everything a young lady would need in

288

the way of undergarments, had been placed at the foot of the large double bed. There were pretty chintz curtains at the windows, a dressing table with a triple mirror and a padded seat before it, a handsome wardrobe badly in need of a polish, lamps and a cheerful fire crackling in the grate. And there were flowers, great chrysanthemums of bronze and white in a big copper vase. It was quite beautiful and even the dust on the dressing table seemed to add to the charm as though nothing of importance could be spoiled by a speck of dust.

'There, chuck, what d'you think?' Myrtle asked her.

'Oh, Myrtle, I love it, and the children and everything but I shall miss you all.'

'Nay, you'll not have time, Miss Amy.'

*   *   *

And Myrtle was right. From the first she was drawn into the hectic life of the Carstairs family, accepted as theirs, so that even when Dodie, Myrtle and Willy—Willy protesting loudly that he wanted to stay with Mimi and his friends— returned to Manchester she barely had time to miss them. John Carstairs turned out to be as vague and kindly as his wife, accepting Amy as though she were a member of his family. He was not handsome but tall, thin, with a humorous face and twinkling eyes. He adored his children and could see no wrong in them which was probably why they were so wild and happy. Arthur would go to school soon at Knotty Ash, ten minutes' walk away, and hopefully learn a little discipline if nothing else, Myrtle had said privately to Amy.

289

Amy completely took over the care, entertainment and education of the Carstairs children, finding to her own astonishment and satisfaction that she had a knack for it. Perhaps it was due to her early years as the eldest of her own brothers and sisters but now and again she realised, though her governess had repressed her and made lessons tedious and boring, she had given Amy a sound education, basic perhaps, but thorough.

She knew that Arthur and Helen were old enough to be taught to read so with John Carstairs's permission she ordered reading books, along with paints, brushes, crayons, simple jigsaws, pasting books in which she encouraged them to stick the pictures they cut out of Mama's old magazines, which with her careless disregard for anything that smacked of good sense she had piled up in a cupboard, and showed them how to make paste from flour and water. Mrs Topsy, as easy-going as her mistress, allowed them the run of the kitchen, directing Daisy in clearing up the resultant mess. Amy taught them to play simple games of cards, Snap and Happy Families and read to them from *The Swiss Family Robinson,* *Pinocchio* and *Gulliver's Travels* and though the younger ones did not understand a word, they liked to squeeze on to Mimi's knee and drowse an hour away.

For Arthur and Helen she ordered *The Only Way to Make Reading Easy* or *Child's Best Instructor* and while Jack, Angela and Georgie sat at the nursery table swathed in capacious aprons happily sloshing paint on to paper or each other, something they had never done before, but only because their mama had never thought of it, she began the process of teaching the two eldest to read.

Bad Lad Mad Bed Red Bib Nib and under each word was a picture of the object. Mad was a bit tricky but she acted it out until they all fell about laughing, and within a week she had made a little progress. They could only be kept still for an hour at the most, then, wrapping them up against the chill of the coming winter, she put four of them, two at each end, in the enormous and very elegant pram, as they were increasingly called, with their feet in the well, bought when it became evident that Bella was to be a very fertile woman. Amy took them walking on Liverpool's riverfront to see the boats that crowded on the dancing water, with Arthur walking beside her holding Muffin on a lead, Arthur's treat for being such a good boy.

Jericho beach was their favourite place, for there she allowed them out of the carriage, even Georgie who was just walking, and let them take off their boots and socks and they splashed in the mud, made mud pies, ran and shouted and bothered no one except a few offended seagulls then arrived home to hot baths, bread and milk and bed.

Sometimes it was Sefton Park with its wide open grassy spaces, its small woodlands, its lake where Arthur and Jack sailed their toy yachts; the palm house where, if they were very good, she treated them to lemonade and cream cakes; its drinking fountains where they invariably got soaked as they squirted one another and where they admired the statues of James Cook, explorer of Australia and Henry the Navigator, father of Atlantic

291

exploration, for Liverpool, which was, after all, their birthplace, was proud of its maritime past. It took her back to that day when she and Sammy and the others had gone to Princes Park with the dilapidated perambulator given her by Mrs Derwent. Her last happy day with her brothers and sisters. But that was gone though never forgotten and with the help of her new family she would find them again, Ma and Pa and Sammy and the rest.

So, with a combination of fun and discipline she began to tame the children who were put in her charge and of whom she became extremely fond, as she was of their mother. She had never been so contented as she was now, not since she had been dragged from Earle Street so many years ago, but naturally the association with these happy, privileged children invariably brought back memories of her own family who would be quite grown up by now.

The new baby came late, and they were almost into December before she arrived.

'Claire, I think,' said Bella, holding the scrap in the crook of her arm, gazing into the placid little face as though this were her first child, not aware of the pang of pain she was inflicting on Amy whose own Claire had been six years old when Amy last saw her. She would be twelve now and the association of the name and the realisation of the passing of the years added to Amy's determination to search for her mam, her brothers and sisters, though her feelings towards her pa were ambivalent. After all, it was he who had 'sold' her to Mrs Seymour.

'Where would I start looking, John?' she asked, as, several weeks later, the three of them were snatching a hasty dinner one evening in December. She called him John and not Johnny as Bella did, feeling that it was not her place as yet to use the pet name his wife did. The harassed-looking doctor who, even as she spoke, was getting ready to pull on his overcoat ready to rush back to Highfield hesitated for a moment. It was very clear that the war was *not* to be over by Christmas and already hospitals all over the country were beginning to fill up with the unexpected rush of wounded men. And Highfield was already playing its part. It would be Christmas very soon and Dodie, Myrtle and Willy were coming to stay, though Dodie was reluctant to leave Caleb over the festive season. He was still at Somerfield despite his longing to leave and live at Langworthy Road with her and his son but until he was certain that Zillah and Randall Hodge had abandoned their search for Amy he felt it unwise to lead his wife in the direction of Dodie where Randall's wife had sheltered. As he explained to Dodie, if he stayed on at Somerfield not only would it keep his secret life from his wife but he would know at once of any new development in their search for Hodge's wife, if any.

He felt guilt and sorrow that he could not divulge to the servants at Somerfield that Miss Amy was safe and happy in Liverpool, for they genuinely mourned her, thinking her dead, drowned most probably in the Irwell, as they had all been aware of her horror at being married to that awful man. Caleb had heard one of the maidservants weeping on the upstairs hallway, comforted by another and had almost given way but if one of them, not intentionally of course, should let out the secret to the mistress, Amy would no longer be safe.

Now John Carstairs paused for a moment, looking into the anxious face of the young, tragic girl whom his wife and sister-in-law had come to love and who he himself admired. His children, though still noisy and high-spirited, idolised her and would behave for her as they would for no one else.

'Perhaps by making enquiries at the hospital where your mother and brothers were taken, but after so many years and with the wounded flooding in I don't hold out much hope, my dear. Do you know which hospital it was?'

'They were all consumptive, I learned later, so I suppose it would be . . . I seem to remember my pa saying the Royal Infirmary but I can't be sure.'

'The Royal Infirmary? Well, if they were infectious they would not be kept there, Amy. They would be transferred to City Hospital East which is just for infectious cases. I could ask a colleague if he might look into it for you, and if the records are still available we might trace them. Give me your mother's name and your brothers', write them down on this pad. Well, I must be off, my darling,' he said, leaning to kiss his wife. 'I have a poor chap whose leg just will not heal. He was lying in what they call no-man's-land for two days and the soil . . . well, it is not fit for ladies.'

'I am no lady, John,' Amy told him quietly, 'and if there was some way I could help these poor men I would do it but . . .'

'You are needed here for the moment, Amy, but later, perhaps when Bella is completely recovered, you might come to the hospital for an hour or two each day. Well, I must be off.'

*　　　*　　　*

It was stalemate on the Western Front and Private Joe Carter watched with his 'pals' on Christmas Eve as the Germans placed Christmas trees on the parapets of their trenches. The temperature had dropped below freezing and they all listened in amazement as the Germans shouted, 'English soldiers, Happy Christmas,' then began to sing a carol which he recognised as 'Silent Night, Holy Night' though it was sung in German. From further along the line, as the Germans finished, 'The First Noel' from the British Tommies rang out clear in the frosty night. He wanted to weep, not just for these lost and homesick soldiers from both sides, but for all he himself had lost in the last months. He would never forget her. His love was as constant as the sun and the moon. He and thousands of others were enduring lice, rats, barbed wire, fleas, shells, bombs, corpses, seeing things that men should not be asked to see. Bodies stacked and rigid like firewood, others no more than bits of human beings, scattered in the most incongruous places, but the deep love and loyalties that had been formed in the trenches, the gallows humour, the knowledge that they would be in the front trench for no more than a week, held them together.

But her, his love, his star, his rosebud, would he ever learn to live with the fact that she belonged to another man? He didn't think so. Never mind, he thought, he might be dead tomorrow and it really didn't matter.

21

She hurried along Victoria Avenue, taking the short cut to the hospital. Her flat black shoes slapped the flagstones and she had to admit that though they were the ugliest footwear she had ever worn, counting even those Mrs Seymour had insisted on, they were comfortable and made walking and running and standing, which she did a lot of, much easier. She was already dressed in what she wore at the hospital, the hideous mauve check frock in coarse cotton with its high starched collar and the billowing linen apron with its wide white belt, and black stockings. Her curling mass of hair was parted in the middle and twisted into a bun such as she once had worn at Somerfield. Her cap, which she would put on as she entered the hospital, was in her pocket.

The war was now bringing in so many severe casualties, many suffering from the effects of gas, that she felt she could no longer stay safely at home and do nothing but entertain Bella's children. John came home with hideous tales of men with destroyed lungs, drowning in the liquid that their own bodies had created. It was an atrocity that could not be tolerated and he had confided to Amy that he longed to get over there and do what he called 'his bit'. Of course he knew it would distress Bella but with Amy to stand by her she would cope. Hundreds and thousands of other women were forced to manage, to let their men go gladly, the men so badly needed at the front to help to get this dreadful war over and he felt guilty that he wasn't where he felt he ought to be.

'But aren't you doing that now, John? The casualties need looking after here and the clearing hospitals in the south are sending more and more to us.' She felt quite proud of the 'us' though as yet she did no more than scrub and polish and empty bedpans. A small part but very necessary. She was sometimes allowed to stand at the elbow of one of the trained nurses while dressings were done, injections given and wounds cleaned and was told that, given time, she would herself be allowed to perform such duties. She had overheard one of the nurses tell another that the probationers were worth their weight in gold and she was damn glad to see them. Though many people pooh-poohed the idea and said that the Red Cross would never use them they had been proved wrong. Amy was proud of that.

But John chafed at the need to stay where he was, agreeing that he was doing necessary work, that he was a married man with children and would not be conscripted but it did not stop him from yearning to be at the front, working in the dressing stations or the hospitals behind the lines. Arthur and Helen had been taken on at the school in Knotty Ash and were dragged, much against their will, along the length of Thomas Lane by Daisy and deposited there, then Daisy hurried back to help Mrs Carstairs with the four little ones. Bella had declared bravely that she could manage without Amy who had fretted about helping the war effort ever since she had listened to the war bulletins, seen the long lists of casualties in the newspapers and wondered why a strong and healthy woman such as herself was not helping to finish this war. John's colleague had been unsuccessful in finding any trace of a Dolly Pearson in the records of the infectious hospital though a child, a Sidney Pearson, had been discharged in August 1908. Unfortunately no address was given as to where he might have gone. Amy longed to roam the streets, the hundreds of rows of look-alike streets, to find some lead as to the whereabouts of her family but she realised what a waste of time it would be. And besides, she was still afraid, even after all this time, that Randall Hodge or Zillah Seymour, unlikely as it seemed, might still be searching for her, or had employed someone to search for her and might they not have deduced she would try to find her own family and be looking in that vicinity.

It was at Christmas 1914 when Dodie, Myrtle and Willy came to spend a week with Bella and John that she managed to have a word with Caleb who was visiting for the day. She still had nightmares about that night she spent with Randall Hodge and knew she always would and still, despite the kindness of men such as John Carstairs, she sometimes shrank from the proximity of a man. She knew it was illogical but it seemed to lurk, that shrinking horror, somewhere just beneath her skin, as though a man's touch might break the surface and release something, a festering boil, a mass of nasty matter that would contaminate the fragile web of protection she had woven round herself. With the women, the children, with John and Caleb, it was held within bounds, but she knew she would never be whole again and the thought saddened her. She would have given anything to be cherished as Bella was, as Dodie was, to have children and a contented domestic life but she knew she never would. But somewhere in the very depths of her, just beneath her breast-bone where she supposed her heart lay, there was a memory of a young man, spare and hard and tanned by the wind and the sun he had worked in all his life. He had always been laughing, gentle, careful with her as though she were a precious piece of porcelain and she knew, though she could not exactly remember it, for it was overlaid with a nightmare, she had loved him. Where had he gone? Into which life, which part of the world had he lost himself and why, which was more to the point, should she care?

She turned to Papa, as she now called him, for the answer.

'Papa,' she said tentatively while the women were seeing to the children at bedtime and John had slipped back to the hospital to check on a difficult case of gangrene.

'Yes, my love?' Caleb said, drawing a cigar from the case he had taken from his pocket.

She waited until he had lit it then asked, 'Do . . . do you remember Joe?'

Caleb felt his heart miss a beat, as he had been waiting for this question ever since he had seen the lad released from prison and watched him stride away into the mists of what would be his future.

'Yes, dearest, I do.' He held his breath and nearly choked on the cigar smoke he had drawn into his lungs.

'Do you know where he went to when . . . ?'

'No, sweetheart, but if I were to guess I should imagine where all our young men are going at this time.'

'The army?'

'I would say so, Amy, but I could try to find out if you wanted to get in touch with him.'

She shuddered and he was appalled as he saw it, for she and Joe had loved one another, first as boy and girl then as a young man and woman. Randall Hodge had killed that, at least on Amy's side, as surely as if he had thrust a dagger into her heart.

'No, oh, no, but I would like to know that he was . . . all right.' She had gone through torment—what a pathetic word—physical abuse, humiliation, degradation, to save Joe from prison and it would be . . . well, she didn't know what she meant or thought, but perhaps that something good had come out of the horror.

She stood up and walked to the Christmas tree that stood in the corner of the room, fiddling with a shining bauble that needed no fiddling with at all.

'I could go to the recruiting office, pull a few strings and see if a Joe Newbridge has passed through their hands.' Caleb said softly. Just then John returned and the ladies came chattering downstairs and into the drawing room, saying the children demanded Mimi go upstairs to say goodnight.

With her hair hidden beneath the shovel into which her pancake hat was transformed and the tapes securely fastened, she began her day emptying the bedpans that had been filled during the night. Their stinking contents no longer distressed her as they had at first. She remembered some of the nappies she had put on her young brothers and sisters, and removing, soaking and washing them in the cold water buckets at Earle Street. She had fastened her mind on these and tried to think of these poor, suffering men as the infants her family had been. This was no worse, surely. She, unlike many of the VADs—Voluntary Aid Detachments—who had never so much as touched anything so down-to-earth as a dishcloth or a sweeping brush, had scrubbed and polished alongside her mam before Mam became ill. She was at the beck and call of the harassed nurses and sisters until her feet swelled in her sensible shoes, sterilising instruments in the operating theatres, holding kidney trays of instruments and later, as she became more experienced and was looked on as trustworthy and not likely to faint, watching as nurses and doctors probed and dressed wounds so terrible that only the most hardened of stomachs could look on with equanimity. Most of the medical staff realised that they could not do without the VADs. Amy took her work seriously and went to lectures, addressed by frock-coated doctors, on haemorraging, arteries, tourniquets, syringes, splints, irrigation of wounds, the last of which everyone hated, and which terrified the patient since it was so painful. She dwelled on the bravery of these young men who had once been postmen, clerks, gardeners, shop assistants and who had flocked to defend their country from the aggressor, unaware of what they faced. What a lark, they said, let's get across the Channel before it's all over and now look at them, mutilated, blinded, choking their lives away, crippled, wondering why they had been in such a hurry to destroy their young lives.

She had begun to notice that the medical staff

treated her in a slightly different way to the other probationers. For one thing she worked regular hours, nine to four each day, six days a week and was allowed to live 'at home', whereas the others slept in the nurses' home behind the hospital and worked in shifts as decided by Matron. She had given her name as Amy Carstairs, posing, with his permission of course, as a young relative of Doctor Carstairs. She could not call herself by any of her three previous surnames, Pearson, Seymour or the hateful Hodge which was her rightful one. She must remain anonymous though by now Caleb was pretty certain that Zillah and Randall Hodge had given up all hope of finding her.

But she must be back at Elmhurst in Victoria Avenue as soon after four o'clock as possible since the two eldest children, Arthur and Helen, returned from school full of energy after a day of being confined, and Bella just could not manage six children, even with Daisy's help. It was perhaps this that made up her mind. She thought longingly of her own sister Becky who would be thirteen now and what a wonderful nursemaid she would have made for Bella, who was resigned to releasing Amy for more hours at the hospital. When thoughts like this slipped through her head in the dark of the night she determined to redouble her efforts to find Mam and the others on her day off. She and Caleb racked their brains to think of some way to achieve this, to think of some person who might have seen them. It was on one such Sunday that Amy decided she would try Mrs Derwent again, for it was a long time since she had been there and perhaps if Mam was recovered she might have gone to visit her old neighbour. It was a risk and Amy was nervous about being seen in Earle Street but surely it was worth it if it led to her mam.

Caleb was on the point, six months after Amy's marriage and flight, of moving in with Dodie. He knew it would cause an explosion of massive proportions, not only at Somerfield but in the business world in which he moved but he was determined to go ahead. He had consulted a solicitor and was about to sue for divorce but the trouble was that Zillah gave him no grounds for ending the marriage. True, she would not share his bed, but on every other score she was, in the eyes of the law, a perfect wife and she had the doctor's testimony that any more children, especially at her age, would kill her. His only hope was that she would divorce him on the grounds of his adultery with Dodie once he had moved out of Somerfield. But he told Amy he would give her time to call on Mrs Derwent before he stirred things up—his own words and completely inappropriate when considering his wife and her beliefs—with Zillah.

It was the first Sunday that John had off in weeks; he was exhausted, drained, but willing to remain at home with Bella and the six children while Amy took a cab to the Town Hall where she would alight and walk the short distance to Earle Street. But what to wear? What disguise, if you could call it that, could she assume to hide her identity should Earle Street still be being watched by Mrs Seymour or Randall Hodge? She knew in her heart and mind, where sense was supposed to lie, that she was being paranoid, but her terror, her *horror* at what had been done to her was still so great she knew that unless she was completely unrecognisable she could not venture into the city.

Mrs Topsy who, unlike so many cooks, was a thin thread of a woman, wore the usual working woman's black. The fashions of the twentieth century were of no interest to her and the garments she wore had been made to last: a decent skirt and bodice, good quality, a warm shawl and a deep-brimmed black bonnet. She always carried a large, furled umbrella and an enormous black bag. Black boots and stockings completed the outfit.

Mrs Topsy was astonished when Mrs Carstairs approached her and asked her for a great favour.

'I cannot go into details now, Mrs Topsy, since the secret is not mine to divulge but I think I can safely say that we have all become extremely fond of Miss Amy. Yes?'

'Oh, yes, indeed, ma'am,' Mrs Topsy replied, completely mystified but ready to help if possible.

'She . . . oh dear, how am I to explain?'

Perplexed, Mrs Topsy shook her head.

'She needs to go across Liverpool to visit a friend of hers,' Bella went on, 'but she must not be recognised. Not that she has done anything wrong, you understand.' Mrs Topsy didn't. 'She has had a . . . a great wrong done her and must stay incognito, that is to say no one must recognise her. Now what I wished to ask you was . . . well, I know it sounds peculiar but would you lend her your . . . er, garments—your shawl and bonnet and gown—so that she might cross Liverpool without drawing attention to herself? Yes, you might look amazed but we honestly cannot think of any other way to get her to where she is going. She must call on someone; believe me, it is all quite above board or Doctor Carstairs and I would have nothing to do with it but . . . well, what do you say?'

*   *   *

February was nearly over when she walked along Earle Street for the first time in three years.

Mrs Derwent was scrubbing her scullery floor, whose tiles came up a treat if you used elbow grease and Mrs Derwent was a great one for elbow grease. They were a mixture of faded pink, grey and a pale brown and though many of the women of Earle Street had let theirs go until the colours were indistinguishable Mrs Derwent never had. When a knock came on the front door, a gentle knock as though the caller wanted to be heard but not noticed—and Mrs Derwent was not quite sure what she meant by that—she tchhed-tchhed irritably and hauled herself to her feet. She had planned to give the scullery a good going over and a caller was not welcome.

She opened the door and glared at the little old woman who stood on her recently donkey-stoned doorstep. 'Yes?' she said abruptly. 'I'm not buyin' owt nor 'ave I time ter listen ter any clap-trap about religion so say up and let me get back ter me scullery.'

'Mrs Derwent,' the little old woman whispered, 'it's me,' glancing up and down the street anxiously, then turning back and waiting patiently.

'Oh aye, an' oo's that then?' Mrs Derwent stood with her hands on her hips but at the same time she had a strange feeling that she knew this woman on her doorstep.

'It's me, Amy, Amy Pearson,' the woman whispered, taking another quick look up and down the street.

At once Mrs Derwent shrieked to high heaven with delight. 'Amy! Eeh, child, we thought we'd seen last o' yer, we really did. I said to our Edie—'

'Oh, hush, Mrs Derwent, I beg you.' With a mighty push Amy had Mrs Derwent, protesting loudly, inside her own kitchen and the door shut behind her. 'Please, be quiet, I want no one to know I'm here, that's why I'm dressed like this. A disguise you might call it.'

'Well, yer certainly foxed me, lass, but why fer God's sake are yer dressed like somethin' outer a pantomime? See, tekk that bloody daft 'at off an' let me gerra look at yer; eeh, yer that bonny . . .' as Amy shook out her hair, throwing Mrs Topsy's bonnet to the kitchen table. 'Wharra lovely girl— nay, woman—yer've turned out, but then yer was always a pretty lass. Now sit yer down an' us'll 'ave a nice cuppa. Lor', it must be wha' . . . I dunno . . . 'ow long since yer was 'ere?'

'I'm seventeen now, Mrs Derwent, so I suppose it must be about three years but I've never given up hope of finding Mam and the family. I know my . . . my aunt, Pa's sister, moved them somewhere but I could never find out where and neither could Mr Seymour who is, I suppose, my uncle though I call him Papa now and . . . well, I was hoping . . .'

Mrs Derwent stood quite still, the tea caddy with the old Queen's poker face on it clutched to her capacious bosom. The kettle was bubbling merrily on the fire, the steam hissing and spitting on the bright coals and the teapot, this with a picture of the old Queen's dear husband on it, stood ready to receive the tea.

'Eeh, lass, lass, all this time an' that auntie o'

yours said nowt.'

Amy leaned forward agitatedly in the chair where Mrs Derwent had put her, clutching Mrs Topsy's shawl about her.

'What is it? Oh, please, Mrs Derwent, is it Mam? She's not ... oh, please don't say she's gone?'

'Oh, no, chuck, yer mam's fine now as far as I know but, well, yer pa died a couple o' years back. Pneumonia, doctor said. 'E weren't strong, just like the boy Eddy, the one who died of consumption. Not like yer mam an' t'other boy. Yer mam's a cottage out Old Swan way, Fir Tree Cottage, an' the older ones are workin' an' yer mam as well. She works in a cotton mill an' they manage fine. That sister o' yer pa's left 'em alone when yer pa died but they're all well an' doin' champion.'

Amy felt the joy and the sadness merge and run through her veins like wine, at once heartening her and at the same time casting her down into sorrow. Pa dead; Eddy, poor little Eddy gone too, but Mam and the rest all thriving, working, with a decent roof over their heads and without that woman's help. Sammy and Elsie, both of them bringing in money, all of them breathing the good, clean, country air, perhaps with a garden attached to the cottage, hens, plenty of eggs, flowers, daffodils in the spring for Mam, vegetables fresh from their own patch, safe, safe but Pa gone. Poor Pa who had fallen apart when Mam was ill and, it seemed, never recovered.

She jumped to her feet and to Mrs Derwent's delighted astonishment threw her arms about her and cavorted round the spotless little kitchen next to the scullery, almost knocking over the bucket of water Mrs Derwent had been using to attack the floor and which she had set down when Amy knocked at the door.

' 'Ere, 'old on, my lass, let's gerr our breath back, like. Don't go off half blown. There's things yer don't know . . .'

'What things, Mrs Derwent?'

'Things what 'ave 'appened since yer was last 'ere. That woman what yer ses is yer auntie, she's bin round ere askin' after yer.'

Mrs Derwent opened the caddy and put three teaspoons of tea in the pot, forgetting in her flummoxed state to warm it. One teaspoon for her, one for Amy and one for the pot. A nice cup of strong tea would put a heartener in both of them, as there were many things that needed straightening out.

Amy was all of a fidget, wanting to get to the main issue, the whereabouts of her family, but Mrs Derwent wouldn't be hurried and not until she had a cup of the invigorating tea in her hand and her shins to the fire did she begin.

'It were about three months, November time, I reckon, since she showed up, yer auntie. Knocked on me door bold as brass an' asked for yer. Said she'd bin ter yer mam's first in Old Swan where she purrem, yer pa an' the kids when yer mam an' little 'uns were purrin the infectious 'ospital. Course, yer mam were 'ome by then an' yer pa 'ad gone. Well, ses her ladyship, seems yer'd married some important chap, like, then run off. Reckoned yer were mad or summat, an' she thought yer'd found yer mam. Accused me o' telling yer where yer mam was. As if I would. I knew there were summat not right. Oh, I 'eard from yer mam. She came ter see me right away after yer auntie 'ad given 'er what for but we didn't know yer was wed or owt really. Well, there was this bloke 'angin' about an' yer Mam said same at Old Swan. Bloody 'ell, she's a right one that auntie o' yours. She'll 'ave 'er own way, choose 'ow, but luckily me an' yer mam didn't know where yer was, not that we'd've said if we 'ad. Yer mam were out of 'er mind wi' worry about yer but there were nowt we could do but wait an' 'ope yer'd gerrin touch. But, lass, yer must be on yer guard. Jesus, what yer done to 'er ter purr 'er in such a paddy? An' wharrabout yer usband? What did 'e—'

'Don't, please, Mrs Derwent. I have no husband. There is a man whom I was forced to marry but our . . . our wedding night was . . .' She gulped, almost choking. 'He abused me . . . I will never forget it but I have some good friends who have sheltered me. I'm still afraid to go out but'— she smiled, that sweet, shy smile Mrs Derwent remembered from years ago—'that's why I'm disguised like this.' The smile deepened into a mischievous grin. 'Don't I look a sight, but my friend's cook loaned me the clothes. Now, if you will give me Mam's address I'll go right away.'

Her face was a picture of joyous anticipation. After all these years of waiting, longing, heartbreak and worry and now, in perhaps an hour, she would be in her beloved mother's arms again. It was sad about Pa but somehow, after his betrayal when he let Mrs Seymour take her away for money she could not quite feel the same about him or his death. She knew he had done what he had considered best for *all* his children without the support of the mainstay of the family. *Mam!*

Mrs Derwent rose to her feet and put her arms about Amy. 'Promise me summat, chuck.'

'What?' Amy wanted to struggle away from her, though this kind woman was only thinking of what was best for her.

'Go back ter yer friends afore yer go ter yer mam's. Talk to 'em. This chap yer call Papa sounds like a sensible sort. Think first, lass, mekk a plan. Don't go runnin' ter Old Swan all of a tremble ter get ter yer mam. Yer've waited this long. Another day or two can't 'urt. Promise me.' She peered anxiously into Amy's face then bent to kiss her cheek. 'Promise me.'

22

He and the rest of his battalion crouched in the shallow, narrow trenches, shoulder touching shoulder, the contact giving them courage. As usual there had been an argument over who should stand either side of him, and Pip and Corky, who had jostled with the others, won. There was a belief that whoever stood next to Joe Carter would remain unscathed and come out of the carnage alive. He had become a legend in the 2nd Lancashires, for he had been at the front since September 1914 and now, over six months later, he was not only alive but unhurt unlike the great percentage of new recruits who had lasted a bare three months in the first bloody months of the war. 'Their Joe' as they affectionately called him could walk into a barrage of bullets and pass through them as though they were no more than an April shower. When the first yellow smoke of gas came over they had been told to piss on their handkerchiefs and cover their mouths to save their lungs but only Joe and a couple of his mates survived the attack. They didn't even know why, they only knew that Joe seemed to bear a charmed life and if you were within an arm's length from him you would survive.

But for all their fears and the terrible conditions in which they lived, the filth, the lice, the rats as big as house cats from living off the bodies of the dead, the mud and the dirty water teeming with little black things, they all felt the spirit of optimism and excitement that day as they waited for the whistle to go over. This battle, every battle, had been carefully planned and prepared for. There had been hours of intensive artillery bombardment intended to obliterate German trenches and eliminate resistance and when the whistle blew they were glad to struggle out of their trenches. They climbed up the scaling ladders and through the holes in the front of the trench. As they had been trained, they formed up in a line with their rifles in front of them and started to move slowly forward. They didn't run though they longed to. Joe and Pip and Corky were aware of the men going down around them but they didn't stop. A man in front of them had his legs blown off by a shell. All Joe could see was his white thigh bones, the rest of his legs gone, but thankfully the man was unconscious.

They plodded on through the haze and smoke, walking across no-man's-land, doing their best to keep a steady pace so as not to become disorganised.

311

But the bombardment had failed to crush the enemy defences. In many areas the enemy barbed wire was uncut and the three soldiers, bonded together through months of fighting together, stolidly marched on until they came to this wire. Though they were accustomed by now to sights that no man should be asked to see, they could not but be shocked by the number of their comrades who, tangled up and crucified in its lethal hold, had been shot by the steady stutter of the German Maxim guns. The German counter-barrage was murderous, and on that first day of the battle the number of dead and wounded ran into tens of thousands.

Joe knew that he been ordered not to stop for a fallen comrade but 'Pip' Pippin was only seventeen, a lanky, good-natured lad from Liverpool, who had lied about his age to join up. He was screaming in agony, doing his best to free his hands to get to the bloody mass of his intestines which hung from his stomach.

Joe dropped his rifle and knelt on one knee, leaning towards the boy, their helmets touching.

'Come on, Joe,' Corky yelled, 'there's nowt yer can do.' But Joe either did not hear him in the din or chose to ignore him.

The shrapnel splinter scythed through Pip's head scattering his brains and ricocheted into Joe's temple. They slumped together, one unconscious, one dead, locked in a grotesque embrace where they lay until nightfall, over twelve hours, when the stretcher bearers found a man breathing, heaved him on to a stretcher and conveyed him to the regimental aid post, virtually in the line. From there with a cursory dressing to his wound he was taken, still unconscious, to a field dressing-station where he was given an anti-tetanus injection and an ambulance carried him to a casualty clearing-station ten miles behind the line. In a series of moves, hospital train to base hospital, he was to be shipped across the Channel.

A week later, in the same unconscious state, and with the same filthy, bloodstained bandage around his head, he arrived, with hundreds of others, at Victoria Station, the hospital train gliding silently and smoothly alongside the platform to avoid the crashing that distressed the terribly wounded men. As the train drew in, on a platform further across the cavernous station a troop train was about to draw out. It was filled with cheering, whistling, excited young soldiers on their way to the great adventure across the Channel. The VADs who had come to meet the hospital train prayed that the troop train would have gone along with the mothers and sweethearts who had come to see their lads off before the hospital train drew in.

Joe was unaware of those about him. The sister who was in charge of them all was directing, sorting, grading the casualties. Each wounded soldier wore a label, like a parcel about to be delivered and the correct destination must be ascertained. 'Stomach', 'Amputation of legs', 'Burns', 'Gas' and 'Head'. Apparently heads were to be sent further north and through the moans, whimpers and screams as a stretcher was bumped, Joe was oblivious. He was carried on his stretcher across the concourse without even a cursory examination and loaded on to another train bound for the north where, in a hospital as yet unnamed, a specialist dealt with head injuries. A brain

313

specialist, getting on in years and considered too old for front-line duties but still useful in this devastation. The hospital was on the outskirts of Liverpool.

*   *   *

Wearing Mrs Topsy's cloak and bonnet yet again, saying that if she was to continue like this she must get her own disguise, Amy prepared for her journey to her mam's. Seth, the yard man at Elmhurst, the Carstairs' home, had run to the corner whistling for a cab to take her to her destination, Fir Tree Cottage, which lay in a narrow lane off Black Horse Lane in Old Swan. She was in such a state of high excitement that Bella had to tie the ribbons of her bonnet.

'Stand still, Amy; see, pull your bonnet about your face. No, leave Amy alone, Jack, you cannot go with her, perhaps next time, and don't fiddle with those daffodils, Helen. Amy has picked them specially for her mama; well, all right, just one, but you know there are still hundreds under the apple trees in the orchard.'

'I can't believe it, Bella, after all this time. Oh dear, d'you think they will know me? It's seven years almost.'

'Every mother knows her own child, dearest.' Bella turned Amy round, looking her over for any possible flaws in her outfit which, though suitable for women of Mrs Topsy's age and rank, was not exactly what a young girl would wear.

'Perfect, perfect! Now remember what Caleb told you.'

'He said so much.'

314

'I know, but you mustn't run into your mama's arms. Oh, I know it will be hard but if anyone *should* be watching you must appear to be an elderly lady visiting a prospective employee. Step through the door and inside and then, when the door is closed behind you, take off your bonnet and ... oh, my love, what a happy ending. You must remember everything so that you can tell us all about it.'

'I will, oh, Bella, I will.' Amy's face was a rosy pink and her golden eyes seemed to be lit from within, a candle of love and hope, for at last this day had come.

'Now don't forget your daffodils.'

The cab trotted at a brisk pace along Thomas Lane. As they passed the infirmary Amy noticed the ambulances drawn up at the entrance, and registered absently-mindedly that more wounded were being admitted. She would be busy tomorrow, but at the moment she could think only of the next half an hour when she would be with her mam again. They bowled along through Knotty Ash, turning left into Alder Road and left again into Black Horse Lane then right into a rutted lane along which Fir Tree Cottages had been erected. Three of them set in short front gardens, the two at each end having a plot of land at the side.

It was a mild March day, for the month had come in like the proverbial lamb, the first warm day of spring. Skylarks were up and singing in the blue arc of the sky. There was a little stream running on the opposite side of the track where a carpet of primroses stretched along the bank. Coltsfoot and speedwell were in flower.

315

Everywhere birds were active, hopping and singing from every hedge and tree, and elm blossom opened out wide in the tree in the end garden.

The cab came to halt and several children busy in the gardens of the cottages stopped whatever they were doing to stare at the unusual sight. None of their faces was familiar but as Amy climbed down, the descent made awkward by the daffodils in her arms, she remembered the years between then and now. The children she had known and loved had grown up as she had.

She chose the cottage at the end of the terrace, smiling at the small boy who was pushing a box on wheels, playing some game of his own contriving. She didn't know him but perhaps Mam and Pa had had another child or children in the years between. Her heart was thumping madly in her chest wall, so madly she could hardly speak.

'Hello,' she said, 'is your mam in?'

He plugged his thumb in his mouth and stared at her with wondering eyes. The other children in the next two gardens had come out into the lane and the horse that pulled the cab was getting restless. Chickens strutted about in the plot of land to the side of the cottage, clucking and pecking, but there was no sound from the curious children.

'Shall I wait, ma'am?' The cabbie broke the silence. The children, country children who probably had never been into the city and certainly were not used to cabs, began to collect along the dry-stone wall that bordered the cottage.

Amy felt the first stirring of alarm. Their Phyllis and Annie, who would by now be nine and ten years old and would be 'playing out' since this was not a school day, were nowhere in sight. There was not a familiar face among the curious ones that looked at her as though she had dropped from another planet. A very pretty lady in funny black clothing carrying a huge bunch of daffodils was not something they saw every day. In fact no one except the rent man even came down their track. Their pas worked for Farmer Jackson at Fir Tree Farm close by and the fields about their homes were full of fine-looking cattle.

'Can I 'elp yer, chuck?' a female voice asked and from the back of the end cottage a rosy-faced woman emerged, wiping her hands down her apron. Her face wore the same expression of bewildered curiosity as the children's.

Amy turned to her in relief. 'Oh, I do hope so. I'm looking for Mrs Pearson—my mother. She lives in one of these cottages and I would be obliged if you could tell me which one?' She smiled radiantly and the woman blinked, quite bowled over not only by the young woman's beauty but by the way she spoke. Not that she was dressed like a lady but she certainly spoke like one.

'Yer'll mean Dolly,' she answered, and once again was almost blinded by the young woman's illuminated expression.

'Oh, yes, my mam's called Dolly. I've been separated from her for seven years but now, at last, I'm free to be with her. Oh, please tell me which is her cottage.' She looked about her at the row of fascinated faces and again that twinge of trepidation ran through her. Where were Claire and Billy, Dick and Annie and Phyllis? Surely, surely, on this lovely spring day they would be out here; or were they working, earning a few bob? Please, Mam ... where? But from the other

317

cottages two more women appeared, drawn by the sight of the cab and the drama that was taking place in their normally uneventful lane. Neither of them was Dolly Pearson.

The daffodils fell in a golden cascade at her feet and she swayed against the gate post. The first woman moved towards her, her hand out to steady her but Amy drew herself upright. Her face was the colour of putty and her eyes were a flat muddy brown. The horse whinnied and the cab-driver cleared his throat impatiently.

'She's no longer here, is she?' Amy's voice was no more than a croak.

'No, lass. Not for months now.' She turned to call over the wall to the other woman, the one in the middle cottage.

' 'Ow long you bin 'ere, Mrs Fryer?'

'Since last November. Farmer Jackson ses there's a cottage goin' to our Bert; we was livin' in a terrace on Oak 'Ill Park. A long tramp fer Bert so this were a godsend.'

The first woman turned pityingly to Amy who stood rigidly by the gate. 'A woman come in a cab just like this 'un. A right owd biddy she were an' all. Called my Alfie a ragamuffin. She were in wi' Dolly fer an 'our or more. Next day Dolly and the kids put their bits an' pieces on a 'and cart an' went off. Nay, lass, I'm that sorry. Dolly were that upset she couldn't speak. Farmer Jackson come over, Sammy worked fer 'im, see, a right good lad, 'e said, but none of us know where they went. Eeh, lass, come in an' 'ave a cuppa tea.'

'No, thank you,' Amy said politely. 'You have been most kind . . . the cab, you see, thank you . . .'

Blindly she turned and blindly she climbed into

318

the cab. The driver had a bit of trouble turning the cab in the narrow lane, watched by the three women and the horde of children.

'Back to Elmhurst, chuck?' the cabbie asked.

She didn't answer so he clucked to his horse and set off at a smart lick. He'd wasted enough time on this peculiar fare as it was.

*   *   *

Bella wished she would cry. After a curt 'she wasn't there' Amy had barely spoken a word. John, coming from the hospital white with exhaustion, had done his best to talk to her, gently coaxing her to tell them what had happened but after those first three words she seemed unable to say anything else. She didn't know, she said, and after the eager expectation and anticipation of the last few weeks it seemed all the lovely life of her had been extinguished. All she felt was hatred. Hatred of the woman who had done this to her. The woman who had ruined her life seven years ago and continued to do so. She had exacted her revenge in a way she knew would hurt Amy the most. Four months ago, after searching for Amy and being unable to find her and return her to the husband Mrs Seymour had chosen for her, she had turned Amy's family out on the street and they had disappeared.

'We'll look for them, darling,' Dodie, who had come on the first train from Manchester after a frantic telephone call from Bella, assured her. 'Caleb has many contacts in Liverpool and will find them. The youngest must go to school somewhere and the eldest ones will be working

319

and your mother is strong now after all the years in the good clean air of the country. Eggs and milk from the farm ... Oh, Amy, don't give up hope, not after all these years.'

But Amy was lost again in that hidden world where she had retreated in the past. Strangely or perhaps it was not so strange, for did they not suffer far worse wounds than herself, physical wounds, she only came alive when she was caring for the men, boys really, who crammed the hospital beds. The flood of casualties that flowed via the clearing hospitals in the south filled each ward. Along both walls and even in a line down the centre of the enormous rooms beds were pushed close together, each ward filled with bandaged men. Arms, legs on pulleys, but mostly heads totally covered in white bandages, for it was here that the clever brain surgeon worked.

One such soldier lay quietly in his clean bed where he had been for the last week alongside twenty to thirty other critical cases. Though his eyes, the most beautiful blue she had ever seen, one young VAD pronounced, were often open, they saw nothing, as the lad was still in a coma. It had done him no good being in transit for so long from the trenches to the hospital, Mr Hawthorn the surgeon had said irritably as he probed the wound, but he had removed the splinter telling them that the soldier would not, *could* not live another twenty-four hours.

Frankly, he said, he was amazed the next day on his rounds to find the soldier still alive. He took a closer look, skilfully removed another sliver of splinter from the shallow wound and, after replacing the bandages, moved on. The wards were all named after famous Liverpool men, men of a philanthropic nature who had left their mark on the great city. There was the William Brown ward after the man who had endowed the great library, the Lord Derby ward, and so on, at least a dozen of them, and it was not until several weeks later at the beginning of May that Amy had cause to enter William Brown ward, where Private Joe Carter was recovering well from his wounds; at least his body was but his mind was a long way behind it. He had come out of his coma and sat placidly in the chair by his bed, seemingly unaware that though the shell splinters in his head had been removed, a small piece of silver plate had replaced them, thereby saving his life.

Amy had been sent, there being no orderly immediately available, from the ward where she nursed with a message for Mr Hawthorn who was urgently needed on the Lord Derby ward where a young soldier was in great trouble. Mr Hawthorn had just spoken to Joe and warned Sister that the lad would suffer severe headaches, and though he appeared to be on the road to recovery he was on no account to be discharged. Besides, he said, until Private Carter had recovered his memory if he was not to return to the trenches where was he to go? A convalescent home somewhere, he supposed, as he moved on.

He was somewhat startled when a young, very pretty little VAD let out a cry which was beyond describing. She clutched at his arm, which happened to be the nearest—to Sister's mortification—and nearly had him over.

'What the dickens . . .' he growled.

'Nurse, what on earth . . .' Sister began but the

321

VAD ignored both her and the great Mr Hawthorn and sank to her knees before the blank-faced young private.

'Joe ... Joe,' she said over and over again, her hands covering his where they lay in his lap. His eyes, those amazing blue eyes so admired by the nurses, came to rest on her face but there was no recognition in them.

'Joe, it's me ... Amy,' she cried brokenly but though he politely left his hands in hers it was obvious to the stunned patients, nurses and doctors he had no idea who she was.

23

'If you can get Mr Hawthorn to agree to discharge him can he come here, to Elmhurst? Please, John, you could keep an eye on him, and report to Mr Hawthorn on his progress. He's recovered from his head wound but he can remember nothing before he found his friend on the wire. He keeps asking how Pip is and at first Mr Hawthorn kept saying it's early days, putting him off, as it were, but Joe knows something happened. That he and Pip were wounded together so at last Mr Hawthorn told him his friend had died. For a few days he retreated into himself. He'd talk to no one, and then he became frightened. "Who am I?" he asked the nurse and when she told him he didn't seem to believe her. Well, of course, he's not Joe Carter but Joe Newbridge but he doesn't remember. He ... he doesn't know *me*, John, and once, once we were close. But if he could settle somewhere away from the hospital, look after the garden, he's a good gardener, and have one of the rooms over the stable, it might help him. He'd be doing what he did before the war, you see, which might activate his memory and he would ... well, knowing him as I do, how kind and gentle and cheerful he was, he might help Bella with the children. It's so sad seeing him just sitting there, staring out of the window.'

'Whoa, whoa, hold on a minute, Amy. Get your breath and let me get mine.' John Carstairs leaned back in his chair at the dining table while the others round the table watched him intently. Dodie, Caleb and Bella, along with Amy and John had just finished their evening meal. Amy was still in her uniform though she had discarded her cap, and John's white coat, the one he wore at the hospital, was thrown carelessly over the back of another chair. Times were gone now when they had changed in the evening; the war and the circumstances it had brought about had changed all that. John was seldom at the dinner table these days, his work at the hospital forcing him to come and go at all times, to grab a meal, to sleep like the dead whenever the flood of wounded would allow. He was likely to be summoned in the middle of the night to an emergency, or when the ambulances from the hospital trains that pulled into Lime Street Station rolled up at Highfield Infirmary. It was the same for every doctor in the land although the general public must be attended to at the same time.

'How old is Joe, Amy?' John asked abruptly.

'He's a couple of years older than me, I think. He came from the orphanage and was not exactly

323

certain. I don't remember him having a birthday.' She shook her head sadly. 'So he'll be about nineteen. He was always well thought of and a hard worker, and also there's the advantage that he's a skilled mechanic. Papa can vouch for that, can't you?' turning to Caleb who nodded his head. 'You've been talking about that Austin 10 for ages, John, now that you are needed so much more at the hospital, so think what a boon it would be not only to have your own little motor car but your own mechanic as well. He'd be of enormous help to us all.'

She gazed at John imploringly. He looked so tired and here she was heaping more burdens on to his already burdened shoulders. Men from the battlefields of Gallipoli had begun to arrive dying from their wounds and worst of all from disease. The troops had been decimated by fevers and dysentery. With its back to the sea, the army was holding the merest fringe of coastline and the men who came to Highfield had horrific tales to tell. There had been no room for even the smallest casualty clearing-station and many of the Australians and New Zealanders who had been sent to Gallipoli to try to break the deadlock on the Western Front were in a pathetic state. Sister Medlock had been heard to joke that they might have to resort to two in a bed the hospital was so crowded. Amy herself had been on duty for twelve long hours and her feet were swollen like one of Mrs Topsy's puddings.

'It would free up a bed, John,' she added hopefully, and they all smiled. It was wonderful to see Amy's enthusiastic concern for Joe, though Dodie wondered privately to Bella whether it was because his wound had somehow emasculated Joe. He was no longer looked on as a man, one of those who had savagely torn her innocence from her and rendered in her a horror of their gender, but a frail human being who needed help. It was over nine months since Amy had been so brutalised by Randall Hodge, the experience making her shudder away from most men's touch, but the war and the human salvage it had thrown up and her involvement with it seemed to have lessened her terror. The doctors, the orderlies, and John himself were too involved with the work they did to be a threat to her but somehow her past bond with Joe Newbridge had been revived. Caleb exchanged a glance with Dodie who raised her eyebrows.

'Amy, you must not allow your compassion for Joe to blind you to his condition. He is in a state of ... well, what would you call it, John? Mental instability, insentience? I know nothing of such things but there might be danger if he were released from the hospital in his present state.'

'Oh, no, Papa, he is very quiet, not at all violent, is he, John?'

'I have not seen him, Amy. I would have to discuss his condition with Mr Hawthorn. He is the brain specialist. We know next to nothing about the mind. There are cases of men in the trenches going mad, with constant shelling, the terror, the conditions in which they exist. They lose their nerve, you see.'

'But you will consider it, please, John?' Amy persisted.

'I will talk to Mr Hawthorn, Amy, and now I think it's time we both got some sleep.'

*   *   *

' "Be sure your sin will find you out." That is God's word, Randall, and no matter how long it takes she will be punished. She and Caleb, both of them. They have committed the same sin, the sin of forsaking the vows they made before God in His house.'

The man and woman sat one on either side of the garden table under the shade of the oak tree in the garden of Somerfield. The table was set daintily with a white lace tablecloth and napkins, a fine bone china tea service and all the appurtenances of afternoon tea: a teapot, sugar basin and milk jug to match the cups and saucers, and a cake stand on which wafer-thin sandwiches and an assortment of home-made cakes were displayed. The man ate steadily, waiting for his turn to put his point of view, which matched that of his hostess.

'My husband is living openly with that . . . that hussy in Langworthy Road and their bastard son. "Can a man take fire in his bosom and his clothes not be burned?" the Proverbs say, and he will surely suffer for his wickedness. "The way of transgressors is hard," we both know that—'

'Exactly, Zillah,' Randall interrupted her smoothly, for once Zillah Seymour began her fanatical quotations from the Bible it was difficult to stop her. He and his wife's aunt were on Christian name terms now after months of searching for his wife. At first when she had seemed to vanish off the face of the earth, no one, not one solitary person, having seen a half-naked

326

woman running madly in the streets in the vicinity of Weaste Lane during the night following his marriage, he believed she had thrown herself in the river though how she had got there was a mystery. But after Caleb Seymour left Zillah and took up residence with his paramour in Langworthy Road, it had occurred to them both that the corner house would have been the ideal and logical hiding place for Amy. They had had it watched for months after that but nothing untoward had happened. Caleb came and went, so did the woman and their child, quite openly, along with an older woman and an old man, who, when questioned, had been downright offensive.

'I think our mistake,' Randall continued, stuffing another of Mrs Abigail's delicious macaroons into his mouth, 'was turning Amy's mother out of her cottage. If she is anywhere, my wife I mean, she is in Liverpool searching for her family. She will be in rooms somewhere and from there she will be scouring the city. She will have got herself a job. With the war on there is plenty of work about, in a factory perhaps where I believe the wages are good, munitions, that sort of thing. She will have spoken to that woman who lived in the same street as her family, who will have led her to the cottage you put her family in, but finding them gone Amy has herself gone into hiding. What a pity! We might have found her had her mother still been there.'

Zillah looked offended, for she did not care to be criticised but nevertheless she was forced to agree that Randall could be right. Liverpool was a big city and it would be like looking for the proverbial needle in a haystack just to go casting about willy-nilly.

'What do you suggest, Randall?' Zillah's voice was icy.

'Well, in my opinion, for what it's worth, my dear Zillah'—he smirked, his thick lips parting to reveal big yellow teeth, those that had done so much damage to Amy's tender flesh—'the only possible solution is to keep an eye on Caleb Seymour. If he is still in touch with my wife, wherever she is hiding he will lead us to her.'

Neither of them took the slightest notice of Alice as she approached the table with a jug of fresh hot water, since servants to those who employed them were considered to be of slightly substandard intelligence who did not understand their betters.

Alice burst into the kitchen like a stone from a catapult, startling the others who were going about their tasks lethargically as it was a warm day and even warmer in the kitchen.

'Well, if that don't beat all,' she cried bitterly.

'What?' Mrs Abigail asked, her hand to her bosom.

'The pair of 'em talkin' about Miss Amy.'

'Miss Amy?' they all repeated.

'They think she's in Liverpool workin' in a munitions factory, that the master—' who was still the master to them even if he no longer lived with the mistress—'put 'er there an' he'll lead them to 'er.'

'*No!*'

'They must be mad, the pair of 'em. They can't let it go, can they? Miss Amy 'as ter be found an' punished 'cos she couldn't stomach that fat pig out there, nor their damn Methody ways. An' there

328

was us all cryin' 'cos we thought she were dead. An' if she 'ad bin it would've bin their fault. Eeh, what with our Joe, then Miss Amy disappearin' I don't know what the world's comin' to. I've a good mind ter give in me notice an' go to work in the munitions factory meself. Mary Parkins who was kitchen-maid at Pendle Hall 'as gone ter London, I 'ad a letter from her last week—'

'Eeh, lass, yer'd never go ter London?' Mrs Abigail gasped as though Alice had said she was off to Australia on the next boat. 'You've bin 'ere since Adam was lad.'

'Why not? I'd like to 'elp the war effort. Them Germans are evil. Look at the way they sank the *Lusitania*. All them folk drowned, nearly two thousand of them innocent as the day.'

'I'm comin' with you,' Jess announced, taking off her apron. 'Bugger the mistress. I've had about as much as I can stand.'

Mrs Abigail threw her own apron over her head and began to weep.

*   *   *

It was only a small-scale attack in March. The Battle of Neuve Chapelle. Those who had gone over first captured a German trench and though they were machine-gunned and devastated by shrapnel shells and whizbangs and many of them were killed or wounded they held on until they were relieved at dusk.

One of the wounded who finally reached Highfield Infirmary could not stop talking about it, upsetting those who were already there.

'The worst was coming back over no-man's-land

329

which was where I got this,' pointing to an empty space where his left leg had once been. 'It was like a flock of sheep lying down sleeping in a field, the bodies were that thick. You couldn't help stepping on them. Some of them were still alive and they were crying, begging for water and plucking at our legs as we went by. One big chap grabbed me and held on to me. 'Give us a drink of water, mate,' he said, 'and when I was taking the cork out of my water bottle I was hit and fell on top of him. Daftest thing I ever did . . .'

On and on and on he went, bitterly resenting that his moment of compassion had lost him his leg, and in the end Doctor John Carstairs moved him to a private ward.

Then, given the shortage of beds and after talking it over with Mr Hawthorn, it was decided that Private Carter was fit enough to be discharged and convalesce at Doctor Carstairs's home.

'Is he able to work in my garden, sir?' Doctor Carstairs asked the eminent brain surgeon. 'Give him something to do.'

'He's physically fit enough to go back to the Front, Doctor, but I'm reluctant to condemn him to that just yet. Who knows what it might do to his already confused mind. And you could watch him and report to me. I hear there is a very pretty VAD who takes an interest in him. A relative of yours?'

'Of my wife's, sir. We have six young children and having no home of her own she came to us to help my wife. But she wanted to nurse, so who were we to stop her?'

'I see.' Mr Hawthorn clearly did not, nor was interested. If his patient was to be well supervised that was all that concerned him.

330

It was left to Amy to break the news to Joe. The summer had been so good that many of the patients had been wheeled out on to the lawns and placed beside the colourful flowerbeds, which was where Amy and Joe had talked. Well, Amy had talked and Joe listened, since he had nothing, no memories of the past he could share with her. Mr Hawthorn had advised all the staff not to speak to the soldier of his past life. Not to force remembrances from him which would be a waste of time and would only upset him. Sometimes Amy herself wondered what she could say to this quiet man. He listened to her as she talked about her present life since, like him, she could not speak of the past.

'Bella, that's who I live with, is at her wits' end sometimes, I mean she has the most mischievous set of children in the whole of Liverpool. Arthur's the biggest scamp. There's a stream, very shallow and not a danger even to the youngest so when Seth, he's the odd-job man, is about they play there. Well, Arthur found a frog and put it in my bed. Honestly, Joe, I nearly died with fright.'

She was rewarded by a smile on Joe's face. But it was like talking to a stranger, trying to think of something to interest him. He just seemed to want to sit and gaze at the flowerbeds. He wore the blue uniform of a patient, not quite big enough for his tall frame and his hair lay in a dark flat stubble on his shaved skull. He had put on weight through lack of exercise and she longed to get him back to some sort of physical activity, to become the Joe she known over a year ago. She could scarcely remember how she had felt about him then, though she knew they had been very fond of one

331

another. *Fond!* Is that what it had been? Like the fondness a sister and brother felt for one another?

'He reminds me of Sammy,' she said suddenly, then wondered why.

'Sammy?'

'My little brother.'

'You have a brother, Nurse?'

'Yes, I have, five in fact. And I wish you would call me Amy, Joe.'

'Why? The other lads don't,' he asked her passively.

'Well, I just wish you would.'

Another day when she had a rare half an hour to herself they had walked in total silence along the leaf-strewn pathways that threaded the hospital grounds. The leaves were turning the lovely burnished gold and tawny red of autumn and because it was dry they crunched beneath their feet. Suddenly he said, 'I didn't know I was in Liverpool. One of the other chaps said . . .'

'What, Joe?'

'That he'd like to go an' look at the ships an' when I asked him what ships, he said on the Mersey. That's in Liverpool.'

'You knew that, Joe?' She was so obviously delighted, as though he were a child who had remembered a lesson; he turned to her in surprise, and she straightened her face. 'Of course you did and why not? Would you like to see the River Mersey, Joe?'

'I don't know. It's a bit . . .'

'What is it?'

'I don't know really. I . . . I might get lost. I don't know Liverpool like . . . Manchester.'

Like Manchester! A tiny part of his past had

332

infiltrated into his clouded mind but she concealed her elation and continued to walk slowly beside him at the pace he set. The graceful, athletic, long-striding young man who had been Joe Newbridge had gone but she meant to do everything in her power to bring him back.

It was October before John told them, her and Bella, that Mr Hawthorn had agreed to think about Joe leaving the hospital where he had been for almost six months and come to stay, he emphasised the word *stay*, with them at Elmhurst. His headaches, which had rendered him almost senseless, were weakening but the specialist wished to keep him close by where he could monitor his progress.

Joe had been found a few days before studying an old copy of the magazine *Autocar* which someone, probably one of the orderlies, had left lying about. Joe had up looked and seeing Mr Hawthorn at his bedside had remarked idly, 'The war's certainly buggered up the manufacture of motor cars in Europe but the Americans, especially Ford, have caught up and taken over. Ford an' General Motors will be the top manufacturers soon.'

Mr Hawthorn had been astounded. 'You are interested in motor cars, Private Carter?' he asked him gently, while all around them staff and patients alike held their breath.

'Oh, aye, I used ter drive—' He came to an abrupt halt as his memory gave out.

'Would you like to drive again, Private?'

'Oh, I dunno if I could, sir, an' I'm sorry about the swearin.'

'That's all right, lad, I've heard worse in my

time.'

Later that day he called Doctor Carstairs into his office, offering him a seat beside his desk. After shuffling files about then lighting a cigar, he asked brusquely, 'I believe you are considering purchasing an automobile, Carstairs.'

Doctor Carstairs looked astonished then admitted he was.

'And is the proposal to have Private Carter to reside in your home still on offer? You intimated as much a few days ago.'

'Of course, sir. My wife and Amy, Nurse Carstairs, are very enthusiastic, especially my wife in helping in the recovery of a young man wounded at the front.'

'Good, good. I might as well tell you I was confounded today to find him reading some damn automobile magazine and when I remarked on it he said, "I used to drive . . ." then his memory went again and he couldn't remember the name of the automobile he apparently used to drive.'

'That's a good sign isn't it, sir?'

'Yes, it is, but I must warn you that if his memory does return I am bound to report to the authorities that he is fit to be sent back to France.'

'Yes, sir, but may I ask you not to say as much to Nurse Carstairs.'

'Sweet on him, is she?'

'Oh, yes, sir, they love one another devotedly though neither of them knows it.'

'Hmmph!'

24

They were playing the skipping game when John and Joe turned in at the gate, one end of the rope tied to a drainpipe, the other held by Daisy. Amy, holding Helen's hand, skipped in and out of the whirling rope while Bella did her best to prevent the others from enthusiastically joining in. Even the baby in her perambulator was fascinated, clapping her hands and shouting with glee.

'One potato, two potato, three potato four, five potato, six potato, seven potato more,' Amy chanted as she and the little girl, who was red-cheeked with excitement and satisfaction, completed the ritual and darted away from the twirling rope.

'Now you, Arthur, no, hold my hand, darling, you have to be quick.'

'I can do it on my own,' shrieked Arthur, avoiding Amy's hand, for after all he was a boy and boys could do anything better than girls.

'One potato, two potato,' he managed before his foot caught in the rope and, mutinously, he gave way to his mama and Angela, who at three years old could not keep up with Bella.

'Me now,' yelled Jack, but it was all getting a bit out of hand with the older children challenging one another as to whose turn it was.

They were all astounded when Joe leaped forward and lifted Jack into his arms. He jumped into the rope which Daisy was still patiently turning and chanted the ritual chorus before jumping out. He placed Jack carefully on the grass then picked up Georgie and repeated the performance. It might have been bedlam as they all surrounded the blue-suited soldier and began to clamour for a turn but Joe lifted his hand and spoke sternly.

'One at a time, if yer don't mind. I've only one pair of 'ands. Line up, just like soldiers. Now, 'oo 'asn't 'ad a go? Right, littlest first . . .' and without further ado he plucked the enchanted baby out of the carriage and jumped her into the rope. Even Arthur behaved himself, dutifully waiting his turn with the soldier. A *wounded* soldier, for Arthur was old enough to know his papa was a doctor at the hospital where the soldiers who were wounded in battle wore blue uniforms.

Daisy was relieved and went off to make tea and bring milk and biscuits on to the lawn where an impromptu picnic was set out. The children, even baby Claire, swarmed all over Joe until their papa said they must let poor Joe rest. At once they sat on the rug Daisy had laid out for them, gazing respectfully at this lovely stranger who promised to be such fun.

'Where did you learn that game, Joe?' John asked without thinking and at once Joe's face clouded over.

'I . . . I dunno. I suppose I must 'av bin ter school.'

Thankfully, the baby, who knew no better, crawled over to him and settled on his lap and the awkward moment passed. He held her gently and a peaceful expression came over his face and in Amy's heart something lurched painfully, deliciously as it glowed once more into life. The complete and rounded happiness she had known only with this man sang through her and she knew at that precise moment it would last for ever. She had believed that though she had made herself a new life; though she had new friends who cared about her and of whom she was extremely fond, her life as a woman who could love a man, a man who could love her as she had wanted to be loved and with whom she could make a family, that dream was over. What Randall Hodge had done to her had contaminated her and the wounds he had caused had festered, then scabbed over but they were still there beneath the surface.

But Joe was back in her life! They had loved one another once, a young, innocent love that had gone no further than that of a boy and girl before they were wrenched apart. And that love had never died! Despite the past, the future lay ahead and in it would be Amy and Joe. She would bring Joe back to life and if he wasn't quite the Joe she had once known and loved, the man who held the child with such unruffled sweetness would stand in his shoes.

She looked up and his glance met hers. He smiled, a good-natured smile, the sort you give someone you've just met and scarcely know. Polite, mannerly, for she was a relative of the doctor who was helping him to recover by employing him. He looked about him over the baby's silken head, noting that some of the shrubs needed pruning and the grass could do with one last mowing before winter set in. It was October now, unseasonably warm, but time to finish those back-end jobs all gardeners recognise.

He frowned, wondering how he knew this, then the children, good for so long, began to edge up to him.

'We've got kittings,' the little girl told him confidentially. 'Would you like to see them?'

'Yes, I would.'

At once the five of them bounced up, even the baby clinging round his neck like a little monkey. He raised questioning eyebrows at Bella who had been dozing in the wonderful peace.

'Go,' she told him, 'and don't bring them back until the baby's fourteen.'

He laughed, for someone, somewhere, used to say that to him.

John got to his feet. 'I'd better go with him,' he told Bella and Amy, 'before they eat him alive. I don't want to face old Hawthorn if I tire him out. And I'll show him his quarters at the same time. Did you leave him something to wear besides the hospital blues, Bella?'

'I did but he's taller than you.'

'Thanks, my love. I don't suppose he cares if his pants are at half mast.'

*   *   *

He settled in and made himself so useful that Bella, Daisy and Mrs Topsy, even old Seth, were heard to say they didn't know how they had managed without him. He set to work on the overgrown vegetable garden which had got beyond old Seth, feeding the ground with manure from a nearby farm and planting potatoes which would be ready for eating in spring. He sowed peas, which again would be first crop early next year. Cabbages were sown in neat rows for spring picking then he began on the flowerbeds. All the colourful flowerbeds were cleared and weeded and in their place he planted winter-flowering pansies in a variety of colours, daffodils and crocus bulbs for spring. He told Mrs Carstairs that he wanted to try honesty which flowered in April but later the fruit discs split to leave a silvery membrane.

'You do just what you want, Joe. Doctor Carstairs and I are no gardeners but if you were to go up to the nurseries at Walton you might see something that would make a nice show during the winter. I'm sure my husband would be glad for you to take the motor car.'

That had been the most exciting event in Joe's new life, going with Doctor John, as he was told to call him, travelling to Coventry by train to the factory where the Morris Oxford—popularly known as the Bullnose—was manufactured. The train was packed with troops, as was every railway station they passed through, some of them waving and cheering and eager to be away across the Channel, and others, who had been on leave and were returning, grim-faced and unsmiling, knowing what to expect. Joe was quiet on the journey, some darting thing inside his head telling him he knew this mixture of emotions but not remembering exactly what it was.

He was enchanted with the factory, moving along the assembly line, watching with fascination the putting together of the chubby little automobile. One that was actually finished and ready for sale had gleaming brass lamps, four of them, two between the front wheels and one on either side of the windscreen and a splendid brass-trimmed horn. It had a canvas hood and two leather seats—not exactly a family car, Doctor

John remarked wryly, but then was there such a thing?—and Joe couldn't wait to get behind the wheel. John wondered whether it had been wise to bring a man who had been wounded in the trenches on such a journey, but then that had been over six months ago and Joe, after the exercise he had known in the gardens at Elmhurst and the good food prepared for him by a doting Mrs Topsy, was physically as fit as he had ever been. He wore his hospital blues since he was still in the army and the mechanics and men at the factory made a great fuss of him, offering him cigarettes and asking him what it was like 'over there'. He refused the cigarettes and wouldn't talk about the war, which he knew disappointed them. His loss of memory had begun when he regained consciousness in the hospital bed so he had no experiences to share to feed their vicarious appetite.

They made the journey back by easy stages, giving Joe the chance to recapture the driving skills he had learned with Caleb Seymour's machine. But Joe was a natural driver and was relaxed and comfortable behind the wheel. They set off from Coventry, skirting Birmingham and Cannock, avoiding Stoke-on-Trent where, just north of the town, they put up for the night at a small inn. John thought he had never seen Joe look so bright and well and though it did his heart good to observe the lad's recovery, his spirits sank when he thought of Joe's next review with Mr Hawthorn. The surgeon could not help but see the improvement in his patient, which would probably mean his return to the front.

With a great honking of the horn Joe drove

340

them up to the front door of Elmhurst, careful not to collide with the horde of delirious children who erupted from the house and the gasps of awe and fright from the servants. The baby in Bella's arms held hers out to Joe but it was Amy who got to him first. To everyone's surprise, including Joe, she wound her arms about his neck and clung to him and his instinctive reaction was to lift his own and put them around her. It felt so natural, so right, so *familiar* that he held her for longer than Mrs Topsy—who knew nothing about their shared past—thought decent.

All the children had wanted to go for a spin and it took Joe's gentle tact and their father's stern remonstrances, since Joe was a wounded soldier, to calm them down. He would take them in turn round the block tomorrow, he promised them, one by one, but first he must have a rest, this from their father.

'Me first, me first,' Arthur insisted. 'I *am* the oldest after all.'

'No, it's ladies first,' Helen argued, pushing her brother to one side.

'You're not a lady—'

'Enough, enough. Now Joe will take the motor to the yard and put it in the stable block, and no fiddling under the bonnet, Joe. It needs cleaning you say but not today. You've driven a great distance and I insist you get to your bed. Mr Hawthorn would have my hide if you had a relapse.'

A few days later, encouraged by his discussion with Mrs Carstairs earlier, he asked her if he might take the Morris to the nurseries to pick up a few plants for the newly dug but rather empty garden

341

beds. There was space at the back of the motor under a cover where the plants could be carried. Did she think Doctor John would mind? But he really would like to get on before the ground was too hard.

When it was mentioned that he was to go to Walton Nurseries Amy, whose day off it was, begged to go with him.

'I'd love a ride in the motor, Joe. I'm the only one who hasn't had a spin.' For all the wildly excited children, one by one, even the baby, who sat on Bella's knee, had roared up and down Thomas Lane to Knotty Ash and back. 'Can I come with you for the plants?' Amy added.

He looked somewhat taken aback, she didn't know why. It hurt her that though he was polite, respectful, ready to discuss the bulbs for the spring or indeed any other question she put to him, perhaps about the children or the motor car, he went no further than that. Had she been more experienced she might have noticed that though he laughed and joked with Daisy and the cleaner Lily and Mrs Topsy—which didn't really count since she was elderly—he was never more than correct with her. Nice, smiling shyly, awkwardly restrained, as though conscious she was a young relative of Mrs Carstairs, not even realising he was holding himself aloof. An older, more mature woman, wise in the ways of male and female, would have recognised his manner for what it was. At this precise moment in his wounded life Joe Carter had lost all sense of himself *as a man* and saw her only as she was presented, Mrs Carstairs's cousin, and was surprised when she singled him out.

And she, who had thought herself to be resigned

to a life of . . . well, what could almost be called 'spinsterhood', no husband, no children, knew now that this was not so. Deep within her, under the layers of the damage done her by Randall Hodge, was the clean, untainted loveliness of her love for Joe. Her first love. Her only love! It would return, that love they had shared, that sweetness, that tenderness, but first Joe must be restored to the knowledge of how he had once felt about her, and that would take time. He had nothing left in him of the natural responses of a man towards a pretty woman. The children had brought him some way back to 'feelings'. They loved him and he responded to them. She had realised that they were two of a kind, she and Joe. Both of them impaired by the wounds of life and only through each other would they be healed.

*   *   *

The nurseries were only a twenty-minute drive from Elmhurst. Joe had put the canvas hood down and the winter sunshine coated Amy's hair with a sheen of tawny gold and amber streaked with bronze, honey and silver, as it streamed out like a banner behind her. Her cheeks were a bright pink and her eyes, big, golden brown, sparkled with joy. She was with Joe who was smiling as broadly as she was. She was in a motor car. It was as though she were flying along the country lanes bordered by hawthorn hedges bright with scarlet berries. A dormouse sitting on a tree stump tucking into the ripe haws fled in a flash as they roared past and in fields labourers looked up from their winter tasks in astonishment, as it was rare to see an infernal

343

machine in these parts.

Joe had on an old pair of breeches and a worn tweed jacket over a sweater, an outfit that had belonged to John. He was fed up with people staring and asking questions he didn't want and couldn't answer when he was in his blues, he said, and with John's permission he had discarded them. Amy wore a smart cornflower-blue woollen two-piece: a flared skirt, shorter than once they had been, and a jacket with a basque and shoulder yoke. She wore no hat. By 1915 the outbreak of war had seen a reflection of military styles in a more waisted, youthful silhouette.

As he was about to turn right towards Walton on the Hill she put a hand on his arm. He turned to her enquiringly. She thought how attractive he had become during his months in the gardens of Elmhurst. His hair had grown and fell in a brown tumble over his forehead and his incredibly blue eyes, almost turquoise, were keen and sparkling, for he was doing what he liked best. Driving a motor!

'Let's go down to see the ships,' she said impulsively. 'You said you'd never seen them or been on the Marine Parade. A day out would be good for both of us. Me cooped up in the hospital, you . . . you said you'd never seen the Mersey and the Liverpool shoreline, the docks. And . . . well'— she turned away from him, a catch in her throat— 'it's a long time since I was there. It was on the last day I was with my family. We, my brothers and sisters and me, we had an old perambulator, like the one Claire sits in but a complete wreck, but we thought it was wonderful. I put the youngest in it and we walked, nine of us, can you imagine, along the promenade heading for Princes Park. Sammy swung on the chain beside the water on the parade and a bobby told him off.'

Her voice tapered off and Joe, who had been watching her intently, reached over and took her hand and held it in his own. He barely knew this lovely cousin; was she a cousin? It didn't matter, she was related to Mrs Carstairs. He felt strangely drawn to her all of a sudden, not only because she was exceedingly pretty—why hadn't he noticed it before?—but because she seemed as sad as he did himself. He was lost, his life was lost, but this girl spoke as though she had been deprived of something dear to her, as he had!

'You 'ad all them brothers and sisters, Nurse.'

'I'll hit you if you don't call me Amy,' she said vigorously. 'Now that we are no longer at the hospital.'

He grinned. 'Sorry, sorry.' He still held her hand and she let him. 'Tell me about them.'

So she told him about her mam and pa and her beginnings in Liverpool; her mam's illness and her aunt, Pa's sister, taking her away to Manchester. She said nothing about her life with Mrs Seymour nor the man to whom she had been married.

'So I came to stay with Bella and John, who, by the way, are not related to me but to some friends of mine. I wanted to do something for the war effort so I became a VAD. Now, can we please get down to the river? I long to smell the cargoes that come off the ships and the sea air itself. Then we can go to Walton and the nurseries.'

*   *   *

Joe parked the motor on Sefton Street, which lay parallel to the river. Even as they climbed out of the Morris they could smell the pungent aroma of the timber from the bonded timber yards at the back of Brunswick Dock. It was winter and the sun was low in the sky and as they walked northwards towards Queens Dock it silhouetted the cranes, the black funnels of the great ships at berth and even, here and there, the rigging of the old sailing ships that plied up and down the coast from Scotland to Cornwall. The air was sharp as it came off the river, smelling of all the essences that Amy had grown up with for the first ten years of her life. She sniffed enthusiastically, inhaling the odours of cowhide and jute, the sweetness of molasses and sugar, the sharpness of salt, tar, the fumes from ships' funnels, spices, coffee, tobacco and turpentine, all come from every corner of the world, come on ships that had managed to avoid the German submarines that lurked below the waters to trap merchant shipping.

Gulls floated serenely on the currents of air above their heads and for that moment they were both sublimely happy.

At Queens Dock they skirted the dock itself and reached the parade that ran along beside the river. The water, because of the lowness of the sun, rippled in grey, silver and golden waves. They did not speak until they reached Princes Parade where Amy stopped, leaving Joe to walk on a few steps before he realised she was not beside him. He turned.

'What is it?' he asked her.

'It was here that Sammy swung on the chain,' she said, pointing to the chain that separated the

346

parade from the river. A seagull was perched on one of the stanchions to which the chains were attached. 'The bobby told him off.'

'Amy ...' was all Joe could manage, not knowing how to comfort her for her unutterable loss.

They walked on, the gladness somehow gone from the day. Princes Dock itself was crowded as a troop ship readied herself for departure. The decks were lined with khaki-clad soldiers, with various expressions of emotion on their faces. Some were elated, others subdued, cheering, or silent as they looked down on those who had come to see them off. The war was no longer the great adventure it once had been and many of the mothers, wives and sweethearts weeping on the landing stage felt they would never see their beloved sons, husbands or lovers again.

They walked the length of dockland as far as the Huskisson Dock where timber was being unloaded. Joe barely glanced at the fort which was supposed to guard the estuary, then, without a word, they turned and walked back, avoiding Princes Dock and the departing troop ship, until they reached the motor. Again they did not speak as they made their way through the city and out into the country until they reached the nurseries at Walton. It seemed they had become set apart by the sight of the troop ship.

They wandered silently side by side studying the plants on display, Joe's keen eye picking out and discarding what were unsuitable. A pretty, rather low-growing bloom in a beautiful deep magenta pink caught his eye. It had curled green leaves and a delightful smell. He looked at the small sign beside it which said it was in flower from January to March.

'That there looks as though it might be a good 'un,' he said as though to himself.

'What's it called, Joe?' she said, eager to ease their estrangement.

'An ivy-leaved cyclamen, it ses.'

'It's very pretty.'

She walked a few steps ahead of him, pointing to where a young man of about fifteen or sixteen was watering a row of plants in pots. 'I wonder what that's called?'

The young man continued his task, not even turning his head. 'A Christmas rose, miss,' he said. 'Flowers Febry ter April.'

'Look, Joe. A Christmas rose. I wonder what colour it will be?'

'White, miss,' the lad told her. 'Great white saucers. Lovely, an' when I get me wages I'm gonner tekk one 'ome fer me mam.'

Amy's skin rose in sudden goose bumps all over her body. She felt the hairs rise on the back of her neck and she had time to wonder why, then the lad turned towards her. She stood rooted to the spot, her blood turning to water in her veins.

Joe came up behind her. She heard his voice from a great distance though none of what he said made sense.

'I like the look o' them, Nurse,' he was saying in the polite way he assumed with her. Though he had been told a dozen times to call her Amy, something in him resisted and even John could not understand it. None of them, not even Amy, knew of Joe's state of mind when he watched her come out of the chapel on Randall Hodge's arm. A state

348

of mind that was somehow connected to his loss of memory, or, to be more accurate, his inability to make a friend of her as he had done with Daisy and Lily, Seth and Mrs Topsy, indeed all the family at Elmhurst.

'What d'yer think? Hellebores, it ses they are, flowerin' Febry ter May. What with them, the cyclamens, Christmas roses an' t'others there should be a nice show all year round.'

Amy did not answer and even the lad was standing, his mouth agape, his watering can sprinkling water on his own boots.

'What is it?' Joe asked hesitantly, his weakened mind beginning to recede from the strangeness of what was happening, whatever it was.

Amy stepped back and took his arm, clinging to it as though should he fail her she would collapse in a heap on the ground.

'It's ... is it? Oh, sweet, sweet Jesus, tell me your name is Sammy.' She leaned against Joe for support and without thought his muscled arm was round her, holding her, protecting her, since it seemed she might be in some danger, though he could see no signs of it from the lad who was helplessly dribbling water on to his sturdy boots.

'Aye,' the boy whispered, 'Sammy. Is it, it's not our Amy, is it? Me mam said . . .'

Amy began to weep. Leaving the circle of Joe's strong arm she clasped the boy in her own arms, winding them round his neck and pulling him to her.

'Oh, Sammy, Sammy . . .' Then in the foolish way that adults have when confronted by a child or a youth, said, 'How you've grown.'

'You an' all,' he murmured into her shoulder

349

while Joe stood behind them in wonderment.

They began to laugh then, Amy through her tears. Holding hands, they capered about, watched open-mouthed by other customers and the men who were working up and down the rows of growing plants. They hugged one another again, the lad who had once been a cheeky-faced boy but had changed to a youth, a young man whose hard life and the tribulations he and his family had suffered showing in his face.

Joe stood back awkwardly until at last, laughing and crying, Amy turned to him, her eyes a glowing amber in her tear-stained face. She still held the lad's hand as though afraid he might slip away should she not keep a firm grip on him.

'It's my brother, Joe. My brother Sammy. I haven't seen him since he was eight years old. Now he's . . . well, you'll be fifteen, won't you, Sammy?' turning again to the boy, who nodded awkwardly.

Joe bobbed his head.

'And Mam? She's well?' Her voice shook a little, for if he said 'No' what would she do? How would she cope?

'Oh, aye.'

'And the others, Elsie and Becky and . . .'

'They're all champion, our Amy.'

'Where . . . where are you living?'

'We've a little cottage. 'Ope Cottage in Spellow Lane, but, well . . .'

'What? What?' clutching at him.

'Pa died, our Amy.'

'Yes.'

Joe shifted uncomfortably but for once Amy was unaware of him.

'We must go now. I must see them . . . all these

years . . . Hope Cottage, you say.'

'Nay, our Amy,' Sammy said, drawing her back. 'I can't leave me work. This is a good job an' I don't want sack.'

'But, Sammy, please . . .'

Joe cleared his throat and Amy turned to him. 'What?' she said almost irritably, resenting his interference in this, the greatest moment in her seventeen years. But Joe knew the importance of decent work.

'Yer brother can't just leave 'is work, lass. 'E might lose 'is job. Let's come back when 'e's finished an' tekk 'im in't motor ter yer mam's.'

'Oh, no, no, Joe. Let Sammy tell us Mam's address an' we'll go now.'

'Mam works at North Shore Cotton Mills, our Amy.'

'Then that's where we'll go. Come on, Joe.'

'No, our Amy.'

'Yes, our Sammy. I'm not waiting another half-hour.'

25

They shuffled through the wrought-iron gateway under a sign that proclaimed it to be 'North Shore Cotton Mill', women almost too exhausted to put one foot in front of the other. Their shawls were draped about their sagging shoulders, their heads bowed, for they had just done twelve hours at their machines making the khaki cloth so badly needed by the government. Their brave fighting boys in the trenches over the Channel required uniforms

351

as more and more of them were called or volunteered to the call of their country. Kitchener's boys, the volunteers were called, and the women were eager to see that they were decently clad. The work was hard and seemingly endless but the pay was good, the women reminded themselves, as was all the pay to do with the war effort. Look at munitions, for instance, but those who worked in the munitions factories were for the most part young women who had once been parlour-maids and worked off their feet even then. But work in the cotton mill was hard and some of the older ones wondered how they could possibly carry on. Of course, many of them had men out there, sons, husbands, sweethearts and if they could keep them warm in the trenches, which they could not really picture in their minds though their Albert or Fred or Willy did their best to describe them, then they were willing to do their bit. But it was hard to be on your feet for so long, day after day.

'Yer've a fair tramp, lass,' one said to another. 'D'yer go through Everton?'

'Well, I tekk a short cut across fields when it's light bu' it gets dark that early this time o't year I don't fancy it burr at least our lad'll 've medd fire up an kettle'll be on. 'Appen 'e'll 'ave got tea on an' all. 'E's a good lad. 'E works 'andy, like, at nurseries.'

'Right, chuck, well, see yer termorrer.'

'Aye, ta-ra, Sadie.'

The women parted, one going towards Boundary Bridge, the other north in the direction of Walton on the Hill. The mill lay in close proximity to the Leeds and Liverpool Canal and the woman had walked alongside it for a while before crossing a small bridge and into Rakes Lane. It was there that she noticed the motor car ahead. It was parked on the corner of the road that led to Everton Valley. On either side of the road the fields had been harvested and in the dim light she could see yellow-hammers feeding in the stubble. Alongside the hedges scabious and red dead nettle grew and on the top of the hedge convolvulus was still rampant. There were a few blackberries remaining and the idle thought that she and the kids might pick some at the weekend passed through her tired mind. A blackberry pie would be nice or she might make some jam. It was funny, although she had been a townswoman for so long she, who had been brought up in the country, could still remember the names of wild flowers and the birds that flew overhead.

As she approached the motor car a young woman got out and stood as though transfixed by the open door and on the other side a young man did the same. Smart they were, both of them, of the upper classes, for working folk like herself did not aspire to motor cars. The young woman, who was dressed in blue, a lovely shade like the cornflowers that had filled the fields in the summer, began to walk towards her. She was a bonny lass, she could see that even in the dark which was falling rapidly.

The girl said something, something so low, so hoarse she could not make out what it was but suddenly for some reason her heart began to beat more rapidly and her breathing quickened. They walked towards one another and when they were face to face she knew who it was. Dear sweet

Jesus—after all these years, after all the heartache, the pain, the horror, the terror—it was not possible. She was ready to fall, her legs turning to jelly but even as she began to sway strong arms came round her, holding her upright and her lass, the one she had thought was lost to her for ever, was whispering in her ear.

'Mam . . . Mam . . . Mam . . . it's me, Mam. I've come home.' It seemed she hadn't the strength to do more than murmur and Dolly Pearson couldn't even summon an answer. Trembling, fiercely clinging, they stood locked together, both beginning to weep. The years they had had stolen from them bit inside them, clawing and yet diminishing slowly, for they had found one another and the joy of it, the rapture, was taking the place of the pain.

At last Dolly dragged herself from Amy's arms though she held on to her hands. She looked and looked into her face, then slowly one hand came up to cup her cheek lovingly. She leaned forward and kissed her.

'I've dreamed o' this day, our Amy. One day, I ses ter meself I'll 'old my lass in me arms again and that day's 'ere. Wha' . . . ? Where . . . ?'

'Mam . . . eeh, Mam . . .' In her intoxication Amy began to speak in the way she once had done. 'I never thought . . . when I saw our Sammy, aye, 'e were workin' at nurseries an' me an' Joe was . . . this is Joe.' She was incoherent in her rapture. She dragged her mother back into her arms as though afraid she might vanish in the deepening gloom. They were still weeping, shuddering in each other's arms while Joe stood and watched, feeling embarrassed to be looking on in such an intimate

354

moment.

At last they managed to compose themselves, half laughing, half crying, and with their arms about one another began to walk towards the motor car.

'This is Joe, Mam, a friend. He was wounded in France and I met him at the hospital where I'm a VAD.' She would tell her mother later about her and Joe's past, and everything else that had happened since last they had been together, but for now all she wanted was to get to her mam's cottage and see her brothers and sisters for the first time in seven years.

Joe smiled at Dolly Pearson and nodded politely. Until today he had known nothing much about the nurse who lived with Doctor and Mrs Carstairs, Amy, as he had been told to call her, but all of a sudden he had been swept into this family drama and he felt a certain shyness as though he were intruding in something that was really nothing to do with him. He was, after all, only the gardener and, before that, apparently, a private in the army and certainly nothing to do with any of these families, Amy's or Doctor John's. Amy had begged to come with him today to pick up some plants and here he was, a witness to two emotional scenes of moving intensity. First the brother and now the mother. He wasn't quite sure what he was supposed to do. Amy was terribly upset and so was her mother, so perhaps it would be best if he got them both back to the mother's home wherever that was!

'Can yer manage ter sit tergether in't passenger seat, Nurse ... er, Amy. I know it's a bit of a squash but if it's not far ... Nay, there's no need ter be fright, Mrs . . . Mrs . . .'

'Call me Dolly, lad, everyone does.' Dolly Pearson looked very apprehensive as she watched her lass ease herself into the machine then was encouraged to squash in beside her while the lad, a nice lad he seemed, fiddled about with unfamiliar bits of . . . well, Dolly hadn't the faintest notion what they were or even what they were for, but clinging on to Amy, not only because she was alarmed by her first ride in a motor car but because she couldn't bear to let go of her, they roared off.

'Oh, dear God . . . oh, dear God,' she kept murmuring while at the same time giving faint instructions on how to get to Hope Cottage which by motor car took no more than five minutes.

*   *   *

The man watched the automobile take off along Rake Lane and turn into Kirkdale Road where he lost sight of it but since he knew where Dolly Pearson lived, it didn't matter. He had followed her times in the last few months, not every day but at least twice a week as the woman had instructed him and now, at last, he had something to report. His job as overseer at the cotton mill was ideal for keeping an eye on this particular mill worker and though he didn't know why, what did he care when the brass the woman gave him for doing it was so good.

The difficult part lay ahead of him. He had to let the woman know that the girl she was looking for had turned up and had linked up with the hand who worked at the cotton mill and that could only

356

be done by telephone! She had given him a number and told him to telephone her when he had any information but the only telephone available to him, only an ordinary working man, after all, was the one in the office at the mill.

He began the walk back up Rakes Lane until he reached the gates of the mill which were closed and locked until the night shift came on. The night watchman sat in his little hut just inside the gate, a good fire in the brazier and the smell of bacon and sausages frying wafting through the bars. A plump cat lay curled on his lap and was obviously waiting for the fry-up the watchman was preparing.

The man rattled the bars of the gate. ' 'Ere, Mickey, let me in, will yer? Would yer believe I forgot me bloody keys an' the missis 'as gone ter visit 'er sister in Blackpool. Tekken the kids an' all which gives me a bit o' peace. Come on, lad, open bloody gates.'

'Yer daft bugger,' the watchman grumbled, tucking the purring cat under his arm and lifting the pan of delicious-smelling sausage and bacon from the fire. ' 'Ere, let yerself in an' be quick about it.' As he unlocked the gate he threw a bunch of keys to the waiting man then went back to his meal. The man's nostrils twitched as the smell was mouth-watering and wasted on a bloody cat but he had something of great importance to do because the woman had promised him a bonus if he found this girl.

It took him seconds to reach the manager's office, unlock it and fumble his way to the telephone that stood on the desk. Hesitantly he lifted the receiver of what was known as a Candlestick model. When he put it cautiously to his ear, hoping to God he didn't get an electric shock, he nearly jumped out of his skin when a posh voice said, 'Number please.' He hastily read out the telephone number the woman had given him and was again startled when a female voice answered. 'The Seymour residence,' she said, and when he asked for Mrs Seymour she asked him politely to hold on.

He did so.

'Yes?' a superior voice said abruptly.

'I found 'er,' he answered.

The woman knew exactly who he was and what he meant. 'Thank you,' she said, just as though it was a missing button he had turned up. 'You will be well rewarded,' then the line went dead.

*   *   *

The reunion with her family was both euphoric and at the same time awkward. When they entered the cottage Sammy was standing at the stone sink peeling spuds for the family's evening meal. He, of course, knew who she was by now though he was by no means easy with her. The ten-year-old sister, pale, thin-faced, big-eyed, anxious, dressed in rags, bore no resemblance to the beautiful, elegant, well-spoken young lady who clung to his mam's hand and Amy knew it would take time for them to be as they once had been. The rest of them, Claire, Elsie, Billy, Dick, Annie, Phyllis and Sidney, came bursting through the door. Becky worked after school for Mrs Ash at Ashes Farm, helping to scrub out the dairy for a few bob and eggs, milk and cheese so she would be last home. Billy had been playing football until the light had

358

gone and the others enjoying various games with their pals in the fields about their home.

They all stopped dead in their tracks when they saw the two visitors who were sitting in Mam and Pa's chair drinking tea and not one of them recognised her. The difference between ten and seventeen is vast and they hesitated, looking to their mother for an explanation.

Amy stood up and moved towards them where they were grouped round the door. At the same time Joe suddenly jumped to his feet. They all turned to look at him.

'I'd best be off,' he announced loudly. 'Yer'll want ter talk an I've things ter see to before ... well, I'll be back for yer, lass'—he found it easier to call her lass than Amy—'ter run yer 'ome.' And before Amy could protest he was out of the door and down the path to the gate where the motor car was parked.

'Were that 'is motor?' Billy breathed rapturously. 'We wondered, di'n't we, our Dick?'

'Aye.'

'Never mind that, our Billy. Look 'oo's 'ere,' Dolly said tremulously.

They all turned to look at the young lady who was standing expectantly at the range, then turned to their mother, their expressions mystified.

'Fer God's sake, will yer look at 'oo it is, after all these years an' not one o' yer ... See ...'

'Never mind, Mam,' Amy told her, choking back her tears. 'It's been a long time and I must say the lot of them have grown so much I would hardly have recognised them so it must seem to them that I'm a stranger.'

'It's yer sister, yer blockheads,' Dolly Pearson

shrieked. 'Yer sister Amy come back to us after all this time. Eeh, our Claire, give 'er a kiss then; all on yer, give yer sister a kiss.'

But still they hung back and Amy realised that what she had longed for, dreamed of, though it had actually happened was not as she had imagined. Her fantasy had gone no further than this moment and what was to happen afterwards had not even occurred to her. They would all have to get to know one another again and it would take time. It was not that they did not trust her. It was that they did not know her.

The door was flung open with a suddenness that startled them all and an attractive girl came in with a basket on her arm. 'I dunno,' she said, 'I'll knock that bloody cowman's teeth down 'is throat if 'e tries it on wi' me . . .' She stopped and the words died in her throat then her gaze fastened on Amy and with a crash she dropped the basket, which happened to be filled with eggs. Flinging herself across the room she dragged Amy into her arms and like her mother began to weep.

'I knew, I bloody knew yer'd come back, our Amy. I sed, didn't I, Mam, I sed. Amy, oh, our Amy.'

And through her own tears Amy managed to say, 'Thank God one of you besides Mam remembers me.'

*   *   *

Caleb had bought Amy a bicycle, not only to get to the hospital but to visit her mother and the family since it was a long walk from Elmhurst in Victoria Avenue to Hope Cottage in Walton on the Hill.

Joe could not be expected to run her there whenever she had the fancy to go, which, let's face it, she said, was as often as she could. She had her duties at the hospital to fulfil and Joe had his job, not only as gardener but teaching the doctor to drive. John was ready to get behind the wheel now and needed the motor car not only to get to the hospital but to meet the hospital trains which came with ever more frequency into Lime Street Station. The bicycle was very smart, a Rover with a sprung saddle, the latest plunger brake and a chain guard, brand new, of course, and on it she was able to visit the familiar chaos of her mam's home. Elsie, now sixteen, had a good position as a parlour-maid at Walton Priory but was in constant argument with her mam since she longed to work in the munitions factory where the wages were so much better, or even, as their recently returned sister had, become a VAD at the hospital. Becky, at fourteen, was ready to leave school and didn't know what she wanted but Amy had her eye on her as a nursemaid for Bella, though she had said nothing as yet. The rest attended Kirkdale School.

She had come to realise that it was going to take time for them to be the family they had once been. Not just because of the years between but because she had changed so unutterably. She was no longer one of the working classes who spoke with the nasal Liverpool dialect as they did but had been turned into a young lady with some ... well, *breeding* was hardly the word but it described the difference between them.

That was why Caleb bought her the bicycle and whenever she had time off she would ride over to Hope Cottage and become one of them again. She

361

was unaware that almost everywhere she went she was followed!

As the new year came in the casualties were appalling. In February 1916 the Germans had launched a major offensive, delivering the heaviest blow they could against France, the objective being Verdun, a citadel town, manned by a permanent garrison and surrounded by impregnable forts. The French urged the British to advance the date of the Allied offensive to relieve the pressure on their forces but it was to be some months before this happened and while the French were fighting for their lives the British Tommies took over part of the line from the French in order to relieve their badly stretched resources. There were no major battles on the British lines because all the strength, the men and matériel, must be conserved for the one tremendous blow that would be struck in the summer.

But the casualties still flowed in, joining the large backlog of men wounded in the first years of the war, the blind, the paralysed, the limbless. With patients requiring long-term care and fresh convoys of recently wounded, many of them found their way to Liverpool and John Carstairs was not surprised when Mr Hawthorn told him that though he did not care for it he had no choice but to return Private Joe Carter to the battlefield before long. He was aware that Private Carter did not take a bed that a wounded man might require but he was able-bodied, physically in better condition than many of the fresh soldiers being shipped across the Channel.

Amy was distraught though she did her best not to let Joe see it. She was still no more than a friend to Joe, the lass who had helped him on the road to recovery; who had ever since they had found her mam and her family included him in many a family event. They were all still shy with Amy and with Joe, but he spoke like them, or something like it, for he was a northerner, he was easy-going and was teaching young Billy to box. He had been wounded in France and in some ways had become closer to them than their own sister.

He was to return to France soon and when he turned up with their Amy in his khaki uniform, his service cap at a jaunty angle, his tunic and pantaloons wrapped around with his puttees, they were enchanted and Amy despaired of their innocence. They thought it was such an adventure that Joe was off to fight again.

'Don't fret, lass,' her mother said as they sat with their feet up to the shining range. She had told her mother the complete story of her life from the day Zillah Seymour had ripped her from her family until the moment she had been brought to live with Bella and John Carstairs. She had not, of course, gone into any detail of the night and the nightmare she had shared with Randall Hodge, for how could she describe it to any woman, especially her own mother, but Dolly was not daft. She knew some men were beasts when it came to women and she had understood.

' 'E don't know,' she said, nodding her head to the small garden where Joe was playing another skipping game, taught him by Amy, with the girls.

'All in together girls, very fine weather girls,' they chanted, while the boys practised the boxing moves Joe had been teaching them.

'No, he doesn't even remember me. I loved him

363

and he loved me, years ago. I still love him but . . .'

'Yer don't know 'ow ter gerrim back.'

'Not without damaging him further, Mam. God knows how he'll cope with the trenches. I've seen some sights, boys who have come back so terrified that any sharp noise sends them scurrying to get under their beds. I can't bear to think . . .' She bent her head and bit her lip and her mother leaned across the hooked rag rug and took her hand, fondling it gently.

'Eeh, chuck, I don't know what ter say. Yer can only 'ope an' pray that the lad's 'ad 'is turn and . . .'

'Yes, Mam. At least I've got you back, and our Becky's to start at Elmhurst when she finishes school. I only hope our Elsie'll come to her senses and give up this notion of going into the munitions factory. She's too young for the hospital.' She sighed deeply and stood up. 'Well, we'd best be going. Joe has to . . . well, he's to be off soon when Mr Hawthorn's given him his final examination. I'll try and get over on the bicycle tomorrow after my shift. D'you know it's taken over a year since I came back to Liverpool for me finally to do something I promised myself I would do one day?'

Since Dolly had taken work at the cotton mill and the two eldest children were working, life had become easier for the Pearson family. The cottage was not big and they had to sleep double or even three to a bed but the kitchen/sitting room was comfortably furnished and with a big fire roaring in the range was warm and cosy. There were the two easy chairs and in the centre of the room a round table at which the family ate. The table was covered with a plush cloth in bright crimson and round it were six chairs and three stools. On the table was an enormous vase brought from Elmhurst containing a mass of golden daffodils, picked that morning from under the trees in the garden at Elmhurst.

* * *

The telephone shook with excitement in the woman's hand as she waited for it to be answered and she was disappointed when a female voice answered.

'Ah, Miss Hodge, is your brother there? It's Zillah Seymour and I'd like a word with him.'

'Just a moment, Mrs Seymour, I'll get him for you.'

A moment later an unctuous male voice came on the line. 'Zillah, how are you?'

'Randall, we've found her!' Triumph ran along the wire and the man and woman on the telephone felt it surge into their veins.

'Where . . . ?'

'I don't know how she found out but she was waiting at the gates of the mill where her mother works. She was with a man in a motor car and they took her mother back to Hope Cottage. Do you realise what this means, my dear Randall? We have only to watch her mother and we, you, will have your wife safely back home with you. Justice will have been served. "The Lord moves in mysterious ways His wonders to perform." Let no man—' But before Zillah could get into her stride on what her Lord said about her and Randall's private problems Randall Hodge cut through smoothly.

'So what is the next step, Zillah? Whatever it

costs I am willing to pay it. A wife should be with her husband, as you and I agree.' His voice shook a little when he thought about what he would do to *his* when he had her alone in his home.

'We need a good detective with an automobile so that wherever she goes with this man, whoever he is, she can be followed. Someone discreet and I will find such a man. Leave it all to me, Randall and I guarantee your wife will be home before the month's out.'

'Very well, Zillah, and thank you.'

Randall Hodge replaced the receiver, wondering idly as he did so why Zillah Seymour was so resolute in her determination to bring back her runaway niece. After all it made no difference to her.

26

The man watched her ride through the hospital gates, turning left towards Knotty Ash, pedalling like mad with her skirts up to her knees. She had removed her nurse's cap and her hair, which she had had cut recently, curled round her head like a chrysanthemum bloom, blowing wildly in a crisp, golden-streaked tumble. Bye, she was a corker and he did not blame her husband for wanting her back. Mind, it wasn't her husband who was paying him. It was some old biddy who had entered his office in Market Street as though she owned the place. She had been so imperious, so grand in her manner you would have thought she was speaking to one of her servants and though he had a dreadful feeling that he should stand up in her presence he resisted it. After all, he was known as the best in his line of work which was—well, how would you describe it?—*retrieving* those who did not particularly want to be retrieved. Errant wives, or daughters who thought, because they were in the twentieth century and that bloody Pankhurst woman had told them they were equal to men, they could go off whenever they liked. Of course he did other detective work besides this rather lucrative sideline and was employed by several businessmen at the moment but this was too good to miss, or even postpone.

Now he was employed not only to find this pretty little nurse but to bring her back, whether she wanted to be brought back or not, to her husband. He had been following her for a week now, in his discreetly sprayed dark green Renault which he had chosen because it seated four, two at the front and two at the back and had a hood that could be put up to conceal what or who he might be carrying. He was staying in one of Liverpool's finest hotels, for his line or work was well paid and the costs all went on expenses. He liked to find out the routine of his . . . well, objective before he made his plans and today he was to put them into action. She had not noticed him as he followed her, some of the time on foot, but even when he was in his Renault, passing her on the country lanes, she had seemed oblivious to him.

He overtook her now, as he knew she was headed for her mother's cottage at Walton. She would cycle across country on narrow lanes, many of them leading to the farms, until she reached Priory Lane then turn into Walton Lane where

Hope Cottage lay.

He parked his Renault several yards round a corner where it was hidden by the burgeoning hedges, sat for several minutes enjoying a cigar then, since he had timed it precisely, knowing she would be approaching, got out of the motor car and stood at the corner, studying a map and scratching his head.

As he had hoped she hesitated when she saw him then applied her brake and stopped.

'Are you lost?' she asked him. 'I don't know my way round here very well but I might be able to help you.'

'That would be most kind,' he told her pleasantly. 'I'm looking for Broad Green but I seem to have completely missed the turn I was told to take.' He was well dressed, polite and gave the appearance of being a threat to nobody. She leaned her bicycle against the hedge and moved towards him, peering over his shoulder at his map and with one swift movement he had his arms about her and a pad across her mouth. She was completely off her guard and for several vital seconds did not even struggle, then with a great surge she kicked backwards in an effort to reach that vital part of the masculine anatomy which Caleb, when she first began to go about on her own and might still be in danger from the monster who was her husband, had told her to aim for. But the pad had been soaked in chloroform and she could feel her senses reeling. Her limbs seemed not to belong to her and her body started to sag, but the man held her strongly and with practised movements began to drag her towards the corner where he had parked his motor. He had some rope in the back of the car; well, not rope exactly, for this girl must not be damaged and rope was inclined to chafe but something with which to tie her up soundly and lay her down on the back seat of the Renault. He must be quick, for who knew what country hick might come along this quiet country lane and demand to know what he was doing.

But it was not a country hick that came upon him but another motor car. He quickly dragged the inert figure of the girl into the ditch and lay on top of her, hidden from view by anyone just passing, but this bloody car stopped, the driver not even turning off the engine and to his astonishment the man leaped from the automobile in a rage so frightening he wanted to jump over the hedge and run for his life. The bastard pulled him off his victim and dragged her to him, holding her in his arms and kissing her face with a passion that held the detective quite fascinated for a fraction of a second and in that second the man sprang up and went for his throat. He would have killed him, throttled the life out of him, for Joe Newbridge was beyond reason, but at that moment a labourer with a sheepdog, coming from Therry Lane Farm to fetch some sheep to another field, stood for an instant, mouth agape, watching the two men grappling in the lane before him and the figure of a girl lying half in and half out of the ditch. His dog began to bark and he set off at a run shouting, 'Ere, what's goin' on an' what's ter do wi't lass? 'Ere, 'old on, lad, don't yew start on me,' as Joe turned on him. 'See, give over, the pair o' yer.' And at that second Joe came to his senses. He turned from the detective who had crumpled to the ground, groaning and clutching his throat, and the labourer, yelling at his dog to 'shut the 'ell up', helped him to his feet.

Joe held Amy in his arms, crying her name over and over again. 'Sweetheart . . . sweetheart, speak ter me, lass. Amy, my little rosebud. Christ, what's that bugger done ter yer, I'll bloody kill him,' turning to the man who had accosted Amy and who was leaning on the shoulder of the bewildered labourer.

'What's goin' on 'ere?' he snarled, addressing Amy's attacker, his lips white with rage and even the labourer, who had nothing to do with all this, stepped back. What a tale he'd have to tell his missis when he got back home tonight!

'It's nowt ter do wi' me,' he protested, but Joe was in control of himself now and the man who had been sent to take Mrs Randall Hodge back to her husband began to edge away towards the corner where he had hidden his Renault.

''Old 'im,' Joe ordered, but the labourer took another step back.

'Nay, it's nowt ter do wi' me, mister,' he repeated, 'so if young lady's all right, I'll be off. I've sheep ter fetch an' my missis'd not be best pleased if I were ter get mixed up . . . Come on, Jess,' he said to his dog and as the Renault roared into life and took off at great speed he continued his hurried walk up the lane towards the field where his sheep grazed.

Joe sat on the grass verge, Amy safely in his arms, watching his love's lifeless face. He kissed it, lingering on her lips, softly, wonderingly, stroking her cheek and whispering, 'My little rosebud, my little rosebud, where have you been? Where have *I* been? What are we doing here in this country lane? I came to find you. You were Nurse Carstairs ... to tell you ... I don't know what medd me come, 'onest. Oh, my little love, and I found my Amy. You are my heart's sweetness; I used to say that to you before ... before ...' He tightened his arms about her and gazed imploringly into her face. She was the colour of suet and suddenly he was frightened. The engine of the little motor car ... Jesus, he couldn't even remember why he had come tearing up here after her. He had known she was coming to see her mother after her half-day shift at the hospital but something inside him ... what the devil had it been, that sixth sense that had told him to get in the motor and drive over to Hope Cottage to see if she had arrived, if she was safe? Why should she not have been and yet his instinct, passive for so long, had screamed at him to come. He looked over at the Morris. The engine was still running and without thinking he lifted her and placed her gently in the passenger seat. She was beginning to sweat and breathe strangely and almost falling over his own feet in his desperation he jumped into the driver's seat, turned the motor car round expertly in the narrow lane and roared off in the direction of the hospital.

There was an ambulance, thank God, only one, standing at the entrance. He almost fell from the motor, then, picking up Amy, he ran into the lobby shouting for Doctor Carstairs.

'That's enough of that, soldier,' a grim-faced nurse who was bending over a stretcher told him. 'There are wounded men here and you—'

'I know that, I were one of 'em once, Nurse, but this lass is ill; she's bin given some drug, I don't

371

know what an' Doctor Carstairs knows 'er and 'e'll 'ave summat ter say if 'e's not told she's 'ere. It's Amy, tell 'im. Dear God, woman, don't just stand there.'

All about them were startled nurses and orderlies, men on stretchers, visitors, all staring, mouths agape, at the maddened young man with the lifeless figure of a young nurse in his arms. It was perhaps her uniform that aroused the enraged figure of the nurse to call out to one of the orderlies to fetch Doctor Carstairs, *if he could be spared*, to the front entrance, and for several restless minutes Joe moved about the entrance hall, his face close to Amy's, murmuring to her, kissing her face, watched by the fascinated spectators.

John Carstairs put up his hands as he approached Joe, who at once began to babble about a man, a pad ... smelly ... a fight and the labourer's help ... and the ride to here and Amy ... Amy ... Amy, her name running like water from a tap through the incoherent tale.

'Bring her in here, Joe,' indicating a small office, and was not surprised when the nurse who had sent for him followed them in. 'Put her on the couch.' And when Joe did so he and the nurse, who had pushed Joe to one side, murmured over her, feeling her pulse, sounding her heart, lifting her eyelids, smelling her breath.

'Mmm,' the nurse said enigmatically as though she suspected something suspicious, then she left the room.

John turned to Joe. 'She's been drugged, Joe. Tell me exactly what happened.'

Joe did so, even mentioning the labourer's dog

as though afraid that if he missed any small thing Doctor John would not have a complete picture.

John sighed then suddenly he became more actively alert, for he had realised in that second that Joe was different. How different? He was looking in the most agonised way at Amy, not as he had done for the past months. Not as the friend they had all made of him, but with such loving passion, such desperate concern he knew, even if Joe himself had not quite grasped it, that Joe was in complete command of his past life and the part that Amy had played in it.

'You ... you remember, Joe?' he asked hesitantly.

' 'Course I remember,' Joe answered irritably. 'I just told yer, didn't I?'

'I mean before that. Before, when you and Amy ... that you knew each other before you were wounded.'

Joe became very still, his eyes focused on something only he could see and his face was totally without expression. John watched him for a moment but this was no time to be discussing how Joe was feeling, for the girl on the couch must be seen to. He thought it was probably chloroform that had been applied on the pad clamped to her mouth but, naturally, he didn't know the amount. She showed no sign yet of regaining her senses but she couldn't be left here. And he must get back to the wounded men who had just arrived in the ambulance, one of whom was in a desperate state. A boy of about nineteen who had clearly not had a bath for weeks. He had been badly burned in an explosion and when they peeled off his uniform his skin came with it and though his mouth was wide open in a scream no sound emerged. He had been blinded by chlorine gas which had also affected his lungs. The burns on his body were the worst John had ever seen in his professional life and he had anguished over man's inhumanity to his fellow man. He prayed to a God in whom he did not believe that the boy would die. The nurse he had left him with, though she was supposed to show no emotion, had been weeping, wringing her hands at the soldier's agony.

'Stay here with Amy,' he said to Joe. 'I'll send someone to examine her.'

'Why can't you do it?'

'I've dying men to see to, Joe. Amy will be all right but watch her for a few minutes.' Then he was gone, hurrying away to attend to the detritus the war had washed up on the shore of his hospital ward.

Joe sat down on the end of the couch and lifted Amy's lolling head, cradling it on his lap. He did not speak for a while then he began to murmur softly.

'Aye, my lovely lass, I remember. I remember playin' tennis wi' yer when yer fell an' scraped yer 'and. Mrs Abigail put a bandage on yer. I remember kissin' yer in t'woods. I loved yer then an' I love yer now but most of all I remember yer walkin' out o' that bloody chapel wi' that bugger ... I were out o' me mind, that's why I joined up. An' I remember poor Pip an' Corky an' all the lads 'oo died on that wire and 'oo sank inter't mud in no-man's-land but though I might've forgot wi' me mind what you an' me 'ad me heart never forgot yer. What 'appened to yer, lovely girl? 'Ow did yer get 'ere?' He placed his lips on hers and the kiss was sweet and reverent, then stroked the satin skin of her cheek, smelling of some fragrance he could not recognise. Not that he knew anything about perfume or soap and such, for he knew nothing about women. He was still a virgin and though the thought harrowed him he did not suppose her to be.

'I love yer . . . I love yer, you're me heart. Eeh, when I think o' that bugger wi' . . . no, no, I can't bear it.' He arched his neck, throwing back his head as he imagined another man's hands . . .

At that moment another doctor, not one he knew, entered the room abruptly. Without looking at Joe he went quickly to Amy. 'I'm an anaesthetist, let me take a look.' He examined Amy's fingernails, took her pulse, sounded her heart, felt her skin, then stood up seeming to be satisfied with her. Already some colour was returning to her face.

'She'll do,' he told Joe casually. 'Take her home and see she goes straight to bed. A light diet and lots of sleep, oh, and make sure she drinks plenty of water.' He left the room as quickly as he had entered.

Joe held her for almost half an hour. No one seemed concerned with the young man who sat in the office with a girl lying quietly in his arms but when she began to stir, to open her eyes, to look up at him, even to smile, he sat her up and held her leaning against him.

'It's all right, darlin', I'm here. No one'll hurt yer but I must get yer 'ome. Doctor ses . . .'

'Joe, Joe, is it you?' she asked wonderingly, gazing up at him, putting a tentative hand to his smooth brown cheek. 'Really you?'

'Aye, lass, I've come back. I don't know what 'appened but some bastard was tryin' ter get yer into his motor, chloroform, doctor said. Well, I saw red. Thank Jesus I came along when I did. What is it?' for she had begun to struggle, doing her best to stand up, terror on her face and in her eyes.

'Joe, it was him . . . him. He's found me and I'd kill myself before I'd go back to him. Joe, take me home. Oh, God, d'you think he's found where I live? I'll have to move, my mam, the family . . .'

'Lovey, lovey, calm down. Nobody's going to hurt yer, not when I'm around, but let's get yer back to Elmhurst. The doctor said yer was ter go ter bed an' rest.'

'Rest. *Rest!* With that monster watching for me. I thought . . . I thought I was safe.'

'You *are* safe! We'll speak ter Mr Seymour. Telephone 'im an' tell 'im what's 'appened. He'll know what ter do but first you must go back ter Elmhurst an' do what the doctor ordered. I'll not leave yer, sweetheart.'

She grew still then and with the sudden light of remembrance in her wide eyes she seemed to see him for who he was. For the first time since the day she had last seen him at Somerfield he was *her* Joe again, the man who, with his combination of gentleness and strength, had cherished her. Every gesture and expression on his face told her how it was to love someone, a woman, to love *her*, to respect and honour and . . . Dear Lord, she didn't know how to put into words what she meant, she only knew that this man, this dear man could be trusted. That between them was the greatest gift given to a man and a woman. A love that was true, unending, unbreakable.

For perhaps five seconds the truth of it wrapped them both in luminous joy. They looked wordlessly into one another's eyes then he helped her to her feet and with his arms about her guided her out of the office, the hospital and into the motor which still stood, to the irritation of a porter, at the wide front door.

'Yer can't park 'ere,' he told them indignantly.

'Thank you,' Joe said politely, leaving the man scratching his head in bewilderment.

*   *   *

'If they know where you work and where your mother's cottage is then they know about Elmhurst,' Caleb told them, 'so we must find a safe place for you to stay.'

'I won't be separated from Joe, Papa. We have just found one another and I—'

'Amy, my dear, I'm afraid you are going to be separated from Joe whether you like it or not,' John said quietly. 'Joe is a soldier who was wounded but he is recovered. Mr Hawthorn was reluctant to return him to the front while he was still missing so much of his memory, including his training in the army, and he was afraid that the pressure of being back in the trenches, even though he was physically recovered, might send him . . . well, you have seen the soldiers, Amy, who were not able to stand the strain of battle. But now that Joe is himself again Mr Hawthorn has no option but to report him fit for duty. He will be sent—'

'I will go with him. They cannot find me in France. I will use my nursing skills at the hospitals

377

there. I know that there is one at Camiers and another at Rouen. I have heard the wounded talking and unless you send me to . . . to . . . well, I don't know, somewhere far away to hide me from them, and where I shall know no one, I cannot hide away for ever.'

They were gathered in the Carstairs drawing room, John and Bella, Caleb, Amy and Joe, the latter hand in hand. Amy had recovered from her ordeal in the lane on the way to her mam's, and Becky, who was now ensconced in the Carstairs nursery where she was a great success with the children, had been sent with a message to Dolly Pearson not to expect to see Amy for a few days. She was well, Becky told her mam and there was nothing to worry about but she was confined to the house on doctor's orders. Becky had repeated the message word for word that Doctor Carstairs had made her memorise, and Amy would be in touch very soon. It had been a bit of a mystery to Dolly but she would hear what it was all about before too long.

There was a deep silence after Amy stopped speaking then Joe leaped to his feet and began to stride round the room with jerky steps. 'Oh, no, no,' he declared. 'I'm not 'avin' you in an 'ospital in France. I've bin there, not in the 'ospital or if I were I don't remember it, but I've seen what . . . what men look like when they're wounded, gassed, an' I'm not 'avin' you put in—'

'So have I, Joe. I've seen the men who come to the hospital from the front and I've been sick, literally, running to the sluice room so that no one would see me, but I've always gone back and got on with it. There was a man with . . . his face was hideous in a raw and bleeding state but Sister said to us, "*Always* look a man in the face. Remember he's watching you to see how you're going to react. Smile when you are doing a dressing." And I did it even though later I was ... well ... I want to nurse, I want to help, but more than anything I want to be as near to you as I can. When you get leave from the trenches and, dear God'—her throat closed up and she was near to tears—'I want to be able to be with you. And have you thought that though you say I will be in danger it will be nothing to the danger I shall be in if I stay where Mrs Seymour and that man ... that man who is my husband and has a perfect right to do with me as he pleases, which is what he did on our wedding night. Oh, no, Joe, my love, I'm sorry.' She got up and ran across the room to where Joe stood by the window, his face twitching in horror and hatred and all the emotions he felt for the man who had taken his lovely girl and used her ... He couldn't stand it. *But she did*, his appalled mind told him and if she stood it so can you. He felt her arms go round him. They were unaware of the others who sat and watched, unable to move, their faces showing their deep distress for this young couple who had suffered so much.

She laid her cheek against his rigid back and clasped her hands across his chest holding him to her until gradually she felt him relax, sighing, for he knew that there was little choice between one danger and another. The hospitals in France, at Camiers and Rouen, were well away from the front line and, unless she was sent to one of the tented casualty stations where many of the wounded were first despatched, she would be safe. If she was to

379

stay here at Elmhurst she would be forced to live the life of a recluse and even then her husband could come knocking on the door and demand she return. He was not sure of the legalities. Once upon a time a wife belonged entirely to her husband and had no choice but to live under his roof but surely things had changed since then? However it was a chance he was not prepared to take. And he had no right, no legal right to prevent her applying to go to France. Who did? She was under age, of course, and had been adopted by Zillah and Caleb Seymour so perhaps Mr Seymour, but when he turned to Caleb who sat quietly on the sofa, cigar between his lips, Caleb shook his head as though he knew what Joe was asking him.

'They will have her, Joe, whatever is said and done. I know my wife. She is obsessed, mad even, and as for that beast who ... well, I will say no more but their religion rules them. The Methodist beliefs are on the whole totally innocent and hurt no one unless taken to extremes as Zillah has. I really think, though I hate the very idea, that Amy would be better leaving, going to France where she can continue her nursing and she will perhaps have the opportunity of seeing you. And I will look after her family, see no harm comes to them and that they stay in their cottage. I have a certain influence in the city.'

He was rewarded with a radiant look of gratitude from Amy, though Joe still looked undecided. He had been in battles before he was wounded. He could remember vividly poor Pip crucified on the wire. He could see men who had been blown into so many pieces not a scrap of flesh had ever been found, but then she had worked in the hospital all this time and had also witnessed broken men and had done her best to mend them. She was not going into the unknown as far as that was concerned. He could not even protect her by marrying her, as she was already married to another man. When this was all over they would have to find a way to free her from him. Mr Seymour would know. Hadn't he had the answers to so many of Joe and Amy's awful predicaments? He had protected Amy and brought her to what he had thought was a safe harbour during the past year and his advice was sound. He loved Amy as a father loved his own child and when Joe thought back to the days when he had worked at Somerfield and the woman who was Mr Seymour's wife he wondered why his employer had ever married her. Miss Dodie, the mother of his young son, was the sweetest, gentlest of women and Mr Seymour was happy with her and it suddenly struck him that Amy and Mr Seymour were in the same boat. Mr Seymour was married to the mistress of Somerfield and Amy was married to . . . he didn't know the man's name and he didn't want to but somehow the thought of it gave him courage and the strength to turn and take Amy in his arms.

'If I find yer've tekken the slightest risk yer didn't need to I'll . . . oh, my love, my dearest love . . .' Then his voice broke and Bella turned and put her face in her husband's shoulder to hide her tears.

27

She stood at the rail in the lifejacket that had been handed to her as she boarded the Channel steamer with strict instructions to wear it at all times. All about her were excited young soldiers going out for the first time, laughing and joking among the grim-faced men who were returning from leave. She wished Joe was among them but he had gone back months ago and she had heard from him only once.

She stared down at the racing grey waters beneath the steamer, watching the pale gleam of sunshine catching the waves formed by the bow. Two sleek destroyers raced beside the steamer, their bows cutting the water in a froth of curling foam; she supposed they were there to defend the convoy which was carrying the thousands of troops who were to take part in what they knew would be a major battle. It was the end of April and she was getting closer and closer to Joe.

She remembered with an intensity that made her glance about her to see if anyone noticed her trembling the last time they had been together. It had been in his room, the room above the garage block where the Morris was stored and where Joe had lived since he left the hospital.

From the moment she had known he was to return to France and that they might be parted not only for a very long time but perhaps for ever she had become aware that if she were ever to demolish for good the night she had spent with Randall Hodge she must know the real meaning of physical love, that of a man who truly loved a woman with a love that was returned. She and Joe, though she had known Joe would never consider it since he loved and respected her, and if he did consider it would make no attempt to persuade her, must be united in the act of love. Even as she said the words to herself, in her mind, of course, she knew it made Joe sound pompous, a prig even, not a true male. Although she was afraid after what her monster of a husband had done to her, at the same time she longed for Joe's touch. It had been growing quietly and lovingly for months and as she thought back to the hours she had spent with him in Manchester, in the woods and gardens about Somerfield, she now knew that it had been in him for many years.

He was to leave within weeks and make his way to Dover, there to board the boat to the coast of France along with others who she supposed would have been very much like the group who were about her now.

Anyone looking out of a window overlooking the yard at Elmhurst that first night might have believed they were seeing a ghost floating across the cobbles, a ghostly figure in white, an insubstantial entity that would have had Daisy and Mrs Topsy shivering in their beds. She had worn, as she always did now, a diaphanous nightgown of lawn trimmed with lace which had been a gift from Dodie who wore such a garment to please Caleb. There had been a light in the window of Joe's room and as she made her way quietly up the steps on the outside of the building she could see a thin line beneath the door. She tapped on it with her fingernails and it had opened at once as though he

383

had been waiting for her immediately on the other side. He wore no shirt and the skin of his chest was a warm brown.

For perhaps five seconds they had looked at one another without words then his hands had reached for hers and drawn her inside and closed the door behind her. It was the first time they had ever been completely alone in a room, private, secret, just the two of them, then without speaking she was in his arms and anything that may have lingered from the horror of her wedding night drifted away like early morning mist as the sun rose. She burrowed into his arms, doing her best to get deeper and deeper into his embrace, making soft little sounds in the back of her throat and he gripped her so fiercely he hurt her. His mouth came down on hers, not in one of the gentle, reverent kisses he had bestowed upon her in the woods at Somerfield but with the fierceness of a man, urgent, demanding, parting her lips, caressing, folding, holding, ready to bite and snap in his need, but not with the cruelty that her husband had shown. But he could tell what it was she wanted and that she wanted it as much as he did.

'Darling, my dearest love,' his mouth murmured against hers while she shifted her body in an effort to get closer to him. He was a man with a man's needs and she was his woman, willing, more than willing, her desire as fierce as his. He loved her mindlessly, his male body dominating his thoughts and could he refuse what she was offering?

Stepping away from her for a moment he lifted her nightdress and pulled it from her so that she stood completely naked before him, glorious, her breasts peaked and rosy pressing against his bare

384

chest and when he shook off his breeches which had dropped about his ankles, his manhood reared against her belly. She was life, warmth, vital and strong, a lustrous shade of burned honey in the candlelight. Their hearts tripped and hammered as they parted a bare inch to look into each other's eyes as though they must both know that they were equal in this, then he lifted her and placed her on the narrow bed. They neither of them thought of the past, nor the future, for who knew what it held. There was just *now*, this magic moment, this closeness. His body was hard and yet there was tenderness, for his love made him so.

'I love you.'

'I love you.'

His lips explored her eyelids, her cheeks and jaw and then back to her mouth which was full and moist and ready for love. Then the softness of their lips became hard, even cruel in the savagery of their need. His penis butted against her for a moment since it was his first time, then he was inside her and Amy and Joe loved one another in a way that had been denied them for so long and which had been their destiny from the beginning. The strokes of him, long, hard, insistent, forced her head back into the pillow and she cried out, and in the room further along the block old Seth heard it, and smiled.

For a full five minutes they remained fast together, their bodies cooling, then she drew his head down to her breast and she thought they slept for a while though time had no meaning. He loved her again, then again, but in the pale light of dawn she crept back to her room and into her bed, her body aching, not with the pain she had known once but with joyful weariness.

She had gone to his room every night until the last one before he left for his unit and they all knew about it in the house. It was not that Seth informed on them, nor that anyone actually saw her glide across the yard, but it was evident in the way they were with one another, looked at one another, smiled at one another that there was a bond, the physical bond, the look on Amy's face that told the world she was a woman who was well loved.

And when he went she thought she would die. They had said a wordless goodbye in his room, held fast in one another's arms, he in the full uniform of a soldier, with a rifle, webbing belts and straps which held rounds in pouches, water bottle and back pack, and wore the soft-topped version of the khaki service cap. She kept her back to him as he quickly left the room. He said emotional goodbyes—on their part—to Daisy and Mrs Topsy, to Bella and the children who were wildly excited that their Joe was off to fight.

Their innocence cut them all to the heart. He was driven to the station by John Carstairs who shook him by the hand without words. They had all become attached to Joe but they did not grieve as she did and she had plenty of time to brood. She was not allowed to leave the house, following Caleb and John's orders, unless she had someone with her. The children took up much of her time though she thought Becky resented her for what she saw as interference in what was now Becky's job. She no longer worked at the hospital but John and Caleb pulled many strings to have her transferred. Caleb especially, who was a man of great influence, power and wealth, tipped the balance. He walked into Matron's room at the hospital and sat down uninvited, perfectly charming, and before many minutes had passed the Medical Officer now in command was summoned and with a substantial cheque in his hand, which would go a long way to purchasing equipment badly needed in the care of limbless soldiers, he was more than willing to assist Mr Seymour in his request to get his niece, a VAD, to France.

At last the day was here; she was safe on the steamer to France. She was part of the British army now, carrying an army identity certificate in her pocket. It bore an unsmiling photograph of her and recorded her name, Amy Carstairs, her age, army rank and the number of her detachment. The number was repeated in brass on her shoulder straps. She wore, like the other fifteen who were travelling with her, a white shirt and black tie, an ugly hat, a dark blue coat and skirt and a wide Red Cross band encircling her arm. She was a VAD nurse on active service.

She was posted to Rouen with five others, to a hospital on the edge of a great forest, sharing a bell tent—the erection of which caused hysterical laughter, perhaps the first phase in what was to be a deep and lasting friendship—with a girl a bit older than herself whose name was, aptly, Mercy. Mercy Andrews was the daughter of a Yorkshire parson, well educated by her father, shy, soft-spoken and apprehensive. She was a little bit of a thing and Amy could not imagine her lifting wounded soldiers, but she had a gentle, compassionate nature. She was attractive with the pale skin that goes with bright, fox-coloured hair, with small golden freckles across her nose. She had worked in a hospital in Huddersfield but like Amy had a reason to be transferred to France, though it was several weeks before she told Amy of her love for a Yorkshire lad who was a pilot in the British Royal Flying Corps. She was twenty and so was he. He had been in France since December 1915 flying a BE 2c and though the life expectancy of a British pilot was seventeen and a half hours, he was still alive, and a hero, Lieutenant Richard Steele. He was stationed at No 8 Squadron, RFC, near Cambrai.

'I wanted to be near him, you see. I haven't the faintest notion how we are to meet but he knows where *I* am now so he will let me know when he has leave and we can see one another.' Amy knew exactly what she meant by that statement!

'Do you have a friend?' she asked innocently.

Amy wondered what Mercy would say if she told her what she and Joe were to one another but then perhaps Mercy and her 'friend' had already anticipated their 'wedding night' as it was euphemistically called.

They did not have much time to talk, for despite what the authorities called a 'breathing space' for the British army it was not noticeable in the hospitals. Between December 1915 and May 1916 the number of killed and wounded amounted to 83,000 and the casualties were gathered in by Amy and Mercy and the other medical staff at the military hospital at Rouen among many dozens of other hospitals. Casualties flowed in but did not quickly flow out, so that the staff were all run off their poor swollen feet, the wards were so crowded. Amy became adept at turning off her mind from the sickening thought that one day she would look down at the soldier in the bed and find Joe's face looking back at her from the pillow.

She had been there weeks and the rumour of the 'big push', the biggest battle of the war, was rife about the hospital, when she received the first precious letter since her arrival in France. It had been censored but it was as though the officer who had read it had sympathised with the young lovers and most of the words he had drawn a line through were very faintly crossed out.

My love, my dearest love,

I am doing my best to shut my ears to the terrible ding-dong that is going on here. [Ding-Dong had been crossed out but she could still read it and knew what it meant.] *I have thought of you every minute of every hour of each day and, of course, all night, with wonder, delight and joy for what we shared before I left. I don't know how we will manage it, my love, but when we are both home again we will be together for always, I promise you. Please, please take care and if there should be shelling* [shelling had been lightly deleted] *promise you will hide under a table or bed. If anything should happen to you I would not want to live. I love you. Dear God, I love you. Take care for my sake. Joe.*

The letter was tucked inside her brassiere, the very latest form of underwear, next to her bare breast, giving her an almost electric shock between her legs every time she had a moment to think

389

about it for it was where Joe's fingers had been. It brought back sharply the beauty and grace of his body, the bones and flat muscles she had caressed, the hard lines of him which had been shaped by the physical work he did. His long lashes fanning his cheek as he slept, the curling tangle of his hair as it grew, his broad back and muscular forearms, his large, blunt-fingered hands, his young, strong face, the spring of hair on his chest and his thighs, hard and lean. When she was in her narrow bed she dwelled on the nights she had spent with him and fell asleep with him in her arms as she had done then.

*   *   *

Joe had been here before with Pip and Corky but both of them were gone now and his new mates— for you soon made pals of the men around you who were, after all, in the same boat—were Wally Dixon and 'Lanky' Dawson, called Lanky not because of his height or build, but because he came from Lancashire and had such a broad accent and spoke in so many Lancashire idioms they could hardly understand what he said. He liked a good 'fradge' which meant a chin-wag to the others; he wore a 'ganzie', a woollen pullover, despite the warm weather, and the 'petty', the primitive toilet arrangements in the trenches, didn't bother him because he had one at home in the back yard! He pointed out the 'sugar stealers' that floated across the trench, which turned out to be floating dandelion seeds, but he was a kind and generous lad who shared all his parcels from his mam with the rest of them. As did they all and Joe

390

Carter received more than any of the lads, since Mrs Topsy, Daisy, Bella, Dodie, and even the children who sent him little packets of their sweeties, posted something to him every week.

At half past seven on the morning of 1 July, as soon as the barrage that had deafened them for days had lifted, they went over the top, starting towards the enemy lines. They attacked shoulder to shoulder, line after line, wave upon wave, straight into the sights of the German machine-guns. The rum had warmed them up and given them a lift but in the face of the enemy fire it soon evaporated. Joe looked to left and right, seeing the long line of wavering khaki moving forward but then they began to drop, going down into the ground like puppets whose strings had been cut. He saw Captain Armitage fall to his right and Wally bent to help him but the captain's head opened with a bright red haze and Wally straightened up and walked on, the captain's blood splattered all over him. On they went and the crashing and whizzing of bullets went with them and the man next to him suddenly screamed and fell. Joe felt nothing as he crossed the pitted land, dropping into old craters and out again until they reached the German wire. He was amazed to find himself still alive. Men were roaming up and down the wire, which had not been cut by the bombardment, looking for a way through but the machine-guns scythed among them, their bodies jerking and twisting and writhing. One or two still standing were ineffectually trying to cut the wires, then they were through and he, Wally and Lanky, laughing hysterically, fell into the German trench, falling on to German bodies.

But their hysteria was short-lived. 'Keep going,' their officer yelled, and they had no choice but to climb out of the trench and trudge onwards, until they fell into the second enemy trench, again carpeted with the dead.

*   *   *

Medical arrangements had been made with care. Advance dressing-stations were clustered along the length of the line with well-sand-bagged collecting centres a little distance behind them. As the day wore on the walking wounded began to arrive and queued four deep for attention. All the medical staff and transport that could be spared were waiting, ready to move quickly to where they were needed most. Operating theatres were sent forward, situated near the line to deal with the seriously injured, but they were swamped within the first hour and the hospital trains were running a shuttle service; in the first four days after 1 July the hospital trains carried 33,392 patients from the casualty clearing-stations to the bases at Boulogne, Rouen and Le Havre.

Amy and Mercy hardly had time to look at what was going on, nor to think of their own men who were out there somewhere, perhaps in the same condition as the soldiers who poured into their ward. It was only possible to keep an eye on and care for the most dangerously wounded. The others must go to England and in most cases there was no time even to clean them up or change the rough field dressings that had been clapped on them in the heat of the battle. The push was still going on and the frantic doctors, nurses, drivers and stretcher-bearers worked round the clock in the wards, tending to men who had had their legs blown off, their faces blown apart, their heads and eyes bandaged, some with drainage tubes in their wounds, the sound of their helpless moaning a constant source of tension, the screams as they were jostled, exhausted, men with red labels attached who were likely to die and most did.

There was one soldier who had been splattered all over with shrapnel. It took five of them to do his dressings, little bits of him at a time. His leg was fractured and they had to roll him over on to his side to do his back and though it must have been agony for him he never murmured.

'What's your name, soldier?' Amy whispered to him when Sister was at the other end of the ward.

'Wally, Nurse. Private Wally Dixon. Me an' me mates copped it a few days ago. I think Joe made it but poor old Lanky got blowed up an' we never saw 'im again.'

'What was ... was Joe's surname, Wally?' she asked carefully, holding herself stiffly to attention as though afraid she might collapse. How silly, there must be a thousand Joes in the army, her racing mind told her.

'Carter, Nurse.' He was quite astonished when the nurse turned away and was violently sick at the end of the bed.

Though the sister was sympathetic there was no way they could spare Nurse Carstairs to go and look for her ... her fiancé, she was told. In the chaos that ruled on the Western Front how could she possibly search for a wounded soldier who could be at any of the hospitals that were flooded with men, half of whom didn't even know their own names. She was brutal in the face of Nurse Carstairs' outbreak of hysteria. She knew several of the sisters at Boulogne, Le Havre and casualty stations on the Somme and would do her best but Nurse Carstairs must pull herself together and when this big push eased a little she would see that she got some leave.

'I can't go on until I know, Mercy,' she moaned. 'I'll have to desert.'

'But where will you look, love? The front stretches for miles. There are dozens of casualty stations, besides which he might not have been wounded seriously and be back in the line. That private you spoke to didn't know what had happened to him.'

'I must find him, I must. You would be the same if it was Richard, you know you would.'

'Yes, but please, Amy, wait; you might have a letter.'

'Oh, dear God, I can't live . . .'

'You can. You must. There are men needing you.'

'Bugger them, It's Joe I want.'

'I know, dearest, I know.'

There came a day when the two VADs, who had done the jobs trained nurses usually did and which in normal times they would have been hauled over the coals for even attempting, found themselves in their little bell tent, both having slept for eight hours, being awakened with cups of tea by a sympathetic orderly.

'Sorry, lasses, but it's time and you'd best get cleaned up before you go on the wards. There's a fresh batch just on their way. Time for a shower and a bacon buttie and then back to work.'

Amy fought the temptation to tell the orderly to go to hell. She didn't care about one more damned patient but she dragged herself from her camp bed and began to pull on the uniform she did not remember removing, throwing a clean, capacious white apron over it that reached to the hem of her skirt and had the Red Cross insignia on the bib. Her cap had a turned-back cuff, an improvement on the hideous contraption she had worn at the hospital in Liverpool. She was glad she had had her hair cut before she left England as all she needed to do was brush carelessly through the short mop of curls and stuff it under the cap, unlike Mercy who wore hers long and needed to plait it before winding it round her head.

They walked together across the grass on which their tent, along with dozens of others, was pitched and as she approached the hospital Amy felt the despair flood her. How could she possibly enter this building where so much suffering was taking place and calmly attend those who relied on her and the other VADs to take care of them, when Joe might be lying in a hospital bed somewhere, or, worse, in a crater in no-man's-land, wounded and needing her. At least before Wally had been admitted to the ward she had harboured the belief, false though it might have been, that he was alive and whole even if in great danger. Dear God, she had known of the terrible things that could happen to a man from all the appalling weapons of war but she had had *hope* that he would come through unscathed. That very soon they would both get leave and find some quiet corner in this war-torn land to be together until it ended. Now he was missing somewhere, perhaps already dead and there was nothing she could do about it. She had her duty to these men who needed what she could give them and, as Sister had so sharply pointed out, even if she was given permission, where would she begin to search for him? Wally would probably know where they had been and with which battalion when he was wounded but even so it would be an impossible task.

There was an ambulance column lined up outside the hospital taking the most severely wounded to the hospital ships where they would be packed into every inch, not only in the wards and saloons below but into the sisters' and doctors' own quarters and even on the decks alongside the 'walking wounded'.

She heard her name spoken just as she leaned over a stretcher that carried a man whose whole head was bandaged apart from a slit for his mouth. He wanted her to light a cigarette for him and she was looking round for an orderly, since she could not leave a wounded man with a lighted cigarette, when she saw a soldier, barely recognisable as a human being, standing by the doorway. He was covered in mud and dried blood and his face was a mass of cuts. He wore no cap though his helmet was strapped to his webbing belt.

'Amy,' he murmured, his eyes fixed on her face, his hand, which he seemed to find some difficulty in lifting, reaching out to her. 'Amy,' he pleaded, begging her to recognise him beneath the filth and blood plastered over him.

With an inarticulate cry, and to the amazement of all those who watched, she flew across the space that divided them and into the soldier's arms which had no difficulty lifting now to hold her.

28

Defying anyone to stop her, she took him to the bath house, stripped him and put him in the bath, cleansing his shrapnel cuts, which were the result of the same shell that had killed Lanky and peppered poor Wally from head to foot, piercing his flesh in a score of places and fracturing his leg. Lanky on one side of him and Wally on the other had taken the full blast, unintentionally shielding Joe, apart from half a dozen cuts to his face. His helmet, which lay on the bathroom floor, was dented in a dozen places and his uniform torn and shredded but miraculously he had survived. He lay in the warm water, coloured with his blood and the filth of the trenches, and fell asleep, for it was the twentieth day of the Battle of the Somme and he had been in the thick of it even though he was, strictly speaking, among the walking wounded. His face had been attended to by an orderly at a casualty clearing-station and he had gone straight back to the trenches but since then one or two of the cuts had suppurated. A trench is a place that is not conducive to healing as it is in essence the grave of many decomposing bodies. The soil of France had become contaminated with the mouldering remains of thousands of the fallen and when that soil entered soldiers' wounds they turned putrid.

She looked down at this man who had healed the great festering sore in her life that had been Randall Hodge and she wanted to weep for love of him. Her arm lay under his neck, supporting him in the water, but she knew she could not stay here and sure enough Sister stalked in and demanded to know what Nurse Carstairs thought she was doing attending to one man when there were dozens waiting for her. She had no right, no right at all to commandeer this bath, casting her glance at the naked man her VAD was holding so tenderly, but then Nurse Carstairs was a good nurse, hardworking, efficient, willing to go on until she dropped and Sister, beneath her starched uniform, was a woman who had once known love before the Boer War took it from her.

'Get him out, Nurse, and see if you can find a bed for him in some corner. I don't care where it is but if I find you hovering about him when you should be at your duties I will report you to the Medical Officer and have you returned to duties at home. Do you understand?'

Amy did! Joe was woken and helped from the bath and though he knew her he seemed dazed with lack of sleep and nourishment. She dressed him in one of the hospital gowns that were put on the wounded and led him to a far ward where some were sleeping as though dead, others tossing and moaning, many drugged into semi-consciousness and where only one VAD was needed to keep an eye on them since they were not expected to live. There was a bed near the door where the VAD who sat at a table could watch him and send for Amy if she was needed and Amy led Joe to it, put him tenderly beneath the covers, kissed him lovingly under the bewildered gaze of the VAD and watched for a moment until he fell into the deep sleep that was almost a state of unconsciousness.

'Send for me if he wakes, will you, Jenkins. I'll come at once.' Unless it was a personal friend, as Amy and Mercy were, they called each other by their surnames.

'Who is he, Carstairs?' Jenkins asked curiously.

'My lover, and if anything happens to him on your shift I will personally make mincemeat of you.'

'Carstairs!' But Carstairs was gone because she did not want to get on the wrong side of Sister. If she could wangle it in one of the lulls that occurred between actions she meant to ask for leave. Take Joe to the small inn she and Mercy had discovered on the outskirts of Rouen, put him to bed and climb in with him. His eyes were filled with the sight of crucifixions on barbed wire, with swelling corpses, and his nostrils with the stench of those who could not be recovered from no-man's-land. She had been nursing gassed, burned, blinded men, men whose bodies were no longer those of men and they both needed to look on flesh that was not damaged, that was whole and smooth, young bodies ready to be loved, as Joe loved her and she loved Joe. They needed to *make* love, to *create* it, condensing into hours the weeks they would be parted, for there was no doubt they would be parted again. When they had passed the urgency of physical love then they would regain the harmony of spirit which, though they had not been consciously aware of it, had always been theirs.

He slept for twenty-four hours and she was there when he awoke, telling him to dress in the fresh uniform she had scrounged for him.

'We have a lift into town. Sister has given me

twenty-four hours leave.'

'And I have forty-eight.' He was refreshed, strong again, his face covered in small scars but smiling at her in the way she knew so well.

They found the inn and the innkeeper's wife had a room—she always had room for the warriors and their ladies—and fed him on one of her freshly killed chickens and newly baked bread with a bottle of wine between them. Afterwards they went up the stairs and with the sound of their own voices groaning with desire fell into bed and stayed there until the next day.

He left her at the gate of the hospital after picking up his rifle and helmet and marched away while she stumbled to the tent to change into her nurse's uniform.

The battle for the Somme continued with new offensives carried out by British and French divisions with huge loss of life. Names such as Delville Wood, Albert, Bapaume and Beaumont Hamel became familiar to British readers as battles were reported in the newspapers. As more and more homes in the United Kingdom were receiving the brief and dreaded telegram, beginning, 'It is my painful duty to inform you . . .' the truth was emerging. The British, though pushing forward with undiminished tenacity, were suffering a disaster of gruesome proportions with hundreds of thousands of men perishing for little territory.

The year 1916 was drawing to its end and none knew better than Nurse Amy Carstairs and the newly made-up Sergeant Joe Carter what it was costing, not only to them but to the men Joe served with and those Amy nursed. They managed to get short leaves, perhaps twenty-four hours or a precious forty-eight. Her life became Joe, his letters, the leaves they managed to snatch, the absolute joy of being together, of eating with him in a café in Rouen, of sharing a narrow bed with him in French inns and once, without telling their friends in Liverpool, a cheap hotel in Cornwall for a whole week. They wrote but with each new letter in her hand she was aware that he might already be dead, for was she not in a position to know, reminded of it every minute of every day of the many obscene ways he could die. Shellfire, rifle fire, fire itself, mustard gas, sending him back to her, if he lived, a crippled, castrated wreck.

The Somme offensive dragged on until November when, with the coming of the winter rains, the exhausted men could no longer drag themselves through the deepening mud and the 'big push' died away in disappointment and despair. The British and French between them had lost in the region of 600,000 men; the Germans more than 440,000 and in the words of their High Command, 'The Somme was the bloody graveyard of the German Army.'

It was then that the poppy legend was born. Genghis Khan, the Mongol warlord supposedly brought the white poppy with him in his advance on Europe in the thirteenth century. Legend had it that the flowers turned red with the shape of a cross in the centre when they bloomed after a battle. On the Western Front the scarlet poppy sprang up on devastated battlefields, especially those of the Somme.

In Britain the high cost of the Battle of the Somme led to the fall of Asquith as Prime Minister in December and he was replaced by David Lloyd George.

Early in 1917 the British army numbered 1,200,000 men and the French 2,600,000 and together they launched an assault on the Messines Ridge. On that first day Joe waited with the rest of his division for the attack on Arras. Since the deaths of Pip and Corky and Lanky and the terrible injuries to Wally, who had all been his special mates and who had stood next to him in the belief that he was untouchable, Joe had become what those in his trench called 'a loner'. He was always approachable for a fag or a pinch of tea, he shared the contents of his parcels from home and was trusted in his rank of sergeant, but otherwise he kept himself to himself.

Strangely enough, he was not quite the loner his companions believed, for at the end of the Somme battle when the first tanks had appeared and they were able to protect themselves from the German bullets by walking behind the great lumbering beasts, a scruffy little dog had crept into their dugout from nowhere and attached himself to Joe. The men, delighted with anything that distracted them from the horrors of their existence, tried to make a pet of him calling to him with tit-bits from their food parcels from home but the animal, a scruffy sort of terrier, once white with black ears, huddled against Joe and would not be parted from him. The sergeant said he thought he must once have belonged to a family from one of the pulverised farms hereabouts and lost them in the ensuing evacuation. Even their officer could not get rid of the animal, for every time he was chased off he crept back and found Joe, licking his unshaven face with quiet joy. When Joe went over the top or on a raiding party the dog waited for him in the 'funk-hole' Joe had dug out of the trench wall, patient, curled up against Joe's kitbag and when he returned greeted him with inordinate relief. Joe was glad of him and christened him Ernie, since that had been Pip's real name, or rather Ernest. Well, you couldn't call a dog Ernest could you and Pip didn't seem appropriate somehow.

It had seemed to Joe that those who fought with him or near him were destined to be killed or wounded so he did his best to remain aloof, making no particular pals. Now that he was a sergeant he went over first so no one except his officer was in close proximity to him. The comradeship among the men was really extraordinary Joe had found but, as sergeant, was able to remain a little apart from them with Ernie beside him.

He had been supervising fixing scaling ladders the day before the attack on Arras when the artillery began their bombardment. As the sound of the massive guns split the air about them so that their eardrums were ready to burst, one of the newer recruits, a lad of no more than seventeen who must have lied about his age, began to scream and run up and down the trench as though doing his best to get away not only from the agonising sound but from this life he had been so eager to join. He threw his rifle from him and tore at his helmet shrieking for his mam and pleading to go home. This was the third or fourth time he had crouched in the shelter of the trench waiting to go over the top but with a suddenness that had them

403

all twitching, those who waited for the officer's whistle, the lad simply went mad with terror. He scaled the ladder and jumped over the sandbags, flinging himself forward, and without thinking Joe climbed the ladder, grabbed the lad round the waist, turned to haul him back over the lip of the trench but not before a shot from a sniper caught him in the back. All he felt was a blow as though some unseen hand had punched him then the world went black. A burly corporal by the name of Sandy Williamson caught him as he fell forward on top of the still screaming lad.

'Well, yer caught a blighty there, Sarge,' he told him, though his sergeant did not hear him. He was left for the stretcher-bearers to fetch out of the six inches of water at the bottom of the trench and one was heard to say he wished that bloody dog would bugger off before it tripped them up.

*   *   *

On the same day as Joe was hit Nurse Mercy Andrews received news that her fiancé, Lieutenant Richard Steele, had not returned from a reconnaissance flight over the trenches. She and Amy had just come off duty. They were not trained nurses but in the chaos of the battles and the thousands of wounded who flooded into the hospital, *all* the hospitals, it was, as Sister phlegmatically told them, all hands to the pump. They were only supposed to hold things, pass things, take trolleys round the wards and collect rubbish in a bucket, make beds, watch and wait to be given orders, clean sluices, scrub floors, hover on the edge of what Sister called 'the action' on

404

the bed but it was impossible not to get involved. It started with just holding stumps as the nurse poured the eusol and peroxide over them but as the overwhelming numbers of the wounded flooded in to the wards it became inevitable that the VADs did jobs meant only for trained nurses.

One of the men that day was very badly wounded. A Scots sergeant-major who had lost one eye and was wounded in his arm and leg. The orderly had to lift him up to get his dressing done and Amy and Mercy did the dressing together. The man had screamed, upsetting all the others, most of them extraordinarily brave even though they were in agony, an agony that could not be eased, for they had nothing to give them.

They were about to leave when a young lad was brought in with all his genitals blown off and though they should have left they stayed to help with the dressing, packing the hole where his genitals had been with gauze and as they left him both knew that he would never be any good as a man again.

They removed their caps and lifted their faces to the sunshine that filtered through the greening leaves of the trees in the hospital grounds. They were grateful for the fresh air away from the stink of the hospital which smelled of a mixture of ether, putrefaction, carbolic soap and, though they did their best to neutralise it, the sluices. They were both so tired they did not speak. They had been on duty for sixteen hours and since the start of the offensive convoys of wounded had been coming in and every ward was full.

An officer in the uniform of the Royal Flying Corps was standing just outside the entrance to the hospital as they moved tiredly towards the stretch of ground where their tent was. Amy did not really notice him until Mercy seized her arm in a grip of iron and swayed beside her.

'Oh! Dear God! Dear God, no!' Mercy moaned, her face losing every scrap of colour. 'Please, please . . .'

'What is it, love?' Amy asked her anxiously, putting her arm about Mercy's shoulder, then she too noticed the young officer who was hovering on the drive where ambulances were still disgorging their cargo of wounded.

The officer put out a hand, then, squaring his shoulders as though going into battle or an interview he did not relish, he walked up to them and saluted.

'Please, Arthur,' Mercy moaned. 'I can't stand it, really, please . . .'

'I'm sorry, Mercy. Christ tonight, I'd rather it was me than . . . he's not come back from a flight, yesterday; of course he might just have ditched, no one saw him go down so there's . . .' The last few words came out in a rush and he half turned as though anxious to be away from this awful job. Richard's family would be informed that he was missing but this girl who Richard loved and about whom his family knew nothing must be told.

'I'm sorry. If there's anything I can do . . .'

'Thank you, Lieutenant,' Amy said. 'You have. I will look after her. Let us know if . . . anything further . . .'

He saluted. 'Of course.' He walked swiftly away to where another RFC officer sat astride a motorcycle. He climbed on the back, then, duty done, they sped away.

She carried on with her duties, for Mercy Andrews's delicate frame hid a backbone of steel. Amy had told Sister, quietly begging her not to mention to Mercy that she had been informed, then they waited for news. Amy had not heard from Joe for two weeks, then three and the two friends drew strength from one another. There was no news about Richard though the same flier who had come to tell Mercy of his disappearance was at the gate on several occasions to bring her up to date, he said, but that only meant more of the same. There had been no sight of a crashed aircraft and he and the others kept a lookout when they were on reconnaissance but then, after two weeks, another pilot, a captain this time, was at the gate to tell them the lieutenant who had first given them the news was also missing and this, strangely, caused Mercy to break down completely and Amy was forced to tell Sister that Nurse Andrews was not fit for duty.

'Her fiancé has not returned from a flight, as you know, and now the flier who came to inform her has also disappeared. She is distraught and so I have left her. Do you think we could give her something to make her sleep until ...' Sister looked sharply at her. 'How long is it since either of you had leave, Nurse?'

Amy thought back to the last time she and Joe had spent their forty-eight-hour pass together at the inn on the outskirts of Rouen. Six weeks ago and though she had not consciously admitted it to herself she knew she was pregnant. Twice she had missed her monthlies and her as regular as clockwork. She was prepared to admit that before long she would not be strong enough to continue with the backbreaking work she did day after day and with Mercy seemingly at last broken by the realisation that Richard, if he came back at all, might not be the same. And where was Joe? It was weeks since she had heard from him and no one knew better than she what that meant. She and Mercy were really no longer fit for duty, not unless they had some decent leave away from this chaos. Fifteen hundred wounded had come in during the last twenty-four hours, forty-three of them in B line, where she and Mercy worked, pretty bad cases. The doctors had been working day and night, with the operating room starting at eight-thirty in the morning and going steadily until one o'clock the next morning and that with four operating tables. The operating room nurses were dead on their feet with 273 operations in four days. The fighting at Arras was fierce and the tanks, which were supposed to be the saviours of the battles, had proved useless. One man who had come in with face and hands badly burned, with compound fractures of both legs, told the doctor his tank had been completely riddled by the German guns, the gasoline tank had exploded and all on board but him were dead and it was expected that he would follow them.

Sister looked at the drawn face of Nurse Amy Carstairs, remembering the fresh-faced young woman who had come to her twelve months ago. This nurse had given every ounce of her strength and courage to nursing the wounded but she needed to go home and her next words confirmed

408

it.

'I believe I am expecting a child, Sister,' she said bravely, 'and I also believe the child's father, the man I am to marry when this is over, is, if not dead, then seriously wounded. I have not heard from him for a long time. Would it be possible for Nurse Andrews, who is not herself, to go home for a while? She needs a breather and I shall be no good to you soon. I know that nurses are badly needed but . . .'

Sister sat and looked at this young woman. How old was she? No more than eighteen or nineteen, but it was plain that she was at the end of her strength and so was Nurse Andrews who would be no good to anyone on the wards if she was to have a breakdown. They would both be missed more than she could say but it was rumoured that America was coming into the war and surely that would mean more of everything. Strong, fighting soldiers, to stand shoulder to shoulder with the war-weary men who had been fighting, many of them for nearly three years. There would be nurses and doctors, equipment, ambulances, orderlies and surely these two young women could be spared? She was not shocked that Nurse Carstairs was pregnant. She was not the first and would not be the last. She would not come back again and if she knew that lass she would move heaven and earth to find not only *her* man but Nurse Andrews's as well, if they still lived. Who knew in these terrible times?

*   *   *

They went home together, Amy and Mercy,

409

embarking on a Channel steamer that had just discharged hundreds of soldiers to be sent to the front and was to take back hundreds of wounded to the already overcrowded hospitals in all parts of the country. They stood silently at the rail, the two young women who had seen so much, suffered so much and lost so much. Two young men were missing with no clue as to their whereabouts in the carnage and Amy anguished on what they were to do next. She had sent a telegram to Bella and John but what they would find when they arrived at Dover she did not know. Still, she was a capable woman now who had managed her own life ever since she had begun nursing and she would find a harbour for herself and Mercy until their men were brought safely home. *They would be found and brought home!* Of that she was certain. She would allow no other thought into her mind but that. She was carrying his child, their child and he would live to see it. It kept her sane, it gave her focus, a hope for the future and she just wished Mercy had the same conviction. When she thought about it, she supposed Joe's location would be impossible to find until he himself got in touch, for he had gone to war with no next of kin, no family who would be sent the dreaded telegram should he be wounded, missing or killed, unlike Richard, whose parents in London would have news of him, or of his death.

'Do you know the address of Richard's parents?' she had asked her but Mercy, listless in her misery, had been unhelpful and Amy meant to write to Richards' commanding officer at the airfield near Camiers and explain the situation. They would find the answer and everything else they needed to know when they arrived in Liverpool.

It was chaotic at the port of Dover with troops embarking for France and the wounded being conveyed from the steamer to the convoys of ambulances awaiting them. There was a nurse leading a line of gassed, blinded soldiers down the gangway, each soldier with his hand on the shoulder of the man in front of him, another nurse bringing up the rear.

The two nurses, still in their uniforms, followed until they reached a space where they could look about them and get their bearings, Amy leading Mercy by the hand. She was startled when she heard her name called and turned round slowly, looking for the person who had shouted above the din made by the embarking soldiers.

'Amy, over here, Amy.'

And there was Caleb, *Papa*, with his arms opened wide to receive her and when she flew into them they closed protectively about her and she knew that for now she and Mercy were safe.

29

'We must think first of your safety, my dear. We cannot presume that your . . . your . . . Hodge has given up searching for you. Dodie and I are concerned that he will continue his vendetta, he and my wife who cannot forgive your . . . ingratitude. And, of course, there is Joe to consider. I am in touch with an acquaintance of mine at the War Office. It helps that although I am

411

in the textile trade manufacturing uniforms for the army, I have also invested money in munitions so I have some, shall we say, influence with men in high places. So many men were wounded during the recent battles on the Messines Ridge and sent from the casualty clearing-stations back home and then distributed to various hospitals up and down the country that it might be a while before we can locate your Joe.'

Caleb shook his head sadly, putting his hand on Amy's where it lay in her lap, then he turned sympathetically to Mercy who was slumped in the corner of the back seat of the black, chauffeur-driven Vauxhall he had hired to bring him to Dover. Mercy's blank gaze was focused on the busy scene of troop convoys making their way to the docks and the ambulances going in the opposite direction. The latter were destined for the hospitals in London where they would be sorted into the clinical categories their wounds decreed. Then, when this was done and when they were considered fit enough to travel, they would be directed to hospitals all over the country.

'And you, my dear,' he said to Mercy, 'where are you headed? Where is your family and—'

'She's coming with me, Papa,' Amy said firmly. 'Wherever I go, so shall Mercy. We are both ...' Her voice faltered and Caleb realised that these two were not simply to have some leave from their onerous duties but were both as deeply wounded as the soldiers they nursed. Not physically, like the wrecks he had watched being carried off the hospital ship, but emotionally scarred by what they had suffered during the past twelve months.

'I see,' he said, though it was clear he didn't.

'I have lost ... temporarily of course, Joe. He must be in a hospital somewhere and why he hasn't written I don't know,' she went on bravely. 'And Mercy, her fiancé is a flier and did not return from a ... but they will both be found. I firmly believe that and so does Mercy but in the meanwhile I'm not sure where ...'

'I have the solution, my love. For you and your friend. When we received your telegram I made some enquiries; you are aware that I have many contacts, people for whom I may have done some small favour and they have returned them where they can. We are not going to Liverpool, though I know you are longing to see your mother but to a safe place I have found for you up north. We shall spend a night in London and then motor in gradual stages to a place called Ambleside. You know of it?'

'I've heard of it, Papa. The Lake District is it not?'

'Yes. I have friends, the Buchanans, who have lived in the area for a long time. I do business with them, explosives, gunpowder ... Well, that is another matter and I have rented a small house in the area big enough for two or more so if ... Mercy, is it? wishes to stay with you until ... well, until you are stronger there will be plenty of room. Myrtle—you remember Myrtle?—has a niece. I believe her name is Pansy, who is willing to come and look after you. She ... she lost her young man on the Somme and is eager to help two brave women who have risked their own lives to save soldiers, though ... well, I will say no more. I shall continue my search for Joe and if Mercy will give me the name of her fiancé I will do the same for

413

him. There, there, my dear,' as Mercy burst into tearful life, unable to believe that here was someone who might be able to help her in her devastation. 'I am glad to help a friend of my Amy so please dry your tears and say no more.' Mercy was not sure where Richard's parents lived except that it was in London, she babbled, doing her best to help this kind man who had come to meet Amy and who was now holding her red, work-roughened hand as well as Amy's.

They stayed the first night in a comfortable, one might even say luxurious hotel, for Caleb Seymour insisted on the very best. He had had the sensitivity to book a room with twin beds for the friends, realising that they had shared the hardships and horrors of France together and that they would not now like to be separated. They dined on food the two young women had not tasted in a long, long while though he could see neither of them appreciated or even noticed it. They still wore their shabby nurses' uniforms, their greatcoats plastered with the mud of the battlefields and he noticed that other diners looked at them with great compassion, knowing where they had come from. When they had retired to their room and the baths they were both longing for he spent several hours on the telephone, ringing first his beloved Dodie then speaking to several highly placed gentlemen at the War Office who, when gently reminded of what they owed him, set in motion the assignment he asked of them.

It took them three days to cover the journey from London to the land of the Lakes, staying each night in splendid hotels in Market

414

Harborough, Buxton, Manchester and then on to Kendal where it was but an hour or two to their destination. He had not suggested that he buy them new outfits at any of these places since it seemed to him it was not the time or place to be bothering them about their appearance. Mercy was decidedly more cheerful, well, perhaps cheerful was not the word, but more *hopeful* since he had confided to her that it was all well in hand, meaning the search for Joe and for Lieutenant Richard Steele, whose name she had shyly divulged to him.

They passed through Kendal taking an increasingly narrowing lane, bordered on each side by dry-stone walls laden with summer vegetation and each girl began to sit up and take notice, for they had never seen such loveliness. Mercy had lived in the industrial town of Bradford all her life but she had had little time to wander the Yorkshire moors that surrounded the town. Her father had kept her busy after the death of his wife, taking over her mother's parish duties and from there she had gone, much against her father's wishes, to the battlefields of France where, whatever beauty had once existed was smashed into the mud and muck and muddle of the war-torn landscape.

Amy had known a momentary glimpse of countryside when she had lived with the Carstairs and cycled out to her mam's cottage, which stood near the nurseries but here was a magnificence that took their breath away. They were still in South Lakeland where the hills were gentler and later they were to know the soaring high wonder of the north, but on this glorious summer day it was as though they had wandered into a fairyland

415

which took their breath away. They were to learn the names of all the mountain ranges, the waterfalls, the fells and lakes but just at that moment they were taken out of their deep misery with a small healing that only nature's beauty can bestow: the intermingling of crag and conifer, juniper and bracken, the long slopes of timber, the delightful, white-painted, rose-covered cottages which here and there lay along the road. They passed through a small town which Caleb informed them was Windermere then there it was, the indescribable shimmer of the lake itself and on it the small, white and coloured sails of yachts floating serenely and both girls felt a small modicum of peace enter her heart. There were tiny hamlets on the road that ran beside the lake, the road itself edged each side with a ditch behind which were the dry-stone walls common to the north of England. They were submerged by a rising tide of wild flowers: sweet Cicely fragrant with the scent of aniseed which drifted into the motor through the open windows; hedge parsley, dock and nettle which would be followed in the autumn by meadow cranesbill, ragwort, foxglove and willowherb. Plants even grew on the top of the walls, stonecrop and feverfew and herb-Robert. The leaves and stems of the cranesbill, seen against the light that was peculiar to this part of the world, assumed the beauty of scarlet and crimson from which the plant gained its name.

They entered Ambleside along what was called Lake Road, appropriately enough, turning left and then left again over a bridge that crossed a brisk burbling stream, down a lane so narrow the car brushed the flowers in the ditch and there was the cottage. There was no garden as such, just rough cobbles which divided it from the road but along its front beneath the windows and growing up its walls was a riot of vivid flowers. There was the showy splash of dahlias and stock, country garden flowers; zinnia, sweet william, peonies and pinks and the lovely aroma of lavender. There were actually two cottages, the one adjoining with its door standing open. A woman in a crisp white apron leaned in the doorway and several children played on the cobbles. There was a dog lying in the sunshine and to one side an old pump from which a trickle of water dripped into a stone trough. Smoke eddied from the chimney.

The chauffeur stopped the motor outside the door and the dog barked until a sharp word from the woman in the doorway quietened it. Caleb climbed out, stretching his limbs, which were not as young as once they had been, and wished the woman a polite 'Good day to you'. She nodded briefly, for it seemed 'foreigners' were not trusted up here in the land of the Lakes. Caleb continued to smile and held out his hand to Mercy who stood hesitantly on what they were to learn was the 'threshwood', the doorstep of the cottage, while Caleb handed Amy out then produced a large key, fitting it into the lock and turning it.

They stepped over the threshwood together, the two young women holding hands, which the woman in the next cottage thought very strange!

'Here it is, my dears. Your home for as long as you like. It is owned by the Buchanan family who have land and properties in this part of the world. One of the family, Alex Buchanan, is my contact at the War Office. His wife is an ambulance driver where you have just come from; yes, a brave lady and I shouldn't wonder if you have not met in the course of your work. Anyway, let us get in and bring your luggage,' which consisted of a small rucksack each containing their clean underclothes and nightdress. 'When you feel up to it you must walk into Ambleside and buy yourself some decent clothes No! No! Do not argue, Amy. You and Mercy have done more than could be asked of any young woman to help our lads and for the next few weeks, months, whatever, you are to recuperate here and I shall give you an allowance to cover all your needs. I will brook no argument, Amy. After all, you are my daughter in everything but blood. I command you to recover! I don't know what your neighbours are like but you have each other and I shall keep in touch. Oh, yes, I have had a telephone installed in the cottage much to the amazement of the folk about here and I shall bring Dodie and Willy down for a holiday while summer lasts. And I'm sure Bella will want to see you though how you will accommodate all her tribe I can't imagine. There are, surprisingly, four bedrooms of a decent size ... Oh, for heaven's sake, listen to me babbling on. That chauffeur will be itching to be off and we have rather a long drive.'

'Will you not stay, Papa?' Amy murmured uncertainly, glancing round the flagged kitchen which was small with thick beams in the ceiling. Although Mercy was with her she found the old-fashioned cottage rather forbidding but at least it was peaceful, cosy and spotlessly clean.

'No, my dear. I might put up at Windermere and drive back tomorrow. Pansy will arrive by the end of the week so I will leave you to settle in. I believe there is food for a couple of days; one of the Buchanan ladies arranged that but as soon as you feel like it I suggest you get out and do a bit of exploring. The scenery is magnificent, so I am told and what I have seen today confirms it. I hope you will both recover here and be . . . well . . . as soon as I have news of Joe and your young man, Mercy, I will be in touch. Now then, let me give you a hug, both of you,' which he did, then, as though he were quite overcome with emotion, he left abruptly, waving briefly from the motor which the chauffeur had turned, and made off towards Ambleside.

'Well,' said Amy, still clinging to Mercy's hand, 'shall we look round?'

*　　　*　　　*

They had decided to share the biggest bedroom at the front of the cottage, for after all they had slept side by side in a tent from the first day they had met and were reluctant to be parted though neither could have explained why. It had a splendid view of the river and a copse of hazel and birch and rowan that stood between the cottage and the water. On the far side of the winding river were the mountains which rose steadily before the cottage and at this time of the year were an exquisite purple. It was peaceful in the drowsy warmth of the summer day, though in the lane the children played and the dog romped and from somewhere a small herd of cows wandered into sight driven by a fellow in a cloth cap, a pair of breeches, a waistcoat and a neckerchief. The girls watched fascinated and when the cows had

419

disappeared they turned and wandered into one of the back bedrooms and were delighted to find that at the back of the cottage lay a long garden given over to flowers and a vegetable plot. It stretched up to a belt of trees and in it stood a small building, its purpose unknown, set about with fragrant bushes of syringa, lilac and honeysuckle. Later they discovered it was what was called a 'necessary house' in which generations had relieved themselves, and held an earth closet with a hole and a bucket set below a well-fitted white lid and seat. The bucket must be emptied every day and the sweet-smelling bushes were to disguise the odour that hung about the place. The girls, when they finally inspected it, told each other it was no worse than the conditions they had known at the back of the line of tents in which they had lived in France!

Each bedroom, as they discovered when they peeped into them, was furnished in the old-fashioned manner of the Victorian era, not exactly what might be found in a working man's bedroom and probably furnished with Buchanan family cast-offs. They wondered who, and why. All the rooms had a big double bed with a quilted cover, a dressing table with an oval mirror on a stand, a wardrobe of good quality satinwood and an old cast-iron fireplace in which was set a copper urn filled with dried flowers. On a white marble-topped washstand stood a basin, a ewer and a soap dish decorated with rosebuds and beside it fluffy white towels hung over a towel rail. The curtains at the window were also covered with rosebuds. The floor was of wood, polished to within an inch of its life, and hooked rugs lay beside the bed and in front of the fireplace. Every bedroom in the house was exactly the same though in different colours, all except one, which was smaller and had a single bed, obviously meant for a servant.

They removed their greatcoats and ugly hats, put their bags on the bed and wandered downstairs to peer into a parlour, a scullery, the kitchen where they had entered the house and a small laundry room that led out into the back garden. Apart from the occasional 'hmm' and 'ah' they had not spoken a word.

They both sighed, looking at each other, both thinking that in happier times, meaning with Joe's and Richard's fates known, they would have been delighted with their surroundings. The views from every window were glorious, mountains covered in all the summer colours, trees, paths leading who knew where, sheep moving on the hillsides, waterfalls splashing and gurgling across rocks and just beyond their front window the lovely River Rothay. Beyond the immediate trees across the river they could see tall chimneys from some obviously large house.

They slept that night in the big double bed covered by the lovely quilt of the palest pink, cream and green. The pillows were large, their slips of good linen edged with lace as were the sheets. The mattress was comfortable and the two young women, still devastated by their loss, curled against each other and slept, for the first time in many weeks, the sleep of the dead, or was it the certainty that they were safe? Their men might not be but it was many months since they had lain down knowing that they would not be shelled or woken to the screams of the wounded as they were rushed from the ambulances into the hospital wards.

'I feel guilty,' Mercy had whispered as they pulled the quilt up to their chins.

'I know, I know,' Amy replied, aware of what Mercy meant, 'but we were not much use to any of them as we were, love. Perhaps when we receive news of Joe and Richard we can do something. There must be a hospital somewhere that would be glad of two such magnificent nurses as you and me.'

She was rewarded by a small sigh of laughter as they both fell into the depths of sleep.

*   *   *

They stayed inside the cottage for three days. They were very quiet with each other, speaking only when necessary. There was nothing much to say, for each young woman knew the thoughts of the other as though they could read what was in the other's mind. The weather continued to be dry and warm so, dragging chairs into the garden, they sat among the mignonette and rock rose, the hydrangea and delphinium which some previous tenant had planted and lovingly tended and which seemed content to stand next to carrots and onions, cabbage and newly planted lettuce, and felt their spirits grow calm. Mercy knew by now that Amy was pregnant and that her baby would be born in January of the following year but in the meanwhile as they waited for Caleb to ring them Amy said she was to be known as Amy Newbridge.

'I have had more surnames than there are in the telephone book but this child is Joe's and shall have his name. We shall never be married unless Papa can work another of his miracles and get me a divorce from . . . him. You know who I mean?' Mercy did, for by now she knew all Amy's history. 'But when Joe comes home he and I shall live as man and wife and no one will be any the wiser. I could settle here, Mercy,' she added wistfully. 'Live in a cottage like this with Joe who loves the land. Oh, dear God, I wish Papa would ring. How can you be so patient, my darling Mercy, when . . .'

Mercy sighed. In her heart, though she emphatically denied it even to herself, she knew Richard was not coming back to her. The short flying life of an airman had been well over due where Richard was concerned and the fragile aeroplane he flew in could not withstand a crash. She said nothing to Amy, who was convinced that Joe must have taken part in the Battle of Arras, as it became known. That was in April and now it was summer. They were afraid to stray far from the telephone, both convinced that it would ring the moment Caleb Seymour got back to Manchester but the telephone was distressingly silent. So, their uniforms sponged and ironed in the laundry room, which was equipped with everything needed, they dressed themselves—leaving their atrocious hats— and set off up the road in the direction of Ambleside. They hadn't spoken to the family next door though they heard the children and their laughter. They were watched from the window as they headed for the bridge that crossed the river, turning into Rothay Road which they found ran straight into the town. The friends walked along Church Street and into Market Place where they found a rather smart ladies' dress shop directly opposite the Queens Hotel that sold ready-to-wear outfits. It was a long time since either had worn anything other than their nurses' uniforms and they had had neither the time nor the inclination to study fashions but Miss Adeline, as she was called, was more than ready to help them. Miss Adeline not only longed to receive the money they would pay her but also to spread the news through the small town that she had actually fitted out two of their brave VADs who had served in France nursing their 'boys'.

Miss Adeline's shop window displayed a very fetching day dress with a jacket-like bodice and an open tunic overskirt. It was actually out of date since it was a fashion from 1914 but the girls did not know this and thought it quite elegant.

'Not that I can see either of us having occasion to wear such a thing, can you?' Amy asked as they stood with their noses pressed to the window. 'Something a bit more practical in cotton, I think. I wish I could sew. Can you, dearest?'

'No. I can sew a button on but that's it. Well, let's go in and see what Miss Adeline has to offer.'

They came away with a couple of cotton dresses apiece, ankle-length with a straight skirt, short sleeves and a bodice that sat on the hips. Mercy chose one in a pale green gingham that was just right with her pale, freckled skin and fox-red hair, and another in buttercup yellow cotton. Amy, who knew that very soon she would be unable to wear anything as fitted as those Mercy chose, picked out a pale duck-egg blue and one in clover. They each purchased a long knitted cardigan to match their outfits, as Miss Adeline told them that this warm weather was unusual for this part of the country.

'And shall you be wearing your . . . overcoats?' she asked delicately, because they were so obviously part of a uniform in drab navy blue. They exchanged glances, then gave in to Miss Adeline's coaxing to look over her new delivery of the very latest coat, warm yet light and ideal for Ambleside.

'Mrs Buchanan, Mrs James Buchanan who runs the hospital, bought one only last week. She had a baby last year—'

'There's a hospital near here?' Mercy asked disbelievingly.

'Oh, yes. It's the home of Mr Buchanan who is in France. An officer,' she preened as though an officer's wife buying one of her garments was a real feather in her cap. 'Mrs Buchanan turned their home, Howethwaite, it's called, into a hospital for ordinary soldiers. Not officers, just . . . well, as I was saying . . .'

She was surprised and delighted when both the young ladies bought one of her overcoats, making their minds up very quickly as though they hadn't a moment to spare, the red-haired one in a shade of autumn leaves and the fair one a deep, warm blue, both saying that they needed to get away from the drabness of their uniforms. The fair one paid for the lot and with scarcely a word they hurried out of her shop carrying their purchases. They seemed very eager to get somewhere, barely replying to her polite 'Good day'. She wondered where they came from, all her little hints eliciting nothing but vague answers. She watched them hurry down the sloping brow and turn into Church Street.

'I wonder where it is, Howethwaite, I mean?' Mercy gasped as she did her best to keep up with

Amy's longer strides.

'We'll soon find out. They seem to be a well-known family here.'

'You won't be able to work for long, Amy.'

'I know, but I can do something for a while and we'll get more up-to-date information from—'

'I know, that's what I was thinking.'

There was a woman sitting on one of the rough stones that bordered the flowerbeds in front of the cottage. She had a suitcase beside her. When she saw them approaching she stood up and smiled.

'I've come,' she said simply.

'Oh!'

'Pansy, an' your telephone's bin ringin' its head off ever since I got here.'

30

'He's in the country, my dear. He was wounded at Arras and was shipped home several days later.'

Amy felt her heart give a great bound as though it would burst out of her chest then it continued to beat rapidly but with such joy she could barely contain it. He lived! *He lived!* He was wounded and that could be, *must be* serious if they had sent him home, but he was not dead. Papa's friend had no idea where he was, only that he was back in this country and she, or Papa, more likely, would find him.

'Now, darling,' Papa was saying, 'I have no details but at least you know he's alive. Alex Buchanan, who has moved heaven and earth to find him, says the hospitals in the south are full to overflowing and so he has probably been sent up north but he doesn't know where. It's bloody chaos, lass, after the last battle but the records show that a Sergeant Joe Carter was wounded and sent back home. That's all I can tell you but I'll keep trying to trace him.'

'Oh, Papa, he's alive, he's alive and will see his child.'

'His . . .' Amy could hear Caleb gasping on the other end of the line and in the background Dodie's voice was begging to be told what was being said, but they all had to know the truth some time. The news—what a silly word!—that . . . well, Caleb was going to be a grandfather!

'Yes, Papa, Joe and I are to have a child in the new year.'

'Amy, oh, Amy and what are you to do about—'

'The man who abused me who calls himself my husband? Nothing. What can I do? I hope he rots in hell, for I am to be Joe's wife. I shall call myself Amy Carter for the time being. Oh, Papa, he's alive . . .' She could feel Mercy pulling frantically on her sleeve and she was selfishly reminded that she was not the only woman here who waited for news of her loved one.

'And . . . and have you word of Richard, Mercy's fiancé?'

'I'm sorry, my dear, but fliers are harder to locate than soldiers. They fail to return to their airfields and no one knows where they . . . crash unless one of their comrades sees them go down. No one saw Richard's craft go down but that does not mean he is dead and he could have walked away from it. Others have. Tell Mercy not to give up hope . . .' Caleb's voice faded and broke up, as

the telephone lines were not very reliable. ' ...
Will do ... best ... tell her ... must go, my dear
girl ... love from ...' and then the line grew faint
and he was gone.

Mercy stood behind her, her head bent and
when Amy put her arms about her she felt her
tremble. 'Oh, Amy,' she moaned. 'I'm glad for you,
though I know that with Joe wounded ... but at
least you know he is. Where is Richard? *Where is
Richard?'*

'Come, darling, let's go to the hospital and see
what we can do.'

Pansy watched them step out on to the lane that
she supposed led towards the hospital. She felt a
great compassion wash over her, for did she not
know how it was with them? Her Marty had just
vanished into the hell that was France, buried
somewhere with his comrades. Not that she had
ever seen it but she had brothers who had and the
expressions on their faces when they came on
leave told their own story.

$$*\qquad*\qquad*$$

The small dog, rough-haired, incredibly thin and
dirty, lay with his nose on his paws just outside the
entrance to the doors of Howethwaite. There was
a lot of activity in and out of the house that was
now a hospital, but the dog kept out of the way of
the orderlies who carried stretchers, of the nurses
who oversaw the placing of the wounded men and
the recovering patients who were sitting in
deckchairs on the lawns beside the line of
ambulances waiting on the drive, stretching back
to the gateway and beyond. One or two had tried

428

to tempt the dog to their side but he ignored them all, his tired eyes glued to whatever was happening in the hallway.

The two young women, both dressed in VADs' uniforms, hurried up the drive past the ambulances and entered beneath the porch of the splendid old house. It was an enormous building of silver-grey limestone quarried in the district with a roof of Lakeland slate and had pantries, still rooms, a dairy and a study as well as all the reception rooms and bedrooms. Every available space was needed to accommodate the wounded. The lawn in front had yew trees and box-edged walkways, flowerbeds full of country roses, lavender, peonies and every colourful plant that could be crowded into them, but the two young women did not even glance at them.

In the hallway they came across a scene of such confusion they both halted for a moment, causing the orderlies behind them carrying a stretcher to curse fluently. Stretchers bearing the wounded, who had come, just as they were, from the trenches amid the mud and blood and flies, lay wherever they were put, some men dreadfully silent, some tossing in delirium. Without a word, even to each other, both Amy and Mercy tossed off their coats, tied their apron strings tighter and moved forward to help according to the efficiency of their training.

There was some woman sitting on the bottom step of the wide staircase weeping into her apron for she badly wanted to give the lads a cup of tea at least but those who were carrying the wounded just stepped round her and got on with their work.

It was several hours later when a certain calm had been achieved that a nurse in a sister's uniform noticed Amy leaning over the bed of a soldier whose face was completely wrapped in a dirty bandage. A doctor was about to remove the bandage and the VAD—who was she?—was ready to administer something from the syringe the doctor had just handed to her.

'Doctor?' Sister said enquiringly.

'Sister?' the doctor answered, totally absorbed with his task and Sister hesitated, for this was no time to be making enquiries about a VAD's qualifications to be giving injections, nor who she was. She was doing a very worthwhile job, evidently well used to such situations, and they needed every pair of hands they could muster. The VAD administered the painkiller and the doctor continued his job, watched by the VAD and the sister.

'He's a wound to his back, Sister, and will need to be taken into theatre but he seems to have a head wound as well. Dear Lord, would you look at this foul mess on the bandage. What the bloody hell is it? Horse manure ... mud ... blood; he'll be lucky to have any face left if the infection has—'

'Can I help, Doctor, though you seem to have an efficient nurse here.'

'Yes, I have, thank you, Sister,' the doctor said absently, not caring who it was who stood by to cater to his and his patients' needs.

The bandage was finally removed and the remains of the soldier's face was revealed. It was that of Sergeant Joe Carter, or so it said on his papers, though, as the doctor murmured to the ashen-faced nurse who was helping him, his own mother would not have recognised him! He was seriously displeased when the nurse, who had been so quick and helpful, quietly crumpled to the floor. Thankfully another took her place and the VAD was removed by two orderlies who plonked her unceremoniously in the kitchen where the weeping woman, still at it, lifted her into the armchair where she herself rested at the end of the day.

'It's not often them nurses faint,' she remarked curiously to a maid who was poking the fire ready to make a cup of tea.

'No, an' I can't remember 'avin' seen her afore, can you, Cook?'

'No, you're right. Ah,' said the cook with a knowing look on her face. 'That's the reason why, lass.'

'What?'

'If I'm not mistook she's in't family way. I should know bein' the eldest o' thirteen. Even before me mam began ter show I could tell by her face that she was 'avin' another.'

*   *   *

Ernie had come a long way following his friend on their journey from the battlefields of France to the hospital near Ambleside. He had raced after ambulances, his keen nose picking up his scent even among the sickening stench that hung about such vehicles and the places where they halted, one of them a casualty clearing-station where he lay shivering by the entrance, for they would not let him in. His animal instincts and that peculiar canine sense of smell told him that the man he was after was on a stretcher being loaded on to a train—not that he knew it was called a train—and when the men who had put him there turned their

431

backs Ernie had leaped nimbly aboard, hiding behind some object until the train reached the docks. He smelled water and though he had not eaten since his friend had fed him, he followed where his nose led him, nipping up a gangway, ignoring the shouts that followed him and hid again as he was carried across the water.

Another ambulance, which this time he found hard to follow because there was so much traffic on the roads and so many unfamiliar smells; a hospital for a few hours where he lay just outside the door; another ambulance, racing along at great danger to himself; and then another train. He had begged for food from the soldiers who wanted to make a pet of him and he survived. As long as the scent of his friend was close by he was calm.

At last, panting along country lanes deep in lush vegetation he came to the gates of the big house and the ambulances and watched his friend being carried inside the house. He took up his sentinel duties and when a kindly woman who was offering tit-bits to another small dog offered him a bowl of scraps and another of water he filled his belly, sighed contentedly and fell into that half-sleeping state that allowed him to watch and doze at the same time.

*　　　*　　　*

Amy sipped the tea the woman who seemed to be the cook had given her and in her mind's eye studied the face that had been revealed when the bandages had been stripped off by the doctor. Something had evidently exploded in Joe's face and taken his skin with it, for it had been raw with great patches of bleeding matter encrusted on it. 'Infected' the doctor had said, unaware that the nurse helping him had any particular interest, other than a medical one, in the soldier. His eyebrows were gone and so was his hair over his forehead. His eyes were closed, his long, dark eyelashes gone and his lips were bleeding from burns but he had not made a sound. She had longed to gather him into her arms and hold him, comfort him, since he must have been in great pain, heal him with her love for did she care what he looked like? He was her Joe and she loved him whatever his looks, but her queasy stomach, symptom of the first stages of pregnancy, let her down and she had fainted dead away. The doctor would be furious, was her last thought as she hit the floor, for doctors had no time for nurses who fainted.

She was aware that someone was bending over her and her name was spoken and there was Mercy, her face anxious, her eyes filled with compassion and Amy loved her because though her own man was still missing and Amy had got hers back, Mercy still had time to be her friend.

'Was it Joe?' she asked, to the fascination of the cook and the kitchen-maid who had no idea who either of these two were.

'Yes,' Amy whispered.

'Is he badly wounded?' Mercy knelt at Amy's feet and took her free hand in hers.

'A bullet in his back and his face . . . one of those bloody shells blew up in . . .'

'Oh, darling.'

Cook and the maid exchanged glances. *Darling!* But nevertheless these lasses were nurses and looking after the men other women had seen off to war and with a sad sigh Cook offered Mercy a cup of tea.

'There, lass, get that down yer.'

The door opened and a nurse with a bloodstained apron tied about her poked her head round it. She looked totally exhausted and glanced longingly at the tea the two VADs had in their hands.

'Cuppa tea, Nurse?' the cook asked obligingly.

'Some of us are too busy to drink tea, Cook.' Her voice was sharp. 'Sister wants to see the VAD who fainted and you'd best come as well,' looking at Mercy. She whisked away as if she hadn't a moment to spare, which was true. Though she had been sharp with the two strange VADs she had to admit they had certainly pulled their weight during the last few hours.

The two friends exchanged glances, but since they had done nothing wrong, unless it was wrong to try to help wounded men, they were quite composed.

'Where's the sister's office, please?' Mercy asked the cook, drawing Amy to her feet.

'Just up the hall, lass, an' to yer left.'

They knocked on the door and when a voice told them to enter they did so, still holding hands. They were both somewhat dishevelled, like the nurse who had brought the message that sister wished to see them, with blood and other matter on their once immaculate aprons.

Sister looked up from her desk and leaned back in her chair. Like them all she was tired beyond imagining but she did not let them see it.

'Well, now, would either of you like to tell me

434

what you are doing here?'

'Have we displeased you, Sister, by what we have done for the men?' Amy asked sharply. 'I realise you do not know us but we were on our way here when the convoy began to arrive. You were busy, so Nurse Andrews and myself did what we have been doing *in France* for the past fifteen months. I think we were of some use.'

Mercy squeezed Amy's hand warningly and Sister looked grim, for like all her breed she did not care to be interrupted nor have some lowly VAD answer her back.

'I repeat, what are two VADs who may have been in France for the past fifteen months doing in my hospital? Why are you no longer in France and—'

'Sister, if I may,' Mercy said meekly. 'The sister in charge of the hospital at Rouen sent us home since we were . . . we had come to the end of our usefulness for the time being, or so she said. We had worked with only a day or so off here and there in the hospital and she decided it was time we had some leave. Amy here, Nurse—'

'My name is Amy Carter, Sister,' Amy interrupted before Mercy could reveal the name she had used in France. 'My father has friends here, the Buchanans, who have kindly allowed us to use a cottage of theirs so that we may have a rest before returning to France. At least Nurse Andrews may be returning to France, I don't know. We have had no time to settle in but I shall stay here to be near my . . . my husband.'

'Your husband!' Sister was horrified. 'We do not allow married VADs, Nurse.'

'That may be, Sister.'

'That is the rule, Nurse.'

Amy ignored her. 'My husband is in this very hospital. I have just discovered him in a ward. His . . . his face is . . . that is why I fainted. He has been missing for weeks but now I have found him. Oh, I know I shall not be allowed to nurse any more but I shall remain here to be near him and wherever he is sent—God forbid it is the trenches again, for he has been wounded twice and has suffered enough—I shall go with him. Nurse Andrews—'

'If Nurse Andrews wishes to apply to work here she may do so. We are short of nursing staff as you will appreciate but I shall have to make some enquiries.'

'May I go and see my husband, Sister?'

'You may not. He is in theatre.'

'I'll wait in the hallway until he comes out. Mercy,' as she turned to Mercy and took the hand she was holding in both of hers. Now that she was no longer a VAD, at least in Sister's eyes, she could say and do what she pleased. Sister was glaring at her but hidden in her steely grey eyes was a small light of something that said she admired these two who had not just hung about in the last emergency but had taken off their coats and worked beside the medical staff. Mrs Carter, if that was who she was, looked very strained and with a sudden gentleness Nurse Andrews led her to a seat at the side of Sister's desk.

'Sit down, Amy. You look all in.'

'Don't fuss, Mercy. It's just this . . . well, you know.'

'Yes, but you need to rest.'

'Why should a young woman like Mrs Carter need to rest, Nurse Andrews?' Sister began but

Amy forestalled any further discussion of her condition.

'Because I am to have a child, Sister.'

*   *   *

They allowed her into the ward simply because she absolutely refused to move from the hallway and even threatened to speak to her father's friend in the Foreign Office, the one who was related to the present mistress of Howethwaite whose husband was himself fighting in France.

'Your husband is not awake yet, Mrs Carter,' Sister told her disapprovingly.

'Then I will sit by his bed until he comes to,' Amy told her, and short of getting two orderlies to remove her, kicking and screaming, she threatened, which would upset seriously ill patients, there was nothing they could do. Mercy, since no one told her to stop, continued to tend to the wounded men and help in whatever way a doctor asked of her.

His face was bandaged and when he awoke he began to toss about in terror, for he could not see. Only his mouth, merely a slit in the bandages and unrecognisable as a pair of lips, was uncovered, as he must be fed and given liquids. His hands flailed beneath the sheet and it was only when Amy released them and took them in hers that he quietened. She kissed them lovingly, watched by a dozen pair of eyes, for every man on the ward would have changed places with the soldier whose hands she held.

'Joe, lie still, dearest, it's me. Lie still. I'm here, I'm here. Your face was injured and your back but

437

the doctor has operated and—'

'Thank you, madam, I will tell my patient what has been done,' a voice at the foot of the bed told her. 'Kindly move away and allow me to examine him.'

'No,' the patient mumbled through his bandages. 'No.'

'It's all right, lad, your wife won't go far,' the doctor said. 'I just want to—'

'My wife . . . ?'

'Yes, Mrs Carter is here to—'

'Amy, my love . . .'

'I'm here, sweetheart. Just at the foot of the bed. I won't go far but you must let the doctor talk to you, tell you what has happened and what he has done.'

Immediately Joe relaxed, but his head continued to turn on the pillow as though he were doing his best to determine whether he still had his sight and, if so, to get a glimpse of her.

'Amy.'

'I'm here.'

And so she remained and would do so until her husband was out of danger, she argued. When Joe slept she managed to rest in the sister's office in an armchair, still wearing the uniform that she had put on when she and Mercy walked into Ambleside to Miss Adeline's dress shop. Mercy returned to the cottage, sleeping, eating what Pansy put before her, bathing in the tin tub before the fire and bringing fresh underclothes for Amy.

But Amy was a nurse and when Joe was quiet and did not need her hand to cling to she moved round the ward, bending over restless men, soothing them, administering drinks, holding

438

hands, adjusting bandages and nothing they said could stop her.

'I want to be here for my husband but I cannot just sit in a chair and ignore a man who needs me. I am a nurse as well as a . . . a wife. It seem ridiculous to me that the help I can give should be refused when these men who have given so much need it.'

'Mrs Carter, they are not being refused it but the rules say—'

'Damn the rules, Sister.'

A faint cheer echoed round the room and Joe Carter, who could hear every word that was being said by his 'wife' and whoever she was arguing with, felt near to tears. A miracle had happened and the woman with the precious, valiant heart who was his life had been here just when he needed her most. He had drifted in and out of consciousness for so long now he could not remember how he had even got here, wherever here was. Ambleside, they said, which he knew was in the land of the Lakes. His whole body was in agony. He remembered the kid, the one who had tried to run away from his terror but had jumped the wrong way and had been brought back. Yes, all right, he told himself, *you* brought him back and got shot up for your pains. A bullet in the back and a shell exploding in your face. Bloody hell, they had you coming and going, but really it was worth it if only to have his beloved girl to hold his hand and get him through this. She had told them she was his wife which was all right with him, especially if it kept her with him, but she must have told them that for a reason and he had yet to discover what it was. He could hear her arguing with someone and he slipped back for a moment to the past when she had been totally under the domination of the cruel woman who was her aunt. What a shy, fragile little thing she had been then and would you listen to her now, giving what for to someone who was trying to make her do what she didn't want to do.

'Private Brown was asking for a drink and there was no one here to get it for him. Oh, I know you are run off your feet, Nurse and were attending to another patient and that you would not ignore the private deliberately but I was here, doing nothing, so I gave him a drink.'

'And what if the doctor had said no liquids and you—'

'I was here when the doctor made his rounds and there was nothing said about no liquids. I am a nurse, you know, and am aware that certain rules concerning an individual patient must be observed.'

He smiled beneath his bandages then winced as the movement of his facial muscles lashed him with pain. He worried about that. His face. What if it should be so hideous when his bandages were removed that people recoiled in a horror they could not hide? The doctor had told him he had not lost his sight so that was a bloody relief. They had doctors for every kind of wound now and a man who dealt only with eyes had seen him while he was anaesthetised and told them that his eyes were undamaged, but there was still his face and his back. Spines were tricky things, he had been told, and if . . . Dear God, let him walk again and let his face be reasonably true to how it had been before the battle. If he should see the woman he loved beyond life itself turn her face away from the sight of his he might be sorry that his eyes had been saved!

31

The small dog lay perfectly still in a warm patch of sunlight at the top of the steps leading up to the open front door. To all intents and purposes he was dozing, taking not the slightest bit of notice of all those moving in and out of the hospital but to anyone who might be watching him—and apparently there was no one since by now they were used to his presence—they would have seen that his bright eyes were weighing up every person in his immediate vicinity. He stood up casually and yawned, shaking his back legs in turn and stretching mightily. He watched for his chance, then, like an arrow from a bow following his sense of smell which had not let him down over the past weeks, scurried through the deserted doorway into the equally deserted hall. There were two nurses, heads together at the back of the stairs poring over a patient's chart, that of a young soldier who would be dead by nightfall, Sister Tully had told them, as a result of gangrene which had travelled from his extensive and badly infected leg wound to the lower part of his body. He was heavily sedated and his mother had been sent for.

The dog darted into the first ward on his right, what had once been the drawing room of Howethwaite, his acute sense of smell guiding him again to the right place. He inched himself through the door and under the first bed. The man in the bed was asleep and the nurse was further up the ward bending over a recent admission, doing her best to stop him from leaping from his bed and running down the ward shouting at the top of his voice. Most of the men, with the exception of the one with a bandaged face, were watching the nurse and the patient. He was one of what were being called 'shell-shocked' patients, men who had given way after probably months of trench warfare, bombardments that had driven them mad with fear, with the dread of fear itself, and though he had only a slight wound to his arm it had been decided that he should be sent home. He was yelling for his mam as he struggled with the young nurse who was doing her best to calm him but the shouting had attracted the attention of two orderlies who hurried up the ward and with expert hands held the poor lad while the nurse administered a sedative. But he wasn't fit to be among these badly wounded men. There was a special ward, even a special hospital for these pathetic remains of humanity who had been driven beyond endurance by circumstances they could not cope with. He had fought at a place called Passchendaele where for two weeks the heaviest bombardment of the war had churned up the land into a sodden mass of mud when the good weather ended and the rain began. No wonder he had lost his reason!

The soldier was quiet now and as every patient in the ward watched anxiously—every little thing made them nervous—the patient limped down the ward, helped by the orderlies who murmured comfortingly, sympathetically, for though they had seen it so often, the suffering of these men still affected them.

Only one man did not watch, the soldier with the bandaged face. The ward calmed down and the patients fell into a doze. The dog looked about him and sniffed then began to crawl on his belly under each bed until he was directly alongside the bed of the man with the bandaged face. The bed was placed by the French window leading on to the terrace. Slowly he stood up, put his paws on the edge of the bed and gently licked the hand of the man who lay there. It was as though he sensed the extreme fragility of the wounded soldier but even so the man flinched in surprise and pulled his hand away. He turned his head on the pillow as though to look down but he could see nothing, naturally, so he laid his hand once more on the white counterpane at the side of his supine body. Again the dog licked it but this time he made a small sound, like a whimper, and the soldier gasped.

'Bloody 'ell,' Sergeant Joe Carter muttered in utter disbelief, fondling the filthy, matted fur on the dog's head. The animal shivered in ecstasy and pushed his black, moist nose into Joe's hand as dogs do with those they love.

'Bloody 'ell, Ernie . . . Is it Ernie? No, I must be going daft. Jesus H. Christ, it can't be. Whatever they give me is sendin' me off me head. Ernie! Dear God in heaven, how in hell's name did you get 'ere, yer soft mutt?' he whispered, not wanting to draw attention to his bed, shaking his head in wonderment though the movement sent arrows of pain down his body. 'Last time I saw you yer were in me scrape-hole. That was, I dunno. How many days, weeks 'ave I bin 'ere? Jesus, lad, if they find yer in't ward they'll chuck you out. Where's Amy? She'll tekk yer to her place until I get out o' this bloody bed.' But the animal kept his paws on the edge of the bed and sniffed at Joe's bandaged face, then laid his muzzle on Joe's hand in total satisfaction. For five minutes man and dog remained, peacefully together then footsteps could be heard as Amy approached. By now Joe knew the sound of her footsteps.

'That was Ernie,' he told her simply.

'Ernie?'

'He followed me from France.'

'From . . . ?' She bent over him as though to let him see her expression of bewilderment.

'Yes. Will you look after him, Amy. 'E can't 'ang about 'ere can 'e?'

'Of course, I will, Joe, but—'

'I'll tell yer full story later, an' thanks, sweetheart.'

Ernie slid on his belly from bed to bed until he reached the door where he slipped out and lay down in the same square of sunshine he had left fifteen minutes before. He gave his ear a good scratch, then rested his nose on his paws; and when the lady who had taken to feeding him asked him who he was looking for, or waiting for, as humans do talk to dogs as though expecting an answer, he looked up at her with his bright, intelligent eyes and could not understand her kind words. After all, he was a French dog!

*　　　*　　　*

Amy and Mercy, leaving behind the strenuously protesting Ernie with Pansy, walked up each day to the hospital, always well turned out, for Pansy, like Myrtle and most northern women, was a devil for what she called 'spit and polish', not just as concerned them and their uniforms, but the cottage where she was in charge. She washed and ironed their cotton check frocks every day with the old flat iron heated on the stove, along with their linen aprons, and their high collars were starched to perfection, their black stockings washed and hung out on the washing line in the garden. Their caps were treated with the same care and they told one another that if Sister at the hospital at Rouen could see them she'd be amazed.

Pansy brought them up to date on the servants who remained not only in Manchester where Myrtle gathered all the news about those at Somerfield who had been Amy's friends, but also at Elmhurst in Victoria Avenue in Liverpool where the Carstairs lived. Mrs Abigail was still at Somerfield as were the rest of them, for in the end Alice and Jess, who had threatened to leave and go to work in a munitions factory, had decided to stay with Mrs Seymour after all. They did not say why and neither did Myrtle but in a strange way it was thought, by Myrtle and Pansy, that it was something to do with their little miss, Miss Amy. They felt she was part of their family. They had seen her through bad times and good though there had not been many of those and to leave and hear no more about her was something they seemed to have decided they could not do. It was as though if they kept a finger on the pulse, so to speak, they would be there to help her if she was in trouble, to defend her perhaps, though it was all muddled in their minds, for was not the master there to take care of her. Mind, those two, meaning Mrs Seymour and Mr Hodge, were a couple of devils and the more of them there were to keep watch the better.

It was still chaotic at Elmhurst, Myrtle wrote to Pansy when she returned from a visit with Miss Dodie, Mrs Carstairs's sister who often went to stay with her. Becky, Amy's younger sister, was a good lass and looked after the baby, who was a toddler now, while Mrs Carstairs did some war work with the local women's group. The other children were all at school so it was a bit more peaceful during the day.

'And does . . . Mrs Seymour . . . have any vistors . . . from her chapel?' Amy asked hesitantly, wondering if Randall Hodge was still as thick with her aunt now that Amy had vanished so completely. Were they still plotting together in their effort to bring her back under their domination or had they given up their obsessive search? After all it was three years since she had been given to, and escaped from the man who was called her husband.

'That there Mr Hodge comes, so Myrtle told me.' It seemed Myrtle had a friend in the Seymour household, though who was not revealed. 'They're still as thick as thieves but then they're both Methodys and his sister gets an invite now and again. They say he were given a white feather when he were in Manchester one day. A young woman give it him an' he were madder than a wet hen!'

It was not until Joe was put out on the terrace two weeks later that Amy was able to have what she called a proper conversation with him. The

446

wound on his back was healing well. The bullet had been removed and though he was still confined to bed Doctor Evans was optimistic that it would not be long before he could get up and take his first steps. His face was a different matter! The doctor was heard to say to Sister Tully that he would not allow Mrs Carter to be present when the bandages on Joe's face were changed and then finally removed since he could not have her fainting all over the place as she had done the first time.

'Well, Doctor, she *is* pregnant and so it can only—'

'*Pregnant!* Then what the devil is she doing here?' The doctor was horror-stricken. 'I turned a blind eye to her being married since I know she is an excellent nurse, but pregnant! She must leave at once since in my opinion Sergeant Carter . . . well, a plastic surgeon should have a look at him.' He sighed sadly and shook his grey head. 'So many faces have been wrecked and mangled by shell splinters that a special unit is being set up for facial injuries in London. A small group of surgeons are taking the first tentative steps to develop techniques for skin grafting and bone transplanting.'

Doctor Evans was a clever and compassionate man who gave everything he had to his patients but sometimes Sister Tully was inclined to think he talked like a rather dramatic walking textbook!

'It is said that relatives, wives, children, fiancées, are recoiling in horror at the gargoyles sent back to them whose only recognisable feature can be a shock of hair. This terrible war . . .' He took a deep breath. 'No, keep her out while the bandages are

447

changed and then let's see how he does. The wounds are healing but he is not a pretty sight.'

'I don't think Nurse Carter will shrink from him, Doctor, and would certainly not allow him to see her flinch. She is a strong young woman who has suffered much in her life. And he doesn't yet know about the baby, or so I was led to believe.'

'Mmm, well, she will need all her strength.'

*　　　*　　　*

The telephone shrilled that night and when Amy answered it she was delighted and astonished to hear her mam's trembling voice.

'Amy, is it you, chuck?' she asked as though she were talking to someone on another planet and could not believe it. It was the first time she had ever used this wonderful, terrifying gadget and her voice said so.

'Mam, Mam, where are you? Oh, Mam, it's so lovely to hear your voice.'

Someone in the background was evidently telling Mam to hold the earpiece to her ear and speak more loudly and Amy was so excited that even Ernie, who was at her feet, began to bark with what seemed like joy.

'I'm at Mrs Carstairs's, lovey. Miss Dodie an' Willy're staying wi' 'er an' Mr Seymour came to Hope Cottage an' picked me up an' fetched me 'ere. Eeh, 'e's that kind ... What?' She was evidently being told again to speak up and Amy wanted to cry with happiness.

'Are you well, Mam?'

'I am, chuck.'

'And the children?'

'We're all grand, queen, but longin' ter see yer.'

'So am I, Mam. Oh, Mam, so am I.'

'An' that lad, Joe, is 'e gerrin better?'

The conversation lasted no more than three minutes since it was evident Mam was getting flustered and after Bella came on and chatted for a moment, then rang off, Amy waltzed round the kitchen with Pansy, the dog barking and leaping up with the fun of it all.

None of them would have been quite so elated if they had noticed the motor car which followed Caleb in the Rolls back to Hope Cottage, then, when he had seen Dolly Pearson dropped off at her gate, the driver who motored hell for leather back to his hotel in Liverpool to telephone his latest report to the woman who employed him.

*   *   *

He lay with the sunshine warming his legs which had been freed from their coverings, one hand holding hers, the other caressing the dog's head, the considerably cleaner dog's head, for there was no way Sister would allow the scruffy mutt he had once been even on to the terrace. Joe's bandaged face was turned towards her as she brought him news of the Carstairs family with whom he had once romped.

'Papa still has the Rolls that you drove and he and Dodie and Willy are over there now. And guess what, my darling, he is to bring them to see us.'

He gripped her hand fiercely. 'Don't let them bring the children here,' he hissed through the slit in his bandages, the hiss all he could manage. At

449

his last bandage change Doctor Evans had cut holes in the wrappings to allow him to peer out, since his eyes were no longer a problem. They were still that incredible, brilliant blue and they pierced her with his terror that the children of whom he had grown so fond might be appalled by the sight of him.

She leaned forward, her face close to his, as his vision was rather restricted. The men about them watched breathlessly, envying him, for this lovely woman was not only his nurse but his wife and what would they have given to have someone like her to bend over them in their pain and nightmares.

Amy put her forehead against his, then, after ascertaining Sister was not about, dared a small kiss on his mouth, or where his mouth was almost hidden by the bandages. She could feel the movement of his smile and the nameless yearning in him to be as he was. Desperately his eyes searched hers looking for confirmation that her love was as strong as his. He knew it was, of course, but in his weakened state he found it difficult to believe that she still wanted him. He had no idea what the future held for them. She was still legally tied to the man in Manchester and until a divorce could be arranged, which meant relying on the man to divorce *her*, even if everything worked out all right, by which he meant that his face didn't revolt her, there were so many hurdles to surmount his heart felt cold, turning slowly in the depths of his chest.

'Sweetheart,' she whispered, 'I have something to tell you that might make you feel that there is hope, always hope . . .' She faltered and his hand gripped hers fiercely in sudden fear.

'What? What is it?'

She looked about her again, smiling at the men who were watching closely and trying to listen, too. She put her lips close to his ear and kissed the bandage that covered it. 'Can you hear me?' she asked him.

'Yes.'

'We are to . . . darling Joe, my love, my heart, we are to have a child; and no matter what you say about . . . about marriage and all that, I don't care. I will have you and you will have me and we will both have our child, Joe.'

She could feel him shake. His hand in hers was trembling and his shoulders heaved and she knew he was weeping beneath his bandages, hoping to God that the salty tears did him no harm. Mam had always said that salt was a healer. She used to put it in a bowl of warm water to bathe the scrapes and bruises of their childhood.

'Amy, dearest Amy, I don't know what ter say. If only . . .'

'What my love?'

'We could be married.'

'We *are* married, Joe,' she told him fiercely. 'And when you are recovered we shall live as man and wife with our child. I don't know where but somewhere safe where you shall work, as a mechanic or a gardener or whatever and we shall be together. Doctor Evans is to remove your bandages soon and you will come home to the cottage and I shall have our child and . . . Oh, Joe, I promise, *I promise* we shall be happy. Please, darling, don't cry, the men are . . . please, my love.'

Joe, who had been strong and brave for her

451

when they lived at Somerfield, was now the weak one and she, who had been so brutally treated, had now to be tough, the one to get Joe through this and out the other side to the peace they both needed.

Several days later she had to find the strength to fight Doctor Evans when he decided that the day had come for Joe's bandages to be removed. She was waiting at the door to the ward when he and the sister and another nurse pushing a trolley approached from the back of the hallway. The doctor stopped abruptly when he saw her there. He stopped so abruptly Sister Tully ran into him and the nurse ran into the sister with the trolley. It might have been amusing had the moment not been so traumatic.

'Now then, Mrs Carter, I absolutely insist that you leave this to us. There is no need for you to upset yourself, besides which I don't want my patient upset either.'

'My husband, you mean, Doctor. As you know I am a nurse who has seen far worse sights than a burned face and I shall not—'

'Faint? You did the first time you saw him.'

'I was taken by surprise and also I am pregnant as I'm sure Sister has told you, which did not help. I am prepared now and I know without a shadow of a doubt that Joe, my husband, will take strength from my presence. You can physically restrain me, Doctor, perhaps with a couple of orderlies, but I shall yell my head off and even have Mrs Buchanan, the wife of the owner of this hospital telephone someone ... I'm not sure who but if you—'

'Mrs Carter, have you the slightest notion how it

452

can affect my patient if he sees the … his wife react in a way that will totally destroy him, destroy his—'

'I am aware of that but my husband is the most important person in my life and even if he is left horribly scarred it will make no difference to me. We have loved one another since we were children and nothing has, or will, change that.'

She stuck out her stubborn little chin in a way that the sister and the nurse found most revealing and her mouth thinned to a firm, aggressive line. The brown of her eyes turned almost black and the good doctor, who truly wanted to save his patient any more suffering than he already knew, felt himself weakening. This was a strong woman he faced and had he not seen himself how she never shrank from any task allotted her, even the most appalling of which there were many in this carnage. that had come upon them.

'Very well, Mrs Carter, but promise me you will stand back and not get in my way. I don't want you to react in any way to what you are about to see. No reaching out to your husband, wanting to hold his hand, that sort of thing.'

The screens were already placed round Joe's bed and the other patients were in that state of tension that came upon them all when one of them was about to be tortured, as they saw it. Slowly, inch by inch, the bandages were unrolled from Joe's head and his face was revealed for the first time just as it was. A terrible freak of nature that was red and twisted, his left eye drawn down, his cheeks sculpted into strange lumps and fissures where the flesh had healed. It was raw, shiny, hard-looking but it had healed without infection. There was a pulse beating wildly in his throat which had not been touched and his jaw clenched below his mouth which, strangely, was also untouched and he kept his eyes on the doctor, not looking in Amy's direction as though afraid to see her reaction.

'Joe,' she murmured softly, 'oh, Joe, my love, my love, how wonderful. It is healed, my darling, healed.'

Slowly he forced himself to look at her. His beautiful eyes, blue but clouded now in his agony of apprehension, were just the same, framed by his long, dark eyelashes which had grown since he had been wounded and his eyebrows thick and brown. Even his hair had grown under his bandages and lay in flat whorls about his skull like that of a baby.

Ignoring Doctor Evans and his orders not to touch his patient, she darted forward and before any of them could stop her she had her arms about him, holding him to her in an agony of love. Not pity, not even sympathy for what he had suffered, just an overwhelming devotion that had remained for all these years and would never die. She was in his arms, trying to burrow herself deeper and deeper into his embrace, making soft little mewing sounds of comfort in the back of her throat as she clung to him. His arms gripped her so tightly they hurt her but she lifted a shining, smiling face to him then kissed him passionately on the mouth, her lips travelling to his cheeks, his jaw, his eyebrows, covering his face, his poor, damaged face with her kisses. The doctor and the two women watched in amazement for he really was a horrifying sight, but Mrs Carter didn't see it, or didn't care and they knew they were looking at a

454

love that was true, deep and everlasting. Sergeant Joe Carter would be all right!

The doctor cleared his throat. 'Erm, Mrs Carter, might I just examine my patient and then we will wheel him out into the sunshine, under an umbrella, of course, since he must protect himself for a while, and you can talk.'

But Amy and Joe barely heard him. Joe was dwelling on the wonder of this girl, for she was really no more than that despite what she had suffered, who was looking at him as though he were the handsomest devil she had ever come across. He could see the evidence of her pregnancy now that the bandage was gone. The doctor was still babbling on about further surgery and going up to London to see the surgeons who might be able to do something with the specialised treatments they were devising for soldiers like him, but Amy put up her hand and rested it on Joe's cheek, caressing the ugly red scars then kissing them tenderly.

'He has no need to go to London, Doctor, at least not yet. Not unless he himself feels the need of it. I don't. We have a baby to be born and then we will see.'

She waved them away with a peremptory hand and when Sister carefully arranged the screens round them she was quite astonished when a quiet cheer echoed round the ward.

32

Elin Carter was born on the first day of the year 1918. She came into the world in the bed which her parents had shared for the past three months ever since her father Joe Carter had been discharged from the army. It was as though she were eager to see the magical world her father and mother would create for her and couldn't wait to meet all those who were expecting her and she slipped from her mother as easily as a little fish, smiling, her father swore, as she arrived. He was there at her birth along with her godmother Mercy Andrews, her grandmother Dolly Pearson who had been driven up by Caleb the week before and Pansy Arkwright who looked after them all.

Dolly's mother had been Welsh, she told Amy, her name being Elin, which apparently meant 'nymph' in Welsh though she herself could not swear to it since she spoke not a word of the language. As the baby's doting father said, she looked like a little nymph or perhaps a tiny mermaid and if Amy was happy with the name so was he. Besotted with her, he was.

Joe Carter was always happy these days, for the Buchanan family had taken him under their wing, doing their best to ease his way back to a normal life but to tell the truth Joe was managing that on his own. By which he meant with his precious love, Amy, and now his baby daughter. He wouldn't have got anywhere without her, his Amy, Buchanans or not, but each day he trudged up to Howethwaite, doing whatever was asked of him whether it be digging over the vegetable plot, preparing it for the plants he meant to put in, tinkering with the engine of Mrs Buchanan's motor car, driving Doctor Evans or anyone who needed it wherever they wanted to go, reading to those chaps who still lay blinded in their beds, fetching and carrying and returning each evening to the arms of his blossoming 'wife'. They had even managed with a great deal of suppressed laughter to make love despite Amy's growing girth, which was another step on the way to his increasing confidence.

It had been difficult at first for him to face the startled stares of strangers in the streets of Ambleside, though he had to admit that the burn scars were calming down. The woman next door and her husband, Ted, had been inclined to look anywhere but at his face when he spoke to them, studying a flower or a distant tree rather than look at him, but when he offered to help Ted with a particularly obstinate tree from which he was lopping off branches they talked, as men will, of football and the state of the war news and anything that came into their male minds. Ted told his wife the bloke was really just like other blokes and from then on the pair found they hardly noticed his injuries.

Now and again Amy was aware of a stillness come upon him, a reserve that even she could not penetrate and she decided that at these times he returned in his mind to that hell where so many of his mates had perished or been maimed. In his dreams he yelled to Pip and Lanky to keep their heads down, and seemed to be distraught over his mate Wally and there was many a night when she

457

had to wake him lest he upset the baby. She would hold him in her arms and rock him out of his nightmares with her body, restoring him to his life with her which she begged him to believe was for ever. He was reviewed by Doctor Evans every few weeks and discussed the prospect of travelling to London to the clinic that dealt with cases like his, but since Amy seemed to see no difference in him and if she did was not disturbed by it, he decided that the scars left by the burns would eventually smooth out, or so the doctor seemed to believe. As long as Amy continued to look at him with that shining glow of love in her eyes, apparent to everyone who saw them together, he ignored some of the curious and pitying glances that came his way. The nation knew by now that their men would come home to them if not physically scarred as he was, then emotionally and mentally wounded, never to be the husbands, the sons they once had been.

And still it went on, with the lifeblood of the nation's youth trickling into the soil of the battlefields. Field Marshall Haig was demanding 600,000 more men to bring his outnumbered army up to strength and hold on to the British sector which ran from the Somme to the Yser, the reports dominating the newspapers in the first weeks of the New Year. Amy knew Joe agonised over what was happening at the front and sometimes she wondered if he yearned to be out there with the men in the trenches rather than tucked away safely with her and Elin at the cottage outside Ambleside, but of course the doctor, who reported to the army authorities, would not hear of it. Sergeant Carter had done his bit and though

458

he might be regaining his health he was certainly not fit to return to the front.

Joe had been elated when a number of American troops had arrived in France at the end of 1917 but there had been a problem with transport and they made little difference to the actual fighting but by March, when Elin was two months old, 325,000 American troops were already in France and Joe's spirits rose enormously. It had been a bad winter up in the land of the Lakes with snow blowing across the mountains in great swathes and drifting to several feet outside their snug cottage. Joe could not even get to the hospital, managing only to struggle from the cottage to collect wood for the fires which were kept burning night and day.

When the snows cleared and spring tiptoed across the land, with the baby wrapped up like a little cocoon and strapped to his chest with a harness of his own design, he and Amy began to explore the area about their home. Taking a picnic basket, they drove along the north side of Rydal Water where the birch trees, known as Lady of the Woods, were just beginning to show their foliage and their dangling catkins. The motor car was an Austin 10, made in 1913 and in a sad state of repair when Joe spotted it on the forecourt of a garage in Ambleside and with a degree of bargaining, half believing that the garage owner just wanted to get Joe's scarred face out of his sight, he bought it for £10! With his natural inborn ability—though where it came from no one, least of all Joe, knew—he had tinkered with it for weeks until he had it going smoothly and it was his delight to take his 'wife' and baby daughter for 'spins' round the narrow lanes about their home.

This day, a Sunday, with Elin old enough now to be carried, they decided to be more adventurous. From afar they had admired the vast, empty landscape—empty apart from the sheep—the beautiful, powerful lift of the mountains, shading their eyes to stare in wonder at the peaks of Langdale Pike, of High Raise away to the west, listened to the liquid music of the tumbling waters of the falls, but now it was time they explored further afield. They swept past Grasmere, beyond Dove Cottage where the great poet Wordsworth had once lived, the baby peacefully asleep on Amy's knee. As though she were aware that her parents had need of peace and tranquility, she rarely cried, or perhaps it was Joe's own placid nature that she had inherited. She was, in her parents' eyes, utterly beautiful with a fluff of golden curls rioting over her small skull, eyes that had become a violet blue, the colour hard to describe. She had long silken brown lashes and cheeks that were rosy and rounded. No matter who you were, you had only to look at her and she produced that wavering smile for you just as though she were waiting to be noticed and was delighted when you did. Joe adored her and would have stopped every passer-by on the streets of Ambleside, inviting them to peep into the old baby carriage Mrs Buchanan had passed on to them and admire his child. Elin had completed the return of the old Joe, the one who had loved and protected Amy for so many years. Gradually he became, not the protected, the guarded, the one who leaned for support in her overflowing love, but what he had been in the Somerfield days, the champion, the knight errant who would defend her and their child with his life. His body had recovered and so had his self-esteem, his self-respect. He was a diffident man, modest, and had proved his bravery on the battlefields of France but beneath that gentle exterior he had an iron will that would defend those he loved to the death. He might look different in the shape and colour of his face and now and again his eyes might tell their tale of his damaged inner soul, but that soul was gradually being restored by Amy's steadfast love.

It was a splendid day, clear and mild with a hint of the summer to come in its warmth. They parked the motor on the verge of the road where primroses were raising their shy heads and climbed steadily, following sheep trods between the growing bracken until they reached the summit of Sergeant Man. They sat side by side leaning against the enormous grey pitted rock which formed a circle with others, their shoulders touching, not speaking but now and again turning to smile at one another, ready to marvel at their happiness then turning back to gaze with awe at the silvery calm of the rippling sunshine on Rydal Water far below. The birch trees flew their new leaves, a waterfall cascading from Easedale Tarn played them the music of its thundering spray and when Elin had been fed from Amy's bounteous breast, then fell asleep again on the dry bed of bracken beside them, Joe lifted Amy's skirt about her waist and entered her as naturally as though mother nature were encouraging them to be a part of life here in this bleak but lovely wilderness. In the beauty of what was rapidly becoming their home Amy was at that moment made pregnant with her second child; neither of them knew it at the time, though later it seemed appropriate that it should have happened when it did. It was not the first time they had made love since Elin's birth, for they could not get enough of the sheer wonderment of being together and alone.

All the years they had been parted, the memories of the suffering inflicted upon them both were fading and as they drew up in front of their little home where the lamps were already lit and welcoming in the windows they were both smiling. Pansy was at the door to meet them as was the smell of the fresh bread she had baked. With Joe discharged from the hospital and coming home each night Pansy had taken the chance to go back to Liverpool to spend a few days with her family and meet up with Myrtle. Her brother had been on leave, looking as though he were not really there at all, his mother complained, as all soldiers did when back from the battlefields of France and with him had been his pal, the pal who stood beside him in the trench, covering his back as Arthur covered his. His name was Jack Cassell, a sergeant who had gone through the war without a scratch, as had Arthur, and like all the soldiers who fought side by side they were highly superstitious, believing that if they were not together on the fire step or in their scrape-hole, one of them would be done for. Jack, whose parents lived in the Shetlands and were too far away for Jack to visit in the short leave he and Arthur were granted, had taken a shine to Pansy and his feelings were reciprocated, as Pansy was still a young woman, the bright, cheerful young woman and the dour, dignified soldier so completely opposite in nature that they were like two halves of one whole.

'I'd not leave yer in the lurch, chuck,' she told Amy, 'but me an' Jack . . . well, we hit it off an' he's goin' ter write ter me and I think it might come ter summat so . . .'

'You might be leaving us, Pansy?'

'Well, yer see, since Marty were killed . . .'

Amy put her arms round the older woman's shoulders and hugged her before planting a kiss on her cheek. 'Yer daft 'apporth,' she said in a fair imitation of how she had spoken when she was ten years old. 'Do you think I would stop you from finding happiness again? And now that Joe and I are together we . . . well, we . . .'

'Want ter be on your own.' Pansy smiled shyly, quite overcome by a lady, as she thought of Amy, giving a hug to the likes of her who was, after all, her servant.

The telephone began to ring as Joe carried the baby, who was awake and smiling now, over the threshwood. He sat down with her in his arms in the warm, fire-glowed kitchen and cradled her to his chest, blowing raspberries on her rounded cheek and making her smile some more and even to chuckle which he thought was enormously clever. He let Amy answer the telephone's insistent ring. It was Caleb.

'Amy, my darling girl, there you are. I've been trying to get through all day but the telephone system is very unreliable.'

'Papa, this is a lovely surprise.' She was ready to laugh and cry but he interrupted her almost curtly.

'How is my granddaughter?' he asked and before she could reply began at once to pour into her ear such a tale she could hardly comprehend him.

' ...And so you see she must go at once to ...'

'What, Papa? Who? I can't hear you properly ... What is it?'

'Darling, it's your friend's ... Was in touch with Alex Buchanan, you know at the War ...'

'Papa, stop, stop. Please begin again. Are you talking about Mercy and Richard?'

'Yes, yes, as they advanced the Americans found him in a German hospital ... prisoner of war ... both legs, I'm afraid. God knows why it wasn't reported ... too badly injured ... suppose but his parents ... can she come to London? He's to be sent to a London hospital ... home ... parents ... address is ...' The line faded completely then but Amy hung on and at last she managed to grasp it. She began to cry broken-heartedly and both Joe and Pansy shot into the tiny cramped space where the telephone stood and even the baby began to wail.

She waved them away, her smile shining through her tears but they both stared at her, wondering what could be making her laugh and cry at the same time.

'No, no,' she managed to gasp at them. 'Tell me again, Papa,' waving frantically at Pansy for a pencil and when she hung up she put her arms about not only Joe and the baby but Pansy as well, jigging them round the kitchen, to the delight of Elin Carter.

'Give me the baby, Joe, then get the motor out and go like mad up to the hospital and fetch Mercy.' Mercy, since Joe's discharge, now lodged with the other nurses. 'It's Richard, *her* Richard.

He's been found and she's to go to London.'

'Dear God in 'eaven,' Pansy exulted, for Amy was not the only one to have known how much more difficult it had been for Mercy to see Amy's happiness when her own seemed burned to ashes.

Mercy's face was waxen when Joe almost carried her over the threshwood, then just as suddenly it turned the colour of a rising sun, glowing with joyful anticipation. She grabbed Amy and hugged her as though it were all her doing, the return of the man she loved, returned from the dead, so to speak.

'Now dearest, you've no time for that,' Amy began, for she was aware, as Mercy was in normal circumstances, of the dreadful injuries her Richard might have sustained. A crashed aircraft . . . Dear God . . . his legs, Papa had said, but it seemed Mercy did not even contemplate what she might be facing. Richard was alive and that was all that mattered.

'Joe will run you to the station in Windermere and find out about connections for you. I will send on your things as soon as you've seen Richard's parents and let me know their address. All this time, oh, Mercy, I can hardly believe it. Oh, darling, I pray that he, Richard, will not be—'

'Don't, Amy, please don't. Like you with Joe I just want to have him back no matter what his . . . his injuries are. I'm a nurse and I will heal him. How long is it? I had begun to believe that he was gone. All those young fliers, Albert Ball and James Childs, Richard knew them both and now, now my Richard has been returned to me. I swear I'll bring him back to health just as you have done with Joe.'

They wept for a moment, then with a small

465

overnight bag clutched to her Mercy was whisked off in the little motor car, waving until the last moment to Amy and Pansy who held the child in her arms. The day was fading and the baby needed a feed and both of them sighed as they slowly moved indoors, in thrall to the marvel of it, to the wonder of Mercy's joy. Pansy's Marty had been lost in the carnage at the front but she had found a man who might replace him in some way and it all seemed unbelievable that so much happiness could come out of so much sorrow.

Pansy stayed with them until the beginning of June when, realising that she was no longer needed by 'Mrs Carter' she returned to Liverpool and took up work in a munitions factory, saying that with Jack at the front and her own mam fretting for Arthur, who was now the only one of her sons still alive, she felt she should return.

'Pansy, Mercy and I will be for ever grateful for what you have done for us. When we were so low, with Joe and Richard missing we ... well, thank you. Now, will you telephone us and let us know how you are. You and Jack.'

'Well, I don't know,' Pansy said warily, eyeing the telephone, for there was not one of her people had anything to do with such modern contraptions. She brightened. 'Can I write ter yer?'

'Of course you can and I'll send you photographs of Elin. And if ever Joe and I get to Manchester'—shuddering a little at the thought—'we'll come and see you. Perhaps you'd invite us to the wedding.' She smiled.

'Eeh, gerraway with yer ...' Pansy giggled but she was pleased nevertheless.

Amy settled down to her life as a housewife and

466

mother—and a mother-to-be—for she and Joe knew now that she would have a second child in January when Elin was a year old. Joe was somewhat dubious, saying that Amy was such a little bit of a thing would she be able to manage two babies but she laughed and called him 'Mr Worrier' and he grinned sheepishly, for what woman was ever born who could be stronger than his Amy.

Mercy telephoned regularly with news of Richard who had lost a leg when his aircraft had crashed and his other was badly injured but he was being fitted with a false leg and was recovering the spirit which had deserted when he was in the depths of despair and made him keep his identity to himself while he was in German hands. He had believed that Mercy would no longer want him, she told Amy, but she had soon disabused him of that idea when she had simply climbed into his bed at his parents' home and made love to him until he laughed weakly and begged for mercy.

'You've got Mercy, I told him, and, Amy, from that day he began to recover. His parents are so grateful to me, as if I were doing something wonderful for them when it was what I longed to do. Not that I told them exactly . . . well, you know what I mean. So we have agreed to a wedding before the year ends. He is determined to walk up the aisle with me on his arm, he says and my dearest wish is that you will be my bridesmaid . . .'

She went on in this vein for half an ecstatic hour and Amy could only sigh with the sheer wonder of it. Both she and Mercy were home!

*   *   *

Amy and her next-door neighbour with whom she was now on friendly terms, since Sally had discovered that Mr and Mrs Carter were not the foreign 'toffs' she had first thought them to be, had been chatting at their front doors, comparing their experiences as mothers—Sally had five and was free with her advice—when the motor car passed by and went on towards Rothay Bridge, turning right on to Borrans Road. They both stopped talking for a moment to watch its passage, for it was unusual to see such a vehicle on their bit of a lane, then resumed their chat. Sally hitched her apron higher up her waist, as she too was pregnant, which made another bond between her and her neighbour, then moved reluctantly indoors. It was a lovely day, warm and sunny, and she had washing to get out, she said, what with five children and a husband who worked up at the copper mine where filthy overalls were the order of the day. Amy peeped under the canopy of the perambulator where her lovely child was sleeping in the sunshine, leaving her plump legs uncovered to let the sun touch them, then like Sally went indoors to put Elin's nappies in to soak. She changed the bed where she and Joe slept and, when she had given the bedding a good 'possing', put it through the mangle and heaped it into her laundry basket. She hung it out on the line and then sauntered to the side of the cottage where the baby carriage stood to check on Elin. It was quiet except for the hum of insects and from next door came the sound of Sally singing one of the popular songs that the soldiers had made their own.

The garden was alive with the buds of early

468

roses some previous owner had planted and she stopped for several minutes to admire them, thinking of Mam and wishing she could get some to her. Next to daffodils, roses were Mam's favourite, though she had told Amy that their Sammy had planted out the cottage garden a treat. Already here, and apparently in Mam's garden too there were country garden flowers, periwinkle, bright yellow daisies, rock cress and aubretia and a brave show of wallflowers. Joe had created this loveliness for her and Elin and for the new child, and others they would have, and had helped Sammy with advice in the short time they had known one another. Mam was going to brave the train and fetch Claire with her on a visit to River Cottage, she had written—she still distrusted the telephone—because she was longing to see her grandchild again and she might as well get used to it, she told Amy, as she meant to come for the birth of the second child.

Bella had telephoned to say that Dodie had been delivered of a little girl and that both she and Caleb were filled with joy. He still had high hopes of a divorce from Zillah but it was a long and arduous task since Zillah was proving awkward and that was an understatement! She herself had finally persuaded John that she wanted no more children and he had found a safe and wonderful means of contraception so if Amy ever felt her family was big enough she only had to apply to her.

Amy smiled as she walked towards the baby carriage. She and Joe, as though to weigh against the death they had seen, were intent on producing life in the form of the children they would have. She placed her hand on the ever so slight mound of her stomach, imagining the tiny life inside her, then leaned under the canopy to smile at her baby who would surely be awake by now. She had been surprised at how quiet she had been, for if she was not gurgling, she was chuckling or talking to the leaves in the trees that swayed above her baby carriage.

'Where's Mummy's girl, then?' she asked smilingly.

Mummy's girl was not there! Amy began to scream, looking wildly round her as though her child might, at the age of five months, have climbed from the carriage and be strolling about the garden admiring her daddy's flowers.

'Elin, Elin, where are you? My baby, my baby, where's my baby!' Her screaming rose to a fever pitch, for Amy Carter had known terror, horror, the full gamut of what might be called nightmares and this surely was the worst.

It brought Sally scrambling from her door and across her bit of garden to stare in the same mortal fright as was emanating from Amy. 'What's up? What's all't lowpin' about, my lass? What?'

'Sally, my baby, my baby!' Amy shrieked.

'Bairn, whar's ter do wi't bairn? I very near 'ad an 'eart-attack when I 'eard—'

'Elin, Elin's not in the baby carriage. I put her in and—'

'Not in't baby carriage? Give ower, yer've not looked proper.'

'Get Joe, send your lad for Joe. She's got her, she's got her . . .'

'Who?'

'Send for Joe. Dear sweet Jesus, she's got my baby.'

33

'Can you not stop that child from screaming, Nurse, and I would appreciate it if you could change its napkin. The smell is appalling.' The woman who spoke shrank further into the corner in the back seat of the motor car, an expression of deep disgust on her tight face.

'She is not used to the milk, madam, and until we are stationary I cannot change her. It is difficult—'

'I appreciate that it is not used to the milk—what is it you recommended, Mellin's Food?—well, all I can say is that it will just have to get used to it, for it is all there is. The child's mother is not available so it's that or starve. It is up to you and as an experienced nurse I am trusting you to see to it. Thankfully we are nearly there and then you can do what is necessary.' She peered through the window. 'I believe we have just gone through the village of Low Hesket so Carlisle should not be far. When you are settled I shall take the first train down south and will keep in touch with you by telephone. I have arranged for a machine to be installed at the house and if you have any problems, which I do not expect, you will telephone me on the number I have given you. You have your instructions. There will be a perambulator, though you must not leave the garden, a bassinet and whatever else is needed for it. I'm sure you can leave the infant in the care of the maid should you need to go into town to purchase anything else you require. It is a big town and you will not be noticed. Make sure you are not. That is why you are being paid such a good salary.' She rapped on the glass which divided the two women and the distressed baby from the chauffeur. When he opened the small window she told him to drive a little faster as she had a train to catch, then turned back to the woman struggling with the child.

'Now you must not speak to your neighbours or in any way draw attention to yourself and if anyone should take an interest and question you, the child's father is wounded and in hospital in London and the mother gone there to be near him. I've explained all this to you before, I know, but I want you to be absolutely sure of your story. The house you will live in is detached, small, but in its own grounds. There is one maid, a girl I brought from the orphanage in Carlisle, a bit simple, which is all to the good, but your job is to take care of the child until I send for you. You understand?'

'Yes, Mrs Turnbull.' The nurse, who had no right to call herself such since she had no qualifications, held the child tightly, her lips thinning as she looked down into its frantic little face. 'Don't worry. The child is in good hands.'

*　　　*　　　*

Doctor Evans was the first to admit that Joe Carter had improved beyond recognition since he had been discharged from the hospital, thanks mainly to his lovely and loving wife and the birth of his child, but he went to pieces when the stuttering lad told him he had to come at once.

'Why? What's 'appened? Is it Amy? What? Fer God's sake, lad, speak up.' In his desperation he took Sally's eldest by the shoulders and began to shake him so that the boy's head, held on a fragile neck, lolled about quite alarmingly.

'Joe, Joe, let the boy speak,' the doctor exclaimed but Joe had lost all reason because Amy would not send for him in the middle of a working day without some good and serious reason.

'Alfie, speak out, lad,' shaking the boy even more and not until Doctor Evans took Joe by the arm and attempted to pull him off did he release his grip. Joe had been helping an orderly to assist a nervous patient to the doctor's office where it was to be decided whether the soldier should be sent to the special hospital for cases like him when Alfie had burst in through the front door, shouting Joe's name.

' 'Ere, what d'yer think you're doin'?' the porter had demanded to know but Doctor Evans's office was just along the hallway and the commotion was heard by him, by Joe and Sister Tully and by the soldier who began to shout for his mam. For a moment it was total confusion until the patient was led away and Joe had a chance to grab Alfie. Doctor Evans, as he watched Joe, realised that the man who had once been a soldier and had suffered in the trenches could still easily be tipped over the edge of reason.

'Steady, lad,' he told him. 'Now, boy, what is it?'

'Bairn's gone,' Alfie gasped.

'Bairn?'

'Aye, Joe's little lass, stolen from 'er pram, Mrs Carter ses an' me Mam ses . . .'

But Joe was out of the office and down the

473

hallway, through the front door and into his little motor before Alfie could finish. Like Amy, he knew exactly who had taken his beloved child. He accelerated towards his home and the woman who shared it with him, and knew exactly what Zillah Seymour was capable of. He was only surprised that it had not happened sooner. Not kidnapping his daughter but exacting revenge which, in her madness, Zillah wanted, needed. She had found them before and had done so again.

There was a police constable just getting off his bicycle, leaning it against the side of the cottage as Joe drew up, scattering dust and gravel all over him.

''Ere, watch out,' he began but Joe was out of the motor, leaving the door hanging open, and into the cottage where Amy was standing, like a small and paralysed animal in the glare of a torchlight, with Sally bobbing about her. Sally had a crying toddler on her hip and another clutching her skirt but she was doing her best to bring Amy from what seemed like a state of stunned shock. Sally turned in great relief as Joe entered and at once took Amy into his arms. He was the strong one now. The policeman gawped about him. At the station he had been told by some incoherent woman on the telephone that a child was missing but kids wandered off all the time and were always found nearby and what all the bloody fuss was about he couldn't imagine.

He changed his mind when he was informed by the man with the distressingly disfigured face that the 'kid' in question was five months old and when last seen had been asleep in her baby carriage! He'd better get his sergeant in on this, he said, but the man, the father, with his arm still round his stunned wife, was on the telephone and speaking to someone called Mr Seymour.

'It must be 'er, sir. Who else would want ter take our Elin? . . . Yes, there's a bobby 'ere now but it needs someone . . . yes, sir, if yer would . . . ' For a moment the father lost his composure and the constable was quite taken aback when he began to tremble and almost was ready to fall down.

Poor sod, he must have been at the front, the constable decided, to have a face like that but then the mother came to life and together they clung as one and who was holding who up he couldn't decide.

'Sir,' he began, 'if I could 'ave a description of the . . . er, bairn, what she weer wearin', like, an' then I'll telephone the station an' get some 'elp.'

'Amy, love, what was . . . ?'

'Did Papa say what he was to do?'

'Yes, he'll 'ave the whole of the country's bloody police force out, startin' with the Chief Constable of Lancashire but first he's off ter Somerfield.'

The constable scratched his head in bewilderment. The Chief Constable of Lancashire! Who was this child and who were this couple related to that they could command such service? The king?

'Sir,' he began, taking out his pencil and pad, ready to jot down anything the father or mother could tell him, for they were both steady now. The other woman with the grizzling children was making them all a nice cup of tea, she said. He waited a moment, then, without asking permission, telephoned the station and brought his sergeant up to date on the matter.

'Yer'd better get down 'ere, Sarge. There's more to this than meets the eye.'

*   *   *

Alice was speechless when she opened the front door and Mr Seymour pushed roughly passed her. It was years since they had seen him and here he was looking like thunder and totally ignoring her as he marched into the drawing room. He glared round him and finding it empty turned on her in such a ferocious manner she cowered away from him, convinced he was going to hit her.

'Where is she?' he hissed menacingly. He was white-lipped in his madness, what Alice thought was a murderous madness. 'Hell's teeth, woman, where is she?'

'Oh, sir, sir, please,' she began, wishing she had let Jess answer the door as she had wanted to.

'That bloody woman, I'll see she's put away for this. She's insane, out of her bloody mind and I'm not surprised. She's been heading that way for years. Now where is she?'

'How dare you enter my house and threaten my servant,' a voice from the stairs asked icily and there she was, the woman who had caused more heartache to the people he loved and to himself, who loathed her, than if she had been a descendant of the dreaded Inquisition. And yes, was afraid of her. Not for himself, but for those others she had threatened in her madness. All these years she had not given up, following like a bloodhound every escape route Amy had taken, viciously persistent, merciless in her belief that Amy owed her allegiance and infuriated that

476

despite all her efforts she had not turned her niece into a good and obedient chapel-goer. And who had deserted the decent husband Zillah had found for her. But he had come here to retrieve the child, not to castigate this insane woman.

'Where is she?' His voice was like a stone hitting a rock and Alice, who was trapped by the front door, flinched and wondered if she should run out of the door, round the house and return to the sanity of the kitchen.

'Where is who, Caleb?' Zillah's own voice was soft with triumph and Alice was aware that her mistress knew exactly who the master meant and Alice wished she herself did.

'You know who I mean, woman. I have informed the Chief Constable of Lancashire, who happens to be an acquaintance of mine, and the whole of the police force is looking for her so it might be as well if you give her up now.'

'Really, Caleb, if I knew who you were talking about I might be able to help you but as I don't I would be obliged if you would leave my home and return to your slut in Langworthy Road. Oh, yes, everyone knows of her and her brats, *your* brats and I must say . . .'

'You bitch, you bloody evil bitch, you'd do anything to hurt those who are defenceless against you but I am not one of them. If you don't fetch my granddaughter here at once I shall see that—'

'*Your granddaughter!*' Zillah shrieked. 'Is that what you call her? You and that girl. Have you any notion . . . have you not heard, "The wicked flee when no man pursueth: but the righteous are bold as a lion!" That is how—'

'Don't you quote your damn—'

477

'"Happy is the man that feareth alway: but he that hardeneth his heart shall fall into mischief."'

With a roar Caleb Seymour leaped at the woman who stood at the foot of the stairs, reaching for her throat, but Alice began to scream, the sound piercing the air and bringing Matt and Barty running from the kitchen where they had been enjoying a glass of Mrs Abigail's home-made beer. Not as good as the real thing, they said to one another, but grand on a hot day such as this. For a moment they could not believe their eyes, since it seemed to them the master was actually strangling the mistress, which they had longed to do many a time, but instinctively they sprang forward and dragged him off. The rest of the servants crept from the kitchen and Mrs Abigail cradled the hysterical Alice to her bosom and watched as Mrs Seymour collapsed to the floor. Not one of them rushed to help her even though she was moaning and clutching at her throat.

With their undivided attention centred on the scene in the hallway they did not hear a motor car draw up and park next to Caleb's Rolls-Royce and when a policeman walked in they stared in amazement. He wore a smart uniform adorned with elaborate frogging, a hat like a pillbox but with a small peak decorated with braid and silver lace and was obviously of a high rank in the force. He was accompanied by another police officer who kept respectfully two paces behind him.

'Mr Seymour?' he asked politely, looking with interest at Caleb who was still being held by the gardeners. They immediately set him free, as they knew they were in the presence of authority.

'Yes, and thank you for coming so promptly,

Whitworth. My granddaughter has been kidnapped and I believe this woman here has had a hand in it. Yes, yes, I know she is . . . was . . . still is my wife but she has pursued my daughter, the child's mother, with a relentless tenacity and, having failed to retrieve her, has turned her attention to the child.'

'Mr Seymour, sir, if we may go somewhere private . . . no, no, my sergeant will stay with Mrs Seymour but we must all remain calm and—'

'Hell and damnation, man, there is no time to be having private talks. She may have killed the child. God almighty, you don't know her like I do. She is capable of anything.' But the policeman was having none of it. If the child was already dead, which he did not believe, it was too late, and if she wasn't it needed information, judgement, calmness and the undivided attention of all those involved in the matter.

'Let us go into your—'

'Mr Seymour's study is just along the hallway, sir,' Mrs Abigail obliged, the policeman noting that she seemed to be a likely witness to anything that might have occurred in this house. She was apparently unexcitable even now with maidservants ready to burst into tears or standing with their mouths open about her, fascinated as bystanders often are at this unexpected thrill in their daily lives.

'Very well, let us go there now and would someone attend to Mrs Seymour. It is Mrs Seymour, is it not?' nodding at the woman who still floundered at the bottom of the stairs. 'Perhaps a doctor . . . ?'

They clung to one another through that long night, not weeping, not speaking much, just with a great emptiness dragging them down, tearing them with such pain it was as though a jagged hole had been opened up inside them as they waited pitiably for the return of their precious child. Doctor Evans came, which was saying something about the seriousness of this occurrence, for he very rarely left the hospital premises so committed was he to his patients. He knew about the catastrophe that had come upon them and wanted to give them something to help them sleep but neither of them would take it.

'We might be needed, Doctor, if she ... if something ...' Amy nearly broke then, for that woman who had made her life hell was capable of anything, even harming an innocent child. That is what Amy had been, an innocent child when she had been taken to Somerfield and from then on the woman had shown her no mercy, giving her, when she was no more than sixteen, to the animal who had nearly killed her. Now, in her frenzied need for revenge on Amy, who had run away from her, from the life into which Zillah had forced her, she had taken Amy's child, presumably to inflict the same fate on her. But she must be mad to think the servants at Somerfield would accept Elin as *another* relative their mistress had rescued! No, her child would be found and returned to them. She must believe that or she would go mad. *She must!*

'Why don't yer take the draught, lovely.' Joe held her close and murmured into her ear. 'I'll wake yer if owt happens.'

'No, Joe, I can't, really. Thank you, Doctor, but I can't ...' Her voice trailed off and the doctor rose to leave.

'I'm so sorry, Mrs Carter.'

There followed days when the whole of the country was made aware that the grandchild of one of Manchester's most prominent citizens had been kidnapped, almost knocking news of the war off the front pages of newspapers. It had been felt that Germany had shot its bolt, as in its attack on the Allies from March to June its casualties were not far short of a million men and although a thousand pieces of artillery had been lost by the British army Great Britain's massive industrial superiority had replaced them by the summer. It was looking hopeful, dare they say, the newspapers were suggesting. And where was Mr Caleb Seymour's grandchild who had been missing for two weeks though no ransom had been demanded?

Amy and Joe spent hours, though they knew it was fruitless, driving along country lanes, looking for they knew not what, since it was foolish to imagine Zillah would take their child and just leave her to perish under a hedge or in a ditch, but they must do *something*. They could not just sit at home and wait. And the beauty of the Lakeland as June passed into July made the agony of waiting even worse. Evening with its long shadows, its subtle colouring, the green sunlit carpet of the fells and the richer hues of the crowded woodlands. It was time to bring down the ewes and their lambs for clipping and the dales were jammed with a jostling, steaming throng of the animals flowing

481

round the little motor car. Dolly had come to make sure they got a decent meal inside them, she said, her face growing old before its time as she suffered her daughter's sorrow.

Caleb dashed up in his motor to report on Zillah whose home and grounds had been searched and who had been interviewed a dozen times but had continued to declare her innocence in this stupidity. What would she want with a baby, even if she was capable of kidnapping it? It was ridiculous and she would bring her minister and many people who attended chapel with her to testify to her integrity. They could not shake her. She continued to go about her daily routine, chapel, meetings on this and that, her good works with fallen girls and alcoholics, and her servants, who were also interviewed several times, could honestly say they had seen nothing out of the ordinary in their mistress. She had been away in June, but only for the day to some meeting; no, they didn't know where, for the mistress did not confide in them. When it was checked by the indefatigable chief constable, she had been seen to board a train to Liverpool early that morning but she had returned from the same city later in the day!

Dodie and Bella and even Mercy telephoned regularly. In a way Amy and Joe wished they wouldn't, for every time the machine shrilled out their hearts would stop then race again with hope that it might be news of their child.

How was she, that lovely, laughing, placid infant who was an essential part of her father's recovery and her mother's joy? Was she being properly cared for? Was she fretting—of course she was—

without them to soothe her? Was she having the sustenance that she had formerly received from Amy's breast? Was she being treated kindly by whoever was looking after her, thanking God it was not Zillah who was seen every day at Somerfield? Or, or—it could not be thought of, let alone spoken out loud—was she still alive?

*   *   *

In the house in Carlisle Nurse Richardson sat the fretful baby on the potty, as she was a firm believer in beginning training from an early age. The child could only just sit up so she had to lean against the nurse's ample stomach, her small, pinched face woeful in her distress. She had not taken to the baby food which was all that was available to her and already had lost that plump, rosy look of health that had been hers in the love of her parents.

'Will you stop that noise, you little beggar,' Nurse said harshly. 'Honestly, you're driving me mad and if it wasn't for the money that woman sends me I'd be off. Come on, for Christ's sake, and get on with it. You know what you're on the thing for, you should do by now. *Will you shut up* or I swear I'll land you one,' and in her temper she slapped the child on her bare leg and at once the baby stopped crying, slipping, as she did more often each day, into a kind of shocked state. In the kitchen the simple little maid put her hand to her mouth and wanted to cry herself. That woman was cruel to that poor little baby and though she herself had been brought up in an orphanage she had never seen a child treated as this one was.

She was startled when the nurse suddenly erupted into the kitchen.

'Bloody hell,' she shrieked, 'you take over. I've had enough of the brat and if I stay with her another minute I swear I'll swing for her. She needs her nappy putting on and while you're at it give her a bath and change her. I'm going out. If I don't have a break from the everlasting whingeing and grizzling I'll go out of my mind. Push her round the garden then perhaps she'll go to sleep.'

Mary, for that was her name, almost knocked Nurse Richardson down in her dash to get to the baby and the woman who had been employed to look after Mrs Turnbull's kid, or whoever she was, left the house and hurried off to the public house in the middle of Carlisle where she had made a few friends.

The baby lay on her back on the bare floor of the small parlour, her eyes wide open but with a sort of glaze on them. She had on only a small vest and had wet the wooden floor about her. She did not even turn her head when Mary dashed into the room but cowered away.

'Oh, sweetheart, sweetheart,' Mary crooned, 'what's ter do then? See, come ter Mary an' have a cuddle. There, don't cry,' though the baby made no sound in her traumatised state. Recognising Mary, her arms went round her neck and she clung to the maid in a desperation that was terrible to see in such a young child. Mary rocked her and kissed her cheek and the baby began to whimper.

'Eeh, I've had enough, I really have. They think 'cos I come from the orphanage I'm nowt a pound but I'll not stand fer this. That woman wants thrashin' and the one what brought yer here. See,

484

let's get yer dressed, bugger the bath, an' then . . .
Oh, Lord, I'll have ter think before she comes
back. I wish I could use that tele . . . thing in the
'all but . . . well, I can do summat an' I bloody well
will. Someone can set me on the road ter the
nearest police station. Eeh, I wish I could read
proper . . .' And all the time she was dressing the
baby in her warmest clothing. When she was
satisfied, she threw the nurse's cloak about her
own shoulders and set off down the short drive,
the baby in her arms. She did not think to take the
perambulator which had barely been used, for the
nurse couldn't be bothered, she said, to push the
thing. Besides which, the baby, whose name they
did not know, clung to Mary like a limpet.

She left the garden and began to walk up the
street and, wonder of wonders, there was a police
constable standing on the corner. With a beating
heart Mary walked up to him.

'I want ter report a . . .'

'What, chuck?' the policeman said kindly,
eyeing the baby in some concern.

'I don't know but it's not right, the way this
bairn's treated.'

34

They squashed into the little motor car, even
Dolly, for she would not be left out of this
wonderful moment, she told them flatly, and did
they care who came with them; Sally and her tribe
if she wanted. They left Sally in tears of joy as she
waved them off at the door of her cottage when

485

they sped away in the direction of Carlisle. Even Ernie, as though sensing the lift of mood in contrast to the dread that had lain over them all, barked in excited anticipation and did his best to jump into the motor and sit on Amy's knee! The child was safe, their treasure was safe, but they must prepare themselves for a bit of a shock, the kind constable who had telephoned the news to Caleb Seymour told him and he had passed it on to Amy. Caleb was ready to jump into his Rolls and make his own emotional way on the road to the north. What did the constable mean? he had asked him and the constable, looking at the listless, seemingly underfed bairn in the maid's arms, could not really bring himself to tell him. He had men out now looking for the woman in whose charge she was supposed to be but the sooner the mother . . . well, best make it nippy, he told him. Caleb did not pass this last bit on to Amy and Joe.

At the police station the young woman and the passive baby were surrounded by police constables, most of them family men, incensed, it seemed, by what had happened to this scrap of humanity who had obviously been a lovely infant, and when the mother and father burst in through the doors of the police station they stood back respectfully.

'Sweet Jesus,' Joe whispered and Amy hesitated, for was this woeful little thing on the young girl's knee really her bonny child?

'Elin, sweetheart?' she mumbled, tears beginning at last. The baby heard her and looked up disbelievingly, then, having grown men in tears, she held up her arms to her mother and began her desperate baby babble, telling her mother of all the terrible things that had happened to her. In a

486

second she was in Amy's arms which closed hungrily round her and Joe knew he would have a hard time convincing Amy that she should let Elin out of her sight ever again, even for a second. He hovered for a moment, then Amy dragged him into the circle and with his arms about them both he wept along with the rest of the men.

But after all this time Amy's milk had dried up and when they were led into a little room to be alone, the three of them, the child nuzzled up to Amy's breast, but there was nothing there.

Amy raised a terrified face to Joe. 'What shall we do? I have nothing for her and she is desperately underfed. Look at her, Joe, she wants to nurse but I can't.'

'We shall have ter try and coax her into taking the baby food that yer can buy in't chemist. Perhaps the girl . . .'

They had, to their eternal shame, forgotten the young girl who had brought their child back to them and at once Joe leaped to his feet and hurried out to where Mary still sat with Dolly beside her, being questioned by the sergeant in charge.

'Mellin's Food, it were, sir,' she faltered, 'but she wouldn't 'ave it but 'appen cow's milk'd do. There's a good dairy on the edge o' Carlisle. I could show yer.' Dolly, who had been holding back her impatience to see her grandchild, stood up and hurried into the room where Amy was cradling her daughter.

'He's goin' wi't lass ter try fer cow's milk, queen; eeh, will yer look at 'er, poor little mite. Jesus wept, if I 'ad that woman 'ere I'd kill 'er wi' me bare 'ands.' Her normally mild voice was savage.

'Let me 'ave a 'old of 'er, chuck,' but Elin Carter, having found the safety of her mother's arms would not let her go. A chemist had been found who provided them with a baby's bottle and a packet of Mellin's Food and when Joe returned from the dairy he had to fight his way through the crowd that had gathered outside the police station, for word had got out that the kidnapped baby had been found. Joe poured the still warm cow's milk into the baby bottle and Elin, after a tentative taste of the teat and never taking her trusting eyes from her mother's face, drank half of it. One of the bobbies even ran out into the street to tell the crowd that the bairn had taken her first feed. The cheer that went up could be heard right down the street.

*　　　*　　　*

Mary was overwhelmed. She was the only one who could identify the two women who had stolen the baby of whom Mary had grown quite fond, so she had been taken in the gentleman's motor car, the first time she had ever been in one, all the way to Manchester where she identified the woman who had taken her out of the orphanage as 'Mrs Turnbull', the one who had brought the baby to Carlisle. Nurse Richardson had been found and had positively gabbled, it not being her fault since she was not to know, was she, that this was the same woman and that the baby had been kidnapped. No, she hadn't read the newspapers and anyway, she had said defiantly, she was led to believe the kid was some relative of Mrs Turnbull.

Zillah Seymour was arrested, screaming her

rage and swearing to have the lot of them put in gaol. They would all be punished by the wrath of God and as for that hussy she would burn in the pit of hell for eternity.

'"Whoso hearkeneth unto me shall dwell safely, and shall be quiet from fear of evil," so sayeth the Bible and I shall condemn every one of you to everlasting purgatory if you do not take your hands off me. How dare you come into my house and accuse me of such nonsense. Do you know who I am?'

'We are here to question you about the abduction of the child Elin Carter,' the chief constable said patiently, for he had decided to question Mrs Seymour himself. Mr Seymour was a very important gentleman.

The servants were confounded, leaving the kitchen door ajar so that they could hear what was going on. It had given Alice a real fright, she kept telling them, seeing the two bobbies on the doorstep, but the sight of the mistress getting what they considered to be her 'come-uppance' was a real treat for them. After the way she had treated their Miss Amy and apparently, could you credit it, had been involved in the kidnapping of Miss Amy's daughter who they were longing to see, it only seemed right that she should answer for her evil. Oh, yes, she was evil all right, even if she was a member of the Methodist Chapel and for all her so-called 'good works'.

'I see you have left the paths of righteousness to walk in the ways of darkness, sir, and since this is obviously a foul calumny on my character I absolutely refuse—'

'You have no choice, madam, but to come with

489

me to the station to answer the charges.'

'Get out of my house or I will telephone my minister and fetch him here to—'

With a nod at his sergeant the chief constable indicated that Mrs Seymour was to be put in the motor car; and when she fought him, screaming of her God and the retribution that would be heaped on his head, he had no option but to handcuff her!

After being questioned she was arrested and removed to the women's gaol at Strangeways but the general opinion seemed to be that she was out of her mind and it might be the loony bin for her, the mental institution at Prestwich. Those at Somerfield positively rocked with it, wondering what was to become of them but without Mrs Seymour to serve it was like a holiday. Everybody relaxed, even Mrs Abigail, but, as she said, Mr Seymour would be back to see to things so they were to go on as usual.

*　　　*　　　*

In Weaste Lane Randall Hodge, with Zillah put away and no longer able to encourage him, finally gave up all hope of retrieving his errant wife and as he said to his sister he might as well divorce her on the grounds of her adultery with the odd-job lad from Somerfield. After all, it was in the news about the child she had and if that wasn't proof enough of adultery, what was? He'd look about him for a decent wife, perhaps from among the young female members of the chapel who had been brought up to know their place and to follow the teaching of John Wesley. There was one in particular, not particularly pretty but with a

490

magnificent figure, whose father had a bob or two.

'I'll go and see the solicitor in the morning,' he said to Elizabeth rather glumly, for the night he had spent with Amy had been the most exciting he had ever known and would that ever happen again? The young woman on whom he had cast lascivious eyes had a father who would object to his daughter being . . . well, manhandled as he had his wife so he would have to be more circumspect. But there it was, he needed a wife and he wanted a son so best get the thing in motion.

*   *   *

Caleb had been shocked when he saw what had been done to his granddaughter but after a few days in Ambleside, staying with Amy and Joe who after all were well set up in the furnishing of their spare room, once occupied by Mercy, he had returned home to report to his Dodie that already, with the resilience of the very young, Elin was beginning to look better. She clung to her mother and had been taken into her parents' bed for the time being until she was fully recovered. Amy was blooming now she had her child at home and Joe, reluctantly, had returned to his work at the hospital, for his instinct was to stay with his family and protect them from further crisis.

'Zillah's locked up now, lad, and can do neither of you harm and I was told on the quiet by a friend of mine in the legal profession that Amy's . . . er, the man to whom she was married has made enquiries about getting a divorce. Your name will be dragged through the courts, yours and Amy's, but she will be free which is all that matters to you,

I'm sure. And the pair of you have enormous sympathy after what happened to Elin. Who knows, you might be wed before the year's out.'

It was true that they were almost celebrities after the publicity about the kidnapping, for by every post little gifts, even big ones, arrived on their doorstep from well-wishers. A brand-new perambulator from a London firm; dozens of soft napkins; beautiful hand-sewn, hand-embroidered little dresses; toys enough to open their own shop—which Sally's children were delighted with—hand-made matinee jackets; little knitted cardigans made personally by innumerable ladies; layettes that would come in handy for the new baby; and more, too numerous to count. It seemed the kidnapping of the Carter baby, grandchild of the well-known businessman and philanthropist from Manchester, had stirred the nation's heart, and the capture of the woman who had instigated the whole affair had every reader rubbing their hands in satisfaction.

'You could come and visit Dodie now, sweetheart,' Caleb said hopefully. 'She is longing to see you and show off our own new little one and Willy is, of course, forever asking when Mimi is to come.'

But Amy knew she would never feel entirely safe until . . . well—when would she ever feel safe?—and for the moment could not be persuaded to leave her cottage. Her child was beginning to thrive again but still would barely let her out of her sight and was shy and even fearful of strangers. Amy and Sally had formed a firm friendship, helped, no doubt, by the gifts Amy pressed on to her and Sally was speechless with gratitude over the baby garments, all so beautiful, and so useful when her own baby was born. Amy helped her with her children from time to time, for was she not experienced in the care of youngsters and had been, even before she was ten. Joe was close by at the hospital, ready to dash back home if Amy should need him and gradually she began to feel the tight knot of tension, of fear, of the unknown, which had been in her for years, dissolve. She and Joe were to be married as soon as the divorce was made absolute. Even news of the war was encouraging. In August the British attacked and smashed through the front line at Amiens from which the Germans never recovered and by the end of October the French had revived and with the support of the Americans it seemed the game was up.

In November the Germans requested an armistice which came into effect at eleven o'clock on the morning of 11 November—'the eleventh hour of the eleventh day of the eleventh month'. In the fighting lines it brought a sort of bewildered relief when the guns ceased to fire but there was little rejoicing among the soldiers.

Joe became very emotional, stroking Ernie who had gone through so much with him, and remembering all those pals of his who had disappeared in the mud of France. He kept in touch with Wally but he was the only one left of those who had served with him, for the others, Pip, Lanky, Corky and many more of his mates, were gone. He held his little daughter in his arms and she looked up at him in astonishment when his tears fell on her bright curls. She was ten months old and was doing her best to walk but she struggled from his knee and crawled to where her mother sat and climbed on to her lap. There was not a lot of room for her with the new baby due in January but she managed it. She was still inclined to be alarmed at anything that was out of the ordinary, but her mother's lap was safe.

Joe smiled and blew her a kiss and she responded by crawling back to him and lifting up her own face to his. She and Amy had healed him, at least mentally, for his face was still scarred but it was nevertheless, though a happy day, a sad one for all the soldiers who had survived when their pals had not.

In January their second daughter was born, this time called Dorothea, shortened to Thea in a token of love and gratitude to Dodie who had saved Amy's life and sanity when she was at the lowest ebb of her life, at least until the day Elin was kidnapped. The christening was to be in Ambleside at St Mary's Church and they were all to be there at Caleb's expense, staying in the Waterhead Hotel in Waterhead overlooking Lake Windermere. Dodie and Caleb, Willy and Lucy his new sister, Bella and John with their six, Dolly, Becky, Claire, Elsie, Annie and Phyllis who were so excited by the prospect they could barely speak. Sammy and the other lads were to stay at home, saying christenings were not for *men*! Sammy was seventeen and beginning to court a maid from the Fern House not far from the nurseries, or rather she was beginning to court him! There was a shortage of unscathed young men, for the war had scythed through a generation of them and Sammy had a good job with prospects even if he was a bit young.

There was some talk of the servants from Somerfield being invited to the christening but Caleb jibbed a bit at that, not because of the cost but saying there were too many of them. When Amy and Joe were married and the baby a bit older then she and Joe could come and stay with him and Dodie and visit Somerfield.

And of course, there were Mercy and Richard who were only waiting for Amy to say the word, which was that she would be bridesmaid, and they would be married.

The next day she and Joe received notification of the decree nisi and Amy felt the long years that had begun on the day of her marriage to Randall Hodge start to recede. It was as though a heavy cloak which she had been forced to wear had been lifted from her shoulders. In six months the decree would be made absolute and then she and Joe would be free to marry.

'Do you realise that we can be married in July, dearest Joe. How long have we known one another? I was ten years old when I was brought to Somerfield and I shall be twenty in June. Ten years and in all that time you have always been my one immutable guiding star. My lodestar. Oh, I know Papa kept me safe when . . . when she and that man . . . well, you know what I mean, but if it hadn't been for the hope you gave me I would not have survived—'

'Give over, my lass,' Joe interrupted lovingly, taking her in his arms. 'You're strong as steel an' yet at same time you were able ter . . . ter *bend*. Like the little sapling what grows in the wood, whippy, an' no matter what high wind blows it don't fall down. Dear sweet Jesus, I dunno where

I'd be without you in me life. I'd have stumbled an'
fallen, my little love, my rosebud. I bless the day
yer came ter Somerfield even if . . . yer know what
I mean, don't yer? The time you were there was
hell for yer but it brought us together so I can't
help but be glad.'

Amy looked at the tall, lean young man who was
soon to be her husband, the easy-going, unhurried
man who had made her feel safe and loved years
ago. His face was intent with how serious he felt.
He leaned against the surround of the range,
pushing his hand through his thick tumble of hair,
a trick he had when he was deeply moved.

'Joe, my love.' She moved to stand before him.
Her soft coral mouth parted as she leaned forward
to kiss him, tenderly, softly, sweetly, reassuring
him that she loved him beyond anything, beyond
her family or indeed any other soul in her life. She
watched the long, slow drooping of his thick
lashes, the assertive twist of his mouth and the
faint lines that fanned out from the corners of his
eyes. The scars were actually smoothing out, she
thought, revealing the wrinkles that had formed
though he was only—what?—two years older than
herself. Time had raced by since they had first
known one another but dear, dear God, they had
the rest of their lives together. Who knew what
hardships the future held but whatever they might
be surely they were both forged to the strength of
steel, which would see them through. How
beautiful he was; yes, beautiful to her and always
would be. He wore a pair of old riding breeches
which fitted smoothly to his lean hips and neat
buttocks and strong muscled thighs. She had
scarcely noticed how attractive he was in the

months gone by, absorbed as she was with her children and the horrors they had both known. She took him in her arms and held him close, feeling some tension that she had not been aware of drain out of him.

He sat down in the comfortable, sagging old armchair which was a particular favourite of his, pulling her down on to his knee and for while he held her in the circle of his arms, both of them staring into the leaping flames of the fire, their eyes filled with the memories of the joy they had brought to one another over the years. His hand fondled her breast, then, as her milk began to flow, he opened the front of her bodice and put his lips to her gorged nipple.

'Save some for Thea,' she whispered as she arched her neck in pleasure, then with a breathy sigh he lifted her in his arms and carried her to their bed where they spent an enchanted hour before the baby woke them.

But it seemed their troubles were not yet done with, for as the war against the Germans was ending and the country was beginning to rejoice another enemy had marched towards them in the form of a virulent influenza, an epidemic spreading across the world, starting apparently in the Near East, reaching Europe and over the winter months it struck down three-quarters of the population. Lloyd George himself was ill and confined to bed, the country appalled that they might lose the man who had, in their opinion, played such an important part in the defeat of Germany. But they rejoiced as he recovered and the country began slowly to accept that it was all over. The horrors, the terrors, the loss of millions of men would always be there, at least in their generation but it was over, and the recovery of David Lloyd George seemed to confirm it.

* * *

The folk of Ambleside said they had never seen anything like it, a christening of such proportions with more guests than any of them could ever remember seeing, but they had to admit it was all very entertaining and you couldn't help but feel that the poor chap who had been in the trenches and who had come back with his face a right mess deserved the happiness that shone from him. And *she'd* been a nurse over there so they'd both done their bit. A friend of hers, another nurse, was there with a chap on her arm who, it was whispered, had only one leg. A flier who'd crashed in one of those flimsy and mysterious flying machines in France.

Amy held her bonny daughter in her arms, dressed in the exquisite christening gown Mrs Buchanan had loaned her, said to have been worn by generations of Buchanans. It was made of muslin sewn into tucks, with embroidery in between, and edged with frills and satin ribbon. Mrs Buchanan was a guest, of course, and even Doctor Evans and Sister Tully managed to slip away from the hospital for half an hour, for though the war was over it didn't mean the flow of patients had dried up. Joe carried Elin as they walked to the church which wasn't far—'Thank God for that,' murmured Richard as he hobbled along with Mercy—and behind Amy and Joe were the family she had lost and found again. Her mam was there holding Phyllis's hand, who was nervous among so many of the gentry, and behind her were Becky, Claire, Elsie and Annie who were so excited their usual exuberant Liverpool wit was completely missing. They were all dressed in new outfits, probably the first the younger girls had ever had, since they usually wore hand-me-downs! They were all good-looking with the same colour hair and eyes as Amy, inherited from their mother. Dolly smiled and was ready to nod at every onlooker, of whom there were many edging the path to the church, sorry that her lads had decided not to come.

It was a lovely service and when Dolly cried, tears of joy, of course, Joe put his arm round her and Amy fell in love with him all over again. So many of her family and friends crammed into the pews, Dodie and Caleb with Willy and Lucy, Willy running his new toy train along the seat, the wheels winding up the mechanism which in turn worked the hooter, causing the minister to look somewhat startled. There was laughter as well as happy tears and a bit of a squabble when Bella's youngest wanted a go but then they were all family, weren't they, so what did it matter. Bella and John were just the same, carelessly allowing their children to be themselves as usual and on the walk back to the cottage, the company, including Sally and her noisy gaggle, agreed that the day so far had been grand.

They snatched a moment by themselves, Mercy and Amy, in the bedroom where Mercy changed into her travelling outfit ready for the train journey back to London.

'And you and Joe and the children will come to our wedding in July or I'll never forgive you. Yes,

499

darling, the same month as yours which seems appropriate when you think what you and I have shared. Amy, dearest Amy, how would we have managed without one another to come through to this?'

'Yes, it's been a long road but we made it. I don't know how, dearest Mercy, but we did it together. A long road but we're both home now.'

They had their arms about one another as they stood at the door of the cottage where Caleb was waiting to take Richard and Mercy to the railway station in Windermere. Richard was already in the motor. Though it was January it had been a mild winter and already in the banks across the lane primroses and aconite and snowdrops were pushing through their hopeful heads and among them were the first spears of daffodils.

'Daffy-down-dilly,
Went up to town,
In a . . .'

warbled Mam from the kitchen where she nursed her grand-daughter and Joe's voice joined in. Amy kissed Mercy's cheek, then turned to smile at Joe as he joined her on the doorstep.

CHIVERS LARGE PRINT
-direct-

If you have enjoyed this Large Print book and would like to build up your own collection of Large Print books, please contact

Chivers Large Print Direct

Chivers Large Print Direct offers you a full service:

• Prompt mail order service

• Easy-to-read type

• The very best authors

• Special low prices

For further details either call
Customer Services on (01225) 336552
or write to us at Chivers Large Print Direct,
FREEPOST, Bath BA1 3ZZ

Telephone Orders:
FREEPHONE 08081 72 74 75